Charmed Lives

Susannah Bates was born in Suffolk in 1970. While reading English at Durham University, she co-wrote her first play, *Smoke*, for the Edinburgh Fringe where it was nominated for the *Guardian* Student Theatre Award. She then went on to study law in London and qualified as a solicitor in 1997. She practised law in the City until she gave up to become a full-time writer. *Charmed Lives* is her first novel.

Charmed Lives

Susannah Bates

ARROW

Published by Arrow Books in 2001

3 5 7 9 10 8 6 4 2

Copyright © Susannah Bates 2001

Susannah Bates has asserted her right under the Copyright, Designs
and Patents Act, 1988 to be identified as the author of this work

First published in the United Kingdom in 2001 by Century

Arrow Books Limited
20 Vauxhall Bridge Road, London, SW1V 2SA

Random House Australia (Pty) Limited
20 Alfred Street, Milsons Point, Sydney,
New South Wales 2061, Australia

Random House New Zealand Limited
18 Poland Road, Glenfield
Auckland 10, New Zealand

Random House (Pty) Limited
Endulini, 5a Jubilee Road, Parktown 2193, South Africa

The Random House Group Limited Reg. No. 954009
www.randomhouse.co.uk

A CIP catalogue record for this book
is available from the British Library

Papers used by Random House are natural,
recyclable products made from wood grown in
sustainable forests. The manufacturing processes conform to
the environmental regulations of the country of origin

ISBN 0 09 9 41504 6

Typeset by SX Composing DTP, Rayleigh, Essex
Printed and bound in Great Britain by
Cox & Wyman Ltd, Reading, Berks

for my grandfather

Acknowledgements

Thanks to the following for the help they gave me during the research and writing of this book: Clare Alexander; Grainne Ashton; Simon Berry; Charlotte Bicknell; Tim Booth; Charlotte Bush; Katie Collins; Anna Dalton-Knott; Ian Dutton; Kate Elton; Sue and Chris Hewitt; Manya Igel; Luciana Lussu; Katie McKay; Alex Oddy; Michael Owen; Kate Parkin; Gina Pollinger; Sarah McLeod; Victoria Sebag Montefiore; Kate Shaw; John Stockdale; Katharine Thornton; Clare de Vries; Selina Walker; and Algy & Pasha.

In particular I should like to thank my brother and my parents, whose encouragement and support have been and continue to be fundamental to every aspect of my writing.

One

It was Friday. Shutdown day. Time to switch off and head off – at least, it should have been.

Kate took off her glasses and rubbed her eyes. Around her, the office was packing up for the May Bank Holiday weekend. She slouched over her desk and watched, tempted to join them, but now was the time for serious work. Not the practical, answering telephones, correspondence kind of work, but the other kind. The studious sort of work that needed a silent office and no interruptions. Weekend work – and it needed to be done.

'Is it okay if I . . .?' Adam, her trainee, hovered in the doorway. He was wearing his coat and swinging an under-employed briefcase.

'Have you done that copying?' Kate asked.

'I've left it to be done by the operators over the weekend.'

It occurred to her to insist he wait until it was finished. He was being entirely reasonable. There was no need for him to stay and, officially, he didn't even need Kate's permission to go. He was just being polite, but Kate was too tired to appreciate this. Exhaustion tugged at her. Professional obligation bound her to the desk – and, while she could not herself escape, it was now within her power to inflict the same hold over him. It was not in Kate's nature to take advantage of this – the very sight of Adam dressed to leave and standing at the door told of his confidence that she would let him go – but today, tonight, some weakened part of her, irritated by his overcoat of assumption, was tempted by thoughts of forcing him to take it off, of hearing him call his girlfriend to say he'd be late.

'Don't you think you should . . .'

Her telephone rang. Kate raised one hand to signal Adam to stay, and held him with her gaze while lifting the receiver with the other hand. She rattled out her name in a low, professional monotone.

'Is that Kate?'

She couldn't place the voice. 'Who's speaking?'

'Tom Faulkener. I was just wondering whether you'd decided to wear stockings or tights . . .'

She flicked her raised hand. Adam made no attempt to hide his joy. She heard him bid loud farewells to the late-night secretary and let the security doors bang in triumph.

'Stockings,' she said. 'How did you get my number?'

'You told me you worked at Willis & Storm, which probably made the subject of stockings even less appropriate. I'm sorry.'

Kate laughed. 'Don't worry. Solicitors like us talk about lingerie all the time, and you should hear some of the things we discuss in the pub on Friday nights,' she looked around her, 'not that I can remember being anywhere other than the office on a Friday night . . .'

'I'd like to see you again,' he cut in, with a change of tone that sharpened her attention. Feeling the tiredness fall away, she stopped and waited for him to continue.

'Are you free tomorrow night?'

'No.'

'Okay . . . what about next Wednesday?'

'Hang on,' Kate's diary was under a pile of unread Law Society Gazettes she had set aside to throw away. 'Got a meeting at five but it should be over by about seven.'

'Good. Why don't you just come over when you're ready?' He gave her his address, said he'd see her then, and hung up.

Kate replaced the receiver slowly. Writing 'Tom Faulkener – dinner' in on Wednesday evening, she tried to picture him in her mind – as he was at last night's party . . .

———◆———

She'd been late. In spite of leaving work sooner than she should, it was still after nine-thirty by the time her cab pulled up outside Charlie's flat.

With a strained expression, she gave the driver a twenty pound note and waited for her change. She wasn't up to a party – not tonight. There was far too much for her to be doing at the office, besides which she didn't even know the guy particularly well. Charlie Reed was a friend of her flatmate, Louisa, and it was only because Louisa had forgotten about his invitation to dinner when she booked her ticket to Paris that Kate was there at all.

'Please,' Louisa had said on the telephone from the station that morning. '*Please*?'

'I'm sorry, Lou. I can't. I know you're stuffed, but I've got a meeting.'

'You're not asked until eight-thirty.'

'It's a completion meeting. It won't be over until nine – nine at the very soonest. And I –'

'Charlie won't mind if you're late,' Louisa interrupted. 'Don't think I can remember eating before eleven there. Ever. Oh go on, Kate. It'll be fun. It's a wonderful flat – you remember that drinks party he gave last Christmas?'

Silence.

'And there's one girl short already so there'll be *loads* of spare men around . . .'

Kate ran a pale finger between the rows of grey buttons on her telephone set. She collected a dark rim of dust over the tip and looked at it.

'Oh Kate, *please*. I promised him. I promised I'd . . .'

'You promised him I'd come, didn't you?' Kate said, half amused.

Louisa hesitated.

'What were you *thinking*?'

'I was thinking you might like it.'

'Of course I'd like it, Lou – that isn't the point.' Wiping the dirty finger across the page she'd been reading, Kate rubbed at the mark she'd made and sighed. 'I don't have the *energy*.'

'But I thought you said . . .' Louisa faltered into unaccommodating silence. 'You know, Kate – just the other day, all that stuff you were saying . . .'

'What stuff?' said Kate, knowing exactly what Louisa was talking about. She was referring to an evening the previous week when Kate had been

4

upset because she hadn't been invited to some party. That on top of not being invited to Rob Turner's weekend in Dorset – it was as if she'd ceased to exist. Louisa had reassured her: it wasn't that Kate wasn't liked – it was just that she'd refused so many invitations recently that people assumed she wasn't interested. It wasn't Kate's fault, of course, but if Kate wasn't prepared to make the effort with them, then why should they make the effort with her? Fair enough, Kate had thought at the time – but it annoyed her that Louisa was now using the point to her own advantage. And it wasn't as if Kate knew these people. Not well, at any rate.

'You know,' Louisa persisted. 'All that stuff about losing your friends from university. I thought you wanted to go out more.'

'I was talking about keeping in with existing friends – not about making new ones.' This wasn't strictly true. Kate knew that her problem was making space for friends – new or old – and that tonight presented a good opportunity for her to do something about it. But it had become so much easier to blinker herself – to say no – than to complicate her life with a social dimension, with parties and drinking and staying up late, with being a bit hung-over some mornings, failing to concentrate, getting into trouble, risking accusations of irresponsibility, risking her career.

Kate knew all this, but she'd forgotten the effect of her tone – so trained in self-assurance that Louisa, wrong-footed, simply said, 'Oh'. And then, 'Oh yes, of course. I see what you mean.'

'I'm sorry.'

5

'Doesn't matter. I didn't really expect you to say yes. I'm sure Charlie's got loads of girls he can ask instead of me. All those models, for a start . . .'

As Louisa spoke, Kate flicked back through her diary. It hadn't always been like this. There was a time every evening had been crammed with entries. Splodgy biro spelling out someone's address in Camden. Eight-thirty, and bring a bottle. Or a weekend in Cornwall, firmly pressed in blunt pencil, with details of lifts and telephone numbers stretching sideways, back up into a working week that didn't care if it came second.

Today's diary was neat. A memorandum would come round from her boss's secretary detailing what lectures were happening when, and who was giving them, for the next six months. And Kate would take a sharp Willis & Storm pencil to the crisp pages of her Willis & Storm diary, find the relevant line, and write out the entries in small, even letters. Not too hard. In case something higher priority came up – a last-minute meeting perhaps – and she needed to rub it out. And that was just the start. Then there were completion dates for her own projects, for her boss's projects, for projects in other departments that relied on banking advice. And these dates were preceded by whole weeks blocked out to accommodate the inevitable workload. There were pre-completion dates. Dates for finalising preliminary documents. There were meetings with clients, business development lunches, corporate events, committee meetings, international conference calls booked for two in the morning. There was as much of her secretary's rounded handwriting in there as there was of her own.

It would really make sense for her to get an Electronic Organiser. That way, she and Janet could streamline her life into perfection. It could bleep reminders, direct every move and she wouldn't forget a thing. Only that would have meant absolute defeat – and Kate wasn't done. Here and there, the odd personal entry remained. She'd ring it with a square sometimes, or scribble doodles in and around its letters. More often than not, such entries were postponed, postponed again, and then cancelled with a call that ended with, 'well call me when you're less busy' – which of course she never was.

'When's the very latest I can turn up?' she said to Louisa, taking the top off her pen.

Charlie Reed was a photographer. He lived in a studio-style apartment on the first floor of what had once been a Victorian family house. The walls were crimson and the lighting low – it shone through yellowing lampshades and crooked lanterns brought back from trips to Morocco.

At one end of the room was a fireplace. When it was cold, Charlie burnt real logs. He tried to justify the pollution implications of this by reminding people that he did not drive a car and Kate, liking the twisted logic, had warmed to him and laughed.

And it was true about the car. Charlie had never learnt to drive. He rode an old butcher's bicycle with an enormous basket on the front. It was kept heavily padlocked to the iron railings in the street outside. Kate found herself smiling at it as she waited for him to answer the bell. Charlie had spent more on securing it than he had on the bike itself.

A warm voice greeted her on the intercom. 'Hello, darling . . .'

The door buzzed and she let herself in.

Charlie was standing at the top of the stairs, his thin arms dangling over the banisters.

She ran up. 'I'm so sorry. I hope you started without me.'

'Of course not, darling. How could we? Anyway, it's only ten o'clock.' He gave her a light kiss. 'You look lovely! Let me see those trousers . . .'

Kate waved a glittery leg from under her coat.

'How gorgeous. I bet you don't wear those to work.' He took the bottle she was holding and helped her with her coat before bringing her through to the others.

Kate saw to her relief that there were only three of them – and that she recognised two. Charlie's broader brother, James, and his wife, Violet, rose together to greet her. 'Hello, Kate,' said James. 'How are you?' He kissed her cheek.

'I'm well . . .'

'And you remember my wife?'

She turned to Violet, who'd cut off all her hair since the Christmas drinks party so that she now looked like a boy. The change was too extreme for Kate to say nothing, but nor was she able to say that she liked it.

'Look at your hair!'

Violet touched the back of her neck. 'All gone . . .' she replied, with a hint of regret.

'It's nice,' said Charlie, ruffling what was left.

Violet pulled away to examine herself in the mirror. 'James doesn't like it . . .'

8

James said nothing.

The third person was sitting deep in a threadbare armchair, watching them.

'Hello,' she said. 'I'm Kate.'

'The solicitor . . .'

The solicitor. Kate frowned.

'Tom Faulkener.' He stood up and held out his hand. She didn't need to look to know that he was smiling.

'If it makes you feel any better,' said Charlie, 'Tom's unemployed. He does absolutely nothing, don't you, darling?' Charlie turned from Tom and handed Kate her glass of whisky. 'He just kills animals in the winter and suns himself in the summer.'

Kate sat down and returned Tom's smile.

'Really? Nothing?'

'Really. Nothing.'

She'd met beautiful men before. A split-second dark distraction – black eyes, black hair, black shirt rolled up at the sleeves – nothing more. She had only to remind herself of the sexlessness of male models to make herself immune.

It was the contradictory way he spoke – the accent cut with the careless precision of an expensive education that had then been battered by travel to get rid of the glossy whine of privilege – that held her attention. She looked at him again, trying to understand the attitude beneath his, 'Really. Nothing.' Was he proud of it? And Tom looked back at her with a face that was clear – too clear – so free from any additional expression that Kate found it impossible to read.

'But you must do something.' Violet gave the fire a

poke. 'I mean, you simply can't just do nothing, waste your life . . .'

'But I don't think I waste my life,' he said, watching her white hand as it pushed the iron rod into the logs, pointlessly shifting them around. 'What do you do?'

'Me?' Violet released the poker with a clatter and perched herself back on the edge of a sofa that should have been comfortable. Her face was flushed from being so close to the heat. 'I work for—' she named a famous interior designer. 'I'm her PA.'

'That's nice,' said Tom Faulkener.

They were silent.

'She's an amazing person to work for. I mean, she is demanding but her work is brilliant,' Violet took a breath. 'Last year I co-ordinated an entire spread in *Dream Magazine*. Did you see it? The one with the safari theme? It . . .'

'Charlie,' said James, over her. 'Your wine. Where's it from?'

Charlie was standing at the far end of the room, lighting candles on the table and calculating where he wanted everyone to sit. 'France – I think,' he replied, putting a hand on the back of one of the chairs and looking up. 'Now Kate, why don't you sit here?'

James swirled the burgundy around his glass and smiled as he sniffed. 'That's not what I meant and you know it. It's that stuff you get from Hobbes, isn't it? Not bad, you know. How much – how much would a case of this set me back? Two? Three hundred quid?'

'James – if you go on her right, then Violet, Tom – and me. You don't mind sitting next to me, do you, darling? And that's a very vulgar question,' he added to his brother. 'Come and sit down.'

Dropping the subject, James looked at Kate and rolled his eyes as they approached the table. There was a general scraping as Charlie's mis-matched antique chairs were pulled out from the round dining-room table, but it failed to drown the voice of Violet telling Tom about her job.

'. . . of course I used to be in fashion,' she was saying as Tom held the chair for her to sit down.

'Really?'

'Only it got so bitchy, you can't imagine – thank you,' Violet smiled sweetly round and up at him as she would at a waiter and continued talking. 'All those women criticising each other's dress sense and gossiping . . .'

Kate sat where Charlie had placed her – between himself and James. Half-listening to the brothers tease one another about wine, she found her attention flickering over the curves of fruit in the middle of the table and on to the man beyond.

Tom had picked up his napkin. Still leaning his head towards Violet, he was putting it on his lap and smiling slightly.

'. . . in the end, I decided that there was more to life than fashion,' she informed him.

'More to life . . .?'

Violet nodded.

'And that was when you decided to go into interior design?'

'I had to do a course first at the Institute – which by the way is simply marvellous, Tom. Really. You should do it. It's only a year, and you meet all kinds of fascinating people. And you get to learn all about

11

great men like Robert Adam and what's-his-name who did that . . .'

Tom looked directly at Kate, all the symmetry of him, all the angles in the structure of his face down to the deliberate double-targets of his eyes, all smoothly centred on her. He wasn't going to look away until she did, and the quick high she got from that secret connection shot across her senses. It wasn't an unfamiliar feeling. It had happened with Mark, and Toby, and that tutor everybody fancied at law school, but that did nothing to dim the pleasure. Catching the half-smile from him and carrying it into her own expression, Kate looked down. Thank you, Louisa, she thought. *Thank you.*

'. . . I can't tell you how much happier I am.'

'That's nice,' said Tom for the second time. 'Still. I'd have thought that working in fashion would have at least some advantages.'

'Like what?' said James, his mouth full of bread.

'I don't know – knowing what to wear, how to wear it, how to cut your hair.' Tom turned back to Violet, whose hand played again at the back of her neck. 'And all those crucial questions, like whether to wear tights or stockings this season, or nothing at all.'

He was still talking to Violet but he was doing it for Kate's benefit now, she knew.

'Nothing at all,' Violet shifted away to show him. 'See? Touch it – go on. That's just skin.'

'Oh yes,' said Tom, bringing his hand back to the table.

He looked again at Kate – and Kate, lowering her gaze, grinned stupidly into her glass of wine.

Smiling to herself in much the same stupid way, she looked down at the document she was amending. It was the size of a telephone directory, and she was stuck on page ten: the definition of 'Relevant Outstandings'. Kate put on her glasses and willed her mind to focus on the print.

It didn't make any sense. With her red pen, she drew a wobbly line in the left margin, wrote 'Explain,' and looked up again.

She chewed the pen and smiled. But the smile disappeared as she turned to 'Utilisation Request – means a notice given to the Agent pursuant to Clause 10 or 18.1 in the form set out in the relevant part of the Fifth Schedule . . .'

She'd had enough. She was going home, too.

Kate's battered document-case was full and she was putting on her coat when her boss – the head of Willis & Storm's banking department – hurried in.

'You off already?'

'Yes. I'm late.' She turned her back to hide a smile as she started sifting through her handbag. She took out various items of make-up, a hairbrush, a couple of tampons and scattered them over her desk.

Michael retreated to the door. 'Oh well . . .' He rustled the papers he was holding.

Kate looked up. 'Is that the fax from Fraser Cummings?' she said.

'Yes. I thought we'd agreed the point about confidentiality.'

'We have. The fax is just confirming it.'

'It is? I must have mistaken . . .' Michael sat at Adam's desk. He put the fax between his elbows and,

13

supporting his balding head in his hands, studied the words in detail.

In the silence that followed, Kate hesitated behind her own desk. Then, slowly, she started putting everything back into her handbag. He was still bent forward when she slotted the last item – her tube pass – into the outer pocket, next to her keys. He was taking forever.

Still wearing her coat, Kate sat down. She suddenly felt tired. She wanted a drink. She thought of everybody in the bar downstairs, celebrating the start of the weekend. She thought of Louisa, back now from Paris, and wanted more than ever to be there too, right now, sharing that bottle of wine she knew was sitting in the fridge door, thanking Louisa for making her go to Charlie's last night – for making her see sense. And then she thought of Tom Faulkener doing absolutely nothing somewhere in Knightsbridge.

It wasn't fair.

Michael pushed the fax away from him and looked at Kate very seriously. Beneath the unforgiving strip-lighting he looked skeletal. 'They've missed the point about press announcements.'

'It's not there?' She knew it wasn't.

'No.'

'Okay,' she sighed. 'I'll send out a redraft now and copy you in.' Throwing her coat over a spare chair, Kate sat at her desk and switched the terminal back on.

Michael arranged his expression into one of concern. 'But what about your evening?'

'It's all right,' she replied, not looking up from the computer. 'I was supposed to be seeing my mother

14

for dinner, but she'll understand.'

'Your mother?'

She nodded. 'Don't worry. If anyone's used to it by now, it's Mum . . .' Kate had had to cancel numerous plans with her mother on account of work. To begin with, they had been trivial enough for Michael to overlook: plans to go shopping, to have lunch, to catch the six o'clock so that she'd be back in time for dinner on Friday night. But then there was the time she'd been late for her mother's last birthday. Michael had had to give her a lift in his BMW so that she'd be there at all, and that was part of the problem. He'd met Mrs Leonard now. He knew that she lived alone, that she seemed to live for Kate, and that made it harder for him not to care.

And then a few months later Michael had gone skiing at Christmas. He'd left Kate in charge of a series of documents to do with the financing of a mining project in India – documents that had to be delivered before the holiday season set in. Additional complications had meant that Kate had had to spend Christmas Eve in the office, working into the night on Michael's documents to get them off in time. She didn't have a car, and it meant that she couldn't join her mother in Norfolk until the day after Boxing Day, because there were no trains. In fact, it wasn't so bad. Kate's brother Peter, his wife and children had come back from Hong Kong to be with Mrs Leonard that Christmas. She wasn't a bit lonely. But Michael didn't know that.

The project had later collapsed. The sight of Michael's guilty expression, and the greedy lunch that followed, had almost made the whole mess worthwhile – but Kate knew there was further mileage to be had from it.

Michael remembered all this, and sighed. 'Well then, you must go. I'll do it.'

Suppressing a smile, Kate turned back to the screen and typed in her password. It wasn't exactly ethical. There were colleagues of hers – Annette, for example – who'd be shocked to hear that Kate was escaping work on false pretences. But she knew there were others – perhaps even Michael – who'd bend the rules far more than this if they could get away with it, and so long as they did a good job. She didn't take false sick leave (she'd never even taken genuine sick leave). She didn't doctor her time-sheet. And she put in some of the longest hours in the department. It was about time she gave herself a break. It just needed a bit of care.

'No really,' Kate tapped at a few more keys, pressed *enter*, and waited for the computer to beep, 'it's fine.' Turning from the screen, she lifted the receiver of her telephone. 'I'll just call to let her know I'll be a bit . . .'

Michael blocked the call with his index finger. 'I'll do it.'

'Sure?'

Still fresh from the rush of escape, of tricking the system, of schoolgirl naughtiness brought to the point of not caring if she was punished, Kate let herself into the flat.

Three suitcases in the hall told her that Louisa was back. 'Lou?'

Louisa rushed out of her bedroom in a towel and

leant over the banisters. Pale hair, newly dried, flopped about a bright clean face. Pushing it back behind one ear with her free hand, Louisa raised both eyebrows at her friend. 'Well?' she said. 'How was it?'

The scent of aromatic bath oils had followed Louisa on to the landing and down into the hall and for a second Kate didn't answer. She just stood among the suitcases and inhaled the luxury. Whatever make-up she'd been wearing had worn off. Her skin was tired, her hair – pulled back in a clip – needed washing, and she was feeling without thinking for the knots in her neck, one elbow bent up and round at a funny angle as she reached to press away the tension. But she was grinning as their eyes met.

'Fun then?'

Kate nodded, still grinning, but saying nothing.

'Fun, and – and – oh my giddy God, you *met* someone?' Louisa screwed her face up for a second before stretching it into her broadest smile and leaning forward again. 'You cow. You total cow – he was meant for me. Charlie *told* me there was someone he wanted to introduce to me, and you – *you* . . . Call yourself a friend? You go and . . . what's his name?'

'Tom.'

'And he's gorgeous?'

'Yes.'

'And he rang?'

'Yes.'

This was greeted by a short wail and then, 'What else? What else?'

'Put on some clothes, come downstairs, and I'll tell

you,' said Kate, turning a provocative back and walking into the sitting room.

Louisa did as she was told, fumbling around and shouting questions. 'Oh, how exciting. I can't wait to hear . . . What does he do?' She stumbled down the stairs, doing up the zip on a pair of jeans and trying to walk at the same time. 'Can I come to the wedding?'

'No.'

Kate went straight to the fridge and found the bottle of wine she knew was there. She lifted it out, found a corkscrew and a pair of wine glasses on the draining board and took them all into the sitting room

'Drink?'

'What are you having?'

'This,' Kate looked at the label. 'This singularly unremarkable bottle of white wine someone must have brought to the last dinner party.'

'It was probably me.'

Kate opened the bottle, poured out two glasses and handed one to Louisa, who sat with it on the floor, leaning against a sofa while Kate sat in an armchair – still wearing her coat, her briefcase on her lap.

'So?' Louisa demanded.

Kate smiled. 'What do you want to hear?'

'Everything.'

Half-looking at her fingers as they played with the combination locks on the briefcase, and half-looking at Louisa, Kate told her. Not that there was much to tell: they hadn't talked a great deal – they weren't even sitting next to each other.

'What were you wearing?'

'Glittery trousers.'

'The Joseph ones?'

Kate nodded. 'And that cashmere cardigan you lent me – the one that's way too small.'

'Perfect. And did you give him your number, or did . . .'

'He found it – knew where I worked.'

'Oh, great!' Louisa clapped her hands together and rubbed them. 'And what does he do?'

'Nothing.'

'Nothing?'

'Nothing. Just like you, in fact.'

'That's not fair . . .'

Louisa had been a model. But after a few bookings for supermarket magazines and mail order catalogues she'd realised that getting anywhere in modelling involved hard work, and Louisa was prone to laziness. A private income allowed this fault of hers full rein because there was no real need for Louisa to work at all.

Kate wasn't surprised when the modelling was dropped. Louisa took to eating and drinking what she liked when she liked. She posed occasionally for features on eligible young women, and she went to a lot of parties. And although the complete absence of work made Louisa's existence more self-indulgent than ever, it was preferable to the frenzy of achieving physical perfection. Louisa's diets, her exercise regimes, her beauty therapies, had shrunk her self-esteem to the pitiful proportions of her figure – and Kate was simply glad to know that her friend was well again. Happy to see her happy, regardless of the indolence – so long as Kate could tease her about it.

'It's completely fair,' Kate laughed.

'I earned five hundred quid for that last shoot.'

'Five hundred quid for Cancer Research.'

Louisa shrugged. 'It's better than being shackled to a desk, don't you think?'

'Mm,' said Kate, picking up her glass.

'Go on then,' said Louisa, bringing the subject back to Tom.

Well that was it, really. He'd rung her at work – and they were meeting next Wednesday. Big deal.

'It *is* a big deal.'

'It's just a date.'

'And when was the last time you went out on a date? I don't think there's been anyone since Mark,' and here Louisa wiggled her little finger, '- shrimpy – Newton, has there?'

Mark Newton and his ego had almost destroyed her friendship with Kate. Louisa had loathed him. He was a barrister and, so far as Louisa could see, he thought that anyone who didn't have a job as important and intellectual as his wasn't worth treating seriously. His behaviour towards Louisa had been contemptuously flirtatious and she was almost glad when Kate discovered about his affair – except of course that, after telling him it was over, Kate had been so appallingly miserable. It infuriated her that Kate had minded so much, and she leapt at any chance to undermine him.

'He wasn't shrimpy,' Kate insisted.

'I think he was.'

'And how would you know?'

'Size of his feet. Anyway, there hasn't been anyone since him, has there?'

'No.'

'And that was almost a year ago.'

'Nine months.'

'Well, it's felt like a year. It's been nine dreary months of never seeing you – you work so hard. And when you have been around you've been so damn depressed – beats me how you devoted so much time to mourning the loss of Shrimpy. Oh, come on,' she refilled their glasses and raised hers. 'Welcome back to the land of the living!'

Kate smiled and drank. 'It's just dinner,' she said.

'Of course. Just dinner.'

'It is.'

'This gorgeous guy's just giving you dinner because he thinks you need to eat a bit more, because that's what nice men do – not because he fancies you?'

Kate waved her right foot at Louisa in a vague kick, knowing that she was out of reach. 'You're just jealous.'

'Too right I'm jealous, if he's as divine as Charlie said.'

'But what about Georges?'

'Oh Georges . . .' Louisa slashed at her throat with her hand.

'Then it's au revoir?'

'Au revoir indeed.' Louisa finished her glass of wine. 'Au revoir and out. This morning. At the Gare du Nord.'

'And not a moment too soon.'

'I'd only been seeing him for a couple of weeks,' Louisa protested.

'Lou, he was dreadful.'

'You didn't even meet him.'

'I spoke to him on the phone – remember?'
Georges had called at three in the morning. Kate had
come in from work at two and had just fallen asleep.

'Oh yes,' said Louisa. 'Well, he's gone.'

There was a sudden silence. And, in that space,
each felt the creaking see-saw of their friendship tip
once more – sending one sky high while the other
prepared to squat on the tarmac. Ever since they'd
met – aged ten, at school in London – it had been like
this. Kate could not think of a time when things had
gone well for them both, simultaneously. Louisa had
always had more money, but that hadn't stopped the
weight of fortune shifting between them. First it had
been Louisa. Sporty and extrovert, she was in all the
first teams – particularly diving – which was all that
seemed to matter then. But as their priorities
changed, so had their luck and soon it was Kate on
the up – good reports, good grades and then getting
to Oxford while Louisa realised she'd never be able
to compete seriously. Then Louisa had discovered
modelling and a string of sophisticated boyfriends at
about the time Kate was living in a grotty house in
Oxford and failing to get a first. Then Kate again,
her career beginning to flourish at just the time
Louisa's was fading. Then Louisa, more recently,
with a life that gave her time to live it. It never
seemed to stop.

All that had happened here, of course, was that
Louisa had got rid of a tiresome man, and Kate had
found an exciting one. Both were fortunate. But in
that silence, and after quite a bit of wine, it felt very
different.

Aware of a turn in her favour, Kate tried to think

of something to say that would balance it. 'But I'm not even sure he's really my type,' she said.

'Charlie said he was devastating.'

'He's almost too good-looking.' Kate looked at the blank shiny surface of her briefcase and saw Tom lean towards her over the bowl of fruit. 'You know what I mean?'

'No.'

'A bit androgenous really, except that he's so tall – he could be in a Calvin Klein ad.'

Louisa laughed. 'And he's taking you out to dinner, this – this *God*. Why?' Noticing that Kate was taking the question seriously, Louisa leant forward and touched her arm. 'I'm joking.'

'I know you are, but still – why me?'

Louisa got up and went into the kitchen. 'Because you're beautiful and clever,' she called back through the door. 'Because you were spilling out of a cashmere cardigan. Because you didn't drool over his looks . . . I don't know. There must be hundreds of reasons why he'd want to take you out.'

Rubbing her neck again, Kate listened and considered.

'Can't you just *enjoy* it,' Louisa went on, coming back in with a bottle of red and forcing in the corkscrew. 'It's supposed to be fun – and it's got to be better than Shrimpy. Now where's your glass?'

Kate held it out. Neither of them spoke as they watched the red splashing in. Then Louisa filled her own glass, put the bottle down and sat on the sofa. Looking round the room, she saw the telephone. 'Oh – someone from your office rang,' she said. 'It's still on the machine.'

23

Kate went over to the desk and pressed the play button of the answerphone.

'Kate. Michael here – calling about Project Cannon. I've just been speaking to what's-his-name Dalziel. We've decided we need a meeting to iron out those final points, so I've arranged a conference room here for ten-thirty tomorrow morning. That's *ten-thirty*. You'll need to bring the latest draft of the Deed of Guarantee. We'll need a copy for Henry Hazel and . . . two for Dalziel and his client and I suppose a couple for ourselves . . .'

Louisa joined her at the desk. 'Still in love with your job?'

Kate said nothing.

'Does that mean no weekend?'

'Probably.'

'They work you so hard . . .'

'They pay me, too.'

Two

Kate could never get used to the City at weekends. The underground station was deserted and the newspaper booths were boarded up. When she arrived at the office, most of the doors were locked. She signed in at the security desk and walked up a lifeless escalator with heavy feet. Her floor was silent: no telephones ringing, no chatter from the secretaries. Michael wasn't in yet, but she noted dully that most of her colleagues were. Annette and Gavin, both bent over papers. Steve at his computer.

Throwing her coat over Adam's chair (there was no chance he'd be in today), she started searching for the Deed of Guarantee and found it on Michael's desk, covered with rough pencil comments. Was this the only copy? She couldn't photocopy this for every-body. They needed clean ones.

She searched without success for a clean copy, resenting the wasted time and wondering how to charge the client for this kind of work. The rule at Willis & Storm was to charge the usual hourly rates, irrespective of the activity, but she felt uncomfortable with that. Was it right to ask them to fork out £250 – or whatever it was – for her to find a document that she might have lost? Was it right that a woman of her expertise should be on her hands and knees rifling through cardboard boxes of papers? In the end she called Simon Dalziel, her counterpart at Fraser Cummings. It was a Fraser Cummings document, and Simon could print it off their system. Kate felt she knew Simon rather well. They'd spoken every day for almost a month in connection with this transaction but had never met.

'Simon. Kate Leonard.'

'Hello, Kate Leonard,' he said. 'Isn't this the perfect way to spend a Saturday morning?'

'Perfect.'

'What the hell's your boss thinking of, arranging meetings on Saturday mornings?'

'I wasn't the one who agreed to it.'

'I mean, fine – bearable – if completion was in sight,' he continued, ignoring her, 'but I've got the awful feeling . . .'

'That you're going to have to go on speaking to me, every day, *ad infinitum*?'

He laughed. 'Well, at least I'll get to see you now.'

'Don't get your hopes up.'

'You mean you don't look like Demi Moore?'

'No, Simon. I don't.'

'What? No long black hair?'

Kate pulled a strand – smooth and nut-coloured – around her shoulder and inspected it for split ends. 'No long black hair.'

'Not even a short black skirt?'

'Simon,' she said, laughing, 'we seem to have mislaid the Deed of Guarantee. Do you think you could bring some clean copies to the meeting?'

'Mislaid?'

'All right. Lost.'

'That's better. How many copies?'

Kate dropped the strand of hair. 'Better make it six.'

Putting the receiver down, she turned to Michael's copy of the Deed of Guarantee and tried to refresh her memory, but her mind lingered elsewhere. It refused to part with images of Tom Faulkener, doing nothing. Tom not answering a telephone, Tom having a massage, Tom sleeping.

They were in Room 4. With Michael behind her, Kate pressed her face against the window in the door to check it was the right room, and saw one man at a table for ten. He was bending over a yellow Fraser Cummings file. As she opened the door, the man looked up and then stood up slowly, leaning on the table as he did so.

Michael almost pushed Kate in his enthusiasm to get past. He couldn't resist other people's clients.

'Mr Ross? Hello. I'm Michael Preston. It's a pleasure to meet you after so long.'

The man smiled briefly, and shook the offered hand.

'I'm Simon Dalziel. The others have just gone to the toilets.'

Kate stared at the sallow face, failing to connect it to the voice she knew. The man had to be anaemic, she thought – or trying for partnership – to look that drained.

Unruffled, Michael withdrew his hand and made for an area of the table that was still empty of files. He settled himself in one of the seats and began to arrange his papers.

Kate couldn't shake Simon Dalziel's hand because she was carrying too many files, but she threw him a warm smile. 'And I'm Kate. As you see, I don't look anything like Demi Moore!'

Simon considered her for a second. 'No,' he said. 'You don't.' And then he turned to Michael. 'Was there anything you wanted to discuss before our clients return?'

Kate bit her lip, hoping that Michael had been too busy with his files to notice the way that Simon had carelessly flicked the switch, exposing her familiarity, shrinking her credibility. But, to her relief, the signs were good. Michael's head was bent. He seemed intent on finding something in amongst the pile of paper in his hands.

'Actually,' he said, not looking up, 'there was something troubling me. In the Guarantee.' He turned to Kate. 'Did you get those copies?'

Kate turned to Simon. 'Did . . .?'

'Over there – help yourself.' Without looking at her, Simon pointed to a pile of papers on the floor by the door. 'I did send Kate a couple of copies last week,' he said to Michael, 'but it's no problem bringing extras. We all know how easy it is to lose documents.'

So it wasn't anaemia. Kate knew men at Willis & Storm like this. They'd fool around and chat her up in private, but they'd think nothing of trampling over her if it furthered their careers. She picked up the deeds, wondering what Simon's friends would think if they could see him like this. That's if he had any.

Michael was buried in his marked-up copy. 'Simon,' he said, 'I've got a number of small points to make, but my big problem is with clause nine on page five.'

Kate and Simon turned to page five.

'All your client needs here is a straightforward guarantee of the borrower's obligations. Not an indemnity.'

'Anything less than an indemnity would be quite unacceptable to the Bank.'

Kate put on her glasses and skimmed the term sheet at the front of the file which set out the basic parameters of the deal and had been signed by both parties. She took it out and waved it at Simon. 'There's nothing about an indemnity in this. And anyway,' she frowned, 'I think you'll find PLC can't give indemnities. Somewhere in the memorandum . . .' she turned to her copy of the company's constitution.

'Clause 3(k),' said Michael. 'I drafted it.'

'In that case, your client must pass a resolution to amend its memorandum,' said Simon.

Michael shook his head. 'Not if we're sticking to the current timetable. You should have raised the point before.'

Simon coughed. 'I'll have to take instructions.'

Which was as good as admitting they were right.

'Fine,' said Kate, putting the term sheet back into her file and clicking it shut. 'No problem. We all know how easy it is to forget the basic points.'

Michael looked up in surprise.

———◆◆◆———

Tom Faulkener hated asking girls out. He loved taking them out and had an extensive address book full of the names and numbers of women whose faces he could no longer remember, but he never got used to the moment of asking. It offended his pride.

After speaking to Kate that Friday, Tom called Douglas. He'd known Douglas all his life and he decided that a drink with Douglas was what he needed to recover his self-esteem. But he'd forgotten that Douglas wasn't going to be in London until Saturday – so they agreed to have lunch then, instead. Douglas' name was, in fact, John Douglas. But there had been so many Johns at one stage of his schooling that the boys concerned had all taken different names. The other Johns had reclaimed their name when they moved on, but Douglas stuck.

He'd once been very fat. Because he was also very tall – taller even than Tom – people tended not to notice, but it had affected his confidence, even now that he was slim – with encouragement from Tom he'd managed to lose about a third of his body weight. He'd had to get a completely new set of clothes, and even these had begun to hang from him, not that he cared terribly. It was nice, of course, not to worry about a protruding stomach any more, nice to be able to eat and drink what he liked, and once he'd got his fitness back, Douglas actively enjoyed the exercise.

But in spite of this, and in spite of what recent photographs – and his reflection – told him when he was alone, Douglas still felt the way he'd always felt when he was with other people. He'd forget how much he'd changed and the result was that he still had the voice and presence of a large man. He still thought of himself as overweight, and held himself that way – sitting with his legs slightly too far apart and his feet flat on the floor at ten to two.

Douglas had never had a serious girlfriend. He didn't know how to spot the girls that fancied him, unless they made it so obvious that he found it funny, and slightly alarming – and the ones he fancied were invariably distant. He wasn't prepared to settle for second-best, and best always seemed to be with Tom.

Douglas and Tom both belonged to Gibbs's, a Piccadilly club. Tom never used it. The advantages of its wine list never quite outweighed the tasteless food, and he had nothing in common with the other members. But Douglas, who lived in the country, often stayed there when he came to London – it was more convenient than his own house, especially on short visits – and it was here they decided to meet. So as Kate and Simon Dalziel battled out the unresolved provisions of a Syndicated Revolving Loan Agreement, Douglas and Tom lingered over their burgundy at the club.

Tom leant back in his chair and stretched his legs in front of him. 'You don't need a girlfriend, Doug. You need a wife'.

Douglas spread some Camembert on a water biscuit and smiled at it. 'What would I do with one of those?' he said.

'Well,' said Tom, watching him, 'for a start, she'd do something about Waveney.'

Douglas had inherited Waveney from his grandfather, who'd died when Douglas was in his twenties, and it was one of the most beautiful houses Tom knew. Douglas had spent a fortune updating the farms and renovating the stables, he'd rid the house walls of dry rot, and had completely replaced the roof, but he'd done nothing about the interior.

'What's wrong with Waveney?' he demanded.

'What's wrong with it? Well, for a start, it's cold.'

'Only to dagos.'

Tom laughed. 'You Anglo-Saxons . . .'

'Celts, actually.'

'. . . mongrels – have been learning about civilisation from dagos like me since time began. It's too cold. And the state of the plaster in the hall's a disgrace.'

'Even if it is,' said Douglas with a smile, 'what difference would a woman make?'

'She'd care. She'd want it properly heated and decorated and so on. And she'd pester you about it, refuse to live there with you, probably refuse to have sex with you – just rub her cold toes against your legs and snivel a bit until you agreed to sort it out.'

'Not all women are like . . .'

'Yes they are.'

'No, Tom. Really. I know your wife had a problem with Waveney. And she wasn't ever warm enough, even in June – but that doesn't mean that all women are fussy. I know lots of girls who wouldn't change a thing.'

'My *ex*-wife isn't the only woman in the world with, er – nesting – instincts, Douglas. She was rather less rational than most about getting what she wanted, granted. But the things they want don't differ. Believe me. And the second one of these girls has you shackled to her, she'll be renovating, plastering, adding conservatories, gyms and God knows what. In fact, I've changed my mind. Don't get married. Ever. You're better off in your frozen ruin.'

Douglas caught the tone, remembered his friend's failed marriage, and frowned. 'But I thought you and Arabella were over that. She's asked you to her party.'

'Oh, we are. We are.'

'Then why. . .'

'We're friends – just so long as we don't have to live together, or make decisions together. All right?'

Douglas knew Tom well enough to know when to stop. He poured some more wine into Tom's glass and changed the subject.

'Did you know that if you marry a member of the club, then she has to give up her membership?' he said.

Tom smiled. 'Who told you that?'

'Ron did.'

'Ron?'

'The doorman. Last night – moaning on and on about the women members using the billiard room for parties – lipstick on the baize, or something. Said the only good thing about it was that their membership expired when they got married. Thought I might propose to Sarah Knowles, on that basis.'

'Oh God. Not the one you were telling me about – the one with the mother?'

Douglas nodded.

'Don't you dare.'

Douglas chuckled at Tom's expression. 'Okay,' he said. 'But who, then?'

As they discussed a number of improbable candidates, Douglas' laughter carried down the stairs and the doorman, hearing it, smiled. But his smile dissolved as the doors of the club swung open to

33

admit Sarah Knowles herself. The doorman was not happy about women members.

'We're just here for tea.' Sarah Knowles was accompanied by her mother, and they both hurried upstairs to the dining room.

Douglas gave Tom a sudden significant look. Tom frowned in question.

'It's her,' said Douglas, under his breath.

Sarah Knowles and Douglas nodded at one another across the room.

'Who's that?'

'Sssssh, Mummy! Not so loud . . .' but Sarah Knowles failed to lower her own voice sufficiently. 'That's John Douglas.'

'As in, *Waveney*?' Mrs Knowles cast a delicate second glance in their direction.

Douglas turned his chair so that its back was squarely against them, and changed the subject. 'So what about you, Tom? Seeing anyone at the moment?'

'Seeing' was the right word. Tom liked it. It implied lack of commitment with regular sex. 'Not really.'

'Not really?'

Tom smiled and told him about Kate. 'Have you heard of Willis & Storm?'

'Solicitors,' said Douglas, wiping his mouth with his napkin.

'That's right.'

'She's a lawyer?'

'Well she's not a secretary.'

'Good income, then.'

Tom smiled doubtfully, and looked at his finger-nails.

'Nothing wrong with a good income.' Douglas polished off his wine and then looked at his watch. 'We should get the bill . . .'

Later, Douglas accompanied Tom home. They walked across Green Park in silence, their eyes drawn to the sun as it sank through a mesh of branches and disappeared behind the Lanesborough Hotel. The clear sky had made it cold, and they walked fast. Douglas was thinking about Tom's money. He'd watched Tom spend nearly four hundred pounds on shirts in one afternoon and he wondered where it was coming from.

Tom's father had suffered losses from being a Lloyds Name. No-one had known the extent of the problem until the old man had died, suddenly, in February. Since his own divorce, Tom had been living in Rome – close to where his Italian mother had settled with her third husband. Tom had rushed back for the funeral but it was clear within days that the estate was a mess, that the administrative burden was going to be vast, and that he would have to stay.

Douglas was one of the executors of Tom's father's estate and he knew Tom's circumstances intimately. He'd offered Tom the use of his own London mews-house, and some money to cover the time it would take for probate to complete.

Tom had been shocked. 'I don't need that, Douglas. Really. I'm fine.'

'You're not fine. The debts are mammoth.'

'I know. But I'm selling Audley Crescent, and the shares. Then there're those horses of his which I'd give away. Did you see the vets' bills?'

Douglas could not convince Tom that this abundance of assets still did not meet his father's liabilities. In the end, it was the arrival of an unexpected overdrawn bank statement at the end of March that did it.

Tom was staying alone in the house in Audley Crescent. He had breakfast in the kitchen and opened his post, while listening to the news – a special report on hospital closures. Tom poured himself some coffee and sat at the table, overlooking the garden. He tore open the first letter, unfolded it, and spread it on the table. Never having been overdrawn, he did not at first understand the meaning of the letters 'DR' near the bottom right.

But as the coffee cup grew cold in his hands and the toast hardened to rock, Tom absorbed the significance of his bank statement. There was no monthly payment from his father's agent. He didn't hear the end of the news report, nor did he hear the weather forecast. Leaving the Filipino maid to clear his breakfast, he took the statement and a fresh cup of coffee into the study, and shut the door.

Much later, he rang Douglas.

'What is it?'

'My bank statement . . .'

Douglas came over directly. In the study, he and Tom sat at the desk and discussed Tom's options. Some years earlier, Tom had inherited a modest sum of money from his maternal grandparents. It would buy him a flat, but that was all. Tom was going to have to provide for himself.

They agreed that it was best for Tom to live in Douglas' mews-house until he found a place himself.

No money would change hands but, each month, Douglas would pay off Tom's credit card bill until it was no longer necessary.

'I won't use it unless it's an emergency,' Tom promised.

'Don't be silly. Use it whenever you like – within reason.'

They'd laughed, and then Tom had taken his friend's hand. 'Thank you, Douglas. I can't tell you how much . . .'

Their hands held with the moment, and then the moment passed. Douglas returned his to his pocket. 'How about lunch?' he said.

He did not expect to see that money again. But nor did he expect Tom to abuse their arrangement. He'd assumed that Tom would find himself a flat, get a job, and move on. Instead, Tom had done nothing. There was no sign of a job. Not even a job application.

Maybe it was too soon. Tom was still coping with administering his father's estate – not to mention getting over his death – and house-hunting could take years. But Douglas was worried about the areas Tom was looking in. He'd never be able to afford South Kensington or Holland Park.

'Come on.' Douglas waited as Tom panted to the pavement. 'God, you're unfit.'

'I'm getting a taxi.' Tom threw his arm out at a passing taxi. It swerved across Hyde Park Corner towards them. 'Thanks,' he said opening the door, 'Knightsbridge Mews.'

'You're not walking?'

'We'll be late for Arabella's party.'

Douglas got in behind him and looked at his watch.

'We're late anyway. Didn't the invitation say eight o'clock?'

Tom laughed. 'Arabella certainly won't be ready at eight. I say we aim for nine.'

Douglas shrugged. 'Whatever. She's your wife.'

'Ex-wife.'

Their cab pulled into the traffic.

———◆———

Tom was right about Arabella not being ready.

While he and Douglas sat in traffic, surrounded by shoppers who swarmed over the pavements and onto the street, oblivious to the architectural patterns of purple and grey thrown in ever longer lines across the creamy edges and surfaces of the upper walls of the buildings around them, she was sitting on one of the graves in Brompton Cemetery with her eyes shut. She sat very still, given how cold she was, so that Barry could dab light-reflective concealer around the corners of her eyes and up into the dark pockets at each side to the bridge of her nose.

Charlie Reed had decided to hold the entire crew. They were waiting for the light to reach its very lowest angle, and nobody – least of all the model – was allowed to leave the cemetery.

Arabella could hardly sit still. People would be arriving in under an hour and she wasn't nearly ready – she hadn't even decided what to wear, and she definitely needed a good long shower after all this sitting around in the dirt. 'I've got a fucking party to organise,' she said.

'Bella, darling – it won't be a second. I promise.'

'You said that almost an hour ago.'

'Did I? Darling, I'm sorry. You'll thank me when

you see the pictures. You really will.'

'*But what about my party?*' her voice rose.

'There.' Catching the eye of Eve, the stylist, Barry twisted the cap back onto the pot of concealer and put it back into his case. 'All done.'

'You'll look so much more hauntingly lovely if we wait,' said Charlie, touching her arm, and going over to his assistant. 'Sam? Are we ready?'

Hauntingly Lovely. Arabella looked at herself again in the mirror. She didn't like Hauntingly Lovely. She didn't like what the stylist had done with her face. She hated the fluid clothes, and the graves were horrid to sit on – musty and flaky, cold and damp with dew.

She wanted to go. Now. But she wasn't sure enough of herself any more to insist.

Like Louisa, Arabella had once been a model. Unlike Louisa, she'd not been a part-time, do-it-if-it-suited-her sort of model. She'd been a full-blown overnight success following a contract to model top-label lingerie. Ten years ago, the girl-woman Arabella – sprawled in sleepy splendour along the back seat of a London taxi – had dominated billboards on motorways, and in airports, stations, bus-stops across the country. Across the world.

Arabella's parents had only had one child, and they were amazed at what they'd produced. Puberty had not brought with it the spots and puppy fat her friends suffered from. Instead, she simply grew into the adult version of a freshly washed child: the colour and quality of her skin just as fresh, her black hair just as shiny, her body longer and curvier, but just as hairless, just as slim.

39

She'd been hit by puberty in other ways. Always mercurial – her moods slithering from sunshine to storms and back again, resting only in the pockets of extremes – the release of hormones into Arabella's blood only intensified the problem. Her parents tried not to spoil her, but found it increasingly difficult to refuse her things. When she was spotted by a scout in a local shopping mall they managed to insist she stay at school until she'd taken her O-levels, but that was the last time they told her what to do.

Within a year, Arabella was on the books of a top London agency, and modelling full-time. Following shows in New York and Milan, she'd been flown to Cuba and then to Iceland for shoots commissioned by some unpronounceable German magazine. Then came the lingerie contract, and people began to recognise her.

Sometimes her parents worried that her style of modelling would lead to page three, or worse. Her father would sit in his car every morning, surrounded by other commuters, stuck in the traffic jam at the station road junction and gaze up at the giant image of little Bella, gazing down at him in a distinctly non-daughterly way, and wonder if it was right.

Her mother would be at the hairdresser's, reading a tabloid newspaper, and see her pictured with someone famous. She'd wonder for a second where it was all going, whether the fast lane was really the place for a girl like Bella to be.

'Is that your Bella there with what's-his-name from the telly?'

'Yes,' she'd say, smiling. 'That's her. Look at those shoes! Her feet'll be in shreds, poor love.'

'Let's see,' the hairdresser bent over the picture and touched it. 'Isn't she lovely? Oh Mrs Dean, you must be so proud . . .'

And really, for all their misgivings, Mr and Mrs Dean were proud of their daughter.

Arabella, however, was not remotely proud of them, and it wasn't long before she moved away to London. She bought herself a house in Chelsea, and paid someone to decorate it for her. She mixed with other models in London and soon found herself at A-list parties, doing a socially acceptable amount of class-A drugs, and meeting other A-types.

It was, perhaps, inevitable that she should have met and noticed Tom. She liked the foreign-ness of his olive skin and black hair, contrasting with his very English voice, and she was mildly provoked by his cool indifference to her own looks and fame – but it was his background that made her decide to fall in love with him. Arabella was a top-label girl. Tom Faulkener had obviously been educated at public school. She felt that, if she went out with him, some of that kudos would rub off on her – and it did. The chameleon quality that had ensured her success as a model also ensured that she was able to recreate herself so that she could fit into her new world every bit as easily as he did. Of course, she never referred to her parents. When she did, she said in her new voice that they 'lived in the country' and hoped that people would imagine a manor house. She was very good at watching and listening, she noticed when other people got it wrong, and she never overdid it.

Marrying Tom was simultaneously glorious and humiliating for Arabella. Glorious, because of the spectacle, the press, and the new surname. Humiliating, because her parents were there, and her Aunt Gaynor – dressed from head to toe in shiny peach.

But in spite of the glory, their married life was unsettled. Arabella's obsession with the right people, with being invited to particular parties, on particular holidays, started to grate. It became clear to Tom, very quickly, that these things were far more important to her than he was. They'd go to New York for a shoot that was supposed to last three days and end up spending three weeks there, so that Arabella could make the launch party of some over-rated film that would never reach the UK.

'I have to *schmooze,*' she'd tell him, standing in front of the mirror flipping up the sling-backs on the Bruno Magli shoes he'd bought for her in Milan. 'You never know who I could meet tonight – and you never know who *you* could meet tonight, darling. I keep telling you you're made for the screen.'

Tom grew to hate it – he hated even the word 'schmooze' – but he loved the flattery. He went to the parties, posed for the diary photographers, and then stood around for hours while Arabella flirted indiscriminately. And it was always Arabella who got the attention. She worked bloody hard for it. He knew that if he tried as hard, he'd get noticed too – it just didn't interest him enough. It wasn't long before he found himself despising her, and some echo of Victorian understatement picked up from his schooling made him question the dignity of it all. Even if he wanted to, Tom felt he couldn't help her rise from English upper class to international jet set –

he wasn't like that – and he began to resent the role of trophy husband assigned to him by the gossip columns.

He resented it even more when she began to act like a child, forcing him to play parent.

'Please can we go to Rio, Tom? Oh *please*?'

'*Why* can't I have that coat? You *promised* . . .'

'Look, Tom! Look at *me*!'

She was always the one to get drunk first, to make the bigger fool of herself, to laugh more loudly, and then, for no apparent reason, to cry with more dark despair.

Tom's response was, eventually, to refuse her on principle. He gave her nothing. He made a point of paying her absolutely no attention. And getting no attention from her husband – particularly in public – was, for Arabella, intolerable.

He knew she was moody when he married her – he'd quite liked it – but nothing could have prepared him for living with it.

He had an affair.

So did she.

And, within months, it was clear that they both wanted out. There were no children, and unravelling their assets had been so straightforward that they'd dispensed with legal advice altogether.

Now, eight years later, Arabella was still living in Chelsea. She hadn't married again, and she lived alone. Her attempts to branch out from modelling into acting and singing had met with no success and now she was trying to return to modelling. Letting the basement flat gave her enough money to live off and she supplemented this with whatever came her

43

way from modelling. But getting back was more difficult than she'd expected. As her agent said, she wasn't getting any younger.

And it was around this time that Arabella began, quite suddenly, to find photographers attractive. First, there'd been Patric Tissot – good, but too similar to her, too much in need of attention. He didn't know how to handle her when she was down, and anyway he was living in New York. Through him, however, she'd got to know Charlie Reed. Okay, so thin men with thinning hair weren't really her type and sex with him was an effort – in the dark she could feel his ribcage, and his skin was cool and lifeless – but he was patient and attentive. More importantly, he was talented. Arabella had every faith in him, every hope that this shoot would resurrect her career.

Charlie stood by a small mausoleum, his thin neck bent, listening to Sam, his assistant. They both looked out at the sun and then at the path that led to the cemetery gates through which the real world thundered by, waiting for the shadow of a cross to fall across the middle of the path and touch the end of the grave that Arabella was going to be sitting on. Then they both nodded. Charlie went back to his camera and looked through it.

'All right, darling. We're ready.'

Arabella was back, all focus on her. Charlie brought the camera very low and tilted it up. He held the edge of the lens between his thumb and forefinger, and twisted it a fraction. Blurred feet? Blurred ivy? Blurred Arabella in the background and perfect purple toes on sharp-cut ivy? He could see

44

the white of her g-string through the muslin of her dress, and a small dark nipple, erect with cold. This was great. Purple lips, grey skin – apart from the thin line of light on the left edge of her nose and the tip of that cheekbone – and her long arm, fingers lost in ivy. A druid, he thought, or a priestess – zooming in – he could air-brush out the slate line from the side of her nostril to the corner of her mouth, and the smaller line that ran in parallel, but leave the smudges under her eyes. She should look a little ill, like she'd been sucking poison from the ivy, perhaps.

'Bring your left arm back a fraction, darling – that's great. Great. Eve – can you do something about that string of hair? Put it behind her ear or something – no – it was better before – okay. Bella, move your leg so that it looks less stiff, can you? Will it bend under your thigh? Or why don't you shift your bottom further up? Great. Great. Now look over towards the stadium. Eve – her hair . . .'

In five minutes, it was over. Arabella ran barefoot to the van. Ignoring the man in the baseball cap staring at her, his mongrel pulling on the lead, she pulled off her dress and stood shivering in the half-light, with only her white g-string cut against her bony hips and concave stomach.

'Where are my clothes?'

'On the front seat, I think,' said Barry's assistant, taking the white muslin dress from her shaking fingers and inspecting it for moss-stains.

Arabella dressed and went over to Charlie, who was supervising the packing up. 'Charlie . . .'

He remained bent over a large black box.

'Are you coming?'

'Darling, I can't. We've got to get all this back to Shepherd's Bush.'

Arabella said nothing.

Charlie looked at her. He ran a hand over his head and stood up. 'Darling, there's just too much to do here.'

'But who's going to help me with the drinks?'

'Don't worry about all this,' said Sam. 'You can leave it with me.'

'There,' said Arabella, smiling.

'Really?' Charlie looked hard at Sam, but Sam was still struggling with the zip.

'Yeah – fine. Just give me the keys.'

'Do you know the alarm number?'

As Sam repeated it, Charlie pulled out a ring of keys from one of his pockets, took off two silver ones and gave them to him. He put a hand on Sam's shoulder and looked at him. 'Are you sure?'

'Sure.' Sam tugged the zip shut and winked at them.

'Darling Sam,' said Arabella, a sunny smile breaking the gloom of her make-up. 'Thank you.'

Sam smiled and waved them off. Then he hauled the bag over his shoulder and took it to the van. Beyond him, the silhouettes of Arabella and Charlie passed under the portals of the darkening cemetery, and out into the street.

———— ❖ ————

Arabella didn't have far to go to get home. Her house backed onto Brompton Cemetery, separated only by a high brick ivy-covered wall, and it was staying with her that had inspired Charlie with the idea for their shoot. From her bedroom, he'd seen the rows of gravestones – all different, yet all part of the same pattern, all those rows – asking to be photographed. Using a frail 'mature' model with evening light, for an early autumn issue, he could satisfy the magazine's pretentious, quasi-academic demands and go all out for religious ambiguity – with that Keatsian Dryad, High Romance, poignant beauty: 'cannot keep her lustrous eyes, Or new love pine at them beyond tomorrow' or whatever it was. Great.

Charlie was tired and excited. Covering the bottom half of his face with shaving foam, he worked the razor methodically, giving automatic flicks of his wrist after each stroke of the blade so that the foam and the small flecks of stubble flew into the sink. He was dying to get at his negatives. Dying to see them, to play with them, to see whether Arabella's face, as it was, with the sad lines, would add to or detract from the 'story' of the shoot. Should she be made 'younger'? It would appeal to a broader market.

On the other hand, he thought, putting the razor to one side and splashing his face clean with cold water from the running tap, the magazine was avant-garde. Perhaps it would encourage him to push for painful ageing – harsh beauty. But would it hurt Arabella to see herself like that? Should he doctor the pictures to save her self-esteem? Or should he work to his own vision, regardless?

Arabella opened the door from the shower and reached for a towel. Her body was warm now, and rosy. Her hair, wet black, was smoothed back from her face – line-free in the more forgiving light. She caught Charlie looking at her in the mirror, and gave him a healthy smile. 'Okay?'

He smiled back and nodded. He was fine. Downstairs, everything was fine. The glasses were all laid out. There had been nothing for him to do. She just wanted him there with her.

'We've got twenty minutes,' she said. 'Will you be ready?'

'Darling,' he kissed her. 'Of course I'll be ready.'

They smiled again.

'I'll bring you a glass of champagne,' she said, and disappeared – wrapped in her long white towel.

Charlie closed the door behind her. Putting a small amount of aftershave on his neck, he thought again of the pictures and tried, uneasily, to link the sight of that fresh pink girl fetching him a glass of champagne with the images of damaged beauty he'd created that day. He could always fiddle out the ageing, he told himself. She'd never know.

But, in the back of his mind, the question remained. What was more important? His girlfriend? Or his artistic integrity?

Tom and Douglas stood on the steps, waiting to be let in. The sound of voices and laughter spilled into the street.

'Do you think they can hear the bell?'

As Tom rang again, Arabella opened the door. Through telephone calls and e-mails, Tom and Arabella were friends again, but they hadn't actually seen each other since he'd got back to London and he found himself staring at her. She was dressed in a red rubber dress he didn't recognise, but there was no mistaking the figure inside it.

'Hi guys,' she said, looking at Tom. 'Come in.'

48

Tom kissed her cheek. 'Bells, you look gorgeous.'

Douglas scuttled past them into a hall full of people collectively engaged in thunderous conversation. They were a strange cocktail of fashion people, aristocrats, masseuses, club owners, students, journalists – all dressed for a different kind of party, but all drunk and mingling easily with one another. Amongst them, he noticed Tom's photographer-friend, Charlie Reed, pushing his way towards them past a group of men – all with very short hair. His shirt sleeves were rolled up and he carried two clean glass jugs. He waved them at Arabella and smiled at her. 'Where did you say you put the orange juice, darling? I can't fin—' Then he noticed Tom and Douglas and extended his smile from Arabella to them all.

'Hello, Douglas,' he said. 'Tom, darling – you were on good form the other night.'

'I was?'

'Just sorry Louisa wasn't there – I'll get you two together another time.'

'That's okay,' Tom put a hand on Charlie's shoulder. 'Whoever Louisa is, she was more than compensated for by her friend.'

'Kate?' Charlie could raise one eyebrow. 'Any luck?'

'None of your business.'

'Oh go on, darling – I introduced you. The very least you can do is fill me in on the . . .'

'There's nothing to say.'

'In other words, you asked her out and she wasn't interested. Oh dear me, Tom. You are losing your touch.'

'No I'm not. I just—'

49

'So she *was* interested?'

Tom gave Charlie a long hard look. Kate struck him as a private person. It was one of the things about her that had attracted him most – that, along with an erotic fullness of body that seemed to run in opposition to the serious nature of her work. He was just thinking that it would be wrong to toss her around like this when he found that he was being scrutinised by Arabella. In sudden reflex, he found that he was laughing, that he had already started speaking.

'Yeah,' he was saying, 'of course she was. Mad for me. Now can someone get me a drink?'

'So what's going on then?'

'Nothing much.'

'Nothing much?'

'It's dinner – all right? Satisfied?'

'Satisfied,' said Charlie with a smirk. 'For the time being.' He turned to Arabella and held out the jugs. 'Darling, what shall I do about filling these?'

'Outside.' Looking away from Tom, she put her mouth close to Charlie's ear. 'In the garden – I'll show you.' She pointed back towards the kitchen and followed Charlie there.

Tom and Douglas watched as they disappeared amongst the guests.

'Here.' Douglas picked a full glass of champagne from a tray and gave it to Tom. He then took one for himself and for a second they stood quietly together at the door. 'What a lot of people. Perhaps we should have come earlier.'

'Or not at all.'

Douglas searched Tom's face, but it was shut.

'Come on,' he said. 'Let's see who else is here.'

In the drawing room, Tom stood by the desk and lit a cigarette, not listening, while Douglas chatted to someone they'd been with at school. He watched Arabella's red rubber dress circulating the room and thought about its contents.

He didn't miss her. She was neurotic to the point of something clinical. She was selfish and badly educated. But that didn't stop him from fancying her. Particularly when he couldn't have her. He watched her approach the man Douglas was talking to and smiled when he thought of how much Douglas had disliked her. She'd treated him like a mascot, calling him 'Doogle', messing his hair, thinking he enjoyed it.

Tom waited for it.

'Hi Rupert,' she said to the other man, 'How's Polly?'

Rupert started to tell her and then, as Tom watched, she turned to Douglas and touched him. 'Oh Doogle,' she said. 'Could you get me a little G&T?'

Douglas stared at her.

'I like one part gin to three parts tonic. Everything's in the kitchen.'

'In the kitchen . . .'

'Just go back into the hall, turn right and keep going. You can't miss it. Oh, and lots and lots of ice.'

She gave Douglas a radiant smile of thanks and then turned back to the other man. 'So, she's pregnant?'

Tom watched Douglas begin the long journey to the kitchen, squeezing round groups of guests and apologising. He smiled. Arabella just expected men like Douglas to defer to her beauty, and Tom couldn't help finding it funny. He watched Douglas' good manners struggle with indignant pride. The former invariably won, which meant that Arabella never knew about the latter.

He watched her listening to Rupert. She still looked beautiful. Douglas said that it was just make-up, and Tom suspected that he was right, but Tom also thought that Douglas underestimated make-up and clothes. He believed all women should make the best of themselves, and Arabella had certainly done that tonight. Looking closely, he realised that she must have lost weight – or maybe it was just that there was more muscle. She was incredibly toned, skin gleaming in the lamplight like a teenager's.

Slowly, he remembered that first night: coming back in the dark with a clumsy Arabella – finding her keys and then dropping them – Tom looking down to see her young hand reach for them and lift them to the door. Not entirely sober.

'Let me,' he'd said, hand over hers – slotting the key in – kissing her neck before twisting both hands and opening the door. Half-falling in – a sharp flash of light as Arabella's fingers found the switch – 'Turn it off,' he'd said. 'Turn it off.'

They'd come into this room. They'd stood by that window over there, both of them half-orange in the light from the street as she pulled up her dress – some sort of silk, he remembered, slipping against his own skin as he fucked her.

Bringing the images from his memory to what lay before him now, Tom felt as if the movement of tonight's party was simply a façade, that behind the display was a dark and empty room. Just her and him in there, sinking to the floor. He felt the stretch of time through the things that had remained, through himself and her, and through the very structure of the room – its sash windows, panelled doors, that chipped ceiling-rose. The walls had since been papered, curtains replaced, sofas refurbished – fashions had changed – but the substance was still there, and so was his desire.

But the rubber dress – now that was new. The old Arabella had enjoyed daring clothes, but she'd stuck to safe materials, materials that no-one could possibly describe as 'common'. Tom remembered giving her a leopard skin coat once, before they were engaged. Arabella's face had not lit up with gratitude, not even with amusement. Instead she'd looked rather hurt.

'You don't think I'd wear that, do you?'

'Well, er,' he'd still been smiling, 'I suppose you could make it into a rug. But since all that effort has gone into the design I think perhaps it would . . .' She wasn't getting the irony. 'Jesus, Bells. *Yes.*'

She hadn't even responded to his impatience and Tom, recognising the signs of imminent tears, softened his voice. 'Oh darling. Have you got a problem with fur? It's fake. Look . . .'

'*Fake?* Fuck you. Stop treating me like some common little tart.'

Tom had gone out of his way to reassure her that she wasn't, and he now realised, with a small smile, that that had probably been the beginning of their road to wedlock. All because she thought he thought she was common. All because of a bit of fake leopard.

And here she was now, dressed in rubber. What had changed? Was it Charlie? Running a finger along the smooth wooden edge of the desk and onto its leather surface, he wondered what exactly was going on between them. He could see Charlie wasn't her type. And then he wondered if, perhaps, it was him – Tom. Was she trying to get him to notice her again?

'Hello, darling,' Tom felt Arabella's hand on his arm. 'Are you thinking what I'm thinking?'

'What are you thinking?' he said, looking at her.

Her lips opened in a lacquered smile.

He moved his arm, so that she would have to move her hand, and half-sat against the side of the desk. Arabella perched beside him, and they looked out at the room. Charlie was at the far end, filling glasses. Aware that he was being watched, he looked up and nodded cheerfully at Tom.

'Are you actually going out with him?'

He watched her smooth the rubber down her body. It was beginning to make her sweat.

'Yes,' she said, not looking up.

They both looked down at her cleavage.

'I thought he was gay.'

'Take it from me. He's not.'

'And how long –'

'Longer than yours.'

Tom laughed. 'I was going to say: how long have you two been together?'

She grinned at him, and said nothing. A drop of sweat trickled between her breasts.

'One month? Two?'

'Tom . . .'

'Well?'

'Are you jealous?'

'How long, Arabella? A week?'

She sighed and the drop disappeared from Tom's view. 'God, it's hot in here. Could you be an angel and open the window for me?'

Tom remained on the desk. 'How long?'

'A few weeks.'

He frowned. 'Then where were you the other night? How come you weren't at his dinner party? The one where he invited that brother of his – what's his name?'

'James,' he told her.

'James Reed. God, he's dull, isn't he? Asks you what you do, and then goes on and on about himself. And that *ghastly* wife of his. I just laughed when she told me she worked in fashion.'

'But where were you?'

'Me?' Arabella brought her eyes to his, delaying the moment before closing her painted eyelids in an expression he knew too well – that look of shattered suffering that could just as easily signify boredom. 'I was ill,' she said at last.

'Poor you,' he replied, in unsympathetic tones.

That was another thing about Arabella he remembered. When things weren't going her way, when she was angry or hurt or wanted something, she was – invariably – ill. And if she didn't like someone, was bored by them, or just didn't want to see them, there'd always be a way out. Sometimes it was 'migraine', or 'laryngitis' (she was very good at sounding throaty-weak) or 'exhaustion'. At other times she was, genuinely, ill – she could make herself sick. She could even make herself faint.

Tom went over to the sash window. Arabella watched him push back the lock and ease down the upper section. It slid open quietly.

'Will it go any further?'

He had to yank it the extra foot. 'There!'

Arabella handed him his glass. 'And how about you?' she said, following him back to the desk, fresh air damp on her skin.

'Me?'

'You and that girl.'

'That – oh,' he said, clearing suddenly and looking away. 'Oh, you mean Kate.' Kate. Kate. Lawyer-girl with tits. Date on Wednesday. Tom remembered her with a jump, and then a strange sense of relief.

'Well?' said Arabella. 'Tit for tat?'

'Come on, Bells – give me a chance. I only met her last week.' Smiling, he looked back and noticed her shiver. 'You okay?'

'I'm fine.'

'Shall I close it again?'

'I'm fine. Really.' And she switched her smile to Charlie, who'd approached them, holding a bottle of champagne.

'Darling,' he said. 'We're running out of glasses.'

'What about those boxes in the larder?'

Tom put out his empty glass and Charlie started to fill it.

'They're empty. I checked.'

'We'll have to move on to the plastic ones, then.'

Turning the bottle up on its end, Charlie let the last drops of champagne dribble into Tom's glass.

'And where are they?'

Arabella put a hand on Tom's arm. 'I'll be back,' she said to him. And then, to Charlie, 'Come with me.'

Arabella's neighbours were used to her parties. They made Arabella promise to entertain only at weekends, and to warn them well in advance – which she did – but that didn't stop them from complaining.

'It's not so much the noise,' said Geoffrey Ripple from next door to Yvonne and Jude from Number 16, as they tugged at their dogs on the way to the cemetery, 'it's the stamina. Don't know how they do it. On and on – music thumping out from in there at four o'clock in the bloody morning. Like bloody Duracell batteries, they are.'

Yvonne and Jude suspected that it was something more than stamina – that substances more powerful than Duracell batteries were responsible – and they were right. As the evening progressed, Arabella's bathroom had turned into a badly run pharmacy. Needing a pee, Douglas had taken one look and decided that it was just too fast. He was going home.

'You can't go yet,' said Tom – he had to shout.

But Douglas shook his head. 'I'll ring you tomorrow. Thank Arabella for me, will you?'

Tom watched Douglas putting on his coat and wondered whether he should leave too. Someone had switched off the lights in the sitting room and spun up the volume of the trance music to fuse-blowing level. The air was heavy with smoke, and people were still arriving. Tom had noticed the entrance earlier of some blond man with a hungry expression and a

57

couple of girls dressed in grubby overcoats that were too big for them, with kohl-ringed glittering eyes and chalky lips – one of them holding an open bottle of mineral water. The black polyester bags they'd brought had been dumped behind the front door, the overcoats slung over the banisters, and they were dancing now by candlelight with about eight men swaying slightly, their arms in the air, and staring into nothing. Arabella was nowhere in sight.

There was a wave of fresh air as Douglas opened the door. Through it, Tom could see that it was getting windy in the street outside. Scraps of take-away wrappings were being blown down the pavement, and someone was struggling with a car door on the opposite side.

'Hang on,' he yelled at Douglas, 'I'm coming too . . .'

It was almost light when the last person left.

Arabella shut the front door and wandered back into her sitting room. She began picking up empty glasses to take through to the kitchen. Her dress squeaked as she moved.

'Leave it, darling,' said Charlie from one of the sofas. 'We can do it in the morning.'

She ignored him.

Charlie heaved himself up from the cushions, went over to her and caught her from behind. 'Come to bed.'

'Stop it, Charlie,' she pushed him away.

'What is it?'

'You go on. I just want to clear everything away before I come up.'

She turned her back on him and continued to put glasses on to a tray.

'But that'll take all night.'

'No, it won't.'

'Darling, it will. You've got all the glasses in the dining room, too. And the hall. And then there's all that food to be thrown out.'

He put a slight hand round her waist and ran it up over the red rubber breasts. 'Come to bed. We can do it together in the morning.'

'I want to do it now.'

'Darling . . .' He looked at her bent neck.

'Will you *stop* calling me *darling*.'

Tom couldn't sleep. He'd never slept well but, since his father's death, it had got much worse and he would often find himself staring at the ceiling of his bedroom at two or three in the morning, wondering what to do about money.

He hated spending Douglas' money. He hated even more the idea of economising. Most of all, he hated having to think about it all the time. He'd always despised people who let it rule their lives and now here it was, keeping him awake at nights. He wanted money of his own.

Tom's father had always said that the only way to make serious money was to have one's own business. So, after his divorce, Tom had lived in his father's house in Audley Crescent and it was during this time that Ralph Faulkener had encouraged his son to set up a gallery. Tom had a degree in History of Art, and it was the obvious choice.

But it hadn't worked. After four months of sitting

in an empty gallery, Tom decided to let it fold.

His father had been furious. 'It would have worked if you'd had any stamina. As would your marriage, I expect.'

They both looked out of the window and thought of Tom's mother, whom Ralph had divorced when Tom was ten. It was such an obviously unfair remark that Tom decided to say nothing.

But Ralph went on. 'No wonder that girl left you. Look at you, sitting there. When are you going to do something with your life?'

You never worked, thought Tom.

'You don't want to twiddle your thumbs forever, do you?'

You did.

'In any case, your private income won't be as extensive as mine once was. You've got no choice.'

For all his insisting, it did not occur to Tom's father to stop the allowance, so there'd been no pressing reason for Tom to earn anything. When the nagging got too much for him to tolerate, he'd simply decided to leave. On the pretext of brushing up his Italian, and researching a possible thesis, he'd explained to his father that he was joining his mother in Rome. Thinking this an excellent idea (researching a thesis was better than nothing, and another language was as good as a qualification), Tom's father offered to buy him a flat.

Tom had bought an enormous apartment with views towards the Vatican. With the exception of the grey stonework round the windows and doors, the wide, irregular floorboards – floorboards that were polished obsessively by the cleaner he shared with his mother – and the black marble fireplace, he had it painted white, and then spent three years making it remarkable by filling it with carefully selected furniture and paintings.

He'd spend whole days in antique shops, examining bevelled glass in a pair of Venetian mirrors, or a set of twelve fifteenth-century dining-room chairs. He'd take measurements and check dates; he'd pick them up and tap them, rub them and stroke them, and hold them to the light.

He read a lot in those days – sitting on the terrace in the morning sun, the oval shadow of his head thrown across the page – and looking up, over urns of jasmine, towards the roofs and clock-towers of Trastevere. Noises from below, the cobbled clatter and horns of motorino-traffic in the narrow streets, the whine of an electric saw in the carpenter's workshop on the corner or the angry voice of the laundrette woman, would blend and soften with the clang of church bells, and create a mild city-music that lulled Tom's laziness still further.

In the parchment-air of evening, he'd join his friends, who tended to be people he'd met through Maya, his mother's god-daughter, or English friends doing art courses. He didn't mind going out, but really he liked it best when they came to him, when he could show off what amounted to his 'work'. They'd admire the tapestry he'd bought that afternoon to hang on the inside wall, then follow him out onto the terrace. They'd drink with restraint and pick at the easy food he'd bought ready-done from the deli while up and around, across the seven hills, the city's floodlights picked its prize buildings out of the gathering dark.

When it got cold, they'd go in. The arrangement of his furniture, his oil lamps, his candles, was such that they would group themselves automatically in pleasing compositions – the chair with the high carved back set against the wall so that the girl on it had to bend right forward to hear what Maya was saying as she lowered herself onto one of a pair of stools, the ones covered in indigo silk that frayed at the edges, and lit a cigarette. In another part of the room, in the cone of light from a standing lamp, the thick walnut surface of a table shone out clear, uncluttered, its line broken only by the silhouette of some man sitting in the foreground.

Tom turned onto his side, remembering the pride he'd felt at the collective beauty of his apartment; and how he'd felt when it was pulled apart and sold.

Three

Kate spent Wednesday in a meeting at the Fraser Cummings offices, perfecting a trick of running a pencil through her fingers and thinking about Tom with the kind of thrill she thought she might have outgrown by now. Sometimes he would come into her thoughts uninvited, that look distracting her, keeping her awake at nights. At other times, she'd summon him up, deliberately reliving that same moment of obvious desire again and again.

The meeting was to discuss the tax aspects of Project Cannon. Michael was not there, but Margaret Stanwyck, a partner from Willis & Storm's tax department, was in complete control. Kate had brought Adam to the meeting. He was sitting on the edge of a chair next to hers, taking down every word. He was terrified of Margaret – a strident woman in her forties with impossibly red hair that frizzed into wisps on her shoulders – and his subservient attitude had not gone unnoticed. Occasionally Margaret would stop the meeting to ask Adam if he'd got a particular point. There was very little for Kate to do.

Switching from thoughts of Tom himself – of what might happen between them – Kate's mind fell to considering what to wear for him that night. That lacy skirt from last year would look fine with the top Louisa had bought back from Paris. She was mentally rummaging in Louisa's jewellery box when she became aware that the entire meeting was looking at her.

'Did you have any comments on the draft Collateral Warranties we sent you?'

What Collateral Warranties? Kate couldn't picture them. Were they her responsibility? Perhaps they had been sent only to Michael? Unlikely. Kate baulked at the prospect of admitting ignorance at this stage of the transaction. She needed more time.

Flushing, she told them she'd faxed over her comments last week.

'You did?'

'About ten pages. Didn't you get it?'

A humourless Simon Dalziel sat at the other end of the table. He was leafing through a large lever-arch file. She watched his pale fingers control the pages. He caught her eye and frowned. 'Are you sure?'

Margaret answered for her. Not only did Kate have a good reputation, but Margaret had worked with her before and knew her to be conscientious. She disliked Simon's condescending tone.

'Of course she's sure,' she said. 'And you've had more than enough time to circulate revised drafts. If anything's holding up this matter it's your amateur document management.'

Kate thought this was a bit harsh. For all his faults, Simon wasn't inefficient. She turned to him, suggesting that perhaps he might like to check his papers when he got back to his room.

She watched as Adam wrote 'SD to check for KL's comments on Coll. Warr. drafts.'

Simon put his file on the table and looked directly at Margaret. 'She couldn't have sent comments on drafts she did not have, Mrs Stanwyck. We only sent them out yesterday. Perhaps Kate had better check her own papers when she gets back to her room.'

Adam crossed out his last sentence.

'But that's ridiculous,' said Margaret. 'If it's taken you until yesterday to produce the wretched things, you can't expect us to give comments within hours.'

Kate could have kissed her.

'This is supposed to be completing on Friday,' he replied. 'We don't have much time.'

'No thanks to you,' muttered Margaret, shuffling her papers.

'Maybe I'm thinking of a fax of comments on some other document, or Collateral Warranties in another matter,' Kate said. 'I'll check when we get back.'

'KL to check for Coll. Warrs.'

The meeting moved on. Kate looked out of the window at a stormy skyline. Fraser Cummings' meeting rooms were at the top of the building, so high up that she could see rain being tossed around by the wind and then flung against the glass. She could imagine people in the street below fighting with umbrellas. The high-rise buildings opposite seemed smaller and blacker in this weather.

Perhaps she'd wear no jewellery – certainly nothing flashy. It was only dinner. On the other hand, her mother had a theory that if you dressed up, men instinctively took you to better restaurants – not that she cared where he took her. She cared only

65

that he'd rung, that he'd wanted to take her out – and that it was happening *tonight*.

Outside, a sudden break in the clouds let brilliant white sunshine pour over the scene. It was still raining but everything shone, and Kate delighted in it. The angles and edges of the buildings and window-panes cut through with such bright clarity that she found herself sketching them on the bottom of her notebook.

She was jolted out of her picture by the mention of her name.

This time, it was Margaret speaking. 'And there was that point about press announcements – Kate? Does everybody have a copy of that fax of last Friday?'

Kate was handed a copy by Adam. He was wearing a large digital watch, and she noticed it was after five o'clock. This was going on forever. Nearly a whole day, and they hadn't even got to the main tax provisions.

Once more, she was the subject of the general scrutiny of the meeting. She looked at the fax, trying desperately to remember Michael's point, but all she could think was, shit – Shit.

This is why I don't go out.

This is why I . . .

This is why late-night dinners and sexy men are never going to mix with collateral warranties and press announcements.

This is why I should never EVER listen to Louisa.

Press announcements. Press announcements. Well, she had a press announcement of her own. She was having a date with Tom Faulkener and the rest of them could go—

'Kate?'

'I . . .' She put a hand on her forehead and looked with half lowered eyelids at Margaret and then the entire meeting.

'You okay?'

'I'm sorry,' said Kate to the meeting. Then she lowered her voice and spoke to Margaret, who she knew suffered from appalling migraines. 'It's my head. It's been bad all day, but it's suddenly got worse. I—'

'Do you get these often?'

'Quite. I'm sorry, Margaret. I simply can't—'

Kate knew she was being irresponsible, but she decided that – for once – her personal life was going to come first. Sure, she'd lied to Michael the other day about getting back for dinner with her mother, but she'd never had a day off sick, not all the time she'd been at Willis & Storm. She had a faultless reputation, and now was the time to take advantage of it.

'Go home,' said Margaret. 'And if it isn't better by tomorrow, go and see your doctor.'

'Oh no. I'm sure it's not—' Kate sucked in her breath with a sharp gasp, and clutched at her forehead.

'Yes it is,' said Margaret, firmly. 'Now go.'

Simon Dalziel leapt to his feet. 'I'll show her out,' he said, taking her bag from Margaret and helping Kate from her chair.

He escorted her through reception. 'I'll help you get a cab.'

'Please don't worry—' She smiled at him and turned to go.

'I think this is yours,' giving it a second look, Simon

67

handed her her sketch. 'I've never been able to get excited about tax, either . . .'

Kate returned his smile. 'I'll get back to you on those Collateral Warranties.'

And he watched her through the glass as she left the building, hailing a taxi with unconscious self-confidence.

Kate called her secretary from the cab. Janet had expected Kate's meeting to last the day and had agreed to help Heather, Michael's secretary, with his filing.

'That was quick,' she said.

'Oh, they're still in there. But I've got an excruciating headache, Janet, and well, you know how Margaret is about headaches.' Kate couldn't resist sounding naughty, and Janet laughed. She knew Kate had a date that night, she understood completely, and she liked Kate more for it. But she'd exact a price for her silence. Kate could bet that Janet would be off sick with flu within two weeks. It would inconvenience Kate, but three hours to get ready for tonight was definitely worth it.

Tom lived in a badly lit mews-house in Knights-bridge. It had a black lacquered door with no number, and she'd had trouble finding it.

There was no intercom system. Tom answered the door himself, dressed in jeans and a cotton shirt that wasn't tucked in – every bit as perfect, physically, as the man she'd remembered. Then she noticed that his feet were bare and that he was eating from a bag of crisps. Inside, from behind him, came the sound of *Eastenders* music. He smiled as he finished his crisp – and Kate's

68

heart sank. Was this his idea of a date? Or perhaps he'd just forgotten. God, how embarrassing. How—

'Aren't you supposed to be tucked up in bed?'

'What?'

'I was told – in no uncertain terms – that Kate Leonard was sick.' He pretended to examine her face for signs of illness and his amused interest, his proximity, the sheer pleasure of it was such that Kate had to make herself look away. 'You don't look particularly ill to me.'

'I'm not.'

'But the restaurant's cancelled. I've resigned myself to an evening of crisps – crisps and solitude. Just look at me.'

'You'd rather I went home?'

'*No!*' he took her arm. 'No, you're staying right here. Come in. Here, let me take your coat . . . Oh, look at you in your little skirt! I won't ask if you're wearing stockings, I promise. You look lovely. Come in and have a drink.'

Inside, he guided her towards the study and switched off the television.

'Whisky?'

'Thanks.'

'Do you think you could help yourself while I change? Everything's there on the table behind the sofa.' He ran a hand along a row of books by the window and pulled out a well-thumbed restaurant guide. 'Might be a bit out of date, but choose one and book a table. Anywhere. Phone's on the desk. Won't be a second.' He disappeared.

Kate stood there for a second – and then approached the drinks tray.

What freedom!

Unlike Charlie, Tom stocked only whisky, gin and various bottles of tonic, mineral and soda waters, most of which were half-empty. She picked out some ice cubes from a bucket and poured in water from a plain glass jug.

The study was functional. Its total lack of fuss spoke of an indifference to decoration, and Kate liked it. She liked what it implied about Tom. He might look like a Calvin Klein model, he might pretend that his life was one long party, but there was obviously a side to him less trivial than that. She could hear him moving around in the room directly above, and wondered if his bedroom was the same.

Sitting at his desk, she contemplated the restaurant guide but was no nearer reaching a decision when Tom reappeared in dark trousers, polished leather shoes, and a crisp white shirt. He smelt strongly of cologne and Kate, who'd never liked aftershave, found herself changing her mind.

***

They walked to a small Italian restaurant nearby. Because it was the middle of the week, it was almost empty and Tom was greeted like an old friend.

'I eat here most nights,' he explained, 'even when I'm alone.'

'You don't cook?'

'I'm lazy.' He said this without shame.

They studied the menu. Kate made a quick decision, put the menu down and looked around. A couple of middle-aged men were joking to each other in Italian. The taller of them was leaning forward with both elbows on the table, listening to the other who sat back in his chair and spoke rapidly, waving his right hand for emphasis. His back was to her, but she could see the expression of the other as he listened, his head tilted.

'They're talking about women.' Tom had been watching her.

'What are they saying?'

'Well, the tall one's wife has very large and beautiful breasts. The other man is, er, complimenting him on them.'

'Isn't the tall one offended?'

'Not at all. He's flattered.'

'How can he be flattered? They're not his breasts.'

Smiling, Tom picked an olive from the bowl between them. He held it between his thumb and forefinger and looked at it. 'I suppose he thinks that they are, poor deluded fellow. Little does he realise how very well acquainted his friend is with those fabulous breasts.'

Kate was laughing now. 'How can you tell?'

Tom put the olive in his mouth and grinned at her as he ate it. 'Nobody speaks with that kind of enthusiasm without a working knowledge of the subject.'

'Of course,' she said and, still smiling took an olive too. 'How come you speak Italian?'

As Tom explained about his mother, and his life in Rome, she felt drawn in. She found men like Michael Preston or Simon Dalziel, even Mark, predictable. She understood what motivated them, or thought she did. At heart, they were governed by the need to earn a living. But Tom's apparent private income placed him outside that jurisdiction. His needs were different. His purpose more elusive.

He was explaining something to her, using the salt cellar, the pepper grinder and their wine glasses to illustrate his point. It was something to do with sailing, and how you had to give way if you were on the wrong side. But Kate wasn't concentrating. She was nodding and smiling and looking at his brown hands as they moved across the table, and into eyes that insisted she paid attention.

She was wondering what would happen later, wondering if she'd resist, wondering if it was really necessary to resist. Not when it was as right as this. And anyway, she was grown up. She could do what she wanted, and she wanted him. What on earth was the point of all those silly games?

'So what happens if the boat behind goes in through here?' she said, moving the pepper grinder from under Tom's fingers to the left of the salt cellar. 'Like this.'

'Like what?' he said, looking at her and not at the table at all.

'Goes in here – see?' She wasn't really looking either. Both of them were smiling.

Shall we just miss out the food thing altogether?

'Signore? Ah, signore – I must tell you what we 'ave as specials tonight. You see, we 'ave delicious seafood linguine, with clams – yes – and scallops and juicy prawns and salmon, and – I think, coriander – yes, and just a little touch of saffron? We 'ave veal – lovely veal marinated in aceto and lime and then grilled – just as you like it . . .'

***

It was late by the time they left the restaurant and returned to the black lacquered door. Tom was smoking and Kate was smiling to herself with her head bent towards the pavement.

'Have you got an early start tomorrow?' he asked.

'Not bad. Eight o'clock.'

'Come in. I'll call you a cab.'

Smart move, Kate thought, following him in. To her surprise, he went straight to his study and picked up the telephone.

'Can I order a cab on my account? Three four seven seven one. As soon as possible. Going to?' He looked at Kate.

'Bayswater.'

'Bayswater. Thank you.' He put the receiver down. 'It'll be ten minutes. More whisky?'

He gave her a glass and lit a second cigarette.

'Can I have one?'

He gave it to her and lit another.

Kate didn't like the silence. He couldn't be that interested, not if he was calling her a cab. And just sitting here, waiting for it to arrive . . . had something gone wrong? What should she do?

'Tell me what you're doing tomorrow,' she said, smiling. 'You can't literally do nothing, can you?' She hoped she didn't sound like Violet.

Tom leant on the back of the sofa, facing her. 'I'll probably get up at about eight. I'll go for a run and get the papers on my way back. I'm seeing my accountant at eleven, and then I'm taking you out for lunch.'

She found it impossible to stop herself from looking pleased.

'If that's okay?'

'That would be lovely.' Kate felt a kick of desire. She wanted him to put his cigarette down and come towards her, and lean with his arms on the arms of her chair, and kiss her.

But he sat by the bookcase, smoking and watching. If she wanted it, why didn't she initiate it? Kate could not articulate to herself that what she wanted was for him to want it, and that the only way she'd be sure was if he made an attempt.

She jumped when the telephone rang. Tom came over to the desk and answered it. 'Hello? Yes, thanks. Out in a second.'

'Come on,' he said, giving her her bag. 'Cab's outside.' He opened the door for her. 'I'll pick you up at one.'

'Do you know where my offices are?'

'I'll find them.'

Holding her shoulders, Tom kissed her on both cheeks, 'Good night.'

'You're late.'

Michael was in Kate's office when she arrived at ten o'clock the following morning. He was sifting through her papers again. 'What kept you?'

Kate frowned. She hated people asking her to explain why she was late, and the mild hangover she was suffering from didn't make it any better.

'I'm sorry,' she said. 'I was sick yesterday.'

Janet had told him about Kate being sick, but Michael had forgotten. 'Oh yes. Yes of course.' He looked up. 'You do look a bit pale. Are you sure you should be in?' Kate wondered how sincere this was, and then remembered that if she looked ill it was completely self-induced. 'Flu is for secretaries, Michael. Isn't that what you say?'

'And I'm right – you should see the statistics. But if *you're . . .*'

'I'll be fine. What are you looking for?'

'Those Collateral Warranties. Adam told me about yesterday's meeting. It appears from the correspondence file that we did receive them.'

Adam wandered in with two boxes of documents and started to sort through them.

'I've asked him to go through your sub-files, to see if they're in there,' Michael explained.

Kate felt useless. 'Okay,' she said. Leave it with me.'

When Michael left the room, Adam asked her how she was.

'A bit better. Thanks.' Kate took off her coat and hung it in the cupboard next to Adam's. 'How was the rest of the meeting?' she said. 'Did you get your minutes typed up?'

'That's being done at the moment by Janet. Margaret Stanwyck sorted out the tax provisions and they'll be sending a fresh document later today. Ah . . .' Adam fished some crumpled papers out of the bottom of the box and waved them at Kate. 'Are these them?'

'I hope not.'

They were. She instructed him to photocopy them twice while she took three painkillers. Knocking them back with the remains of a bottle of mineral water, Kate found that she was thinking of Tom – of last night – of why he hadn't wanted to sleep with her. Jesus. It had kept her up all night, first talking to Louisa about it, and then lying there in bed, her eyes open to the darkness, searching for clues and reasons as the red clock digits by her bed rolled on to the morning alarm. And now she hadn't been in for five minutes, she hadn't even begun to look at what needed to be done today, and already she was . . . Did he find her unattractive? Had her breath smelt of balsamic vinegar?

'Of course not,' Louisa had said last night, after she'd got back, as they'd chatted over mugs of peppermint tea.

'Just check for me, will you?' Kate had breathed – hard and loud – over Louisa's nose.

'No, you idiot. It *doesn't*.'

'Then why? He didn't even kiss me, for heaven's sake!'

Louisa's theory was that he was just playing the game. Of course he wanted her, but he wasn't like other men she'd dated. This man knew exactly what he was doing. He'd wait and wait until she was begging for it.

'Oh Gawd,' Kate had said, rubbing her head. 'I've never begged for it in my life.'

'You won't have to beg, literally. But you'll be wanting it so much when he does pounce that you'll fall into his hands like a ripe plum.'

'Over-ripe,' Kate had muttered. 'Rotting.'

Her telephone rang. It was Simon Dalziel. 'How's the artist?'

'Artist?'

'Your little sketch, remember?'

'Oh – oh, terrible. Terrible artist. Feeling terrible.'

He laughed. 'Well, you missed nothing. We had your delightful colleague batter us for a few more hours on, er, withholding tax, double tax treaties and grossing up.'

So he was back to being fun and charming. Kate picked up her pen. 'I understand from my trainee that all the outstanding tax points have now been agreed, and that you'll be sending us a final draft later today,' she said.

Simon hesitated. 'I'll try to get it to you as soon as I can but it might not be until tomorrow morning.'

'I'm afraid that's not good enough,' she replied, doodling a sailing boat on the cover of her internal telephone directory. 'Tomorrow's Friday. We'll need more time to check it.'

Janet came in while she was speaking. Smiling broadly, she handed Kate a slip of paper.

While You Were Out . . . Tom Faulkener – Can you meet him at the Savoy Grill at 12.30? He'll see you there unless you call.'

Kate grinned back at Janet and nodded.

'I'll do what I can,' Simon was saying.

'It's only a few amendments. You said in the meeting that you'd get it to us today and we're relying on you to do that.'

'This isn't the only transaction I've got on,' he whined.

Adam came back with the photocopies. Kate smiled at him and raised her eyes to the ceiling.

'Simon,' she said to the receiver. 'I'm quite sure you don't need me to tell you how to organise your work. That's your problem. The point is – as you yourself said – we're running out of time. I'm expecting the document today and, obviously, the deal will suffer if you can't get it here when you said you would.'

And her day took off. Mechanically, she answered calls and responded to faxes. She dictated attendance notes and more chasing faxes to Janet, corrected them and then scribbled her signature at the bottom when they came back. And she kept a weather-eye on Adam, who was sorting out board minutes, certificates, letters from insurance brokers. Couriers were dispatched with last-minute documents for Simon Dalziel, but no sign from him of the main Loan Agreement. When she paused for breath and looked at the clock on her telephone it was twelve-thirty.

'Shit.'

Adam looked up. 'What is it?'

'I'm late for a lunch appointment.' Kate felt for her bag and stood up. 'Call me on the mobile if anything unexpected happens. I'll be back at three.'

'I don't have your number.'

'Janet's got it.'

Putting on her coat as she galloped towards the security doors, Kate nearly collided with Michael.

'Kate!'

'I'm late. I'll be back at three. Adam's got my number.'

'Kate, listen we're not signing tomorrow. Client instructions. I've been speaking to Henry Hazel, and there's been some disagreement over which management accounts the bank gets to see.'

'You mean they want to wait for the next set?'

Michael nodded.

'But they won't be out until the end of the month. What's wrong with the protections we've given in the financial covenants?'

'I know. But there's not much we can do if Henry's agreed . . .'

'Damn Henry,' Kate slammed her right hand

78

against the wall by the security doors. 'Does he realise he's just ruined the last month for us?'

'Some of us . . .'

'What do you mean, *"some of us"*? I was sick yesterday for God's sake. And I've not had a weekend out of the office for weeks.' She looked defiantly at him. Janet and another secretary had stopped typing and were looking at them with interest.

'Okay. Okay. I wasn't referring to you.'

'When did you speak to him?'

'Shall we continue this conversation in your office?'

'When did you speak to him?'

'Oh, I don't know. About an hour ago and then I had to do an interview.'

'Does Simon Dalziel know?'

'Yes.'

Kate shut her mouth to stop herself from saying something she'd regret. Instead, she made a strange internal noise as she turned on her heel and strode out.

'Kate . . .'

'I'll call you later.'

The security doors closed between them.

She knew she was being unprofessional, but so was he. Why couldn't he have let her know? Even bloody Simon Dalziel knew before her. Wasn't she relevant?

She hailed a cab in the pouring rain. 'The Savoy Hotel, please. As quickly as possible.' She jumped in, hair already wet and hanging in strands around her coat. She was pink with anger.

'You okay, love?' The young cab driver was looking at her in the rear-view mirror.

'I'm fine,' she snapped, and then smiled. 'I'm

sorry. It's my job. Sometimes I wonder why I . . .'

'Don't we all?'

They reached the Savoy in ten minutes. Kate over-tipped him and skipped joyfully up the steps.

Douglas was feeling embarrassed. 'You shouldn't have brought me,' he said. 'She's coming to see you.'

'I want you to meet her.' Tom offered him a cigarette and lit one for himself. 'It'll be fun.'

Douglas looked at his watch. 'What time did you tell her?'

'Twelve-thirty.'

'Look. It's nearly ten to one. Can't I meet her another time? The poor girl . . .' Douglas broke off. While he was speaking, the doors had swung round to admit the subject of their conversation. She bounded over to them, fresh and wet and glowing.

'Tom!' Her energy filled the foyer.

'You're late.'

'I know. It's been a dreadful morning.' She was about to kiss him when she noticed Douglas, standing up beyond him – large, and in the way.

He was looking at her.

Tom stood aside. 'Kate, this is a friend of mine: John Douglas.'

'Hello, John.'

Douglas offered her his hand. But he found that, when she was looking at him, he couldn't look at her properly. Instead, the direction of his gaze fixed itself somewhere between Tom and the uniform of a waiter walking towards the bar. Embarrassed, he released her hand as quickly as possible and put his own hand back in his pocket.

'Please call me Douglas.'

'Douglas?'

Tom explained. But to Kate, and to Douglas, the circumstances of his name sounded affected.

'Okay,' she said. 'I'll call you Douglas. Just please don't call me Leonard!'

Douglas smiled at the floor and asked if the traffic had been bad.

'Not really. Apart from that bit at the top of the Strand.'

'So what kept you?'

'A transaction. Just cratered . . .'

As she spoke, he felt able to look up. She was taking off her coat, shaking off the drops. With her wet hair dripping onto a smart, tight navy pinstriped suit, she looked a strange combination of beach babe, career girl and ripe rustic – and Douglas was taken aback. Not fully listening to what it was she said, he realised that he'd been expecting something tougher. Hardened glamour – the kind that went with Tom's taste in women – welded to a career, and a disposition of iron.

That suit might have fitted his expectations had it been less – stretchy. Perhaps. But the absence of make-up, of anything artificial, and the damp hair spread across her shoulders.

'. . . working on it for weeks – completion set for tomorrow and we had it all agreed down to a couple of points on the confidentiality undertakings . . .'

Douglas nodded politely but Kate trailed off. She hadn't come here to talk about work.

Tom lifted the coat from her shoulders and threw it over the side of the sofa. 'Drink?'

'Whatever you're having.'

'Bloody Mary?'

'Perfect.' She wrung out her hair and wiped her face.

'I'll get it.' Douglas made for the bar.

When he returned, they were sitting very close to each other on the sofa. She looked up as he approached and held out her hand for the glass.

'Here,' he muttered, handing it to her.

'Thanks.'

For a moment, they were silent. Douglas put his own glass on the table and sat in the armchair at right angles to the sofa. Kate was sitting between them. She couldn't see them both at once.

'Tom tells me you're a lawyer.'

Kate smiled. 'What else has he told you?'

'Nothing,' said Tom. 'Nothing at all.'

'Is that true?'

Douglas hesitated.

'What have you told him, Tom? What?' Kate turned to Douglas, laughing. 'Well, whatever it was, he must have been lying. There's nothing to tell.'

Douglas drank the remains of his Bloody Mary. 'He's been very discreet. The only thing he told me about you is that you work at Willis & Storm, so all I know is that you're clever.'

'Have you met anybody else who works at Willis & Storm?'

'No.' Douglas shook his head.

'You don't need to be clever, you know. Just crafty.'

Douglas didn't believe this but he decided it was better not to contradict her. Clever or crafty, she was bound to win.

'So,' she said, pushing forward. 'What do you do,

Douglas? Absolutely Nothing? Like Tom?'

'No,' he said, amused. 'No. I farm.'

'You farm?' The Bloody Mary was starting to have an effect. 'You farm?' she repeated into her glass. 'Where?'

'In Norfolk.'

'How funny – my mother lives in Norfolk – in Diss.'

'Oh,' said Douglas, without thinking. 'Wrong end.'

'Wrong end?'

'I'm on the north coast.'

'Well,' Kate smiled. 'Who knows. Perhaps *you* live at the wrong end.'

Douglas had not seen the smile. Worried that he'd been rude, he was eager to agree that perhaps he did live at the wrong end when Tom interrupted.

'You won't be able to convince him that there's anything wrong about Waveney, Kate. It's his life.'

'That's not what I . . .' Kate felt Douglas's embarrassment and turned to him. 'You were saying that you farm, right?'

Douglas nodded.

'I've never met a farmer before,' Kate examined him as she rested her elbow over the edge of the sofa. 'You don't look like a farmer.'

'That's a relief.'

He looked up, but she wasn't listening. Her body was still turned to him, but already she had twisted her neck back to Tom. Her hand, which rested on the arm of the sofa, was completely hidden by his. Douglas watched them smile at one another. He finished his drink and stood up. 'I must go.'

Resisting attempts by both Tom and Kate to make him stay, he put on his coat and said goodbye. They watched him as he walked towards the door, his arms swinging out slightly. He stood aside to let in a porter carrying a heavy suitcase and then he waved to them as he passed out into the rain.

Later, over lunch, Tom asked Kate what she thought of Douglas.

'Well, he must be nice if he's a friend of yours . . .' she stretched out a finger to steal one of Tom's chips, 'but I suppose it's difficult for him, living in your shadow.'

Tom guarded his chips with his hands. 'Flatterer.'

'He didn't even look me in the eye when we shook hands.'

'He's shy,' said Tom. 'He was probably intimidated.'

'Intimidated?' Kate tried to get to his chips under his hands, but he caught her fingers. 'By me?'

'Yes.'

'Why?'

Tom released her. He picked up his knife and fork. 'Because you're pretty. And you're clever,' he waved his fork like a fan. 'Sorry: crafty.'

'Oh shut up,' she said, snatching a chip – and wondering again how long he was planning to wait. It seemed to her that Louisa had to be right. He had to fancy her. What other explanation was there? Dinner, lunch, meeting his friends, and now – here – telling her that she was pretty and clever. It *would* happen. He *would* make a move, for sure.

Kate held the fillet steak firm with a fork and ran her knife clean through.

It was just a matter of time.

Four

It was about four o'clock when they left the Savoy. Tom put up his umbrella, he gave her his arm and they crossed the Strand. As they reached the other side, he kissed the top of her head.

It was as if he'd told her a secret.

Overcome with excitement, Kate stopped and raised her face. He was looking down.

'Did you say you were free this afternoon?'

She smiled. 'I'd better check.' Enjoying the light sensation of Tom's hand in the small of her back, Kate pulled her mobile out of her bag. There were two messages.

The first was from Michael.

Under Tom's umbrella, Kate felt a squeak of guilt and a thud of dread.

'. . . deal's on again. Completing tomorrow as planned. They suggested some small amendment to the financial covenants – not unlike the one we had in the Schelner Project – which seems fine. And Henry's happy if I'm happy, so . . . anyway, Adam's sorting out the CPs, and I'm dealing directly with what's-his-name Dalziel. Would you call me when you get this? There's a meeting set for eight-thirty tomorrow morning . . .'

The second message was from Adam, looking for bank mandates.

She turned to Tom. 'It's on again.'

'Your deal?'

She nodded.

'But so far as they're concerned, you're ill.'

'It doesn't work like that. They want to complete tomorrow, they complete tomorrow.' The orange light of a free taxi caught her eye. Kate stuck her arm out and turned to him. 'I'm so sorry,' she said, 'I . . .'

The cab was waiting. Tom opened the door for her. 'Don't worry. I'll call you.' He closed the door and waved her off, watching the rounded rear of the cab as it diminished down the Strand.

What now?

Under his umbrella, Tom stood watching her taxi shift lanes and pull away down the Strand. The red bulk of a double-decker heaved itself past, throwing up a jet of muddy water from the gutter, and stopped at a light. A crowd of chattering tourists leapt off, pushing themselves around him, splitting and rejoining, complaining about the wet.

Tom merely stood, watching, getting in the way of the street. Someone tried to squeeze a pushchair past.

'So sorry . . .'

Tom stepped aside.

'Get out the fucking way!' A sexless cyclist wobbled up. 'Move!'

Tom moved.

All London heaved around him. They were digging up the road on the other side. Filthy men in fluorescent jackets and ear protectors rammed their

86

motors into the tarmac. Passers-by frowned. Some blocked their ears. But to Tom, from his side of the street, they were all part of the same bustle.

What now?

His watch, speckled with rain, told him that it was four-thirty. He knew what he should be doing. He should be calling the estate agent to find out about that flat in Pimlico – whether they'd accepted his offer. But Tom didn't want to know about the flat in Pimlico. He liked the house in Knightsbridge.

He pulled out his mobile, and noticed he had a message from Arabella.

' . . . can you call me when you get this?'

Putting the mobile back, he let the crowds carry him towards Charing Cross. He cut down Villiers Street towards the Embankment, then under the railway and over the road. In spite of cars screaming past, and the intermittent crescendo of trains overhead, it was calmer. He lit a cigarette.

It had stopped raining, but the sky still hung dark and heavy over the crazy coloured lights on the South Bank. Tom fixed on their disturbed reflections in the water, and let his thoughts drift to Arabella. He watched a motor launch work its way to the other side, and thought of the way that rubber dress had held her body.

Tom felt again for his mobile, pulled it out and dialled her number.

'Arabella?'

He could hear the clipped voices and shaky orchestral music of a black-and-white film.

'My darling, you know I love you . . .'

'Bells?'

'Tom?' the voice was thick with emotion. 'Tom! Oh Tom, thank God . . .'

'How much longer? I don't think I can bear . . .'

'Shall I call back?'

'No . . . no, hang on.'

'You must be strong . . .'

He heard her switch it off.

'There. Oh Tom, thank God you rang,' she said. 'You're not busy, are you?'

'Not particularly,' he threw the end of his cigarette onto the pavement and put his hand in his coat pocket.

'I have to see you,' she swallowed. 'See, there's something very important. Very, *very* important – you understand? Been thinking a lot, you know . . . I – I can't do it. I can't . . .' she broke up with an odd-sounding choke.

Tom slipped without thinking into the old routine of forcing aside his automatic concern (it was just another one of her tantrums) and then worrying that perhaps this time it wasn't. 'Has something happened?' he said, carefully.

'No, that is—'

'Is it Charlie?'

'Charlie? No. No, but – I have to see *you*, Tom. Please – I . . .'

The motor launch was coming back, its dark form low in the water, the divergent waves of its wake breaking the surface into a thousand watery fragments of crazy neon light.

'Tom, *please*. I need you.'

───────

In the cab on the way to her flat, Tom called Douglas.

'What did you think?'

Douglas was staying at Gibbs's while the spare room at the mews-house was being redecorated. He'd decided to throw out the old spare bed, and the replacement – one he'd found in one of the cottages at Waveney – still hadn't been brought up. He was in his room at the club, packing.

'She's not blonde,' he said.

'Yes, she is.'

'She's mouse.'

'She's absolutely not mouse.'

Douglas just laughed.

'She might not be Scandinavian blonde like you,' said Tom. 'But she's not mouse.'

'Whatever you say. She's still much too pretty and much too clever for you.'

Tom smiled. 'You should have stayed.'

'Certainly not.' Douglas had his mobile propped between his chin and his right shoulder. He leant on the suitcase. 'But I'm glad you rang – forgot to ask if you were still coming on Saturday . . .'

It was Douglas' birthday on Saturday. He was planning on spending it at Waveney with his parents, with Tom, and a few others. He'd mentioned it to Tom some weeks ago, but he'd not yet got round to asking the 'few others'. He wondered if it was too late. People always seemed to get booked up for weekends so far in advance.

Tom held onto a handle as his cab shot round a corner. 'Of course.'

'Want to bring her?'

'Who – Kate?'

'Yes.'

Tom was tempted by the idea of a weekend with Kate – Kate at Waveney looking at the paintings, Kate dressed for dinner, Kate walking on the beach. All that time for talking, for finding out more about her. And time to watch that brain of hers wondering – will he, won't he? To drive her mad by not coming on too strong.

'Who else is coming?'

'No-one at the moment. Apart from my parents. I might try to get a few more people. Maybe Charlie Reed. It won't be very exciting.'

Tom knew how much Douglas hated his birthday. He could hear Douglas' anxiety.

'Come on, Doug,' he said. 'It'll be great. Last year was tricky because there were people there you didn't know from Adam – and most of them were those profoundly thick, unattractive, dreary little Sloanes the Wentworths brought with them – the ones who ought never to have been let out of boarding school. They were truly ghastly – remember those party games they made us play? It wasn't *your* fault.'

'Mm.'

'And it won't be like that this year, not with you and me and your fabulous parents – all of us deeply clever and physically irresistible.'

Douglas smiled.

'And maybe Kate – who I think I can safely say is up to standard. And Charlie, who isn't really, but every party needs a dud.'

'Do you think he'd like it?'

'Of course he would. And he'll fucking adore Waveney – probably want it for his next shoot. Come to think of it, Doug, I expect you could make a fortune letting the place for stuff like that. You ask him. Get him to bring his camera. And I'll ask Kate – I know she'd love it. She really liked you, you know.'

'Silence.

'Well?' Tom persisted. 'Are you going to ask him?'

'I don't know . . .'

Douglas.

'Oh all right. And you'll let me know about Kate?'

'I'll let you know tomorrow. First thing.'

Tom's cab pulled into Arabella's street. It was full of sodden blossom.

'What number, Guv?'

'Sorry Doug, hang on a minute,' Tom leant forward. 'Number Twelve.'

The cab stopped outside Arabella's house. Rain had darkened the afternoon sky, and lights blazed from every window like a dolls' house. Tom could see her in the kitchen.

'Doug?'

'Still here,' said Douglas.

'I'll call you tomorrow. Okay?'

'Great. Bye.'

Douglas continued to sit on his bed. Far away, through two layers of double glazing, the sound of muted traffic reached him. He put his hands behind his head and lay on the bedspread, a relic from the seventies with zig-zag stripes in shades of brown. He raised his eyes to the net curtains at the window and then out to the slate-washed rainclouds beyond.

Flat, looking up at the sky, his eyes stretching into nothing, Douglas felt his spirits sinking. He hated his birthday. Each year, it reminded him of how few friends he had. And it made him cross that he minded.

He knew that his lack of friends was due entirely to the fact that he made no attempt to encourage them, but that didn't stop him feeling inadequate. The truth was that while Douglas adored his family, his housekeeper and his tenant farmers, he felt awkward with the people he met socially. He couldn't *do* that kind of small-talk. He couldn't half-know people. Either there were very close friends like Tom and – well, like Tom. Or there were the people he came to know through various projects at Waveney. These were the people with whom he had something real to talk about. They didn't lure him into saying something stupid, just to be interesting. They didn't look suddenly and significantly riveted when he told them where he lived – or look bored when he really couldn't bear it, and just told them that he farmed.

He could hear himself breathing very slowly. In and out. He was almost asleep when the telephone by his bed rang with single rings. The caller was in the building.

'Hello.'

'Is that John Douglas?' A brisk voice. It made him feel defensive.

'Who is this?'

'It's Davina Knowles. We met at the Beaumonts' party last summer. Remember? You know my daughter, Sarah.'

'Of course.' He sat up. His head hurt.

'I see you're booked in for the night.'

'That was last night, I—'

'And I was wondering if you were free.'

'I—'

'Oh, so you are. Great. The thing is, poor Sarah's

here by herself tonight, and I was hoping you might be able to look after her. I've been speaking to Mr Tait.'

'Mr Tait?'

'The Secretary. And there's one table left for dinner.'

Douglas was obstinately silent.

'You should really grab it now.'

Douglas pictured Sarah's little moon-face, and found himself feeling sorry for her. Nobody deserved a mother like this.

'I'd love to,' he heard himself saying, 'but don't trouble Mr Tait. I'll take her out.'

'Well!' breathed Mrs Knowles. 'That's terribly kind of you. Are you sure?'

'I'll meet her in the Ladies' Sitting Room at seven.'

'Or go to Sarah's room. It's number—'

'No. No, really. The Sitting Room's much easier. I – er, I get lost,' he said.

'Do you?'

'Much too big.'

Mrs Knowles thought of what she knew of Waveney and wondered what he was on about.

'Whatever you prefer,' she replied. 'I'll make sure she's there. In the Sitting Room. At seven.'

Douglas undid his suitcase and fished out his last clean shirt. While he waited for his bath to fill, he booked his room for another night and called the housekeeper to let her know he'd not be home until tomorrow. Then he called a restaurant, one recommended by Tom for dinners à deux, and booked a table.

That done, Douglas wrapped himself carefully in a

93

very small chocolate towel. He picked up his wash-bag and took it into the steamy bathroom, locking the door behind him.

———◆———

Arabella did not look like someone on the verge of a crisis as she stood against the light. She was resting on one leg, waiting for Tom to say something.

He kissed her cheek. 'Are you going to let me in?'

She stood aside and let him past. He headed straight for her sitting room. Slowly, Arabella closed the front door and followed him in. She watched as he helped himself to a cigarette from the box on her desk with the intrusive familiarity of an ex.

She poured herself a glass of left-over champagne from her party, and looked at him. 'Drink?'

'Go on then.'

She gave him her glass, poured herself another and twisted down on the floor with her back against the wall, wriggling her toes into the carpet.

Tom sat in an armchair, his glass in one hand and unlit cigarette in the other. 'That was a good party,' he said.

'It was too crowded.'

'Better than being too empty.'

He put down the glass, lit the cigarette, and blew a smoke ring in her direction. 'Where's Charlie?'

'Madrid.'

'Still?'

'They couldn't shoot the first day. It was raining, or something. I don't remember.' Arabella shifted her position on the floor by lifting her hips slightly and curling one leg under the other. Her skirt was made of some sort of flimsy material that slipped as she moved.

'Are you missing him?'

'Not half as much as I miss you.'

Tom said nothing. Dragging on the cigarette, he looked at her hard, and then shook his head. 'Arabella, I . . .'

'Oh stop pretending, Tom. You were watching me all night.'

Tom reached for the ashtray. 'Is this why you asked me over?'

Arabella didn't reply. She drained her glass and rose in one movement to fetch the bottle. Tom watched her bottom twitch away, under the slippery skirt. '. . . Bells?' He lit another cigarette and waited for her to sit down again. 'Things not working out with Charlie?'

'Everything's fine.'

'You're still together?'

She nodded.

'Then why . . . ?'

'Because you want me to.'

'But I don't.'

'Yes you do. I know you do. I just can't understand why you're being so . . .' Smiling slowly, she tipped half her champagne into her mouth, swallowed, and looked at him. 'Is there someone else?'

Tom said nothing.

'What about that girl?'

'Kate?'

As he told her about Kate, Arabella felt physically weak. She had to let the wall support her back. Aware of his relaxed legs, one bent at the knee and one stretching towards her, she listened quietly to the sound of his voice rising and falling. But while her

95

face held an expression of mild interest, her brain spiralled. All she could think was that she wanted him back.

'Sounds *awful* to me.'

'She's not. You should meet her . . .'

'Why should I want to *meet* her? *I hate* her.'

Tom put his glass down. 'Bells . . .'

'*I hate her. I hate her.*' Screwing up her nose and eyes, Arabella worked her arms around like a frustrated child.

Remembering why he'd wanted a divorce, Tom got up. 'No, darling. You don't hate her. It's me you hate.'

Arabella sobbed. She tried to look at him, but he was swimming in a blur. 'What's wrong with me . . .'

He was holding her now. 'I can't hear you,' he said softly.

She caught her breath. 'What's wrong with me?'

'There's nothing wrong with you.'

'Then why won't you come back to me?'

Now she was pressing against him, taking him still further back, reminding him of her body, of why he'd wanted to marry her.

'Why? Is it because I'm ugly now?'

He wiped her eyes with the end of his tie and smiled at her. 'Stop fishing . . .'

———◆———

The faded chintz curtains in the Ladies' Sitting Room had been drawn, but the room remained cold and empty. Glossy magazines had been carefully scattered on a table in the centre. Douglas picked one up and sat down. He ran the pages through his fingers, flicking past images of perfect women coiled around scent bottles, wrapped in chiffon, confidently lovely and right out of reach.

The tapping of Sarah's shoes on the floorboards drew his attention. He put down the magazine and stood up to greet her.

'Sarah –'

'I'm so sorry I'm late . . .'

'Are you?' Douglas looked at his watch and then back at her with a smile. 'Let me get you something to drink.' He ordered two glasses of champagne and sat right on the edge of the sofa, looking at his feet.

Sarah arranged herself in the other corner. 'So,' she said. 'Where are you taking me?'

He was about to reply when a waiter bent forward with their drinks on a tray. Douglas picked up both and gave her one.

'Thanks.'

Smiling weakly as he raised his glass, Douglas then drank half of it at once and started to feel a bit better.

'I thought we could go to Caratello.'

'In Bolton Terrace?'

'You know it?'

'Of course,' she said, face full of enthusiasm. 'But I haven't been there in ages.'

Douglas let more champagne slip down his throat. He enjoyed the bubbles tickling. 'Did you like it?'

'All I can remember is that it has a rather peculiar door.'

'And the food?'

'I . . .'

'You're a cook, aren't you? You're supposed to

pay attention to that sort of thing. Or was the food so dreary you—'

Sarah laughed. 'I wasn't a cook then.'

'What were you? A deb?'

'God no. Not for anything. And not for want of trying on my mother's part.' She smiled suddenly and Douglas, putting down his empty glass, smiled back at her across a barricade of chintz. 'I'm so sorry about her,' she faltered, 'about that. You must have hundreds of things you'd rather be—'

'No. No,' he insisted. 'Not at all. It's lovely to see you.' And much to his surprise, Douglas found that he meant it. It was lovely to see her. Okay, so she wasn't glossy magazine material and Tom, no doubt, would find her utterly mundane. But nor was she like her mother. She was shy – and she reminded him of himself.

Douglas finished his glass of champagne. 'Tell me more about the cooking,' he said, putting the glass down. 'Does your mother approve of that?'

Sarah nodded. 'Oh yes. Just so long as I don't do it too seriously, you understand. I'm what she calls a *fashionable* cook. You know: I mustn't *ever* take on permanent work, I must only cook for *people like us*, I mustn't let anyone treat me like a servant,' she dragged her eyes from the ornate ceiling back to Douglas, and laughed. 'I'm surprised I get any work at all.'

———◆◆◆———

Caratello, a basement restaurant in Earls Court, made no attempt to advertise itself, hiding behind a large oak door at the bottom of a flight of mossy stone steps. Sarah was right about the door. It was covered with carvings of creatures, half-human, half-animal, entwined in explicit sexual positions – but the lamps on either side were so dim that few entering the establishment were aware of this.

Philippe, the proprietor, was having a busy night. Most of his twelve tables were booked and he had been forced to turn regulars away. He hoped Mr Faulkener was going to turn up. It was nearly ten o'clock and the table in the grotto still sat empty.

Moving at double speed, carrying pudding menus, damask napkins and fragile wine glasses, Philippe crossed the room. He put the napkins and the glasses on a table that needed resetting and brought the pudding menus to the couple at the table in the corner.

Douglas smiled. 'We don't want any pudding. Just a couple of cups of coffee and the bill, please.'

'Cappuccino for me,' said Sarah.

'And for you, sir?'

'Oh . . .'

'Would you like filter, sir?'

'That sounds perfect.'

Philippe caught the eye of his youngest waiter, relayed the order and continued resetting Table 6. As he did so, the carved door swung open to admit Arabella.

'Sarah,' said Douglas, 'I think I will have one of your cigarettes after all.'

'Of course.' Sarah offered him the packet. Douglas bent forward to let her light his cigarette for him. Through the reflection in a mirror, he watched Arabella hand her coat to Philippe. He heard Philippe say, 'Faulkener? Of course, Madam. The grotto. Please follow me . . .'

Tom was coming in.

'What is it?' Sarah stretched her neck to follow Douglas' gaze. Douglas lowered his eyes, but it was too late. Tom had seen them.

'With you in a minute, Bells.' He ambled over to Douglas' table.

Douglas put down his cigarette and stood up. 'I don't think you know Sarah Knowles.'

'I don't think I do,' Tom shook her hand, and grinned at his friend, 'but I've heard a lot about you.'

'We're about to leave,' said Douglas.

'Really?'

Philippe was standing near with their coffee. Tom moved aside to let him put the cups on the table. 'Philippe!' Tom clapped him on the back. 'How's things?'

Philippe pulled back from the table and smiled politely at Tom. 'Hello, Mr Faulkener. Things are very good. I have shown your – your friend to your usual table.'

Tom turned to Douglas. 'You're not about to leave, Doug. You're just starting coffee. Won't you join us for brandy later?'

'Oh yes!' Both men looked at Sarah in surprise. 'Don't you think so? Douglas?' she broke off.

Douglas could see Arabella in the grotto, complacently reapplying lipstick. She looked glamorously messy. So, for that matter, did Tom.

'. . . Douglas?'

'He's miles away,' said Tom.

'Well,' Sarah got up. 'I'm going to the loo.'

Tom stood aside. He and Douglas watched her ask Philippe for directions and disappear behind a screen.

'What the hell are you doing?' said Douglas, unable to look at Tom.

'I could ask you the same.'

'This is different. There's nothing between me and Sarah.' He looked firmly at Tom.

'Really?' said Tom. 'Why take her to Caratello then?'

'I felt sorry for her. And if I'd known it was going to be like this, I certainly wouldn't have come here. The carvings on the door are obscene.'

'What carvings?'

Douglas snorted. 'Don't pretend you haven't seen them.' His voice was getting louder.

'But I haven't. Anyway, I told you it was like this.' Tom gave his friend a knowing smile, put a hand on his shoulder and spoke softly. 'You can do a whole lot better, Doug. Really. Don't compromise yourself.'

But Douglas wasn't listening. 'What about Kate?' he said.

'Kate?'

Douglas shook his head and his hands with frustrated vigour. 'Kate. The girl you introduced me to at lunch. Today. Remember? The lawyer?' He took a breath. 'Why are you doing this?'

'I'm having dinner with my ex-wife. What's so wrong with that?'

Douglas felt his cheeks burn. Tom was waiting. So was Philippe, with the bill. So was Sarah, behind Philippe, wanting to get back to her chair. Even Arabella was watching them from her table in the grotto. She waved at Douglas as women wave at babies on trains. He ignored her and bent down to his jacket for his wallet. He pulled out his credit card with a shaking hand and gave it to Philippe.

'I'm sorry,' he said to Tom. 'It's none of my business.'

'What's none of your business?' Tom let Sarah past, Douglas pulled out her chair and she sat down. They ignored her question.

'You're right,' said Tom, with a hard smile. 'And Arabella's waiting. I should go.'

Douglas couldn't bear it. 'I'll see you on Saturday?'

'Of course.'

'And Kate?'

Tom shrugged. 'I'll call you tomorrow.'

He made his way over to the grotto.

Sarah put her coffee-cup back onto its saucer and looked into Douglas' absent face. 'What's up on Saturday?' she said.

'What was that?'

'Doesn't matter . . .'

'I'm sorry,' he shook his head, as if clearing it of something, and smiled. 'It's my birthday. I've got a few friends coming for dinner.'

'How nice.'

'Yes.'

He watched her help herself to another cigarette. Noticing she was in need of a light, he struck a match and brought it close to her cigarette. 'And what are your plans?' he said, watching her exhale. 'Anything nice?'

'Nothing much, really.'

'Oh well in that case, do you . . . ? I mean, if you're really doing nothing, would you like to come too?'

'Are you sure?' She was beaming at him.

'Yes,' he laughed. 'Yes, completely. If you're not busy.'

'Oh I'd love to.'

'It won't be very exciting, I'm afraid.'

Maybe not to you, thought Sarah, picturing her mother's expression when she explained why she wouldn't be coming home this weekend after all.

Philipppe brought a slip of paper for Douglas to sign.

'Is service included?'

'Yes, sir.'

Douglas wasn't concentrating. He added a hefty tip and won a smile.

'Thank you, sir.'

Five

Kate, meanwhile, was in the office – and knew she'd be there all night.

Michael had left for Poland shortly after six. He'd patted her on the back and told her she'd be fine, but this was not a simple transaction. With £100 million at stake, she felt twinges of vertigo. Her time was spent reading and sending more faxes, negotiating last-minute points with an uncooperative Simon Dalziel, checking redrafts and arranging couriers. She even found herself in the library at one stage, checking a point of law on taking security over shares.

I should know this, she thought, desperately flicking through Goode on 'Legal Problems of Credit and Security'.

At eleven, she and Adam shared a pizza. It was cold, but they ate it with relish and joked about Henry Hazel's moustaches.

She sent him home at two. Soon after, revised drafts of all the documents came through by fax, and she spent the next four hours working through her final comments. Then, with her eyes half shut, she copied them to Henry Hazel's boss in California for final approval. As she waited for a response, the cleaners arrived. They worked without speaking. Kate heard only the rattling of computer keys as they were dusted and the humming of industrial hoovers.

At seven, she showered and changed back into yesterday's clothes – they still smelt of pizza. And by eight, she was at her desk with her head resting awkwardly at an angle on a pile of paper files, sleeping.

A messenger came in with a fax from California and placed it quietly in her in-tray. He'd seen them like this before. Mad. He made no attempt to wake her, and closed the office door softly behind him. But she was woken soon after by the telephone ringing.

'Hello, Kate!' said a bright voice. 'It's Liz from Reception. We've got a Mr Ross and a . . . I'm sorry sir, what was it? . . . a Mr Dall-zeel for you. Shall I show them straight into Room 4?'

'Thank you, Liz. I'll be down when Henry Hazel gets here.' Kate rubbed her eyes. Then she noticed the fax in her in-tray. She picked it up and smiled. They'd got approval. She forwarded her calls to Janet and was concentrating on putting her papers together for the completion meeting when Adam wandered in. 'Hello.'

She looked up. 'Hi.'

'You look awful.'

'Thank you, Adam.'

He grinned. 'An all-nighter, then?'

As Kate nodded, Janet put her head round the door. 'Oh dear. Look at you . . .'

Kate pulled a face.

'Henry Hazel's in reception.'

Kate rubbed her eyes again and looked at Adam. 'Do I really look that awful?'

He continued smiling.

'That means yes!' she wailed, grabbing her make-up bag and running to the loo.

Five minutes later, she was in reception, where Mr Hazel was sitting very upright. He was a small neat man with bushy moustaches who wore off-white shirts striped in browns or greys, and the trousers of his suits were too short. He'd met Kate before and thought her unnecessarily glamorous. He wanted a sound lawyer like Michael Preston. Not a pussycat. He felt that the glamour would somehow be factored into his bill, and that he was being made to pay for something he did not want.

Kate went over and offered her hand. Hesitantly, he shook it.

'Where's Mike?'

'He's in Poland.'

'Poland?'

Kate gave him a tired smile. 'He sends you his regards Mr Hazel, and his apologies for not being present. I'm afraid it's just me.'

Henry Hazel grunted.

'I've got his number, if there's a problem. But there shouldn't be,' she added, noticing his expression. 'You saw head office approval? Today's just a signing session.'

'Heard that one before,' said Mr Hazel, opening the door for her. 'After you.'

Kate smiled her thanks, and went through. 'You brought the company seals?'

'All in here,' he tapped at his briefcase. 'Weigh a ton.'

And the door swung to behind them.

Charlie got back from Spain that morning. He ought to have been developing his latest photographs but, instead, he was watching morning television when Douglas called. He turned down the volume and picked up the telephone, expecting Arabella.

'Darling—'

'It's Douglas.'

There was a pause. 'Douglas, darling. How are you?'

Douglas had a problem with being called 'darling', particularly by a man. He coughed and got to the point. 'Charlie, it's my birthday tomorrow . . .'

'Many happy returns!'

'Thanks. I was hoping you might . . . I don't know . . . It's a bit last-minute, but are you free tomorrow night to come to dinner at Waveney?'

Charlie sat back in front of the television and watched as the silent celebrity chef showed the silent blonde presenter how to make hollandaise sauce in silence.

'Just a very small group of people,' Douglas continued, 'And not very exciting I'm afraid. I'm sure you'll have got something planned already, but—'

'Douglas, darling, I can't think of anything nicer.'

'You can come?'

'We'd love to. At least, I would and I'm sure Arabella's free. Can I check with her, and get back to you?'

'Of course.'

Crippled by his own good manners, Douglas was unable to refuse. But the assumption that Arabella was included in the invitation provoked inexpressible rage. The fact that Arabella had invited him to her party, and that he'd accepted, somehow made it worse.

Cursing Tom for encouraging him to go to her party, and for encouraging him to invite Charlie at all, Douglas slammed shut his suitcase with unnecessary force and took it down to his car.

Meanwhile Tom was looking at Arabella, asleep on her stomach, with her head twisted round and her mouth wide open. Her right hand was resting on his stomach and he was wondering if he'd be able to leave now without offending her. It was almost ten o'clock and he needed to speak to Kate about Douglas' weekend.

He looked about the room. It hadn't really changed. Different magazines and different bottles on the dressing table, but the same silver mirror and brushes he'd given her that time they went to Prague, and the same pair of lamps on her chest of drawers – the ones they'd been given by his parents, the ones she should have returned to him. And, between the lamps, a picture of them cutting the cake. And then some larger photographs on the walls. All black and white. All, shamelessly, of Arabella.

Tom knew he had to get up and speak to Kate. He was about to extract himself from underneath Arabella's hand when the telephone rang.

Her left hand shot out from under her pillow and pulled the receiver towards her. 'Hello?' She rolled round and rubbed her neck. '. . . Oh, darling no, don't worry, should be getting up anyway. Yes, did you?'

Tom got out of bed.

She glanced at him and put a hand over the receiver. *It's Charlie*, she mouthed.

Tom waited as she listened to Charlie.

'What? Really? Well that sounds great.' She stared at Tom questioningly while speaking to Charlie in detached tones, 'How nice of him. Yes, I'd love to come down to Waveney this weekend . . .'

Tom frowned.

Arabella frowned back. She put an arm forward, with the palm of her hand turned up, and mouthed: *What should I do?*

He shrugged.

'Yes, Charlie. Still here. Just trying to think if I'd made any other plans this weekend . . .' Tom nodded at her: *That's fine. Come if you like.* '. . . but I don't think that I did – at least, nothing I can't cancel. So what's the plan? Okay. What time shall I pick you up?'

Tom headed for the bathroom. If Charlie was going to bring Arabella, he was bloody well going to bring Kate too.

In spite of his determination, Tom had trouble getting hold of Kate on Friday. He decided it would be tactless to call from Arabella's flat, so it was almost midday when he called her office.

He got Janet.

Kate was in a meeting. No, she didn't know what time it would be over. Could she take a message? He left his mobile number and waited for Kate to return his call.

At four, she still hadn't called. He tried again.

'Is that Tom Faulkener?'

Tom was annoyed. He didn't want anyone,

particularly not Kate's secretary, thinking that he was desperate.

'Did you give her my message?'

'It's on her desk, but she's still in the meeting, so she won't have got it.'

'Can't you take it to her?'

'What? In the meeting? Not if it's a personal call.'

'Have you any idea when she'll be out of the meeting?'

'I'm afraid I don't. But I can say you called again . . .'

'Don't bother.' He rang off without saying thank you or goodbye. Janet couldn't bear people who did that. It was plain rude.

Tom tried her home number, but it was permanently engaged. In the end, he got into a cab and went round to her flat. He didn't trust that secretary to pass on his messages. If necessary, he could drop a note through the letterbox.

———◆◆◆———

It was getting dark. Louisa put aside her magazine and switched on the light, feeling heavy-hearted. The article entitled, 'You *Can* Have It All' reminded her of Kate with her career and now a proper love life. And she couldn't banish the strong sense of injustice she felt. It was she, Louisa, whose love life should be flourishing. Kate could have her career. She could even, eventually, find domestic happiness. But not until Louisa was settled. The idea of Kate potentially having it all, while Louisa had nothing, flattened her.

She went into the bathroom, turned on the bath taps and put in the plug. Watching the water splash down and seep along to the far end, she wondered why it was that she was still so attracted to the idea of marriage. Her brother, Alex, had not been with his wife five years before their marriage fell apart – and that wasn't bad really, compared to some of his other friends. The fact that there were two children to consider made it worse – for the children, of course, but also for Alex. He'd fought furiously for joint custody – but now that he had it, he had hardly any time for parties and fun. Louisa could see that there was nothing romantic about getting married for the sake of it. And yet she wanted it.

With her little finger, Louisa tested the temperature of her bath water. She took off her clothes and stepped in. Bending her knees, she sank to a sitting position, then lay back, immersing her shoulders, then her neck and finally her hair.

Tonight she was seeing Richard Hastings – a good friend of her father's and a married man of fifty-two with no signs of leaving his wife. She knew he was no good. She didn't fancy him much anyway. She just liked knowing that he fancied her. It wasn't her problem if Anne couldn't keep him to heel. Perhaps she was having fun and games of her own? Louisa didn't care much. She closed her eyes.

And then, above the flapping of the extractor fan, she heard the doorbell ring. She waited, but the ringing was insistent.

Dripping, her towel only just covering her, Louisa picked up the intercom receiver.

'Hello?'

'Kate?'

'No. Who is this?'

'Is Kate there? It's Tom. I'm a friend of hers . . .'

'Oh,' said Louisa in a voice that told Tom she knew exactly who he was. 'She's not back yet.'

Tom hesitated. 'Would you mind if I came in? I've been trying to get hold of her all day.'

Louisa pressed the buzzer to let him in. He climbed the stairs, up and up, and then through the open door, into their flat. 'Hello?'

'Down in a minute.'

Tom waited, looking up. He didn't have to wait long. He was still looking up when she emerged from her bedroom, dressed in an oriental silk dressing gown, her hair wound into a turquoise towel.

'Hi,' she said, leaning over the banisters. 'I'm Louisa.'

'I'm Tom.'

She noticed his suit first. Perfect. Then she noticed the rest of him, and wondered if she'd seen him before. Tom. Tom. Tom who?

Below, Tom looked up at the smiling face, framed by its towel. Then he saw that the action of leaning over had caused her dressing gown to slip open.

Louisa looked down and giggled. 'It's always doing that.' She came down the stairs towards him, pulling it together, still smiling. 'Come through.'

Tom stood aside as she opened the door to the sitting room.

'Drink?'

He shook his head. 'Don't worry. I won't keep you. I just need to get a message to her.'

Louisa poured herself a glass of wine and sat down as Tom continued. 'I've been trying all day, but her wretched secretary won't pass on my messages.'

'Join the club.'

'And I tried calling here but you were permanently engaged.'

Louisa giggled again and crossed her legs, saying nothing. Then she bent her head forward, unwound the turquoise towel, and rubbed her wet hair. It was much blonder than Kate's, almost white. Her face was flushed when she looked up.

'Your message?'

He looked down at the floor. 'We've been invited for the weekend by a friend of mine – Douglas. Kate met him the other day. It's his birthday, and he and I were both hoping she might be able to make it.'

'I'm sure she'd love to.'

'I thought perhaps we could catch a lunch-time train tomorrow but I really need to speak to her about it.' He wrote his mobile number down on a scrap of paper. 'She can call any time.'

As Louisa took the paper from him, the doorbell rang. She picked up the intercom receiver. 'You're early.' She grinned at Tom through her wet hair as she listened, and then continued, 'Is it really? Well you'd better come up then.' She pressed the buzzer.

As Tom left, she heard defensive 'Hello's as he and Richard passed one another outside, and she was smiling as Richard entered.

'Who was that man?' he said, shutting the sitting-room door behind him.

'A friend,' she said, looking at the scrap of paper in her hand. *Tom Faulkener.* Why did that name ring a bell? Where had she met him before?

'A particular friend?'

'Just a friend.'

It was after nine o'clock that night by the time the documents were signed. No sleep, not much food and a glass of champagne sent Kate sailing back to her office, light-headed and over-excited.

Adam was clearing his desk. He looked up. 'All over?'

'Yes!' Kate punched the air, and he grinned. Then, putting her papers on her desk, she sat down. 'That was the good news. The bad news is that there's lots of post-completion stuff to do.'

Adam stopped still. 'Now?'

'No,' she said. 'Don't worry. It can wait until Monday. So you can go home or to the pub or whatever it is you do on Friday evenings, but I want you here first thing on Monday so that we can get started. And so that that dreadful Simon Dalziel isn't on my back hassling us for things to be done and getting smug.'

'Is eight-thirty early enough?'

'That'll be fine.'

Kate watched as he retrieved his coat from its hanger in the cupboard. He zipped up a battered holdall, dug out his squash racquet and looked at her tired face.

'Well, I'm off. Have a good weekend.'

'Yes. And you.'

Slowly, Kate put on her coat and picked up her bag. As she left her desk, the telephone rang. Without thinking, she picked up the receiver.

'Hello, Kate. It's Simon.'

'Simon.' Kate frowned. 'Please don't tell me about any last-minute disasters now. I couldn't bear it.'

He laughed. 'No. No. Don't worry. Nothing like

that. I mean, the fact that the documents weren't executed properly and the powers of attorney you produced are out of date really doesn't matter. I was hoping you might feel like a drink.'

'I hope you're not serious.'

'I am about the drink.'

Kate fiddled with the messages in her in-tray and noticed Tom had called twice. 'I'd love to. But not tonight. I'm so tired I can hardly walk.'

'You wouldn't need to.'

'The answer's still "No". I'd be drunk in a matter of seconds.'

'I wouldn't mind.'

'No!'

He laughed and suggested lunch the following week. Surprised by his persistence and lacking the energy to think of a polite way out, Kate accepted.

She looked at Tom's messages again – two of them – and smiled. So much for playing it cool. So much for stringing her out until she was on her knees. He was keen. *He was keen!* Turning back in her diary, back to Wednesday's entry – where she'd written his number next to his address – Kate began to dial. But she hadn't got to the end of the first three digits – the smart '5-8-1' that told he lived in Knightsbridge – when she thought again and put the receiver down.

It was late. Almost nine-thirty. He was bound to be out now, and she didn't want to leave a message. That would mean that she would then be the one waiting for him to call. No. No way. Not now she had the upper hand.

It would do her no harm – no harm at all – to make him wait. In the meantime, she was going home to a hot bath, maybe a video and a long sleep.

She left the office smiling. A gust of wind picked up a strand of her hair. She made no attempt to settle it, but huddled into her coat. Yellow lights shone through the glass walls of her regular bar. Inside, she could see a bunch of people from her department, secretaries and lawyers, arranged around a table full of bottles of lager and wine. Flirting, laughing, deep in conversation.

Kate moved unhurriedly through crowds of commuters. She found a stream of them moving in her direction and, pulling her bag closer to her body, let herself be carried along through the barriers down the escalators and onto the platform for trains heading west.

It was Saturday morning, and Louisa was making breakfast. She moved decisively, the steel of her saucepans and utensils flashing in the sunlight. Under the grill, bacon was curling and spitting. Beyond the sink, a Dualit toaster ticked like a bomb. Louisa watched a pat of butter melt in the centre of the frying pan, waited for it to bubble and then flicked two eggs into the middle. She loosened their edges with a fish slice, watching the transparent rims harden and turn white. Having satisfied herself that they wouldn't stick, she returned to the bacon.

Kate, in her dressing gown, with nothing on her feet, was drawn to the smell. She poked her head round the door. Louisa heard her, but did not look up. Flinching from the heat, she picked the rashers off the grill-pan and divided them equally onto two plates.

'Is one of those for me?'

Louisa nodded – and returned to the eggs. Kate stood watching, her feet cold on the kitchen tiles.

'Did you see the message?'

'What message?'

Louisa tested an egg and smiled. However big the bit of paper, however large the writing, Kate never seemed to get her messages.

'The one I left on the hall table? The one about Tom?'

'Tom?'

'He turned up last night.'

'No! When?'

There was a final click as the toast was done. Louisa took the slices out and put them in front of Kate.

'When? What did he say?'

Still saying nothing, Louisa picked up the messy packet of butter and passed it to Kate. 'Here.'

Kate forced herself to exercise the kind of patience she'd learnt at work when clients made unfeasibly heavy demands without realising it – and took the butter. Stopping herself from running to the hall table to look for the message herself, she stood next to Louisa and buttered the toast in sweeps. Louisa wasn't being difficult – not deliberately. She simply wasn't able to do so many things at once – and right now, to her, the eggs were more important.

Noticing the rough way Kate buttered the toast, Louisa decided not to say anything. She'd never been able to make Kate understand about presentation, and it wasn't worth insisting now. She'd probably have to do it herself, and then the eggs would be ruined. She eased her first egg off the bottom of the pan – it was perfect – and waited for Kate to throw the first slice of buttered toast onto one of the plates of bacon.

She put the egg very carefully on top. 'That's yours.'

Kate put the second slice on the second plate, picked up her own plate and took it to the table. 'What did he say, Lou? Did he leave a number?'

Louisa put the other, less perfect, egg on the second plate and brought it through. Kate watched Louisa sit at the table. She watched Louisa take a little bit of everything and put it all into her mouth.

'Well?'

Louisa paused to chew, then looked at Kate and smiled. 'He wants you to spend this weekend with him in Norfolk. At his friend's place. Some guy you've already met.'

'Douglas?'

'Think so. It's all in the message.'

As Louisa went on, Kate's thoughts raced. A weekend? A whole weekend? She pictured the scene – walks across ploughed fields in gum boots, thick jumpers, and the shabby sludge-coloured coat she'd had since she was fifteen. There'd be mugs of good strong tea in an Aga-heated kitchen, and an ever-present Tom who'd be turning that experience from something ordinary into something so intense she wouldn't sleep.

Her only problem was how all this might affect Louisa. Kate didn't want to shut her out, but it was important not to rub her nose in it by going on and on.

'He tried to call you at work, he said, but you were in a meeting. There's a number . . .'

'Did you like him?'

'Mm,' Louisa chewed. 'Better-looking than Shrimpy, at any rate.'

Kate laughed. 'That's not terribly difficult.'

Louisa watched Kate crash into the perfect egg. It bled its yolk over the rest of her plate. 'Actually,' she said, 'he looked slightly familiar. I'm convinced I've seen him before, but I can't think where . . .'

'Sexy people always look familiar. Think of how many times you've been approached with the *haven't I seen you somewhere before?* line.'

Louisa grinned. 'Will you go?'

'Of course.'

Later, after breakfast, Kate called him. They arranged to meet at the station that afternoon.

Louisa put on the kettle and stood at the window, waiting for it to boil. The window needed cleaning, and her focus narrowed in criticism – onto the detailed smears and dots of dirt that covered its surface – and remained there until some outside movement drew her attention out through the glass to the gardens below. There, a strengthening wind was blowing away the last of the morning's sun. Light and shade chased each other across patches of grass and through the trellis frames, rattling in the wind. Out of sight, a door was banging. Louisa rested her fingers on the wooden frame of the window pane, level with her face, and continued to stare at the movement beneath her long after the kettle had boiled.

Douglas kicked off his gum boots and padded along the corridor which led from the garden room to the gun room. There, he took off his coat and cap. He went over to a Victorian sink in the corner to wash his hands, and caught sight of his face in the mirror. He switched on the light and examined himself.

Thirty-eight. He was thirty-eight today. Did he look it? He bent his head and squinted at the reflection of its crown. Not bad. But not that good either. He put the cap back on and gave himself a lifeless smile. Unimpressed, he turned his back and threw the cap into the opposite corner of the room. He looked around for his shoes.

One of them was being carried in circles by his dog. Douglas sat on a monastic bench next to the gun safe with his feet turned out. He put out his hand.

'George . . .' he said, in tones of gentle reprimand, 'bring it here.'

George wagged his tail but continued to circle beyond Douglas' reach. Douglas was looking at him with a soft expression. 'You old mongrel.'

George's tail just wagged harder and harder.

'Bring it here . . .'

Douglas sat back and smiled at him.

'George!'

The dog stopped and faced Douglas, shoe hanging from a grey muzzle. One eye was cloudy and blue; the other, sharply focused on his master.

'Drop it.'

Slowly, George dropped it and padded off. Douglas had to get up to reach it. He wiped off George's saliva and pulled on the shoe.

They went through this ritual every day Douglas spent at Waveney. It concluded with Douglas rubbing George dry. George would lie down and then roll over on to his back with his legs in the air, looking firmly at Douglas with his good eye all the time. Using a filthy towel, Douglas would start rubbing while George made little grunting noises.

Douglas found himself thinking of Kate as she was when she had bounded into the hotel last Thursday, so shining and excited. Tom had been right. More than admiring Kate, Douglas was intimidated by her. As he rubbed the wet fur on George's legs, he asked himself whether such a concentration of good fortune in one woman was necessarily so attractive.

Was she slightly pleased with herself? Had life been too easy? He sighed and turned George onto his other side. Why was it that some girls seemed to have it all while others, like Sarah, had so little?

Douglas frowned and rubbed George so hard that the old dog yelped.

'Oh sorry, George . . .'

George gave Douglas an injured look and left the room.

Later, in his study, with George asleep and twitching by the fire, Douglas banished thoughts of his guests from his mind and turned to the estate accounts. The study had been his grandfather's, and it was one of the few rooms at Waveney which did not appear to suffer from neglect. This was due largely to the fact that its walls were covered, floor to ceiling, with bookcases squashed full of outdated encyclopaedias and dictionaries. It was impossible to see the state of the plaster beyond.

Douglas sat at his desk. It was positioned between two sets of French windows – the only place it would fit. The chair faced into the room with its back to the wall, and this arrangement annoyed him. It meant that he couldn't gaze out at the pheasants on the grass or as they picked their way along the curved stone wall beyond. Often, he'd carry his work to one of the small armchairs by the fire. But the comfort and the warmth would overcome him, and Mrs Brady would discover him and George in the study as early as ten o'clock in the morning, fast asleep amongst the estate papers.

So if Douglas had something that really needed to be done, he made himself sit at the desk. By inheriting Waveney directly from his grandfather (his parents had not wanted it, not now that they had renovated the house in Gloucestershire, replanted the garden, and settled there). Douglas had also inherited a full-time responsibility – a business – and the estate accounts were crucial to its success. He ran his eye down the balance sheet. It all seemed fine. He compared it to last year. Expenditure was up, but that was to be expected. There'd been the drainage problem at Rowden but that was more than covered by the profit figures following the improvements at Felton.

Douglas was just about to call his agent to compare notes, when the telephone rang. It was Tom. 'Just calling about Kate. She's coming. We're taking the train, the one arriving at just after eight. Is that okay?'

'That's great. Sarah Knowles is on the same one. Brady'll meet you.'

'Wonderful.'

There was a pause. Douglas shifted a blue glass paperweight from Estate Correspondence to Social. 'Tom . . .'

'Yes?'

'Did Arabella tell you she's coming too? With Charlie?'

'Yes.'

'Will that be okay?'

'Why shouldn't it be?'

Douglas, mystified, said nothing.

'I'll see you at about eight-thirty then.'

'Yes, Tom . . . yes. See you then.'

By the time Kate's cab approached Liverpool Street Station, the rain had stopped. She wound down the window, looked out and blinked. Everywhere, wet surfaces threw back the sudden sunlight with such white-sharp intensity that, in the darkness behind her eyes, a pattern of corresponding shapes emerged and flowered like negative exposures.

'Here's fine.'

Still dazzled by the glare, she paid the driver and ran into the station.

Tom was waiting at the gate to the platform, trying not to feel guilty. It wasn't as if he'd betrayed her: he wasn't going out with her, he owed her no fidelity. Opening a new packet of cigarettes, he pulled at the gold line and the wrapper fell away. For God's sake, he hadn't even kissed her. Taking out a cigarette, he bent forward to put the box in the pocket to his suitcase. He was about to light the cigarette when he saw her. She was standing on an upper level, looking down. Looking for him. He watched for a second, pleased that he was the one she was trying to find. She was wearing a well-cut camel coat and her hair, very clean, almost the same colour, fell round one shoulder.

Tom lifted an arm, and she saw him.

Indistinct announcements of arrivals and departures echoed throughout the concourse as he watched her coming towards him under the diffuse light from the Victorian glass roofs. She was smiling.

'You can't smoke in here, Tom.'

Holding the unlit cigarette in his fingers, Tom put his hands on her shoulders – she was taller than he remembered – and looked at her, close. He looked rapidly, spiralling in round the edge of her head past the collar of her coat, and then up and over the contours of her chin, her cheek and into her eyes. 'Hello.'

Kate let go of her suitcase and smiled.

She felt his hand at her spine, his elbow at her side. Easily, he pulled her forward. He was going to kiss her – completely – right here in the station. Only then, to her horror, and in a movement that would have been imperceptible to him, Kate found that she was holding back.

It's just the natural response after so long, she told herself. Some misplaced sense of caution – of privacy, perhaps – that's all. Stamping away the impulse, weakening it to something he could interpret as merely being coy, Kate pushed at her resolve and lifted her face to his.

But then somebody else's voice said, 'Tom . . .'

Tom released Kate and stared at the speaker with deliberate lack of recognition.

Kate turned from him to see a flat-faced girl looking at them. The girl was more embarrassed than they were. Her stance was uncertain and she was breathing heavily.

'Sarah Knowles – remember? Douglas told me you'd be on the train.' Sarah put a hand on her chest and caught her breath. 'It's about to leave.'

Behind them, the gates were closing.

With the unlit cigarette still lodged between his fingers, Tom grabbed Kate's suitcase, then his own, and the three of them ran down the platform.

'Which carriage are you?'

'Just get on!' Tom opened a door and threw the suitcases in. He held it for Kate and Sarah and then jumped in behind them, laughing.

Six

It had been one of those freak early days in May that could have been July. Douglas had spent all afternoon outside, and he was now sitting further round the low curved wall he could see from his study. He was drinking gin.

His eyes scanned the landscape. It stretched from the garden and the drive, across cultivated fields to the rough dune grasses beyond. On a clear day he could see right out to sea. Today, it was completely still.

He watched long shadows fall across the drive and listened to his parents – or rather, his mother – speaking. They were sitting close enough for him to be able to hear them, and far enough away for him not to feel obliged to contribute. Which was just as well, since she was talking about somebody's wedding. Douglas, whose lack of interest in weddings was exceeded only by his lack of interest in fashion, was grateful to his father for bearing the brunt of her talk.

'Will the Wentworths be there, do you think?'

'No idea. It's months away.'

'Miranda wore the most unsuitable dress at Laura

and Nicholas' wedding last year. Do you remember, John?'

Douglas said nothing.

'Henry?' She touched her husband's arm, 'I know you do. It was semi-transparent.' Henry laughed. 'No, my darling, I don't . . . unfortunately. I can't have been wearing my glasses.'

Douglas turned round and smiled at him. 'You're lying.'

'No,' Henry protested. 'No, really!' He lifted his gin with a stiff hand. 'What time are your friends turning up?'

'Any time now.'

'Do they know it's your birthday?'

'Tom does.'

With a flick of her wrist, Jane swilled ice around her empty glass. 'What's Tom doing at the moment?'

'Good question.'

She put the glass down. 'He's not still kicking his heels, is he?'

Douglas shrugged and looked back at the view. The shadows had gone. Everything was losing definition in the gathering darkness.

Henry sighed. 'The poor boy's parents got it hopelessly wrong. Far too much money, no responsibility. And neither of them keeping a proper eye on him. I suppose he might have been all right if it weren't for Lloyds . . .'

Jane sat forward in her chair. 'What'll he do?'

'Well,' said Henry, 'there's no more family money. If he can't work, and he's as extravagant as John says he is, then I suppose there's only one alternative.'

'Marriage?'

Henry nodded.

Douglas was disgusted. 'Marry someone for their money?'

'People do it all the time,' said Henry.

'That's no reason for Tom to do it too. And don't suggest it to him. He'll end up back with Arabella.'

'I don't think he will, you know. She must be in her thirties by now.'

'So?'

'Well, she won't be earning the thousands she was at the start of her career, will she?'

They all watched as the headlights of a car flickered into view.

'What's the new girlfriend like?'

'Is she rich?'

Douglas kept his eyes on the car. 'Probably not, but she's got a good job.'

'What does she do?' asked Henry, watching his son watching the view.

The car disappeared behind some trees. In a moment, they'd hear it clatter over the cattle grid.

Douglas told him.

'She sounds terrifying,' said Jane, standing up and smoothing her skirt over her stomach.

'She is.'

As the car passed over the cattle grid, George shot towards it, yelping in a frenzy of excitement.

'George!'

Henry laughed. 'Your dog's hopeless,' he said.

'But he's very beautiful.'

'You're biased. He's old and smelly and he can't see properly.'

Douglas grinned as he helped his father out of the

chair and handed him his stick.

Although they lived in Gloucestershire, Douglas'
parents often visited him at Waveney – particularly in
the shooting season, or if Douglas was having a party.
While they accepted the fact that his friends had
active sex lives, Henry and Jane took the view that
'the young' (as Jane called them) should not (unless
of course they were married) sleep with one another
at Waveney while they – Henry and Jane – were
there. That didn't mean they'd object to corridor
creeping, just so long as it was unofficial.

Douglas hated enforcing this rule. The house was
his. In theory, he could have ignored their wishes,
but in practice, there was no question of Douglas
doing anything that might discourage his parents
from coming – and so the rule was observed.

Tom had what was effectively his own room
anyway.

Arabella and Charlie were given separate rooms,
but Arabella's had a double bed.

Kate and Sarah were sharing.

'What are you wearing tonight?'

'This.' Kate shook out a black dress and laid it on
her bed. 'I hope it'll be all right, it could do with an
iron.' She looked up from the dress. 'I'd no idea it
was going to be so smart. Douglas told me he was a
farmer.'

'I expect he told you he farmed.'

'There's a difference?'

Sarah smiled and Kate, understanding now,
smiled back. She looked in the direction of Sarah's
suitcase. 'What about you?'

Sarah was wondering if she was going to be over-dressed. She'd noticed the crumbling plaster in the hall and the peeling wallpaper in their room and she was feeling uneasy. She'd expected it all to be smarter.

'I brought two dresses,' she said, looking at them there in her suitcase, still in the dry cleaners' wrappers.

'Let's see them.'

Sarah held them up. One dress was green and the other, black. 'What do you think?' she asked.

Kate peered through the rustling cellophane. 'Hard to tell, until you put them on.'

With modesty picked up from ten years of school dormitories, Sarah turned round to undress. Kate sat at the dressing table with her pot of foundation, and watched her in the mirror. She found other women's bodies fascinating and observed with interest the revelation of Sarah's short but broad-boned fleshy one, in its unimaginative underwear. Thank God I don't look like that, she thought, and then felt guilty for thinking it.

Sarah tried the green dress first. It was long, and it looked expensive. Kate was impressed with how it managed to hide so many physical flaws.

'You look great. What about shoes and jewellery?'

Sarah dug into her bag and extracted a pair of nondescript shoes and a heavy diamond necklace. Kate turned round on her stool and gazed at it. She walked over to Sarah's bed and took a closer look. 'Oh Sarah, it's stunning . . .'

Sarah threw it on the bed. 'It's my mother's.'

Kate picked it up. She held the necklace at arm's length and admired the waterfall of stones. 'You'd better look after it. I might not be able to resist the urge to put it in my case when I leave.' And, smiling, Kate handed the necklace back.

Sarah put it on. Kate examined her critically, in much the same way as Louisa would examine Kate. Those diamonds would be better with a black dress, she thought. But she, Kate, was wearing black. Resisting the temptation to steer her into the green, she suggested Sarah try the black.

'It's hard to tell unless I see you in it.'

I am so nice, she thought, as Sarah turned her back.

Hating her body, Sarah discarded the green dress. She snatched the black one off her bed and stepped into it quickly. She was zipping it up when they heard a car outside. Kate, who was standing near the window, peered out through the curtains.

'Who's that?'

Kate watched a man get out and slam the door. She recognised the silhouette. 'It's Charlie,' she said.

'Charlie?'

'Charlie Reed. You know. The guy we were talking about on the train. And I suppose that must be his girlfriend.'

Sarah shifted the dress so that it sat properly, and straightened her neck. 'What do you think?'

Kate let the curtains fall and turned back to see Sarah, uncomfortable in the other dress. To Kate's moral relief, it was too tight over her hips. 'Definitely the green. Fits you much better.'

'Really?' Sarah stood with her back to the free-standing mirror and twisted round to see her bottom. 'Oh dear,' she said and, laughing, reached for the zip.

From his bedroom at the other end of the house, Douglas also heard Charlie and Arabella arrive. He listened to the car doors bang and the crunch of footsteps on the gravel. He did not feel like greeting them.

Bow-tie in hand, he stood in front of the mirror, put up his shirt collar and twisted the tie into a bow. He thought of the scene with Tom in the restaurant and winced. Tom was right. It was none of his business.

He heard Mrs Brady's voice in the hall. '. . . he's dressing at the moment, but let me show you to your rooms . . .'

Douglas pulled at both ends of his tie so that it sat firmly, and wondered for the hundredth time what it was that made him allergic to Arabella. If Tom and Charlie both liked her then there must be something he was missing. He picked up his cufflinks and resolved to try a bit harder tonight. He'd sit her on his right. No. Kate was on his right. On his left? But then what about Sarah Knowles?

Mrs Brady was leading Charlie and Arabella past his bedroom.

'Dinner won't be until nine-thirty.'

'Wonderful,' said Arabella's trained voice, 'I can have a bath.'

'There'll be drinks beforehand in the . . .' The voices faded as they turned a corner.

Douglas sat on the bed and struggled with his cufflinks. The slits in his cuffs were too small. He was deciding to sit Arabella next to him at lunch tomorrow when there was a knock at his door. 'Yes?'

Douglas looked up to see Tom in the doorway,

holding a yellow envelope. He was fiddling with it. 'Everything all right?'

Tom looked away. 'I've been thinking,' he began.

'So have I. I was out of line, I—'

Tom came forward into the room. 'Let me finish. I wanted to apologise to you for some of the things I said that night – for putting you in a difficult position this weekend.'

'No need for you to apologise,' said Douglas, returning to his cuffs. 'I was far worse.'

'I don't think that you were.'

Douglas had done the left cuff, but he was failing with the right.

'Can you manage with those?'

'I'm fine.'

They both watched the almond slip of silver as Douglas forced it through one of the slits and began on the next. He was going to be some time.

'I'll see you downstairs then,' said Tom, dropping the envelope beside him on the bed.

'Right,' Douglas looked up, smiling. 'Won't be long.'

Tom went out and shut the door.

Sitting on the bed, wrist twisted on his knee, Douglas stared thoughtfully at the door as if, somehow, it was Tom. He couldn't remember the last time Tom had apologised for anything. And if it had been an innocent dinner, then why was he sorry? Douglas bent his head to the cufflink with a silent sigh. Pushing it through its final hole, he realised that his first instincts had been correct, and the person he felt sorry for was Kate.

As he stood up the yellow envelope slid across the

bed, with 'Douglas' written on it in Tom's small hand-writing. Douglas picked it up. Inside was a birthday card with a picture of a large dog, like George, rolling on its back. Tom had managed to find a photograph of Sarah Knowles in an old issue of *Country Life*. He'd cut out her head and stuck it on top of the dog's body.

Douglas smiled in spite of himself, and put it on the chest of drawers.

On his way downstairs, Tom stopped at the door of Kate and Sarah's room and knocked.

'Who is it?'

'Me. Tom.'

'Hang on . . .'

He heard footsteps on the other side. The door then opened a crack, and Kate's face appeared. 'We're still getting changed.'

She was halfway through putting up her hair. Tom took in the soft neck and arms and cleavage, cut out of the matt velvet, and approved. He then looked up and noticed the enhanced skin of her face and her heavy eyelashes.

'Come here.' He pulled her out towards him, into the corridor and kissed her.

Kate pulled away. 'Not here.'

'Why not?'

'We . . .' she looked around her.

'Nobody's looking at us.'

'I know, Tom. I'm just not . . .'

'Come here,' laughing, he pulled again.

Again, she pulled away. 'Stop it.'

'Stop it?'

'I'm not comfortable.'

Tom let go. 'Well,' he said. 'I'm sorry.'

Kate misread the tone. 'No, *I'm* sorry. I just . . .' Cheeks even pinker, she looked at him and smiled. But he wasn't looking back. She put out a hand. 'Tom?'

'If you don't like me kissing you, why don't you just say?'

'Don't be silly, I'm only . . .'

'You're only more concerned about people seeing us, or your make-up being spoilt, than you are about me.'

'What?'

'Or perhaps you have some middle-class complex about being seen kissing?' He regretted saying it almost before it was out. He tried to see her reaction, but Kate had withdrawn her hand and turned her back. He watched her hand give the doorknob a sharp twist.

'I'll see you downstairs.' She passed into the bedroom and shut the door behind her.

Despite the patchy wallpaper and threadbare upholstery, or possibly because of it, the drawing room at Waveney was striking. Four tall sets of windows stood on the north-east side, with views out to sea. The windows were framed by fraying silk curtains, finely embroidered with pictures of spiky birds and spiky leaves. They gave onto a wide terrace with a balustrade and three fat pillars that supported an upper balcony.

The problem with being north-facing was lack of direct sunlight. And while this meant that the furniture, the curtains and the antique wallpaper were protected from fading, the drawing room was one of the coldest rooms in the house. Even though the day had been warm, it still needed heating and there were fires at each end of the room. Mrs Brady had closed the shutters and drawn the curtains, and the resulting wall of fabric kept in some of the heat.

Above one of the fireplaces hung a large painting of Hong Kong Island before it had been built up. Arabella was looking at it when Tom and Douglas entered. Putting Kate out of his mind, Tom went straight up to her and touched her bare back. 'I recognise that dress . . .'

Arabella turned towards him. 'How terrible,' she replied. 'My standards must be dropping.'

Tom looked at Arabella's breasts underneath the red rubber. 'At least nothing else is.'

It was weak, but Arabella laughed. 'You like it?'

'I love it,' said Tom. 'You never wore sexy clothes like that when you were married to me.' And Arabella smirked.

'Oh Little Doogle!' she said to Douglas who was passing them on his way to the drinks cupboard.

'Hello, Arabella. How are you?'

She was wearing far too much scent.

'Very well,' she said, letting him kiss a cheek. She opened her bag and extracted a cigarette from a packet inside. 'Do you think you could bring me some matches?'

Douglas stared at her.

'Or a lighter?' Arabella smiled at him and returned to Tom. 'Where was I?' she said, 'Oh yes, my standards . . .'

Douglas found a lighter on the mantelpiece and handed it to her.

'Thanks.' Not looking at him, Arabella took it. She put a cigarette between her lips.

'Let me.' Tom took the lighter and flicked his thumb over it. She leant towards him. Aware that his use was over, Douglas left them. What he hated, he decided, wasn't so much Arabella, as the effect Arabella had on Tom.

———————◆◆◆———————

Kate was thrusting the last clip into the pile of hair on her head.

How dare he call her 'middle-class', as if it were something to be ashamed of? Shutting her eyes, she squirted hairspray all over the hair. How *dare* he?

Kate knew she had difficulty accepting criticism. School reports and personal assessments at work had, ever since she could remember, been full of praise. On the few occasions she had been criticised, Kate would (if she agreed with the criticism) just apply herself, solve the problem, and the criticism would stop. It was that simple. The only criticism she'd experienced, and agreed with, and which she'd done nothing about, was that she should stop trying to make things perfect. She didn't react to it because she did not see it as a problem. It was an integral part of her success, and she did not intend to change.

But Tom had criticised her background, and she was disturbed by her inability to reject the criticism as invalid. What was wrong with being middle-class? She was proud of it, wasn't she?

But she wasn't so proud if middle-class meant, as it seemed to mean to Tom, being carefully self-conscious, or too caught up in convention to allow for spontaneity. She wasn't like that, and it grated on her that Tom, whom she found unpredictable and exhilarating, might think that she was.

Twisting her neck, but keeping her eyes on her reflection in the mirror, she jabbed an earring into her left ear. She wound on the back of the earring and then picked up the other. He was deliberately putting her down. He wanted her to feel insecure.

She twisted her head the other way. Jab. Into the right. Was it really just a petty reaction to her not wanting to kiss him, or was he trying to tell her that he wasn't serious, that she wasn't his equal?

'We should go down.' Sarah was waiting by the door. Unmistakably not middle class, with her plain face and her mother's diamonds.

'Fine,' said Kate, winding in the back to her second earring.

Tom was still chatting to Arabella beneath the painting of Hong Kong when Kate followed Sarah into the room. Arabella's back was to the door.

They both looked for a second at the dazzling figure, sucked into its crazy dress, and then Sarah turned away, to the less intimidating sight of Douglas pouring drinks.

Kate went on looking, and found herself warming to the girl Tom was talking to. She looked funky and glamorous. She dressed like she didn't care about class – she was above that sort of thing. Deciding that Sarah Knowles could keep her mother's diamonds, Kate accepted a drink from Douglas and asked him who she was.

'That's Arabella Dean,' said Douglas carefully. 'Charlie's girlfriend.'

Kate stared at Arabella with informed eyes, and recognised her. 'Not the model? The one who did those bra ads?'

'Not a bra in sight tonight . . . come and meet her.'

He led her over, and introduced them. Ignoring Tom, and smiling at Arabella, Kate complimented the dress and Arabella, who was susceptible to compliments, mirrored the smile. 'It's cool, isn't it?'

'Very.'

'I do have to cover myself in talcum powder before I put it on,' she said, holding her cigarette back so that the smoke didn't blow into Kate's face. 'And I can't wear underwear. But I think it's worth it. Don't you?'

Kate laughed. 'It's fabulous. Where's it from?'

Finishing his glass of champagne, Tom left them by the fireplace and went to get himself another.

Arabella offered Kate a cigarette. 'What do *you* do?'

The tone of Arabella's voice told Kate she assumed that Kate knew already what it was that Arabella did, but Kate didn't mind. She took the cigarette and smiled. Tom had taken the lighter with him, so she borrowed Arabella's cigarette to light it.

'Thanks.' She handed it back to Arabella. 'I'm a lawyer.'

'Intcresting.'

'Not really,' said Kate, still smiling. 'I spend most of my time in a room with no daylight, reading contracts between banks and companies. I'd much rather do what you do.'

'Would you?' Arabella finished her cigarette and threw it into the fire. 'It's not as glamorous as people think, you know.'

'What are you working on at the moment?'

Arabella hesitated. The Brompton Cemetery shoot was done now. Charlie was helping her compile an up-to-date portfolio, and her agency said there was a chance of a DIY Store commercial, but she wasn't really working on anything, and she couldn't bring herself to tell Kate this.

'Look who's *here!*' Charlie slid an arm round Arabella's waist and looked at Kate knowingly. 'Hello, darling,' he turned to Arabella. 'I told you he was keen. I *told* you . . .'

They both looked at Kate, who smiled. 'He just invited me for the weekend.'

'*He just invited me for the weekend*. Darling – what more do you want? A proposal?'

Arabella caught Kate's eye and pulled a face. 'Why? Why do men *still* think that the only thing a woman really wants is to get married?'

'You mean you don't?' Charlie asked.

'No!' said Arabella and Kate, together.

Charlie laughed. 'Okay,' he said. 'What do you want then?'

'Another cigarette,' said Arabella as she detached herself from Charlie's arm and went in search of the lighter.

'Char-lie . . .' said Kate, involuntarily imitating his voice as she guided him towards a sofa. 'She's great.'

Charlie grinned. 'Isn't she?'

'How did you meet? Was it work?'

'No, funnily enough, not really . . .' Charlie sat next to her and scratched his head. 'Patric Tissot – you know him?'

Kate shook her head.

'Patric takes pictures too. He introduced us properly last year, but that wasn't the first time.'

'When was the first time?' she asked, indulging him.

'Well,' he smiled. 'She doesn't remember it of course, but I first met Arabella the day she and Tom got married. I was only an inexperienced photographer's assistant then and she was – well, you know. And I was so mesmerised, I could hardly string three words together . . .' Charlie's laugh evaporated as he noticed Kate's expression.

'Married?' she said slowly. 'Arabella and Tom?'

Tom had seen Arabella leave the room. He waited a minute and then followed her into the hall. It was cooler there, and dark. She was standing by the window with her box of cigarettes.

'Arabella?'

She could just see the cars in the courtyard, lit by the lights from the house.

'What's wrong?'

She said nothing.

Tom sat on the window ledge, close to Arabella, but facing in. He rested his hands on his knees.

'The other night . . .' he began.

Arabella put a hand on his shoulder and squeezed it. 'It's okay.'

Tom shut his eyes, feeling her rubbing his shoulder. They stayed like that for some time, with the voices from the drawing room in the distance, and the air cool around them. She looked down. For a moment, because his eyes were shut, she was free to enjoy his face without feeling that she was staring.

Then Tom felt her gaze and opened his eyes. Her

hair was hanging forward, and she was smiling at him – a smile of undisguised desire.

Why could Kate not look at him like this? Why had she not let him kiss her? Where was her passion? He remembered the cold fingers pushing him off, and a face closing down as she looked away. *She's not interested* . . . the mocking tone of Charlie's voice the other night rose loud and clear in his memory. . . . *You're losing your touch*.

Maybe I am, he thought. But not where your girlfriend, *and my ex-wife*, is concerned.

'I don't know what to do,' he said. 'I want you both.'

'That's okay with me.'

'It is?'

'Mm.' She was still rubbing his shoulder, moving her hand in slow circles. Tom couldn't help himself. 'Kiss me,' he said.

She bent forward. He had to push her hair out of his face.

There was a burst of conversation, and the door to the drawing room opened.

'Darling – s,' Charlie waved at them across the hall. 'There you are. Douglas says you've got the lighter . . .' He was walking towards them. 'You'd have thought that in a house this size we'd be well supplied with lighters, or at least matches.'

'Here.'

The lighter passed from Tom's hand into Arabella's. She took it back to Charlie, and they re-entered the drawing room together.

Tom remained at the window for a second, wondering how much Charlie had seen.

He was sitting next to Douglas' mother at dinner.

'Tell me, Tom,' she said. 'What are you up to these days?'

Tom smiled at her. 'Oh . . .'

'I can't remember what John said you were doing.'

'I . . .' Tom filled his mouth with soup.

'You young people are always so busy. John never seems to have a minute to spare.' Jane watched him closely. They both knew that she already knew the answer. Jane didn't know the details, and she didn't know that Douglas was effectively subsidising him, but she did know that he didn't have a job, and she disapproved of inactivity, especially where Tom was concerned.

'I'm still sorting out my father's affairs. We had a lot of trouble with the Lloyds litigation . . .'

'I know. But what plans have you got for the future?'

'I haven't thought.' He took another mouthful of soup.

'What about that gallery?'

Tom said nothing.

'What went wrong exactly?'

Still saying nothing, Tom finished his soup.

'We could have helped you.'

He met her inquisitive eyes. 'As I said, Jane, I haven't decided.'

'But you should.'

The bowl was whisked away as he put down his spoon and reached for his glass.

'. . . I'm your godmother, Tom. Your dear mother doesn't have a clue about these things. Who's going to push it if not me?'

'It's not your problem.'

At this point Arabella, who'd been listening, leant across Tom. 'I agree,' she said to Jane. 'It's about time he got a job.'

Jane considered Arabella in her rubber dress long enough for Arabella to wonder whether she should have worn it.

'Arabella,' she said. 'Forgive me. I can't remember . . . what is it that you do?'

'Well,' Arabella coughed, 'I still model a bit . . .'

Tom laughed. 'It seems to me that the only person round this table with a proper job is Kate.'

They all looked at Kate, who looked back at them defensively from her conversation with Charlie.

'I was just saying that you were the only person here with a proper job,' Tom explained.

'Am I?'

The room was silent for a second.

'And Sarah,' said Douglas quickly. 'You're a professional cook, aren't you?'

'Oh, but it's not a proper job. Not like being a lawyer.'

'Don't be so modest.'

Jane put her napkin on the table and moved her chair back. 'I'm sorry,' she said to Tom. 'I must check the kitchen . . .'

Tom was on his feet. He pulled out her chair as she rose. And as he sat back down, he glanced again at Kate. She was playing absentmindedly with the salt cellar and listening to Charlie. 'I wouldn't be able to forgive someone who deceived me,' he was saying.

Tom looked closely at Kate. There was something in her attitude – in the way she sat, the way she stabbed at the salt – that made him know she was very angry, and that he was the one at fault. He found himself wanting to tell her he was sorry – but why? For what? *She* was the one who'd rejected *him*. Surely she should be apologising. Not him, unless – could she have seen what had happened, in the hall, with Arabella?

He leant forward. 'Nor would I.'

'There,' Charlie nodded at him and looked back at Kate. 'Even Tom agrees with me.'

But, to Tom's fury, Kate didn't even turn her head.

'What – never?' she said, directly to Charlie. 'Even if you loved them?'

'I'd want revenge.' Charlie pulled the salt towards him and started making half-moon patterns in it with the spoon.

'What's wrong with you?' Tom caught her arm.

'Nothing,' said Kate, pulling away.

'Is it something I said?'

'No.'

'What then?'

Shrugging, she walked on across the hall, but again he held her arm.

'Stop, will you? I don't understand.'

'Why didn't you tell me you were married?'

They went into Douglas' study. The fire had gone out and the room was cold. Tom shut the door. 'Didn't you know?' he said.

'Why should I know?'

'I mean, we . . . she was . . .'

'Do I have to read *Hello!* magazine to find out about significant bits of your past?'

'It's not that significant, darling. We got divorced eight years ago.'

'So it's not important?'

'Of course it's important, but I'm not going to blurt it out the first second I meet someone. I'd have told you soon enough.'

'No, Tom. Not soon enough. I had to go through the humiliating experience of hearing about it from Charlie, for God's sake.'

'Oh,' he said. 'I'm sorry. I'm sorry about that. I didn't think.'

Saying nothing, she pulled out a book.

'. . . but it wasn't deliberate. I didn't set out to humiliate you.'

'Then why did you call me middle class?' she replied, looking at her book.

'That was a joke.'

Kate turned a page. 'I'm glad you found it funny.'

He took the book from her and put it back on the shelf. 'Stop being paranoid.'

'I'm not being paranoid.' She moved away from him and sat in one of the little armchairs by the fire. He watched her pick a dog hair off her velvet dress and flick it to the floor. 'I don't like being kept in the dark, and I don't like you telling me I'm middle class.'

'What's so wrong with being middle class?'

'You think it makes people inhibited.'

Tom smiled. 'Well,' he said, moving towards her. 'Does it?' He pulled up the other little chair and sat opposite Kate with his forearms on his knees, gazing at her.

Kate couldn't help smiling back. 'Are you challenging me?'

He nodded.

She raised her eyebrows. 'What – now?'

'Yes. Now.'

He watched her consider it. Then she sat back in her chair and recrossed her legs. 'No.'

He sat back, too, and shrugged. 'There,' he said. 'I was right.'

'You think I'm inhibited because I won't seduce you – now?'

'If you waited, it would be because you are inhibited,' he said

'It might be because I prefer to be seduced.'

'You are being seduced.'

'Not very well,' she began, but Tom was already on his feet, pulling her out of the chair, his hands rough under her arms. Her feet brushed the floor as, laughing, they fell against the encyclopaedias.

Kate's hair slipped from its clips. She shook it with vigour and its weight toppled over one side of her face. With the back of her head resting between Volumes XIII and XIV of the 1854 edition of *Norfolk Farming*, Kate let Tom hold her the way he'd held her at the station and, still laughing, they kissed.

Seven

To the delight of Douglas' parents, Sarah Knowles played bridge.

'Not terribly well, I'm afraid,' she said. 'More kitchen bridge.'

'Wonderful!' said Henry. 'Just like us.'

This was a lie. Douglas looked at him and coughed.

'Just one rubber?' pleaded Henry.

Douglas sighed. 'Arabella? Charlie? Do either of you play bridge?'

Arabella and Charlie, who were sitting at the far end of the room, just laughed and shook their heads. They certainly weren't going to admit it if they did.

Jane was already setting up a table by the fire. 'Where are the good cards?'

Douglas caught Sarah's eye and smiled at her. 'You don't have to play, Sarah. They can be dreadful bullies.'

Sarah looked at Henry, whose face managed to express both enthusiasm and guilt. She smiled. 'I'd love to play, but you must promise to be patient.'

Henry beamed. 'Of course.'

Charlie and Arabella had discovered the back-gammon set.

Kate and Tom had disappeared.

Douglas submitted to the inevitable and produced the good pack of cards from a chest behind the sofa. 'Only one rubber, Father.'

'Of course.'

They were on the fourth game when the double-doors opened and Kate entered, followed by Tom. The drawing room was silent with concentration, from the bridge table, and from the sofa. Tom caught Kate's eye. 'Bit serious in here,' he whispered.

Kate would have smiled at this, if she hadn't already been smiling.

'Armagnac?'

She nodded.

As he poured two glasses, she checked her reflection in the glass on the wall by the door. Hoping it wasn't too obvious what they'd been doing, she picked out a couple of redundant clips and tucked a strand of hair behind her ear.

'You look wonderful,' Tom murmured, behind her.

'I look a disgrace!'

Tom gave her a glass. 'Exactly.'

Kate pulled a face and went in search of bathroom privacy, to repair the damage.

Arabella handed Charlie the dice, and looked up from the sofa. 'Is that armagnac?'

'Want some?'

'Love some,' she smiled.

'Charlie?'

Charlie had thrown an impossible combination, and was staring at the board. 'No thank you, darling . . .' He scratched his head. 'Can't I move at all?'

'No,' said Arabella, scooping up the dice.

Tom poured a third glass and took it over to Arabella. She felt him approach and turned from the board, her face unsmiling, momentarily transparent as she took the glass. Charlie looked away.

'Well,' said Tom, 'who's winning?'

'I am.'

'No, darling,' said Charlie, slowly, 'no you're not.'

Arabella laughed. She kissed him briefly and returned to the board. He still couldn't move and it was her turn again. Tom and Charlie watched her throw a double.

'Yes, I am . . .'

Still smiling, Kate reappeared, her hair brushed onto her shoulders. She approached the bridge table. Douglas was sitting with his back to the fire and frowning. He was too hot. He'd been left to play an absurd hand and he was losing heavily. The table demanded his full attention.

Sarah Knowles, who was playing dummy, twisted round and smiled at her. 'Hello, Kate. We're playing bridge.'

'So I see. What are trumps?'

'Clubs,' said Henry, examining Sarah's cards on the table and calculating that Douglas had to have the five. And that it was his last winning card.

Kate pulled up a chair behind Douglas and noted the state of play with interest.

'There you are . . .' Henry pushed the trick towards his son.

'Did I win that?'

'Yes – but you've lost the rest.'

Henry and Jane gave one another happy looks of

victory and totted up the score.

Douglas threw the remains of his hand on the table and looked round at Kate who was still looking at the table, her face in profile very close to him. He preferred her hair down.

'Do you play?' he asked.

Kate raised her eyes. In a state of drunken love with everything, she decided he was sweet and smiled. 'A bit.'

Her smile had the same distracting effect on Douglas as the expression she'd been wearing the day they'd met, and he looked at his feet.

Then, from the other end of the room, there was a burst of laughter and Charlie stood up. Waving his handkerchief with an imperial flourish, he announced his surrender, and said that he was going to bed. 'Are you coming?'

Arabella began setting up the board again. 'Oh Charlie. Stay. Have another drink and watch me beat Tom.'

'But darling, if I have another drink I shall never make it upstairs. And I have no particular desire to watch you beat Tom. Are you coming with me?'

Arabella didn't look up. 'Just one game,' she said.

Tom was helping her put out the pieces. Charlie looked at them both for a second, and then went over to the door. 'Night all.'

At the other end of the room, Henry passed Sarah a pack of cards. 'Your deal,' he said. Sarah dealt slowly and deliberately.

Douglas, whose chair faced into the room, noticed Arabella get up. She moved so that she was sitting on the sofa, right next to Tom. Douglas watched him light a cigarette and put a hand on Arabella's knee. He bent his neck to listen to something she was saying.

'Kate,' said Douglas, 'why don't you go over and help Sarah to play her hand?'

'Yes. Please do, Kate.' Sarah moved her chair to make room for her. 'I'm in need of all the help I can get.'

Kate picked up her chair and brought it round to Sarah's side of the table, so that her back was now to the sofa. She took Sarah's cards, flicked them into a fan and rearranged them. Then she held them so that Sarah could see them, ran her index finger along a row of six spades and opened the bidding.

'One spade.'

Douglas had four spades to the ace and most of the points in the pack. He waited for his mother to say 'No bid', jumped Kate's bid to three spades and waited for his father. 'Hurry up.'

Henry smiled. 'No bid.'

Kate raised the bid to four spades.

'No bid,' said Jane.

'No bid,' said Douglas.

'What?' Henry had no spades and no points, and he could smell a grand slam. Leaving it at four spades was blatant under-bidding.

But Douglas simply repeated his bid, and prompted Jane to lead.

Jane threw down a low heart. As dummy, Douglas arranged his cards on the table. Henry and Jane and Kate all stared at them. Idiot, thought Kate. We could have got a slam. Henry frowned. He took a breath, and was about to speak when he felt Jane looking at him.

'You'll be okay, won't you?' asked Douglas, standing up.

'We'll be fine,' said Sarah, smiling as she reached for Douglas' king of hearts.

'Are you sure you want to do that?' asked Kate.

Henry's fingers twitched on the green baize of the card table.

Douglas caught his mother's eye and smiled. 'I'll be back in a second,' he said and, picking up his glass of cognac, he wandered over to join Tom and Arabella.

'Anything more to drink?' he asked, leaning against the sofa.

Tom's hand abandoned Arabella's leg as he reached for his glass. He gave it to Douglas. 'Thanks. Bells?'

Arabella shook her head.

Douglas filled Tom's glass and returned with it. 'Here you are.' He handed it to Tom and then sank into a high-backed armchair by the wall that had been his grandmother's favourite. With a cigarette in one hand and his glass in the other, Tom's hands were now fully occupied.

Douglas crossed his legs and smiled at Arabella. The backgammon board, set up for a new game, sat unplayed between them on the floor. 'I'm not interrupting anything, am I?'

'No. Not at all.' Tom flicked his cigarette ash into the fire and looked over at the bridge table. Beyond the little glasses and the nearly empty bottle of warm brown armagnac, sat Kate with her head on one side, guiding Sarah.

'Don't tell me she's a bridge pro, too.' Arabella sat forward and followed his gaze.

They saw Kate sweep a trick towards a small pile on her left. She examined Sarah's remaining cards and then those on the table. The others watched, waiting for her to lead. Instead she threw her cards face up on the table and said, 'The rest are ours.'

Henry glanced at his hand and nodded. 'Well done. A pity your partner didn't have the sense to bid it.'

'I'm so sorry, I—'

'Not you, my dear,' said Henry gently. 'Him.'

From the safety of his grandmother's chair, Douglas grinned at his father and took another sip of armagnac. 'We didn't need to bid any more, Father. It was just one rubber – remember? You agreed. And we won.'

Henry looked at his score card and then back at his son. 'That's not the point.'

'What did you expect? I wasn't going to risk losing a slam when we could win the rubber.'

'But where's the fun in that?'

'He doesn't do it for fun,' muttered Jane, tidying the cards into a pile.

Sarah looked at all the numbers and lines on the score card, trying to make sense of them. 'So we won?'

'Yes you did,' said Jane, putting the cards back into their box. 'And it's time for us to call it a night.'

Henry turned to look at the fine gold hands of the clock on the mantelpiece and the movement caught his wife's eye. She smiled. 'It's almost one o'clock, dear. Come on.'

Bidding the others goodnight, they went to bed.

'Well,' said Sarah to Kate, in the silence that followed, 'I might go up too.' She pushed back her chair and stood up. 'Coming?'

Kate, undecided, looked over at the group by the backgammon board. Tom turned his head and smiled at her.

'Don't go,' he said, ostensibly to them both. 'Have another drink . . .'

'I don't think I could,' said Sarah.

'Of course you can. Have some of this,' he waved his glass of armagnac. 'It's heavenly.'

But Kate could feel him asking for more. She smiled. It was all very well – a bit of kissing in the library – but she didn't trust herself to win, to want to win, the gentle battle that would almost certainly happen if she and Tom were the last ones to go to bed. And why else would she be staying up? Call me middle class, she thought, dragging her eyes from his. But I'm not up to that with you. Not yet.

Douglas was on his feet. 'Let me get some for you both,' he said. 'Come on, Sarah. Kate. You've drunk virtually nothing tonight.'

Kate shook her head. 'That's not true,' she said. 'In fact, quite the reverse. And I'm tired.'

'So am I,' echoed Sarah.

'Do you mind?' Kate looked at Tom, whose face expressed humorous disappointment.

'Of course not,' said Douglas, smiling at them both.

Kate followed Sarah's green bottom up the stairs, glad of her decision. It wouldn't do any harm for her to spend tonight in her own room – and for him to wait.

Douglas sat back in his grandmother's chair. Out of the corner of his eye he could see Tom's right hand stubbing out a cigarette. Tom passed his glass of armagnac from left hand to right and put his right hand on Arabella's shoulder.

'You okay?' he asked her.

Arabella shifted her shoulder closer to him and nodded.

Douglas uncrossed his legs, put his feet flat on the floor, and stretched from his chair to a wooden box that sat on a table just within his reach. He pulled the box towards him and put it on his lap. Arabella and Tom watched as he opened it, and held it towards them. Inside, like a row of missiles, lay twelve fat Cuban cigars.

Tom adored them. He smiled into the box as, with delicate fingers, he liberated one. He clipped off the end, put it into his mouth and retrieved his lighter from the arm of the sofa. There was then a display of patient puffing, checking and puffing again, as it was ignited.

Douglas looked at them both, caught in a cloud of aromatic smoke. 'This is jolly good armagnac,' he said, holding up his glass.

'It's always good,' said Tom.

'Is it? *Is it?* Well. No wonder you always accept my invitations.' Douglas laughed so loudly, Arabella wondered if he'd had too much to drink.

'They've got pretty good armagnac at Gibbs's, haven't they? Tom?'

'I don't remember.'

'You haven't had it? Not as good as this, of course. Blows your head off. But I like it when it does that . . .' Douglas laughed a portly laugh. 'Bill Streetley was really getting stuck into it the other night.'

'Bill Streetley?' said Tom. 'I haven't heard from him in ages. How is he?'

'Back from the Philippines for Laura's wedding. Put on a bit of weight, but on top form.'

Arabella didn't know Bill Streetley. She yawned, listened to them for a few minutes and then gave up. 'Well,' she said, giving Tom's arm a significant press as she stood. 'Good night.'

'So early?' Douglas closed the cigar box with a satisfying snap, and put it back on the table. 'What about your game of backgammon?'

Arabella's room was in the oldest part of the house, at the end of a long corridor. The corridor was dark but, in the distance, the rectangle of her door was visible in the form of a thin line of light broken by hinges. Arabella felt for the handle, opened the door and entered.

Her room was warm. The curtains had been drawn and the bed covers pulled back. Only the low-watt lamps at the dressing table and one at her bedside had been left on. Their old silk shades cast a sepia glow across the room so that everything had the brown tint of an Edwardian photograph.

Arabella kicked off her shoes and sat at her dressing table.

Holding her face at an angle to the mirror, she looked at her reflection and smiled. The combination of the angle and the smile managed to give, to Arabella, a false but pleasing impression of perfect symmetrical bone structure.

To an observer, the coy smile into infinity looked mad. Arabella held the expression until she was satisfied. Then, dragging her eyes from the mirror, she reached for her cream. Absentmindedly slapping it on, she began thinking about Tom, and whether she should try to join him later. She took a ball of cotton wool from a glass bowl to the left of the mirror, and began wiping.

The gloss and colour was falling from her face in streaks when, in the mirror, she noticed Charlie's eyes, and jumped. He was still in his dinner jacket, and sitting in an armchair in the darkest part of the room.

'Charlie –?'

'Darling,' he said. 'We need to talk.'

Arabella threw the cotton wool into a bin and pushed back her hair. 'I'm tired.'

'It won't take long,' Charlie persisted, and she knew he wasn't leaving.

She went over to the bed and sat on it, unrolling her hold-ups. 'Go on then.'

Unsmiling, Charlie watched as she threw first one, and then the other, onto a pile of clothes heaped around her suitcase. 'I want to know what's going on with Tom,' he said

'Nothing.'

But she could tell from Charlie's expression that he didn't believe her, and that this was serious. In seconds, the irritation she'd been feeling at his theatrical voice and affectations evaporated. The prospect of having no boyfriend, no protector, scared her. Not thinking that it was, perhaps, a blessing that Charlie had suspected something, that she'd be free of him and that, maybe, this was a good thing, Arabella clung on without really knowing why.

She gave him a tentative smile. 'Now Charlie,' she

said, as if speaking to a child. 'You have to understand that Tom and I are very close. We go back a long way.'

Without her make-up, Arabella was a different woman. Although it was just the surface that had been removed, the effect was as if she'd lost her guts. There was no energy left. Her tired skin was shiny from the cream, and it was hard to see where her mouth began. Her eyes were small and dim. 'There isn't anything for you to be jealous about,' she went on. 'Tom's with Kate. I'm with you. End of story.'

Charlie said nothing.

'Don't you trust me?'

In the silence that followed, Charlie pressed his lips together slowly, and then released them. 'No,' he said at last. 'Not after tonight. And I don't trust Tom.'

'But what happened to make you so suspicious?'

He shrugged. 'My instincts are never wrong, darling. You were different.'

'But I've just explained. You can't expect two people who've been married just to forget it all.'

'Clearly.'

Outside, in the passage, a clock struck the half hour. Charlie ran a thin hand through his hair. He looked at her and shook his head.

'At least explain what makes you think that there's anything going on between us . . .' Her voice trailed off as they both heard a knock at the door.

Charlie reached the door first and opened it. 'Hello, Tom.'

'Charlie.'

Charlie looked at Arabella over his shoulder. 'She's all yours. Good night.'

Tom stood back. ''Night . . .'

Charlie brushed past him, back along the passage and up a flight of stairs at the end.

'Charlie!' Arabella pushed past Tom, and chased Charlie down the corridor, her rubber dress squeaking as she ran.

Tom watched her bare feet disappear up the stairs.

He was not surprised when, at lunch the next day, there was no sign of Charlie.

'Where is he?' said Kate, putting a napkin on her lap and reaching for a glass of water.

'Gone.'

'What? Back to London?'

Tom nodded.

'Why?'

Tom looked pointedly at Arabella, who was at the sideboard, helping herself to pork. 'There was a row last night.'

'What kind of row?'

'Er. Terminal.'

'Kate,' said Henry, who was hungry, 'why don't you go and help yourself.'

Kate, who was not, put a small amount of crackling and a couple of brussels sprouts on her plate and brought it back. Arabella was sitting on the other side of Tom, listening to Douglas. Watching her, Kate leant close to Tom and spoke quietly. 'What happened?'

'Well,' said Tom, who'd spent all morning thinking about what he was going to say when Kate asked this, 'apparently Charlie thought that there was something going on between us – between Arabella and me.'

Although Tom was whispering, his tone was so

160

casual that the sense of his words was delayed. Kate felt the implication some seconds after she'd heard the words.

She dragged her eyes from Arabella and let them rest on Tom's inscrutable face. 'What?'

Tom stretched for a decanter of claret. 'For some inexplicable reason, Charlie thought that Arabella and I were rekindling our marriage.'

She waited for him to fill their glasses. 'Are you?'

Tom replaced the decanter, and pulled a face. 'Come on. Would I be inviting you here and ravishing you in the study if I was still interested in her?'

But there was something closed – polite – in his expression. And that mild non-communication triggered a bullet-fast series of associations in Kate's brain. Images of Mark, her ex, the one who'd betrayed her, shot up on her mental screen, and her heart seized up with fear. But her reason limped behind, so that all she could think was, Why? Why am I feeling like this? What is wrong with me?

'Kate?'

'What do you think made Charlie think this?' she said at last.

'No idea.'

'Is she still in love with y . . .' Arabella was turning towards them. Stopping abruptly, Kate turned to Henry on her left.

Henry had been preparing himself. 'Douglas tells me you're a solicitor,' he said.

'Yes,' she smiled. 'Yes I am.'

Henry filled her glass with wine. 'I was wondering what you think about Europe. Does the legal profession want a pro-European Government?'

'I'm not an EC specialist,' was her automatic response, 'but I'd say that the profession as a whole is pretty reactionary.'

'Is it?'

Kate looked at him, unsure of where this was going. 'I think we're used to our own legal system – you know, precedent and statute and the House of Lords being the final court of appeal, and so on. The presence of the European Court tends to confuse that a bit.'

'I see,' said Henry, enjoying himself. 'But what do *you* think?'

'Me? Well. I'm a *City* solicitor. And the City's line is much more in favour of Europe, but I'm sure you know . . .'

'And you agree?'

She looked at him again. 'I . . . I can't help thinking that a lot of the scepticism comes from fear and sentiment, which doesn't strike me as a good enough reason for missing out – for missing out on the obvious benefits.'

'On trade and the economy?'

'On trade and the economy,' she echoed, with the uncomfortable feeling that she'd been pulled into an argument.

'Could you pass the salt?' said Arabella, to Tom, while Kate battled on with Henry.

'Of course.' Tom handed it to her, and Arabella took it without looking at him. Digging at the crystals, she put a pile of them on the side of her plate – the correct way, like Tom – even though it made more sense to scatter them over the potatoes – but that was wrong, she knew, because he'd laughed at someone else for doing that, and because she'd read it in some book in someone's loo – not toilet – you never said toilet . . .

Tom lifted the salt cellar from her hands. The air about her was violently quiet. 'You okay?'

Arabella nodded.

'. . . which shows, I think, what happens if you lose control of your own rate of interest Do you really want some German bank controlling our fiscal policy, my dear?'

'But that will happen anyway, indirectly . . .'

As Arabella's attention swivelled towards Kate and Henry's conversation, Tom caught her eye and smiled. 'What's your opinion of the Common Market?'

'I prefer Harvey Nichols.' And then, as if they'd been having another conversation, Arabella put down her fork and said, 'He's taken the bloody car.'

'You can come back on the train with me and Kate.'

'That'll be fun.'

'And Sarah Knowles.'

'Laugh a minute.'

'Come on, Bells. It's not that bad,' he took another mouthful. 'You don't want to be lumbered with someone you don't love.'

'I could say the same to you.'

Tom swallowed and glanced at Kate. She hadn't heard. She was arguing about the government's agricultural policy with Henry, and Henry was definitely winning.

'What makes you think I don't love her?'

'The fact that you fucked me on Thursday night?'

Tom tried to glare her quiet, but Arabella finished eating and pushed back her chair. 'I think most

163

people would agree with me that, if you loved her, you wouldn't be cheating on her. Or have I missed something?'

'*Arabella.*'

To Tom, it was as if she was shouting. Again he checked. Again, Kate hadn't heard.

'Yes?' Arabella met him with a cheap grin. 'Anything wrong?'

'Not. Now.'

'Then when?'

'In London. I'll call you.'

'Promise?'

'Promise,' he echoed, as he'd echoed before – conspiring uneasily in the parent-child language of their past.

Later, walking through dune grasses on her way to the beach, Kate thought of how her imagined weekend had differed from the reality. Okay, so here she was in gum boots and the raggedy coat, but that was the extent of it.

The screening of a James Bond film on television that afternoon meant that Tom had decided not to come. Kate had tried to persuade him. Didn't he want some fresh air before going back to London? Wasn't this the point of being in the country? Couldn't he see old films any time?

But the pleading look Tom gave her as he sank to the sofa – frail coffee cup in one hand, fresh packet of cigarettes in the other – had been enough for Kate to drop it. And she didn't fancy her chances against Ursula Andress.

So it was just her, Douglas and Sarah (Arabella had

left straight after lunch – catching an early train). Watching Douglas in front – climbing the dune with Sarah, George pressing at their heels – Kate wondered if she'd been wrong about him, too. He wasn't going to set the world on fire, but there was clearly more to Tom's quiet friend than she'd originally allowed.

Of course there was 'more'; she smiled at the word. There was a fuck-off house, a massive estate and God only knew how much money – but that wasn't the point. Kate stopped for a second to tie back her hair and thought that, in some ways, perhaps it *was* the point. Or rather, what was interesting was that, in spite of it all, he wasn't proud. If anything, the reverse. And it wasn't that brand of self-effacing behaviour that came from the idea that there was nothing to prove. He didn't have the elegance. It was more to do with the fact that he simply didn't bring those things into the balance when he looked at himself. They weren't important to him.

Noticing this attitude – liking it – she looked at herself and realised how accustomed she'd got to the ways of the City, to a world where, to survive, she'd had to make the most of all her assets. The sight of Douglas with that huge advantage over other people and not using it, even subtly, made her feel a bit ashamed.

She'd found him in the kitchen that morning, sitting at the table with the housekeeper, going through a list. The housekeeper had been teasing him about his handwriting, about the amount of money spent on his education, and what a waste it was if he couldn't even write properly – and Douglas was laughing and agreeing with her. They behaved as equals. The mutual affection and clear lack of tension seemed to boost, not detract from, the underlying respect – and added up to the kind of relationship Kate wished she had with her secretary.

It was a pity, she thought, that Douglas couldn't have been as relaxed with the rest of them, a pity that he was so unsure of himself, so shy. But she still felt a fool for not giving Tom more credit. How could she have expected his friend to be some inbred Sloane, riddled with arrogance and ignorance and banging on about the Empire? Of course there'd be 'more'.

Moving back to thoughts of Tom, to the way she'd felt at lunch, Kate decided that she was being paranoid. Just look at the way he'd chased her last week. And then, inviting her here. She remembered the way he'd kissed her in the study, and the way he'd looked at her last night when she said she was going to bed. It was her – Kate – he wanted. And she wanted him. It was very simple.

Arabella might still be in love with him – Kate could understand that – and of course it would make poor Charlie jealous. No wonder he'd left her. But that was his problem, and Arabella's. There was nothing for Kate to worry about over Tom, except the pleasurable question of when they were going to have sex – and why was she hesitating? It was obviously going to happen at some point, and perhaps she should have been more spontaneous last night. What had she got to lose?

She climbed to the top and looked down. There they were below her, walking out from dune-cast shadows on the sand towards the line of water. The widening distance, and the boom and hiss of the sea, meant that she could no longer hear their voices, but she could see that Sarah was talking, arm swept before her, while Douglas followed its direction, nodding, and then pointing precisely at some landmark while his dog lapped at the shallow water. Kate smiled. They looked like a married couple already.

She followed their tracks down the dune towards where they were sitting on a large branch of bleached-grey driftwood. Douglas shifted up for her.

'It's beautiful,' she said, looking out – and feeling a limit to the word that he didn't seem to notice.

His eyes shone. 'Isn't it? Sometimes I wonder why I ever leave – don't I, you horrid thing,' he added to George, who'd leapt up wet from the sea, paws scattering sand over his jacket, a stick in his mouth.

Douglas pushed him down and he ran with it to Sarah, who threw it. They watched him execute a perfect retrieve.

'*Good boy!*' said Sarah, who took it from him and made him sit while she threw it again.

Douglas looked at Kate. 'Never does that for me.'
'*Fetch it!*'

This time, Sarah threw it far. She had to get up to help him find it.

'It's been a good weekend,' Kate said to Douglas. 'Thank you.'

'I'm sorry there weren't more people.'

'I'm glad there weren't.'

'Really? You mean that? It's not too quiet?'

'No, it's . . .'

'Sometimes I worry that there isn't enough for people to do here. It's a long way to come, just for this. I mean, of course *I* love it,' he smiled at her, 'but then I live here. It must be rather different for any-one staying.'

'Don't be silly. You've got the beach, the billiard room, the stables . . .'

'But do people really *enjoy* all that?'

'I do,' she said.

'That's kind of you to say so.'

'And so does Tom.'

'Tom's my friend. Of course he's going to say he likes it here.'

'Oh come on, Douglas. Do you think someone like Tom – with those looks and those social credentials, his name on every party list in London – would really come here as much as he does if he found it boring?'

Douglas wasn't sure.

'Not that I think he's fickle,' she added quickly. 'But you do know what I mean, don't you?'

'Yes,' he smiled. 'Yes, of course.'

Douglas understood. She meant that if a man as wonderful as Tom chose to come to Waveney, then that was the ultimate endorsement. It was as if her liking for the place depended entirely on Tom. And, to his discomfort, Douglas found he wasn't sure that Tom was a good enough measure – for Waveney, or for Kate.

———————◆◆◆———————

When they got back, the film had finished. Kate and Sarah went upstairs to pack.

'Are you ready in there?' Tom knocked and opened the door. 'Come on . . .'

He smiled at Kate. 'Here. Give me those.' He took their suitcases and carried them down.

Outside, Douglas and his parents were standing on the steps, attended by a subdued George.

'Good bye, George,' said Kate, squatting down and kissing the soft head. George raised his snout and licked her eye. 'Ugh!'

Douglas laughed. 'You can't give him a kiss and not expect one in return.'

'But not in my eye.'

Henry hated goodbye scenes. He listened to the formulaic patter and wondered how it was that perfectly sensible people could allow themselves to sound so banal. He offered his hand and his cheek as appropriate, and waved and nodded as expected. But he could only relax when the car had disappeared.

Then, arm in arm, he and Jane walked back towards the house, while Douglas and George set off across the fields in the direction of Rowden Farm, to check the state of its drainage before tomorrow's meeting.

Eight

It was completely dark. Kate took a few seconds to realise where she was. Then she put out a hand for Tom. She really had to stretch. The bed was huge and he was curled right up at the other end. She touched a warm back.

'What is it?'

'Sorry,' she whispered. 'I was getting my bearings . . .'

He rolled over. 'It's a big bed.'

'I was lost. I haven't got lost in bed since I was four.'

'Why are you whispering?' he whispered.

She could tell he was smiling. 'Why are you?'

'Come here.' Tom arranged her on top of him, into a position he'd shared with Arabella, and closed his eyes. 'Comfortable?'

'Yes.'

'No, you're not. Put your leg there . . .'

They lay in silence. Kate's head was on Tom's chest. She could hear his heart and feel him breathing.

He was perfect. He didn't even smell, except for the remains of that aftershave. When she thought of how she'd flinch from a rank Mark in the mornings –

trying not to make it too obvious – it was wonderful
to inhale freely. And he was warm. She'd forgotten
what it was like just to be with a body again.

And, of course, there had been the sex. Feeling the
length of that same body, the perfect proportions of
its bumps and curves, the bits where it was smooth –
the bits where it wasn't – that same skin, so quiet
beneath her now, made her wonder at her luck.
She'd never been with anyone even half as lovely as
this man. She'd never thought that physical perfection would make such a difference – that the sight
of him could turn her on as much as being spoken to,
or touched.

Her only worry – and it was a big one – was that she
wasn't good enough, physically, for him. With legs
that could do with a wax, breasts that made it slightly
uncomfortable – even now – lying face down, a
stomach that wasn't bad, but wasn't totally totally flat
– she was going to have to make time for more trips
to the office gym, and she was going to have to give
up bacon sandwiches in the mornings.

She thought of the office. It was going to be a long
day. There was all that post-completion stuff to sort
out with Adam on Project Cannon. She needed to
brief Michael. And there were at least two other
matters she should have resolved last week. She was
going to have to get up to speed on those. There'd be
people nagging her about them. And there was the
weekly department meeting in the evening . . .

'Tom?'

'Mm.' His chest reverberated.

'What time is it?'

He took a deep breath and sighed. Her head

crested and sank, and then buzzed as he replied, 'No idea.'

She turned her head the other way and squinted at his luminous alarm clock. Twenty to six. Kate turned her head back and closed her eyes. But it wasn't twenty to six. Instinct pressed her to twist off Tom and to pick up the clock. It was eight-thirty.

She fumbled for the light and switched it on.

'What are you doing?'

Kate looked over at the window and understood why it was so dark. He had shutters.

'It's eight-thirty, Tom. I'm supposed to be at work.'

He groaned.

'I don't even have the right clothes. Can I use your telephone?'

'Of course,' said Tom from underneath the sheets.

———— ❧ ————

Kate got to the office at ten-thirty.

She put her coat in the cupboard and sat at her desk. Weakly, she stared at it. A pile of faxes sat in her in-tray and the message light on her telephone was flashing. Beyond the papers, Adam was watching her.

'What happened?'

'Don't ask.' She shook her hair and tied it back with a rubber band. 'Where's Janet?'

'Called in sick this morning.'

Stupid. Useless. Good for nothing. Unreliable fucking Janet. Couldn't she have waited a couple of weeks?

'Why?' she demanded.

Adam shrugged.

'Who've we got instead?'

'We haven't. They didn't have a spare float.'

Shifting through the faxes and papers in her tray, she arranged them in order of priority. Then she listened to her messages and made a list. She was just picking up her dirty mug to get herself some coffee when Michael strode in.

'There you are. I've had Simon Dalziel on the phone. He wants to know about some undertaking you gave last Friday to provide board minutes. I hope you can.'

Kate put the mug down. 'First: it wasn't our undertaking, it was the client's. And second: faxed copies have already been provided. Henry Hazel just left the originals behind on Friday.'

'Call Dalziel anyway, will you. He obviously didn't understand.'

'Project Scarlet fell through,' Adam told her, shutting the door behind Michael, who had not waited for a response. 'He's been shouting at us all morning.'

'Ah.' She stood up. 'Coffee?'

'Love one,' said Adam.

'Milk, no sugar?'

He nodded.

She took their mugs to the office kitchen.

———◆———

Simon Dalziel sat at his desk, playing with his stapler. The last five or six months had been the busiest of his life, but the completion of Project Cannon and the collapse of two other deals had left him with no urgent work to do. But instead of enjoying the release of pressure, he was bored.

Simon had an office to himself. It was nine storeys up and it overlooked a construction site. Fraser

Cummings provided on-going legal advice to the construction business responsible for that site. Simon himself had dealt with the legal aspects surrounding the financing of it.

He was fond of this office. If he swivelled his chair, he could watch the builders crawling in the dust. Simon came from a family of builders and ever since the divorce of his parents – when, aged ten, he'd visited the offices of a solicitor in Leeds – rising from dust to air-conditioning had been the driving force in his life.

Simon never tired of being reminded of the distance he'd travelled, and there was no reminder more delightful than the view from his window. Today, however, he was facing in and playing with his stapler.

With the exception of his secretary, and a married colleague of his, Kate was the only attractive woman he'd come across in months. She wasn't Demi Moore, but she wasn't bad. She wasn't as clever as him, but she wasn't stupid. More importantly, she was posh – and he was quietly confident she fancied him. Now that Project Cannon was at the post-completion stage, he couldn't rely any more on meetings and conference calls to throw them together.

He pulled the telephone towards him and dialled her direct line.

Kate had forwarded all her calls to Heather, Michael's secretary, who was very pretty and very stupid.

'Kate Leonard's office,' she sang. 'How may I help you?'

'Can I speak to her?'

Heather was silent. She'd realised too late that she didn't know how to transfer calls on the new telephones they'd been issued, unless those calls went to Michael.

'Hello?' said Simon.

Heather panicked. 'Would you like to speak to Michael Preston instead?'

'No. I'd like to speak to Kate. Is she there?'

'Hold the line, please.'

Heather left her telephone off its hook and made for Kate's office. Kate had shut her door. Behind the glass, Heather could see her bent over some papers, chewing her pen. Heather knocked and Kate beckoned.

'What is it?'

'Sorry to disturb you, Kate. There's a man on the phone for you.'

'Who is it?'

'Dunno. Sounded nice.'

'Is he still on the line?'

Heather nodded. 'I asked him to wait.'

'Have you just left your phone off the hook with whoever it is waiting at the other end?'

'Yes.'

'Heather!'

'It's these new phones—'

'But you've had special training for them, Heather. Honestly.'

In the silence that followed, Kate heard the lack of patience in her words and regretted it. She looked at Adam and saw that he'd noticed it too.

'Okay. Just go back, take his name and his number, and explain to him that I'll call him back. Can you do that?'

Heather nodded.

'And I know it's hard, but please remember never to leave a phone like that in future, Heather. It isn't professional.'

Oh God, Kate thought as Heather left the room. That sounded even worse. Remembering Douglas with his housekeeper, and wishing she was better at managing people, Kate bent over her work. 'Don't look at me like that.'

Adam said nothing.

She put down her pen and sat up, looking at him 'It's hard to be nice and patient when you're under pressure.'

'I know,' he said, in mature tones that told her she wasn't trying hard enough.

'You wait until you're four years' qualified,' she said.

Minutes later, there was a sharp knock at the door and Heather returned with Simon's details. She stalked in, chewing gum, and put a Post-it note on Kate's desk. Kate picked up the note and looked at Simon's name, spelt correctly in Heather's careful handwriting.

'Thank you, Heather.' She stuck the note on her telephone and bent over her papers. Heather didn't move. Surprised, Kate looked up. 'What is it?'

'I just want to remind you that I'm not your secretary. Janet's sick and I'm doing you a favour. All right?'

'Yes. Of course.'

'Today, I'm working for Michael, you, Annette and Adam. Not just you. All right?'

'Yes, Heather. I understand.'

Heather towered over Kate's desk. Adam could see her stiletto heels digging into the carpet. It was amazing how women walked in those things. He'd tried on a pair once and hadn't managed three steps without falling over.

'It sounds to me like you're working for too many people,' said Kate. 'What's Daniella's workload like? Perhaps you could share some of yours with her?'

'Daniella's in training today.'

'Okay, Heather. Well, I probably won't have much typing for you to do today anyway. All I need is for someone to take my calls?'

Heather switched her weight to the other leg and went on chewing her gum.

Kate was tired of grovelling for services she thought should be automatic. It was almost lunch-time and she'd only crossed one item off her task list.

'Okay. I won't forward my calls to you. But please take them if I'm engaged, or out.'

'Yeah. I can do that.'

'I appreciate it.'

All three of them knew that Heather had simply agreed to pick up a ringing line, which was general policy at Willis & Storm.

Kate bent her head, indicating their discussion had finished. Victorious, Heather turned round and tossed her head. Her platinum hair whipped gloriously round her neck, and she caught Adam's eye as she swept out.

'And you can stop smiling,' Kate muttered.

'I'm not smiling. I'm not smiling at all. It's very

serious – especially as she still hasn't got a clue how to transfer your calls . . .' Kate put her head in her hands ' . . . do you want me to show her how to do it?'

———————◆◆◆———————

Kate waited until she reached a natural stopping point before calling Simon.

'That's an amazingly stupid secretary you've got there,' he said, laughing. 'She's also amazingly pretty.'

'Ah. And she's not my secretary, a point she seems particularly keen to establish.'

Simon laughed again.

'You're in a good mood,' she said.

'It's Monday,' he replied. 'Of course I'm in a good mood.'

'And you're also extremely weird. If you're calling about those board minutes, I spoke to Henry Hazel and he says he's couriering them to you as we speak. As for all the other post-completion stuff, Adam Lipinsky, my trainee—'

'I know. I've met him.'

'Of course you have. He'll be co-ordinating matters this end.'

She caught Adam's eye as she said this and raised her eyebrows. He nodded.

'I was actually calling about lunch.'

Kate was silent.

'You said you'd have lunch with me today.'

'Oh God, Simon. I'm sorry. I'm up to my ears this morning—'

Simon didn't believe her. He knew too well how easy it was to pretend to be busier than he actually was.

'Tomorrow?' she offered.

'You really can't come today?'

'It would be so much better tomorrow. Except – there might be a meeting tomorrow. Hang on . . .' She opened her diary.

She had a meeting on a new matter with a client in Croydon on Tuesday morning and, if she was back in time, there was Steve's lunchtime lecture on finance leasing – a lecture she'd give anything to miss, but her absence would be noticed, and she wouldn't put it past Michael to go out of his way to find her a finance lease to draft. She had, supposedly, a day off on Wednesday (*Mum – shopping*) which she knew she'd have to cancel – there'd be a mountain of work from the Croydon instructions, and she still hadn't finished that billing for Colin Abrahams.

'What about Thursday?'

Simon opened his own diary. 'Thursday's fine,' he said, resignedly and wrote her in.

Simon Dalziel, thought Kate as they ended the call and she put down the receiver, clearly doesn't have enough work to do. She scribbled some additions to her task list and was about to ask Adam to chase Henry Hazel about the board minutes, when the telephone rang again. She could see Heather's name on the display.

'Yes, Heather?'

'I've got another man for you.'

Kate raised her eyes to heaven. 'Who is it?'

'Wouldn't say.'

It had to be Tom.

'Put him through, then.'

It was.

'Hello, darling,' he said, and Kate was surprised at

the relief she felt that he'd rung. Spontaneity was all very well – following your heart and trusting your instincts – if the other person was serious, or felt the way you did. But if it led to having your fingers burnt and your heart broken – if it meant the kind of humiliation she'd felt over that boy she'd snogged at a teenage party who'd then just gone on and snogged someone else – Kate wasn't sure it was wise.

But that wasn't going to happen this time. The risk had paid off – he'd even called her 'darling'. Adam could tell, just from the intimate way she said 'Hello' back, that this was not a business call. He concentrated on his computer screen and listened to every word.

'Nightmare,' she was saying. 'Didn't get here till ten-thirty. Awful. A pile of faxes and a host of messages.' This was followed by quite a lot of laughter and then, 'It's all right for some. Are you still in bed?'

Adam's focus jumped across the screen. Had Kate got lucky at the weekend?

He was about to send an e-mail to the entire department, alerting them to this, when Michael entered.

'Kate,' he said. 'I need you in my office.'

Kate nodded.

'Now.'

'I'll call you back.'

She put down the receiver and followed Michael into his office.

Polishing the photographs of his children on the shelf behind Michael's large leather-surfaced desk, and watering the yucca plant by the window, were

Heather's favourite duties. There was no standard strip lighting in there. The only electric light came from a smart lamp on the desk, and it made the room seem more like a study. The effect was instantly soothing.

Kate waited for Michael to sit down before sitting down herself. Behind his desk, Michael was less frantic. He smiled at her.

'This is partly about Heather,' he began. 'She doesn't like you treating her *like dirt*.'

Kate bit her lip.

'I know she can be pretty useless with the telephone, but the best approach is to be patient. It just takes her a bit of time.'

'I'm sorry.'

'Don't worry about it. I asked you in here more to keep her happy than to tick you off. But now you're here I can take the opportunity to tell you how pleased Henry Hazel was with your work.'

'He was?'

'Particularly impressed by the way you controlled Friday's meeting. In fact, he's given some new instructions and he specifically asked that you be in charge of the day-to-day running.' Kate's spirits soared. She knew Henry Hazel hadn't liked her to begin with. He was a man of few words and he'd never say something unless he really meant it. A smile stretched across her face.

'It's a sensitive project and we're going to have to keep a careful list of insiders. You'll need to think of a code-name. Project Cannon II is fine, if you can't think of anything better, but check with Henry – clients can be funny about stuff like that. And it's serious money. If the deal goes through we'll be looking at millions in fees. We'll be working in conjunction with the EC Department and the corporate boys . . .' As Michael outlined the new deal, Kate made rapid notes.

'Same bank as before?'

'It'll be a syndicate, with the same bank leading and arranging. So yes – I expect you'll still be working with your friend at Fraser Cummings.'

She looked up from her notebook. It wasn't often Michael's eyes smiled but, for a second, she could see a resemblance to the four-year-old in the photograph behind him.

'Henry's faxing you a term sheet, but you'll need a meeting with him as well before you contact Dalziel. The main difference between this deal and the one they did before is that it's tax driven, so you'll want Margaret to be at the meeting. You really need her right at the start. Don't let her secretary palm you off with Stephen Woods. The issues are too complex, and you must have a tax specialist with banking experience. Henry thinks they'll need to set up an SPV for this. I wasn't sure that was necessary, but if you think it is then you may as well get Adam onto the paperwork right away.'

As they continued, Kate began to realise from the way Michael was talking – from the way he asked her opinion and seemed happy to trust her judgement – that he was expecting her to do this one on her own. And it wasn't as if this was an easy project. Hazel Industries had hundreds of offshore subsidiary companies. There were tricky accounting issues to get to grips with, and interesting points of international law to be researched – she'd need to instruct counsel on some of those. Although it would involve other departments, this was a banking matter, and Kate would be expected to understand all the complexities and make sure that they were dealt with in a few comprehensive documents that the client would understand.

Kate began to feel both the benefits and the burdens of a new kind of responsibility. She would definitely have to cancel her mother now. And there wouldn't be much time for Tom. But at last she had the edge over other solicitors in her department at her level – particularly Annette Latham.

Annette was a year older than Kate. But because she'd taken time off between school and university, and because she'd not read law to begin with, Annette was a year behind – and minded. She tried to make up for this by working alarmingly hard – even by Willis & Storm standards – and by showing off. She'd attend department lectures and ask questions designed to let people know how much she knew, and not because she had a genuine interest in the answer. The suspiciously self-conscious expression she wore on her narrow face while the speaker replied had become a department joke – Gavin did a brilliant imitation. She'd write erudite articles in legal publications, and she'd actively tout for work.

Michael didn't like Annette. She was bright and keen, but she lacked charm. She'd stand too close to him when they were looking at the same document, and her breath smelt of coffee. He made a point of avoiding her at office parties. He did, however, find her useful. Her attitude seemed to provoke the others into working noticeably harder. They were clocking up more hours on their timesheets than ever before, which meant bigger billing at the end of the year. And the more his department could bill, the more clout Michael had in partners' meetings. So he nurtured her instinct for rivalry.

Annette had noticed that Michael gave Kate more files and more attention, and she knew why. It wasn't because Kate worked hard, or billed much. And it wasn't because Kate was particularly clever, so far as she could tell. Well, she, Annette, wasn't going to degrade herself like that. She wasn't going to grow her hair and wear tight suits. She was going to succeed on merit, and merit alone. She was bitterly jealous when Kate was given a trainee. She pestered Michael so hard that she was given her own trainee six months earlier than planned. Kate didn't mind – it meant she had Adam to herself – but she felt that she'd become the benchmark by which Annette judged her own success. Annette was always wanting to know what files Kate was working on, how many chargeable hours she had on her timesheet, and Kate was beginning to lose patience.

That was why this new deal meant so much. It showed Michael that clients liked her, and that she could attract work. It opened the gap between her and Annette, and made her feel valued for something real – and not because of some smart political move.

She was in Michael's office for over an hour, taking notes and discussing fees. It was almost three o'clock when she emerged, thinking about lunch.

From her station, Heather's guilty eyes followed Kate as she passed. She'd been in there, with the door shut, forever. What had Michael said to her?

'Everything all right, Kate?'

Kate glanced back. 'Fine. Any messages?'

'On your desk.'

'Great.'

To Heather's surprise, Kate gave her a warm smile and disappeared into her room. Heather shrugged and reached for her emery board. The nail on her left thumb was starting to split.

Kate was about to call her mother about cancelling Wednesday, when her mother rang first. This happened to them so often that Kate now took it for granted, but Elizabeth went on being amazed. She'd be pulling up weeds in the garden and think – quite suddenly, and for no apparent reason – that she hadn't spoken to Kate for weeks and that now would be a good time to call. By the time she got into the house and washed her hands, the telephone would be ringing. She hadn't yet found the courage to pick up the receiver and just say, 'Darling –', but she was tempted.

Kate picked up the receiver. 'Hi, Mum.'

'How on *earth* did you know it was me?'

'Your number came up on my display.'

'A display?'

'I have a small display – you know, like on a calculator – and it tells me the number of the caller. It means I only get to talk to the people I like,' she grinned. 'I find it more reliable than telepathy.'

'All right, clever clogs. Does it tell you what I'm calling about?'

'Yes, actually, it does. It's saying *Have you Remembered about our Shopping Trip on Wednesday?* and *Can I stay the Night?*'

Elizabeth laughed. 'Marvellous. Well, have you? Can I? . . . Hang on, I'm getting your answer already – the old methods still work. Here we go: *I'm really sorry, Mum. I've got to work.*'

Silence.

'Kate?'

'I'm sorry. Really, Mum, I am. I thought this week would be clear but, if anything, it's worse.' She heard her mother sigh.

'Well, when are we going to get you your present?'

'You don't need . . .'

'It's my daughter's birthday, and I don't need to get her a present? Darling, we've discussed this. You need something fun to wear to summer parties – I can't bear it when you wear your drab office clothes.'

'What summer parties?'

'Your birthday party, for a start.'

'I'm not having a birthday party.'

'But it's your thirtieth.'

'Nothing to celebrate about that, so far as I'm concerned.'

'Darling . . .'

'Mum. Listen. Apart from anything else, I'm not going to have time to organise a birthday party for myself, and it'll cost a fortune.'

'I'll pay.'

'That's not the point.'

Elizabeth shifted the cat from her chair, sat at the kitchen table and opened her packet of cigarettes. 'I know you don't like me saying this, Kate, but you must try to get over Mark. It's been almost a year and you're letting him win if you go on like this, burying yourself in work.'

'What's Mark got to do with this?'

'You seem so unwilling to . . .'

'You can worry about my work and my clothes if you like – even my birthday – but there's absolutely no need to worry about Mark Newton, Mum. He's history.'

'I know, darling,' said her mother, putting a cigarette into her mouth and reaching for the long silver lighter that Peter had given her for Christmas. 'But you . . .'

'I'm over him. Really over him.'

Something in Kate's tone made Elizabeth think that, at last, this might be true. 'Who've you met?' she said.

'Hang on.' Kate got up to close the door to her office, and returned to her desk. 'You remember Charlie?'

'The photographer?'

'That's right. Well he's a great friend of someone called Tom Faulkener . . .'

Elizabeth lit the cigarette and smoked it while Kate told her about Tom, about Arabella, and about her weekend at Waveney.

'Waveney? You actually stayed at Waveney?'

'You know it?'

'Darling, of course I know it, it has a wonderful nursery garden. I get all my lavender there. And what I've seen of the house is simply stunning. Lucky you. I can't remember the name of the family. It was empty for a while I think and then—'

'Douglas.'

'That's right. Sir John Douglas lived there. He *must* be dead by now.'

'It belongs to his grandson.'

'Is the grandson nice?'

'He's okay. Not terribly glamorous.'

'Living at Waveney – not glamorous? What on earth do you mean?'

It didn't take long for Kate to notice that her mother was much more impressed by Douglas and Waveney than she was by Tom or Arabella.

'Do you want to hear about Tom, or not?'

'Yes, darling. Yes, of course. What does he do?'

Kate hesitated. 'Not much, actually. At the moment. I think he wants to be an art dealer, but that's on hold while he sorts out his father's estate.'

'Running an estate can be a full-time job, you know.'

'No, Mum. I'm talking about estate as in *inheritance*.'

Adam came in with Annette. Both were holding boxes of files, and Adam was looking depressed. They put the boxes on his desk. Annette stood with her back to Kate. She opened one of the boxes, took out the top file and began whispering.

Kate knew that her mother was used to their conversations being cut off mid-flow. 'I'll talk to you later,' she said, and put down the receiver. 'What's this?'

'I need Adam to go through these boxes for me,' said Annette.

'Why?'

'Apparently, he hasn't been shown how to do a bill yet, and I thought he could start with this one – the last bill we sent was some time in November.' She turned back to Adam. 'This is the most recent correspondence file – see? Dig around in these,' she indicated the boxes, 'find all the files like this, back to whenever the last bill was sent out – I think it was last November, but it might have been before then, March maybe. You'll have to check . . .'

'Annette.'

'Yes?'

'Can't you get your trainee to do it?'

'Michael's taken her to a meeting. I explained about this bill, and Mike said to see if Adam was available – so that's what I'm doing. He's not busy.'

'Yes he is. And you're supposed to ask me before hijacking him like this.'

'I am asking you.'

'*And I'm saying no.*'

Adam kept his eyes on the floor as Annette put the file back in its box.

'All right,' she said. 'Keep your hair on.'

———◆◆◆———

Louisa was asleep in front of the television when Kate got home.

She woke with a start when Kate switched it off.

'You've got to stop doing this,' she said, taking off her coat.

Louisa rubbed her neck. She'd fallen asleep in an odd position and it hurt. 'I know,' she said. 'But there was the second part of that Channel 4 police drama I saw last night, and then I . . . *And where were you?*' she added, remembering Kate's absence in a rush.

'Last night?'

'Yes, Kate. Last night.'

Kate smiled. 'I was with Tom.'

'All night?'

'All night.'

'You mean you . . .' Louisa stared at her as she nodded. 'You dirty stop-out. You tart. You lucky woman . . . was it incredible? Oh God – I bet it was. I bet he's bloody marvellous.'

Kate just went on smiling.

'Oh go on – tell Auntie Lou. Did he go down on you?'

'Louisa!'

'You did have sex – right?'

'Lou. Please.'

'Oh come on. Don't be such a spoilsport. Just tell me if you had sex – then I promise I'll lay off.'

'Okay. Okay.'

'So you did?'

'Yes,' Kate laughed. 'Yes we did.'

'And?'

'Well, I think there's a strong chance it'll happen again. He rang first thing this morning – called me darling. I think this is going to work, Lou. I really do.'

'But what about the sex?'

'It was great.'

'Is that all?'

'That's all you're hearing.'

Louisa looked away. Ever since the days of snogging at teenage parties, they'd always compared notes, told each other everything. She'd been longing to tell Kate more about Richard – how things were now that Georges was off the scene. She really wanted to ask Kate what she thought about condoms – whether they were something she expected the man to get, or whether she had her own supply. Did having one's own supply look a bit slutty? But it would

190

be a bit one-sided now if Kate didn't talk about Tom.

'I'm sorry, Lou. I just think that this time it's a bit different – you know. I don't think he'd like it if I went into all that with you.'

'Sounds serious.'

'It is serious.'

'No more shrimpy jokes?' she said, and Kate smiled. But it wasn't a proper smile.

Louisa sat in silence while Kate bustled through the flat – switching on lights, sorting through the post, throwing away old envelopes and circulars.

'Kate?' she said. Kate looked up from the pile of letters in her hand. 'What's going on?'

'What do you mean?'

'You always tell me . . .'

'But I have told you – I told you we slept together. I told you it was good.'

'No, I mean really tell me, all the nitty-gritty. Like . . .'

'Like before?'

'Yes.'

Wishing Louisa would mind her own business – understanding why she wasn't – Kate sighed.

'All right,' she said. 'What do you want to hear?'

Her question had the desired effect. Kate appeared completely reasonable, effortlessly accommodating. But the way she asked it made Louisa feel so nosy, it took away her courage.

'I don't know,' said Louise, confused. 'Anything.'

'Anything . . .'

'Just tell me about last night. Or tell me about the weekend if you like – it must have been better than the one I had.'

'I thought you were supposed to be seeing that older man – what's his name?'

'Richard. I was, but he cancelled at the last minute because someone had some free tickets for him and his son to go to a match.'

'Couldn't he take you too?'

'Not exactly,' Louisa followed Kate into the kitchen. 'You see, he's married.'

Kate was shocked. 'What about his wife?'

'What about her?'

'They're still together?' Kate poured boiling water from the kettle into a saucepan and shook in some dried pasta. She took Louisa's silence as a 'yes'.

'Don't you worry that encouraging Richard might split them up?'

'No,' said Louisa, watching her stir. 'Richard's very happy with things as they are.'

'Is his wife?'

'She doesn't know.'

'What if she found out?'

'She won't.'

'How can you be sure?'

Louisa sighed. 'Really, Kate. At the end of the day, it's not my problem. I wasn't the one making promises to remain faithful to anyone. This is something between Richard and his wife. It's got very little to do with me and nothing whatsoever to do with you.'

As she listened, Kate tested the pasta, drained off the water and then flung it into a bowl. Stirring in some pesto from a pot in the fridge, she caught Louisa's altered tone.

'Of course it's none of my business. Except that you're telling me about it – and if I were in your shoes

I'd have had nothing more to do with Richard once I found out he was married.'

Louisa leant heavily on the sideboard, and twisted her neck to look at Kate. 'Life's so simple for you, isn't it?'

'It's only complicated if you make it complicated. You could just decide to do the decent thing and never see Richard again.' She looked at Louisa's back bent over the sink. 'I don't see what the complication is.'

'The complication,' said Louisa, 'the complication is that . . .' she finished scrubbing the saucepan clean and put it on the rack. 'The complication is that I don't meet that many men I fancy any more. It's all right for you. With a perfect job and a perfect boyfriend . . .'

'They're not perfect.' Kate found a fork and went over to the table to eat.

'You always have some problem with whoever it is that I go out with,' Louisa continued, stressing her words. 'Max was too stupid, Georges was irresponsible and selfish. Richard's married . . . Why should I choose my men to please you?'

'I'm not saying you should.'

Kate hated telling Louisa things she didn't want to hear. She didn't want to make Louisa unhappy, and she certainly didn't want to pour cold water on a new relationship. But this was a married man, and Louisa needed to be reminded of the risk, the heartache, and the potential damage of what she was doing. Of course it was far easier to say nothing, let Louisa make the mistake, and stay out of it. But Kate's idea of friendship was stronger than that.

'I'm saying you should respect someone else's marriage,' she went on, her voice quiet and deliberate, as she wound some pasta onto her fork and put it into her mouth. 'Do you love him?'

Louisa finished scrubbing the grater, her back still to Kate, and the limp curve of her shoulders told Kate that she was crying.

'Oh God,' Kate dropped her fork and ran over. 'I'm sorry, Lou. I didn't realise.'

'It doesn't matter.' Louisa pulled out the plug and they both watched the dirty water, circling away. 'I don't love him,' she said, over the gurgling and sucking. 'I don't even fancy him. I just . . .'

'You can't give him up?'

Louisa said nothing.

'When are you next seeing him?'

'Wednesday.'

'Why don't you cancel, and we'll give a dinner party instead . . .'

By Tuesday, the weather at Waveney had reverted to wind and rain. Douglas rose early and took George for a walk. George hated the rain and stuck close to Douglas' legs as he strode over the dunes. Douglas hardly noticed. He was watching the breakers on the sand and thinking of Kate.

Douglas knew. In fact, he knew more than he really wanted to know. Tom had called him about it the second Kate left the flat that Monday morning.

'Success!' he'd cried.

'What kind of success?'

'What kind of success do you think?' Tom had laughed. 'You'd never guess to look at her, she seems so conventional. It was like a . . .'

Douglas had stopped him. 'You shouldn't be telling me these things.'

He reached the top of the highest dune and stood facing the east wind. He shut his eyes and let the rain prick at his face while George cowered in the grasses on the sheltered side of the dune, waiting.

When he got back to the house, there was a message on his desk to call Arabella. Douglas blew his nose. Stuffing his handkerchief into his trouser pocket with one hand, he reached for his address book with the other, and then put it back. No. If she wanted him, she could call again.

She did.

'Did you get my message?'

'Yes. I . . .'

'Why won't anyone return my calls?'

'I'm sorry, Arabella. I . . .'

'Whatever.' Arabella didn't want to hear his excuses. She took a deep breath and got to the point.

She wanted to see Douglas. Would he be in London this week? Would lunch tomorrow be possible?

'Is there something wrong?'

'I'd prefer to talk about it when I see you,' she answered.

Douglas told her to meet him in a café on the Fulham Road – he wasn't going to be coerced into spending a fortune listening to her problems – and hung up.

Thinking that it fitted quite well with going to Kate's dinner party that night – he'd just have to leave Norfolk in the morning – Douglas' eyes rested on George, who was snoring by the fire. The salty wet fur gave off a sour smell as it dried.

Nine

Tom had not expected to get Kate into bed so quickly. It wasn't that he had trouble with girls, but he'd assumed that this one would be tough to crack. She was cautious, she needed convincing – and, in truth, he'd been enjoying the challenge. He'd known instinctively that an indirect approach was better. Make her curious. Make her wonder what was going on. Make her doubt herself until she's almost desperate – then take her.

Instead, it had been effortless, but far from feeling that the chase was over, Tom found himself more involved than ever. What had happened last Sunday? How was it that she'd given everything, yet still he wanted more?

It had been almost nine o'clock when their train arrived back at Liverpool Street. Sarah Knowles (who, on what she earned as a cook, was always trying to save money) had told them she was taking the tube. It was really quick to Fulham – only one change – so no, she wouldn't share their cab.

Kate had been quiet in the cab queue. She seemed tired, and Tom could see that she wanted to get home. He was just going to have to wait. Ring her next week. Another dinner, maybe two. Approaching the next cab, he gave the driver her address, and opened the door for her. He then heaved in both suitcases and got in behind while Kate sat back in her corner, looking out at blocks of concrete. Tom looked at her – at the dormant smile-line at the side of her mouth. She didn't look tired, he thought. She looked unhappy.

He took her hand in the darkness between them and squeezed it. 'You look sad,' he said, and she didn't reply.

He was still holding onto her hand. Bringing it to his lips, he kissed it and then looked at it as he spoke. 'Please don't be sad. We – I mean, if you're not happy, we don't have to take this any further.'

'That's what you'd like?'

'No. *No* . . .' he sighed. 'I wasn't great this weekend, I know. I should never have said those things to you, and then you had to cope with Arabella being there and so on, and of course I should have come on that walk with you, but . . . oh Kate, listen to me, will you? I don't know you very well. I've got no idea if this is going to work, or if it'll be a disaster – but I think we'd be mad not to try. Don't you?'

And he'd meant it. The thought of losing Kate – of losing her when he hadn't really had her – had added weight to his desire, converting it into a need for something more from her than sex. Catching the sincerity in his tone, and finding it impossible to reject, Kate had turned to him. He'd taken her face in his hands and kissed her. And they hadn't stopped kissing until the cab arrived, twenty minutes later. Kate had looked up, out of the cab, to where light shone from the windows of her flat.

'Louisa's in,' she'd said. 'Can we go to you?'

'Are you sure?'

'Sure.'

Her abrupt departure on Monday morning left him with an uncomfortable awareness of her absence. Of course, she didn't have any choice. She had to go to work. But it implied a kind of emotional independence – and it was that, he thought, that kept him longing for her. Sex with Kate had not carried with it the total surrender he'd experienced with other women.

Ringing her at work – her breaking off with that, 'I'll call you back' – had reinforced this. She hadn't been able to see him on Monday night which meant that, by Tuesday, he was in love.

That night, she'd turned up late at his house, thrown her briefcase next to the umbrella stand in the hall, and let him kiss her. He'd felt her light weight in his hands, and smelt the remains of scent in her hair.

'Darling.'

The tired woman leaning on him. The briefcase slotted in between the umbrellas and the wall. Tom felt the beginnings of a simple pattern of togetherness and he loved her for letting it happen. There was no trace of her presence in the mews-house. She kept fresh clothes at the office, arranged her life independently of his, so that he wasn't trapped. Her undemanding disposition gave him nothing to kick against. And it was because of this that Tom resolved to drop Arabella. Disgusted with himself, he made no attempt to contact her and hoped that the problem would just go away.

But Arabella kept leaving messages on his answer-phone.

'*What are you up to today?*'

'*Want to see a film?*'

And then, '*You're obviously still out. Call me when you get this.*'

When, by Tuesday he hadn't called, she left a final message. '*It's me again. You might at least have had the decency to tell me that you want me out of your life.*'

Douglas had told him that she'd asked to meet for lunch.

'She sounded quite upset.'

'Whose side are you on, Doug? I thought you wanted this to happen.'

The café was next to a building site. Dust from the pavement irritated Arabella's eyes. Aggressive drilling penetrated her ears. A group of workmen sat by the door and stopped talking as she entered.

'Hello,' said one. Arabella ignored him. The door swung shut behind her, blocking out the drilling. She looked round for Douglas, recognised the tweedy back and went over – sitting in the opposite chair before Douglas noticed she'd arrived. He stood up anyway, and bent over the table to kiss her cheek.

After he kissed her, he looked at her. 'Are you okay?'

'I'm fine.' Arabella took a packet of cigarettes and a box of matches from her handbag. Douglas watched her stuff the bag between her right leg and the wall, then she sat forward with her elbows on the table and lit herself a cigarette. 'You don't mind, do you?'

'Go ahead.'

She inhaled deeply and looked around the café. 'How do you discover places like this, Doogle?'

Douglas had to fight his instinct to apologise for not taking her somewhere smarter. He handed her a scruffy menu and she took it, but put it flat on the table.

'I'm not hungry,' she said.

'Something to drink?'

Arabella wanted mineral water. Douglas ordered it, and an indifferent waiter dropped a bottle on their table, with a plain tumbler – the kind she remembered from school. The tumbler hadn't been dried properly and Arabella had to shake it, to get rid of the tap drops. Looking back at Douglas, she twisted open the bottle-cap.

'I wanted to speak to you about Tom.'

'Yes,' said Douglas, shifting in his chair. He watched the water fall into her glass, and waited for her to speak. 'About Tom?' he prompted.

'I . . .' Putting down the bottle, she picked at the sky-blue plastic lid. 'I was just wondering . . . has he – has he gone away somewhere?'

'No. He's here. Here in London.'

'Are you sure?'

'I'm seeing him tonight – staying with him, in fact. We're going to dinner with Kate,' he added, hoping the mention of Kate would be enough.

'Why can't I get hold of him then?'

Douglas was silent.

'He doesn't want to speak to me, does he?'

'He's got a girlfriend—'

'But I'm his wife.'

'Arabella,' he bent his head, trying to get her to

look at him. 'You got divorced eight years ago.'

She pushed away the lid and reached for her cigarette, burning itself out in the tin ashtray between them.

'Tom's the only person who's ever understood me, loved me . . .'

'What about all your friends, and your parents? And Charlie Reed – he's mad about you.'

She waved them all away with a sweeping hand, and a trail of smoke.

'Arabella,' he said, very softly, his own hands flat on the table. 'Move on.'

'I can't.'

Douglas looked away.

'You don't have any idea what it's like to feel like this for someone, do you? I can't just *move on*,' she stubbed out the cigarette. 'It's not like getting a new car.'

'I know that. But you have to try.'

'I just – need – someone,' she paused, 'to convince him . . .'

'No.'

The cigarette was out, but she went on stabbing.

'Won't you even ask him to call me?'

'If he wants to call you he will.'

'Why are you doing this to me, Douglas? You're ruining my life.'

'That's enough,' he stood up. 'I won't have you blaming me for whatever went wrong between you. If you've got anything to say, say it to Tom, not to me.'

Arabella let go of the cigarette and put her face in her hands. 'How can I? When he won't return my calls . . .'

Tom opened his eyes and stretched. Time for another cup of that coffee. He threw down a copy of the *Spectator*, and heaved himself out of his chair.

In the kitchen, an open bag of special coffee beans was sitting on the sideboard. Tom had found them in a new coffee shop just opened at the end of the mews – next to the Italian restaurant. They'd told him it was important that he grind the coffee himself, it was too good not to drink fresh. So, after looking at another flat in Pimlico that was too small and too expensive, Tom had spent the rest of his morning looking at coffee grinders in Harrods, discussing them in depth with an Iranian assistant. In the end, he bought two. A big one for him, and a small one for Kate – perhaps she could use it at the dinner party tonight. He went back to the coffee shop and bought Kate a bag of beans, to go with her grinder.

Putting a handful of beans into his grinder, he turned it on and watched them fly round the tinted container. The noise was deafening.

As Douglas let himself in, his first thought was that the spare-room renovations hadn't been completed – that there were workmen still there. He dropped his suitcase in the hall and followed the noise, and then realised it was coming from the kitchen. Hoping it was nothing serious – he couldn't afford to spend any more money on the place, it'd already taken up a disproportionate amount of this year's budget – he opened the door.

Tom switched off the grinder when he saw Douglas enter. 'Hello!' he said.

Relieved and amused, Douglas inspected the

grinder. He switched it on. 'This your new toy?' he shouted.

'Good, isn't it?' Tom turned it off. 'Makes such a difference to the taste of one's coffee.'

'God knows how you lived without one for so long,' said Douglas.

Tom laughed. 'Want a cup?'

'All right. I hope you've got a proper coffee machine, too.'

'Only that ropey one you left behind. The one that leaks. I was tempted by a beautiful one for something extortionate, but I was very good, and I resisted. Oh and look, I got Kate an identical grinder. Just half the size. Thought I could give it to her when we go over later.'

'You're ridiculous.'

Tom grinned. 'Girls like that sort of thing, Doug.'

'Do they.' Douglas watched as Tom made the coffee. He noticed the care Tom took with it, his love of luxury.

'Milk?'

'No.'

They took their cups into the study.

'So,' Tom took a large gulp. 'How was Arabella?'

'She wants you to call her.'

'I know,' said Tom. 'She's been pestering me all week – rings at least three times a day.'

'So why won't you ring her back?'

'Because I know what she's doing, Doug. It's classic Arabella. She knows I'm with Kate, she's mad with jealousy, and she's going to do anything she can to fuck it up. It's typical, especially now that Charlie Reed's disappeared. She can't have me, and she's going to make damn sure nobody else can either. She knows I'll just ignore her, so she's trying to get at me through you – and I'm sorry, but I'm not going to give in.'

'But surely one call – just so that she really understands about Kate . . .'

'Oh for God's sake. She saw us together at Waveney. If that isn't clear enough, Doug, then I don't see what difference in hell a call from me will make.'

'Well, it's up to you,' said Douglas. 'It's your problem. Just don't expect me to do your explaining for you. I don't enjoy it – and anyway, she doesn't listen.'

Tom drained his cup of coffee. He put it to one side and lit a cigarette. Douglas was right, of course. It was up to him – Tom – to tell Arabella what she didn't want to hear and have done. Only it wasn't that simple, he thought. Nothing was ever that simple where Arabella and he were concerned. He found it impossible to control their conversations. He found himself saying things he didn't want to say – agreeing to things he knew were wrong – before he'd even had time to think.

He didn't trust himself to speak to her any more. And it would be even worse to see her. He'd just have to think of some other way. Write, maybe – but something told him that Arabella would not be satisfied with a letter. She knew the effect she had on him, and she was going to make sure she used it.

'I'm sorry,' he said to Douglas. 'And I'm sorry you had to get involved. Leave it to me.'

Kate was late back. And as she opened the door of the flat she could hear Louisa talking and men laughing. They'd arrived.

She threw her briefcase into her bedroom and changed rapidly. But as she slipped on her shoes, she remembered she was going out with someone now. She should think about her underwear.

Everything came off again. At the back of her drawer, she found a black lacy all-in-one thong thing she'd bought while she was going out with Mark, but had never worn. She squeezed into it and glanced at her body in the mirror.

Not bad.

She put on the rest of her clothes and checked her make-up. Kate didn't wear much make-up at work. After the day she'd had today, she expected what was there to have come off, and what was underneath to be pale and strained. Instead it was fine. She looked good. Just a bit more mascara and she was ready.

Tom and Douglas stood up the instant she opened the door. It was only after she'd greeted them that she noticed someone else in the room, besides Louisa.

'Hello?'

'Oh,' said Louisa, 'Kate. You haven't met Richard Hastings.'

Richard remained on the sofa. He smiled up cheerfully. 'Want a nut?'

Kate, unsmiling, shook her head.

'Kate . . .' Louisa moved towards the kitchen, 'I need your opinion on the pork.'

'You don't need me to help you make decisions, Louisa. Do you?' Kate smiled an acid smile she rarely used, and turned away – neutralising her expression for Douglas, who was squatting by the bookshelves with *The Law of Property* in one hand. 'You can't be interested in *that*.'

'Actually,' he said, 'I am quite interested. I want to know more about my rights when trying to evict undesirable tenants.'

'Kate doesn't think I'm undesirable,' said Tom, grinning.

'Kate isn't your landlady.'

'Oh—' smiling in reflex to Tom, Kate turned to Douglas, 'Does the mews house belong to you?'

'I hope you didn't think it belonged to me,' said Tom. 'I'd never decorate a place of my own like that – those awful chair covers and magnolia paint everywhere.'

Douglas stood up from the bookshelves. 'You see what I mean? Undesirable tenants.'

Richard took his bowl of nuts into the kitchen, where Louisa stood at the stove. She was bent over a pan of boiling potatoes, testing one of them with a fork while steam rose into her face, turning it pink and damp. She was dressed, very smartly, in black. But over the top of her suede mini-skirt and tight cashmere cardigan, she was wearing a dirty red apron. The apron came down below the length of her skirt, and above her knees. From the front, all Richard could see was a pair of legs. Louisa looked at him and smiled.

'Hi,' she said, pulling off the cardigan, 'I'm boiled.' She threw it onto a chair and turned back to the stove, bending down to pull the pork out of the oven, her skirt getting shorter by the second. The strappy black silk top was not enough to rid Richard of the momentary impression that there was nothing else beneath the apron. His imagination catapulted.

'I like that skirt.'

Louisa stood up, pushed her heavy, newly washed

hair from her face and smiled again. She was sweating slightly.

He pulled off the oven gloves she was wearing. Dropping them to the floor, he pressed her against the edge of the sink. Her mouth tasted of pork juices. He put a hand on that part of her thigh where apron became stocking.

Louisa didn't move. She just smiled over his shoulder and said, 'Hello Tom.'

Richard turned round to see Tom leaning on the kitchen door with an empty wine glass in one hand. 'I like that skirt, too,' he said to Richard, seriously. 'Especially with the apron.'

Richard, speechless, let her go.

Grinning, Louisa bent her head and wiped her hands on the apron.

'Carry on. Please,' said Tom. 'I was just looking for that bottle of wine.'

'In the fridge,' said Louisa. 'Pour me one too, will you?'

'Of course.' Tom filled her glass and returned to the others.

Kate and Douglas were sitting on the red sofa with *The Law of Property*, closed, between them. Tom gave Kate her glass. He then sat opposite, in the armchair by the window, and looked at his girlfriend.

Kate was sitting directly beneath a standard lamp. Her hair shone, but her face was in shadow. Only the end of her nose and the line of her jaw were drawn by the light. And a pool of it lay on her skin in the 'V' of her jacket.

Douglas was telling an anecdote Tom had heard before. As he watched, Tom trained his ears to the kitchen, but heard nothing. It was, he thought, suspiciously quiet.

Douglas could tell he wasn't listening, but that didn't matter. Kate was on the edge of her chair. He elaborated and gesticulated, turning his anecdote into a performance, while Kate wondered how long she could bear it. She had to get this thong thing off. Her skin would be raw from it scratching every time she moved. Tom would think she had some sort of awful disease.

On and on went the anecdote.

When Louisa asked her again if she could test the pork, Kate leapt up.

In the kitchen, Richard was rearranging her herb pots. She gave him a cool look and then switched it to Louisa.

'Richard,' said Louisa, 'why don't you refill that pot with nuts and take it next door?'

Kate waited for him to leave and then shut the door.

'I'm sorry,' said Louisa, clutching her hair. 'He just turned up. What could I do?'

'Tell him to go away?'

'His wife had to go to a funeral in Wales and we – we've never had a whole night.'

'Louisa . . .'

'You might find that you like him.'

'That's not the point.'

'I know,' she said, her voice light. 'I'm a wicked woman. Is this done?'

Kate gave up, and bent over to see where Louisa had poked a knife into the pork.

'It's perfect.'

As Louisa served, Kate disappeared to her room and took off the thong. Standing naked at her cupboard, she weighed up greying M&S against nothing at all, and opted for the latter.

Tom was sitting next to Louisa. He could see Richard's hand on her leg. Even when he wasn't looking, he was aware of it.

He thought of Louisa as he'd met her, in that dressing gown. And then, in the kitchen just now, which wasn't so far from the thought of Louisa in bed. And the idea of such a beautiful woman in bed with a man like Richard Hastings was so offensive to him, he found it hard not to haul Richard aside and tell him to lay off.

Tom knew plenty of women like Louisa. She was the kind of woman whose beauty came with a guarantee. She'd never look plain, never not look her best. Kate, on the other hand, could look completely unremarkable. The muted colour of her hair, the rounded figure, the skin that was sometimes so pale it simply became grey meant that, at times, it was easy not to notice her. But then with a change in the light, or her mood, or perhaps the right clothes – whatever it was – Kate would transform. Sometimes she'd be lovely for hours at a time. Sometimes, only a second. And Tom found himself transfixed with watching for those moments.

Moments like the one in the bathroom last night – Kate standing at the basin with nothing on while she brushed her teeth, round breasts balanced over an old-fashioned waist, her bottom rose-warm from the shower, flinging her hair back over her shoulder as she spat. Tom loved the way she looked. He wouldn't swap her for a thousand Louisas.

But that didn't stop him from enjoying Louisa's beauty.

Louisa crossed her legs over Richard's hand. Tom watched Richard's face with amusement. Sweat poured into Richard's eyebrows.

'Tom?'

Tom turned his eyes to Louisa's soothing complexion.

'Cigarette?' she offered.

Tom took one. He pulled a lighter from his pocket and held it for Louisa and then himself. He inhaled and then, eyes watering, reached for the packet of cigarettes on the table. It was an unfamiliar brand.

'Are these yours?'

Louisa nodded.

'They're foul.'

Louisa took the packet from him. 'That's why I'm offering them out,' she said.

Tom laughed, and then stubbed his one dead. 'Where are they from?'

'Mexico. I was there two years ago.'

'No wonder they're so bad!'

'As I remember, they were always this bad. But my boyfriend at the time was smoking them and I thought they were deeply cool. Thought I'd grow to like them.' She laughed to herself and exhaled. 'I never did.'

'Did you feel the same way about the man?'

'No.'

It was a shut-out 'No', but Tom didn't mind. He reached for his own packet of Marlboro Lights and offered her one. Louisa stubbed out her Mexican cigarette immediately. She held one of Tom's steadily before her with an outstretched arm and considered it.

'*These*, on the other hand,' she said, tilting her chin, 'are reliable, if somewhat weak and unimaginative.'

'That's me,' said Tom, and Louisa smiled.

After dinner, Kate and Tom decided to go back to Knightsbridge in Douglas' cab. As Kate collected together her briefcase, handbag and tomorrow's clothes, Tom and Douglas chatted to Louisa, thanked her, and complimented her on her cooking.

Richard said nothing. He was standing behind Louisa with his arms around her waist, looking at the back of her neck, desperate for everybody to just go. When Kate reappeared, he opened the door and stood like a footman while Tom and Douglas kissed Louisa goodbye and thanked her again. Come *on*, he was thinking. Come *on*.

Richard was not going to shut the door again. He eyeballed Tom, who was finding more and more things to thank Louisa for.

'Come on, Tom,' said Kate, noticing. 'The taxi's waiting.'

Tom was the first to find his set of keys. He opened the door to Douglas' house and stood aside for the others to go in first.

'I'm sorry about that,' Kate said, putting her briefcase in its usual place. 'If I'd known he was coming, I'd have invited another girl.'

Douglas was hanging his coat on a peg by the door. 'Don't be silly. He's an interesting man.'

'He's a pathetic man,' said Tom, throwing his keys

on one of the chairs in the hall, and climbing the stairs. 'What is he doing with a girl half his age? He should be at home with his wife.'

Douglas looked at Kate. 'Is he married?'

Kate nodded. 'Married with kids. I think Louisa must be mad. It's not as if he's even that attractive . . .'

Tom reached the top of the stairs. 'Come on.'

Douglas looked at her and smiled. 'Sleep well,' he said. 'See you in the morning.'

The spare room was on the ground floor. Douglas opened its door and went in. The redecoration looked good, he thought – glad that he'd saved money on the bed, to spend on the little basin by the window. He undressed quickly, brushed his teeth in the new basin, and climbed into the narrow bed. It was that Victorian one he'd heaved out of the forester's cottage at Waveney to make room for Keith, the new gamekeeper. It had smart brass knobs and a thick mattress, but it was musty. Douglas' mother had insisted it be removed, and now he could see why.

He set his alarm clock and switched off the light. In the darkness, he let the cinema in his mind replay the evening – replay Kate.

And then he thought of Tom. Throwing a pillow on the floor, he lay back and tried to sleep. But he couldn't – the room was stuffy. Douglas got out of bed and kicked over the abandoned pillow. At the window, he opened the curtains and unlocked the catch. The upper window slid down, letting in fresh air and the rumbling of traffic.

He stood there, looking out, and remembered the conversation with Arabella.

Move on, he'd said.

———◆◆◆———

The following morning, Louisa woke first because her sleeping body could no longer tolerate the pillow-case area of bed that Richard had, unconsciously, driven her into. She lay curled up in it, one arm dangling over the side, her fingers playing with the carpet, and began to think about last night. But a soft, continuous tapping told her that outside it was raining. Remembering she'd left the windows open in the dining area to get rid of the smell of smoke, Louisa got out of bed to close them. Last night's room looked flat in the morning light. A faint smell of cigarettes lingered but Louisa was cold and the bookcase under the window was getting wet. She hadn't bothered to put anything on, and shivered slightly as she pulled the windows shut.

But it had been fun, she thought, closing the door and returning to Richard. The pork had been delicious, and she was glad that he'd been there to see how well she could cook. They'd all been so complimentary, especially Tom. She remembered him in the kitchen and smiled. Poor Richard.

Meeting Douglas had jogged Louisa's memory about Tom. She now knew that she'd seen pictures of them both quite recently – like last year – in a magazine article. The article had concentrated mainly on Douglas and a couple of other eligible landowners but there had been a picture of Tom with that model and something about the fact that he was Douglas' friend and that, if the reader didn't mind passing up

213

on a country estate, then he was single again. Louisa remembered noticing Tom.

She pulled back the covers on the other side of the bed and got in.

'Urrr! You're freezing.' Richard rolled over, reaching for her. 'Let me warm you up . . .'

Louisa curled her back into him and let him hold her while her body temperature rose in response.

'Better?'

'Much better.'

He kissed her neck, and she felt a shift of intention in his touch.

Ten

'What is it?'

'Open it.'

With Tom watching, Kate tore off the paper, and two things fell out. Putting the bag of coffee beans to one side, she looked closely at the other object. 'A coffee grinder!' She leant over the kitchen table and kissed him. 'Thank you.'

'Look, Kate,' he pointed to the large grinder by the toaster, 'it's just like my grinder.'

'Only smaller.'

'Oh . . . la-di-dah. Did Miss Leonard want a big grinder? Is Miss Leonard complaining?'

'Not at all,' she shot him a glance. 'I love little things.'

'Little things?'

She nodded.

'So I must be a crashing disappointment – right?'

'Oh God,' she laughed. 'Whatever I say now, I'm in trouble.'

'Just tell me that you fancy me rotten, and that I'm better endowed than any of your ex-boyfriends.'

'I fancy you rotten, Tom Faulkener, and you are – most certainly – better endowed than any of my ex-boyfriends.'

'For that, my darling, you can have a cup of coffee from my extremely large grinder.' He sat watching while she went up to it, took off the lid and looked inside. 'And I don't want to hear any comments. Beans are in the cupboard above the fridge – no, not that cupboard . . .' he got up to help her. 'Can't you tell the difference between a fridge and a freezer?'

Kate let him take charge. She leant on his shoulder as he put the beans in, and blocked her ears as they were ground to powder.

'Smell that, darling.'

Kate could smell it from where she was, but she still bent over the grinder.

'Isn't that the best smell in the world? Now,' Tom took it from her, put it to one side and picked up the old espresso machine. 'We put water in here, see?'

Kate nodded.

'And the ground coffee in this bit – not too much, and you mustn't press it in – see?'

'You sound like Delia Smith.'

'Fuck off. And this bit twists on like that – tight – and where are the little cups? The little cups, the little cups . . .'

The little cups were in the dishwasher. Kate took them out, rinsed them and handed them to Tom. It was getting late, but she didn't want to leave. She wanted her little cup of special coffee, and she wanted to drink it with him.

'Okay. Machine goes on here, cups go on here . . . and here . . . and we light the gas, here . . . and then we wait. You're going to love this.'

Kate did love it. She knocked it back in two gulps,

put down her cup and looked at him. 'It's heavenly,' she said. 'And I must go.'

Tom watched her walk away from him, into the hall. She was wearing a severe black suit with nothing on underneath. He knew this because he'd watched her dress.

He followed her out of the kitchen. 'How do the men in your office keep their hands off you?'

Kate laughed, and took his hand off her bottom. 'They know the law. At least, they know *that* law.'

Coffee grinders forgotten, Tom put his hand back. 'Come upstairs,' he said.

Kate sighed. 'Tom, I can't. I've got to be in by nine today. There's a lot to do . . .'

'I'll drive you.'

Kate was in at nine-thirty. She rushed up the escalators and through the security doors.

Janet was back.

'Feeling better?' she asked as she passed Janet's station.

'A bit under the weather,' said Janet, very quietly, 'but I thought I should come in.'

Bollocks, thought Kate. Bollocks, bollocks, bollocks.

She swung into her office.

Heather was sitting in Kate's chair, chatting to Adam.

'Morning, Heather!'

Startled, Heather stood up. 'I was just checking your post, Kate. I . . .'

Adam turned back to his screen.

Kate took off her coat and put it on a hanger. 'Anything urgent?'

'No . . .'

'Great.'

'Just a message to call Simon Dalziel.'

'Good old Simon!'

'You're cheerful,' Adam tapped something on his keyboard. 'Did you get lucky last night?'

'Yes, Adam. I did.'

Heather's eyes popped. 'You shouldn't be telling him stuff like that, Kate. He'll e-mail it to the whole firm.'

Kate laughed. 'I think I'm allowed to get lucky with my boyfriend.'

Adam looked up from his screen. 'A boyfriend?'

'Don't sound so surprised. Some men find me quite attractive.'

'But I thought you were single.'

'Bad luck, Adam,' said Heather, grinning at Kate.

And then, much to the surprise of all three of them, Adam blushed.

'Coffee anyone?' Kate escaped to the office kitchen with her mug and Adam's Manchester United one. As she stood by the kettle, waiting for it to boil, Michael came in.

'I didn't know you supported United,' he said, putting his mug next to Adam's.

'I don't. It's Adam's mug.'

'So he's got you making his coffee for him, has he? I'd watch out if I were you. He'll be asking you to type his letters for him next.'

Kate smiled sweetly. 'I don't have a hang-up about making other people's coffee.'

'Great. You can make mine. I like it with a cloud of milk and no sugar.'

'A cloud of milk? What the hell's a cloud of milk?'

Michael was on the telephone when she took his mug to his office. He didn't look up. Feeling rather more complicated about making Michael's coffee than she did about making Adam's, Kate put the mug on his desk and resolved not to do it again.

Back in her own office, Kate looked at her in-tray. She could see a mountain of unread Law Society Gazettes and inter-office memoranda about changes in tax legislation. Ignoring them, she pulled out the Bank of Tyrol file.

Adam sat back in his chair. 'So who is he?'

'What?'

'Your boyfriend.'

'None of your business.'

'Does he work here?'

'No.'

'Is he a lawyer?'

'No.'

'How did you meet him?'

Kate put down her coffee cup. 'I met him at a dinner party. Any more questions?'

'Hundreds.'

'Don't you have any work to do?' Kate looked at his empty desk. 'Adam, you must tell me when you've got nothing on.'

'Annette said she might have something for me today.'

'I certainly don't want you working for Annette. She'll give you a lot of mindless crap.'

'And you don't?'

'Oh come on. At least I try not to . . .'

Adam smiled at her.

Kate decided to get him working on a new file – one that was being co-ordinated by a different department, but that had banking points to be checked. Kate now had a whole cabinet full of files. She was working for about twenty clients. Not all of them provided as much work as Hazel Industries, and some of them were so half-hearted she wondered why they bothered with legal advice at all, but so far Adam had only done work on Hazel Industries matters. This was mainly because the Hazel Industries instructions were relatively easy to translate for trainee purposes – the banking issues weren't too jargon-heavy – but it was time he had a shot at something else.

She wrote a name and a telephone number on a Post-it note, then held it out to him. 'This man is an in-house lawyer at Space Vortex PLC. Space Vortex is the client. It's a software company, but it also has a pharmaceutical business. It wants to separate the pharmaceutical from the software by demerging.' She flapped the Post-it note at him. 'This man is extremely nice. Tell him it's about Project Galaxy, and that you're an Insider.'

Adam's eyes brightened at the prospect of secrecy. He took the note from Kate.

'Tell him we need copies of all Space Vortex's financing documents. Explain you're from the Banking Department here, and ask whether it's better for you to go and pick them up or whether they can send them. Try to get an idea of how much paperwork there is.'

Kate opened her Bank of Tyrol file. 'It'll be interesting. It's an important deal and it should make the papers.'

She felt slightly guilty. Adam didn't know that he'd be spending the next three months going through document after document with a tooth-comb, and that it would bore him to distraction. But someone had to do it.

She finished her coffee. Now. Where were those Side Letters?

———◆———

She wasn't looking forward to lunch with Simon. But as she left the closed air of her office and wandered through the early afternoon, she was more than usually thrilled by its brilliance, and glad not to be lunching on grey sandwiches at her desk.

It wasn't as if the day was particularly fine. It was windy. The sunlight came and went in patches, and it wasn't warm. But when it came, it raced down the streets in westward waves, with the shade rolling in behind. Kate, lifting her head, picked up its energy and felt irresponsibly happy.

At the end of the street, in shadow for a second and then suddenly bright, was Simon's restaurant. Kate approached it, thinking that City lunches were worth it only if you could write off the afternoon, and slope home for an early night.

She thought of Tom, under the same sky, only seconds behind. What was he doing now?

———◆———

Tom was calling Kate.

Janet picked up the telephone, and they recognised each other's voices.

'She's not in.'

'Do you know when she'll be back?'

'No.'

Tom lit a cigarette. 'Will she be back today?'

'I don't know.'

He felt the hostility in her tone and injected some into his. 'How do you suggest I contact her then?'

'I can take a message.'

'Does she have an answerphone of her own?'

'Voicemail, you mean?'

'Whatever. Put me through, will you?'

Janet hit the keys on her telephone, and connected Tom to the switchboard instead.

'Switchboard.'

'I was calling to speak to Kate Leonard,' he spat at the surprised operator. 'I have been told by Kate's secretary that she's out at the moment, and I wish to be put through to her voicemail. Her secretary is obviously incapable and has connected me to you instead. Please would you put me through. I'd also like to express a complaint at the appalling service.'

'Of course,' said the operator. 'Would you like to channel your complaint through Kate, or shall I put you through to Charles Kenyon, the partner responsible for client complaints?'

'Put me through to Charles Kenyon,' he said, finishing his cigarette.

'Can I take your name, sir?'

'Tom Faulkener.'

'Of . . . ?'

'Of . . . ?'

'Yes, sir. I need to give Mr Kenyon the name of your company so that he can find you on his client files and register the complaint.'

'Oh,' said Tom in a small voice, and asked to be put through to Kate's voicemail.

'*Kate. It's me. What are we doing tonight, besides the obvious?*'

He rang back five minutes later and left another message.

'*It's me again. Your secretary has no manners. I'm considering voicing a complaint with Charles Kenyon. Is Charles Kenyon as dull as he sounds?*'

He rang again at two o'clock.

'*Who are you having lunch with? Some dreary banker, who can't keep his hands off you? Why aren't you waiting by the phone for me to call?*'

Kate clattered through the swing-doors into a dark panelled dining room. It took a second for her eyes to adjust to the darkness.

'Have you a reservation, madam?'

Kate squinted at the shape of a large coiffure bent over the desk. She watched a pointed fingernail press its way down the reservations diary.

'No idea,' said Kate, bending over the diary too. 'Probably. I'm meeting someone.' She pointed her own finger at Simon's pencilled name. 'That's him. Dalziel.'

Simon was sitting by himself at the far end of the restaurant. Kate could tell from the settings that this lunch was not going to be quick.

'Simon.' She held out her hand. Simon ignored the hand and kissed her cheek, firmly. She had to pull her hand away fast to avoid punching him in the stomach.

'I thought you'd never arrive.'

'Am I late?' She sat down and looked at her watch. Ten past. 'Sorry.'

Simon touched her arm. 'It doesn't matter. What would you like to drink?'

Once they'd ordered, Simon asked Kate if she knew about Hazel Industries' latest project. Kate took a bread roll from the basket between them and wondered what to say. Project Cannon II was top secret. She was having her meeting with Henry Hazel and Margaret Stanwyck on Monday, and felt she should say nothing until then.

'Which project?'

'Come on,' Simon handed her the butter. 'You know.'

'I don't know. I don't know what you're talking about. Hazel Industries has hundreds of projects on the go.'

'What if I were to say that this project is banking-related?'

'Is it?'

'Tax-driven –'

'Really?'

'And involves a bit of restructuring, and a syndicated loan?'

Kate said nothing, but she grinned.

'Will you be setting up an SPV?' he persisted, and she looked away.

'Tell me,' she said, changing the subject, 'are you busy at the moment?'

Simon gave up. 'Are you?'

'Frantic. Sometimes I wonder why we do this job. We're mad not to be working at the banks – their work is far less taxing, they get almost double our salary, and their hours are better.'

'But it's less intellectual.'

'You call our work intellectual?'

Simon filled her glass. 'Let's not talk about work,' he said. 'Let's talk about bars. I bet someone like you goes out a lot. Do you know any good ones?'

It was after three when they got their bill. By that time, Kate was in no doubt of his intentions and she was angry. She found the situation unprofessional and, somehow, it compromised her much more than it did him. She was conscious that, if she rejected Simon, every issue in the next deal would become an intolerable battle. And if she accepted him she'd be risking her professional reputation, and her authority.

Of course she wouldn't accept him. There was Tom. But the question was whether, while having absolutely no intention of letting anything happen, she should draw things out, hint at possibilities, and play him into taking a more indulgent approach with her.

It was asking for trouble. The deal would certainly involve late-night meetings. Many opportunities for Simon to lunge at her. It was unfair to Simon, and possibly to Tom, but the project would be a dream. It was the perfect opportunity for her to show Michael and Henry Hazel what a smart deal she could cut.

Kate let Simon guide her out of the restaurant, into a windy street. The sun had gone in, and the air bit at her neck. She pulled her coat closer and shifted her bag on her shoulder.

'Thank you,' she said.

'We must do it again.'

'Yes . . .'

Kate was not wearing gloves. Wrapping her arms

225

around her body, she nestled her hands in the pockets of warmth at her armpits and watched Simon's cool eyes staring at the sky. She could tell that he was wondering whether to get specific.

'I'll call you,' he said, looking back at her.

* * *

Kate returned to a desk that was out of control. The Side Letters still needed drafting; there was a memo from Colin Abrahams asking her to call up an old file and bring it to his office at five; she needed to put pressure on Simon for the new project; she really needed to get up to speed on the Project Galaxy demerger. And there were three messages waiting on her phone.

She brightened when she discovered that all three were from Tom, and called him back immediately.

'I hate your secretary,' he said.

'She hates you . . . and this isn't a battle you're likely to win.'

'Unless I complain to Charles Kenyon.'

'Don't.'

He laughed.

'Tom . . .'

'All right. What are we doing tonight?'

'I've got to work.'

'How late?'

'Hard to tell.'

'Will you come back here?'

'Might be after midnight.'

'I don't mind. I'll get some food in for you, and a bottle of wine. We can have a little feast . . .'

* * *

It was five o'clock. Tom was getting ready to go out

226

when the doorbell rang. He put his wallet and keys on the table in the hall and opened the door.

Arabella.

'Can I come in?'

'What is it?'

'Let me in and I'll tell you.'

Tom let her in and shut the door. Arabella strode towards the kitchen, talking from lips that hardly moved.

'I take it from your radio silence that you don't want anything more to do with me. I'm here because I want you to say it to my face.'

Underneath her long coat, he could see a tight fluffy polo-neck and a pair of leather trousers.

'. . . rather than your ignore-her-and-the-problem-will-go-away approach. You can't treat me like this, Tom. I'm not going to lie back and take it.'

He took the coat from her and draped it over the back of a chair. 'Can I get you a cup of coffee?'

'No.'

'Something stronger?'

'No.'

'Well,' said Tom, opening a cupboard. 'I'm going to have one.'

He took out some coffee beans, put them in the grinder and turned it on. Arabella flinched at the noise and waited until it stopped.

'Why won't you say it?' she persisted.

Tom poured the ground coffee into Douglas' espresso machine and put it on the stove. 'Say what?'

'Say you don't want me, you don't fancy me.'

Tom stood at the stove, staring at the blue jets of gas curling out from under the coffee machine.

'Say you don't love me, say our wedding vows meant nothing, say that —'

'Stop it.'

'Say it.'

Coffee was spilling from the spout of the machine, collecting in a dark pool at the bottom of Tom's cup.

'You can't say it. You coward. You can't even look me in the eye.'

Tom switched off the heat. Above the spitting and hissing from the machine, he heard a chair scrape. There was a swish as she swept up her coat.

'Arabella . . .'

'Forget it.'

She had to pass him to reach the door.

'Arabella,' he caught her wrist. 'You don't understand.'

'Yes,' she said, resisting. 'I do understand. You're weak.'

He tightened his grip. 'I'm trying to do the right thing.'

Then, quite suddenly, Arabella stopped fighting and Tom found that he'd pulled her towards him.

In the sinews of her wrist, he felt a shift of passion from determined resistance to rough fatalism, and his reflex was sexual. She was too close. He pushed her so hard against the wall that she felt the light switch between her shoulder blades, and the breath she'd forgotten she'd been holding in her lungs tore out in a sigh.

———•◦•———

'Darling. I'm going to be back earlier than I thought. More like ten. Even better, I've got tomorrow off shopping with Mum, so perhaps we can go out somewhere tonight, and lie

in tomorrow morning? I'm meeting her at Oriel's at ten, but that has to be better than the usual six-thirty, doesn't it? We were wondering if you wanted to join us for lunch. Call me.'

They heard her hang up. The answerphone beeped, whirred, and was silent. Tom sighed and looked at Arabella. She was staring at the ceiling.

'What time is it?'

'Don't know.'

He sat up and looked beyond her at the clock. It was eight. 'Did you intend this to happen?' he said.

'No.'

'How did it happen?'

She didn't reply.

Later still, she left. They didn't say much. Exhausted, sitting at the bottom of the stairs in the hall, with his cheek flat against the cool wall, Tom listened to her walking about, collecting her things.

The anger she'd brought with her had produced between them the complete sexual antithesis. He'd never had sex with a woman in tears before and, instead of alienating him, the sight of her crying involved him, absolutely.

'I'm done.'

He turned and watched her come downstairs, face recovered.

'Got everything?'

'Yes.'

He stood up. 'Did you drive?'

'Yes. The car's outside.'

'You got it back?'

She smiled. 'Eventually.'

'You'll be okay?'

'Fine.'

Tom opened the door, and watched her walk up the mews, her coat flapping in the wind. 'I'll call you,' he said. 'I promise.'

The car flashed and beeped as she unlocked it. Tom watched her get in and pull the door shut. He heard the engine splutter into life, and waited for it to move towards the end of the mews. In her rearview mirror Arabella saw him in the doorway, standing very straight against the light.

He stood there for a bit after she'd gone, listening to the traffic. Then he turned and went in.

Elizabeth hated shopping with Kate, almost as much as Kate hated shopping with her.

'What about this then?'

'It's pink.'

Elizabeth put the jacket back. She pretended to work her way along the rail, while watching her daughter to see what she was pulling out – to get an idea of what kind of things she liked. They were all grey and brown and black.

Turning her attention back to the rail, she pulled out a silvery mini-dress. Perhaps Kate would think that this one was sufficiently grey. 'This?'

Kate looked up from the pair of trousers she was holding out and shook her head. 'I'm too fat.'

'Rubbish.' Elizabeth went over and held the dress to Kate's body. 'You'd look stunning.'

She would. She'd look every bit as good as the model in the life-size picture by the fitting rooms. Better. It would show off her legs and there seemed to be enough room at the top for her bust. Elizabeth had a tiny bust and often wished Kate would make

230

more of hers while it was still there. She didn't know how lucky she was.

'Can't you just try it on?'

'What size is it?'

Elizabeth wasn't wearing her glasses. She brought the label close to her face and frowned.

'What's a thirty-six?'

'It's something like an eight – go and ask the attendant to find whatever a size twelve is and I might oblige.'

'Darling, you'll swim in a size twelve. I'm getting you a ten.'

Kate shrugged. She didn't want it anyway. She was feeling depressed. They were meeting Tom for lunch, it was past midday, and they still hadn't found anything. She hated doing this – hated getting in and out of clothes that made her feel unattractive. She had a mountain of more important things to be doing and in the back of her mind she was worried about lunch – about her mother and Tom meeting each other.

An assistant who looked like a younger, shorter version of Arabella reappeared with two silver dresses, followed by her mother.

'Darling, they don't have it in a ten, but she thought you'd fit the twelve anyway.'

'The sizes come up smaller than most,' the assistant added, noticing Kate's expression.

Kate tried on the dress while Elizabeth and the assistant chatted outside.

'Silver's very popular this year . . .'

'I adore those bright pink jackets. How much are they?'

Kate didn't hear the reply. Noticing it was the kind

of dress that would show her bra, she took it off and looked at herself for a second. Shop mirrors were always more flattering, weren't they? How else did they expect to sell their stuff? Stepping into the dress, pulling its straps over her shoulders, Kate watched her reflection, and listened to the conversation outside.

'And what would she wear it with?'

'We've got some little chiffon skirts, madam. She could try a pink one, or – I think a different colour looks better, actually. We had someone in here earlier who bought a red one. She was going to put a bright pink ribbon on the border of the skirt. I know that sounds funny, but she looked really lovely.'

'What a clever idea! I'm sure Kate would look lovely, too. Have you got it in her size?'

'I'll just go and see. Twelve, was it?'

'Ten.'

'How is it?' Forgetting that her daughter was fully grown, Elizabeth flicked open the curtain – exposing her to the shop. Kate stood in front of the mirror, her hair flicked to one side, bending one arm right over her back to do up the zip.

'Let me.'

Elizabeth did up the zip and looked at Kate's reflection in the mirror. The dress was perfect over her hips, and slightly too tight at the top. Elizabeth smiled with pride. Kate fidgeted and twisted to see herself from the back.

'My skin's too white.'

'What about fake tan?'

'Fake tan smells.'

Elizabeth let out an exasperated sign. 'Will you stop being so negative?'

232

'I . . .'

'You've done nothing but whinge and complain. Today was supposed to be fun, sweetheart. Not an ordeal.'

'We've got jackets and skirts in the ten. I brought the skirt in a pink,' the assistant leant across Kate and hung the clothes on the peg by the mirror, 'and a black, and a red – just in case. All right?' She smiled brightly at Kate and Elizabeth.

They waited until she'd gone.

'I'm sorry,' said Kate, in a tone that didn't quite match the words. 'But I hate doing this. You know I hate it.'

'Would you rather I left? Why don't I leave you to find something by yourself, and meet you at the restaurant?'

Kate hesitated.

'I want to go to Harrods anyway, to see if they've got that book on herbs. Why don't you look around for yourself, find something and get them to hold it? I'll come back with you after lunch and pay for it then.'

'Would you mind?'

Kate waited until her mother left the shop, and then left too. Turning in the opposite direction from Harrods, she cut across Sloane Street and went into Harvey Nichols.

The store was packed. Squeezing past cosmetics counters, and avoiding eye contact with self-conscious women offering promotional sprays of scent, Kate wondered what all these other shoppers did for a living. It was Friday. Why weren't they working? Were they all like her, grabbing one day in a hundred before rushing back to work – in which case, what had prompted them all to choose the same damn day? Or were they like Tom – professional sloths, idling away another – yawn – morning, checking the latest hair products, or if the new collections were in yet, before a spot of food shopping on the top floor and then home for a nap, or an afternoon movie?

Finding the up escalator, Kate was lifted to the first floor – to dreamy bits of nothing worth thousands and thousands of pounds, to fragile see-through dresses hung far enough apart to fit a month's wages – in tenners – between them. Less expensive clothes were on the second and third floors, but Kate couldn't resist it.

Just to get my eye in, she thought, heading straight into Alberta Ferretti. Then I'll go upstairs and find something to buy.

Finding nothing in Ferretti, Kate moved on.

She was pulling back a velvet coat of darkest navy – so dark it could be black, and lined with vibrant silk – when she heard a voice say, very clearly,

'*Did you see who that was?*'

Two assistants, standing together at a cash desk, were staring out beyond Kate.

'She's beautiful, isn't she?'

'I love her shoes . . .'

Expecting a celebrity, Kate turned to look in the same direction and saw Arabella.

Arabella, aware of the scrutiny, looked up from the Alexander McQueen dress she was holding. She saw Kate – and then she smiled.

'Hello,' she was coming over. 'How are you?'

Kate kissed her, loving the way the assistants stared.

'There's nothing here,' said Arabella. 'Nothing. Look at this,' she pulled at the coat Kate was holding. 'Just look at that price.'

Kate looked.

'And then look . . .'

Kate looked at where Arabella pulled at a seam. It looked fine to her.

'Crap.' Arabella put a hand on Kate's shoulder and doubled her smile. 'Aren't you supposed to be at work?'

'No,' said Kate. 'I've got the day off – and I've got to find something to wear for my thirtieth.'

'God, how nice. What's the budget?'

'My mother's paying.'

'Your mother? Wow. Wish I had a mother like that.'

'Oh she's not,' Kate laughed. 'I don't have carte blanche, but I'll top up the difference myself if I have to. I think I deserve it.'

'Of course you deserve it, working as hard as you do, and I'll tell you something, there's a stunning silver jacket in Versace. I'd have bought it myself if I had a mother like yours.'

A quarter of an hour later, Kate and Arabella were watching the silvery jacket and a pair of tight black satin trousers being wrapped in tissue paper while they waited for Kate's card to be processed.

'And there's a heavenly pair of shoes I saw in the window at Gina, Kate. You have to get those – and then you're done. You're going to look amazing – when is it?'

'Not until June. Will you be in London then?'

'Expect so.'

235

'Well, I'm not sure yet exactly what I'm doing, but whatever it is you must come.'

'You mustn't feel you —'

'I'll send you an invitation – put you on my list – thanks.' Kate took the pen and signed away eight hundred and fifty pounds. She mustn't feel guilty. She could afford it. She deserved it. 'You must give me your address.'

'Tom'll have it,' said Arabella. 'Just ask him. Now let's go to Gina and then grab a drink before you rush off to your lunch.'

Kate wasn't sure she could really afford the shoes. She tried them on, walked up and down with Arabella cooing at them. She loved them, and she was sure that Arabella would know exactly what was in, but they were over two hundred pounds. So she asked the shop to hold them for her – just until after lunch, when she was sure that a bit of food and alcohol would weaken her into getting them. The assistant smiled and said that was no problem. She'd hold them until the end of the day.

Arabella knew a bar in Beauchamp Place. 'Just a couple of glasses of champagne,' she said.

Kate didn't need persuading. She liked Arabella – Arabella's warmth, the slightly outrageous way she spoke, the crazy sense of style, the total lack of gravity. And, again, the lack of snobbishness. Someone like Arabella must have hundreds of glamorous friends, and yet she was prepared to spend time helping Kate shop – and making it fun. Go on, Arabella had said. Who cares if it's a bit too funky? Who cares if people stare? And who cares if it's tight? It's sexy, and it's cool. Instead of feeling jealous

about, or threatened by, the life Arabella and Tom
had shared, Kate found that it was completely irrelevant. If Arabella could rise above it, then so could she.

But she didn't know what thoughts were running
through Arabella's mind as Arabella pushed one glass
of champagne along the bar towards Kate and
brought the other to her lips. It was too easy for her
to misinterpret the interest in Arabella's eyes, and the
smile that Arabella had picked from the many shades
of smile in her model's palette. This was the *Women's
Monthly* cover – the friendly you-could-be-me-smile –
and Kate was fooled.

The restaurant wasn't far from Harrods. It was small
and bright, with a mass of wine glasses hanging
upside down by their bases over a chrome bar. The
chairs were chrome as well but, for those who arrived
early, there were soft leather sofa-benches around
the edges of the room. It was impossible to sit in these
without being thrown virtually horizontal. If you
drank a lot, it was equally impossible to get out of
them. Douglas had had real difficulties the last time
he and Tom had eaten there.

Tom had managed to find a table in the corner, so
that at least two of them could sit comfortably. He
and Elizabeth were deep in the leather, and deep in
conversation – both smoking – when Kate arrived.

Tom heaved himself up and kissed her. 'Did you
find anything?'

'Silver jacket and black satin trousers.'

'Tight ones?'

'Skin-tight. I can hardly move – and you'll never
guess who helped me find them, who I bumped

into totally by chance on the first floor of Harvey Nichols . . .'

'Go on, then,' said Tom.

'Arabella!'

'Oh yes?' said Tom, masking his reaction with a laugh. 'What was she doing there, I wonder?'

'Who's Arabella?'

'She's Tom's ex-wife, Mum – and she's lovely. I tried to persuade her to come to lunch as well, but she said she had something else on. I want her to come to my party, Tom. She said you could give me her address.'

'Whatever,' said Tom, picking up the bottle of wine. 'Want some?'

'Lots,' said Kate, sitting on the chrome chair and smiling from her mother to Tom.

'Why don't you sit here?' said her mother. 'It's more comfortable.'

Kate shook her head. 'I'm fine.'

Tom filled all their glasses and gave the empty bottle to a waiter.

Elizabeth sat forward and leant for her glass. She drank from it and watched Tom's slim body flop back into the leather.

'So, Tom,' she said. 'What have you been doing this morning?'

'Flat hunting,' he replied, and steered the conversation on to where was nice to live in London, to Mrs Leonard's decision to move to Diss. But he found it hard to remain interested – and Elizabeth noticed. Yet whenever she asked Tom about himself, he seemed reluctant to give much away. So they ended up talking about Waveney, and Douglas.

238

Elizabeth let him refill her glass. 'How long has he been there?'

'Not sure.' Tom refilled Kate's and then his own. 'Eight years? Something like that.'

'And his parents?'

'Live in Gloucestershire – have done since they got married, and that was ages ago. They belong there now. I suppose they've put so much into the house and the garden, and all Jane's closest friends live round there, they didn't want to move back to Norfolk permanently. I think having Douglas there was the perfect solution.'

'Kate says he isn't very glamorous, but I can't believe it.'

'Mum . . .'

'She's right. He isn't. But he is one of the nicest people I know.'

As Tom spoke, they heard the ringing of a mobile telephone. Half the restaurant felt in their bags and coat pockets.

'Whose is that?'

'Mine . . .' Tom kept the numbers of everybody he knew in the memory of his mobile. This meant that if someone he knew was calling him, the display panel on the telephone would give him not only the number of the caller, but also the name. Catching sight of 'ARABELLA' as he switched it off, Tom experienced a rush of excitement so intense that he completely lost his appetite.

At the first opportunity, he excused himself and rang her from the loo. 'Where are you?'

'Claridges. Room three-one-two. Bored. And completely naked.'

'He seems charming, darling. And so much better-looking than Mark.'

'Isn't he!' Kate ate her last anchovy and grinned at her mother.

Elizabeth decided to say nothing about the concerns she felt. Not yet. Just because Tom was charming, that didn't automatically make him two-faced. Mark had been no oil painting, and look how badly he'd behaved. And maybe Tom's reluctance to talk about himself was modesty, and not because he had anything to hide. But Elizabeth wasn't sure. She looked again at her daughter.

'You know, the best thing about him – for me – is seeing you so happy.'

Leaning back to let the waiter take her plate, Kate extended the grin as far as it would go.

It suited them that Tom had to leave promptly. They wanted to get back to the shoe shop, so that Elizabeth could see the shoes they were holding, and help Kate make a decision. They thought it was sweet that he insisted on paying for lunch.

Eleven

As summer came, Kate's working hours lengthened with the days. She was rarely away from her desk before nine and, when she was, it was usually because of some office social – because she had to attend the leaving drinks of Steve's secretary, or because Michael had got Gavin to organise a 'bonding' bowling night in Finchley – rather than because of her private life. It was often after ten when she got back and then it made sense for her to go straight to Tom's flat, which meant that she hardly saw Louisa at all.

Louisa understood about the demands of Kate's job. She could see that there was no point in Kate coming home, just to say hello, before going on to Tom. And she didn't really mind – not while she had Richard. Kate's absence meant that she and Richard had greater privacy and, given that Kate didn't approve of Richard, it was really better all round.

But Richard wasn't always there for her and when he wasn't – when his wife gave a dinner party, or when the children were home – Louisa had time to look at the rest of her life. It was then that she became conscious of Kate's absence. She'd rung Kate a couple of times at work. Kate, or her secretary, said she'd ring back when she was less busy, but Louisa still hadn't heard from her. This time, she decided she wasn't going to be put off.

'Can I speak to Kate Leonard?'

'Kate's on the phone right now,' Janet told her. 'Can I take a message?'

'Oh,' said Louisa, recognising the voice. 'Hello. It's Louisa Edwardes again. Can I hold?'

'She might be some time . . .'

'I don't mind.'

Louisa had to wait for ten minutes before she finally got through.

'Lou – I'm so sorry. Is everything okay?'

'Everything's fine. Just wondered when I was going to see you. It's been over a month.'

'No. Really?' said Kate. 'God, isn't that awful. It's been like a madhouse here, and what with—'

'How about a drink tonight?'

'Lou, I can't. I'm giving a talk tomorrow, and I have to get my slides in order.'

'That won't take all night.'

'I really really can't. There'll be clients attending.'

'Come on, Kate. Just you and me. I don't mind meeting you late – late as you like. They've made me a member of the Virtual Bar, and that stays open until three in the morning – or gives a very good impression of it – so you've got no excuse. Just say yes.'

Kate thought of the time Louisa had last pestered her like this, the time she'd gone to Charlie's party and met Tom. Looking back over the last month or two, she could see that she was slipping back into the work-sleep-eat-work spiral, that she was getting dull.

She couldn't seriously work on her slides after six

o'clock anyway, because the guys in the reprographics department all left on the dot. She figured that, if she stayed until eight, she'd have a working draft for her lecture notes, and she could tidy that up in the morning. Just get up half an hour early. She could ring Tom to explain what she was doing – he'd understand.

'All right,' she said. 'I'll meet you there at nine.'

As it turned out, she had her notes completed by seven, and an hour to spare. So she decided to join her colleagues for a drink in the wine bar first.

Squeezing past a table of about eight people, their coats slung over the backs of chairs, their briefcases on the floor – or reserving other chairs – Kate made for where Heather, Janet, Gavin and Steve were settled in a corner. Janet and Heather were leaning forward over the table together, side by side, both talking to Gavin, while skinny Steve sat back in his chair, drinking lager.

'She's already complained once to Michael,' Heather was saying. 'Thing is, he's got too much on his plate. And he doesn't really care.'

'Care about what?' said Kate, pulling up a chair.

'Annette,' Gavin told her. 'She's driving Daniella mad, keeps telling her—'

'She's made Danni redo her filing *three times*. And then told her to clean up her dress-sense.'

'That's a joke,' said Kate, 'coming from Annette. Did you see the trousers she was wearing today?'

'Now now, girls,' said Gavin, grinning. 'Don't be bitchy.'

'Annette Latham's got the fattest arse in the department,' remarked Heather, finishing her glass and giving it to Kate. 'Your round, I think.'

The other three drained their glasses and gave them to Kate who, protesting, nonetheless went off with them to the bar.

One hour and three glasses later, she joined Louisa at the Virtual. For all her working hours and isolated life, even Kate knew about the Virtual Bar. It had just opened. It had been written about in almost every article in the Style section of last week's *Sunday Times*, and it was typical of Louisa to be a member already.

'I know the guys who own it,' she'd said – as if that made it more ordinary.

Louisa was dressed in her leather jacket, her black suede mini-skirt and a pair of brand-new Prada knee-length boots. The sight of her sitting there on one of the orange sofas with a bottle of champagne cooling in an ice bucket on the table in front of her, a magazine on her lap, made Kate feel faintly square.

'I'm pissed,' she announced, collapsing beside Louisa and kissing her. 'How are you?'

Louisa put the magazine down, poured Kate a glass of champagne and put it into her outstretched hand. 'Don't do things by halves, do you? What happened?'

'Finished early. Had an hour to kill.'

Louisa watched Kate look around the room – at the Louisa look-alikes, the Tom look-alikes, blacked out against a series of vast computer screens and mirrors that made it impossible to see where the room began and ended – particularly if you were drunk.

'It's amazing,' said Kate.

'Hasn't really hotted up yet. And if you want to celebrity-spot, you have to wait until about two.'

'Then I'll have to make do with you. Now tell me – how's Richard?'

Louisa was still telling Kate about Richard when they finished their bottle of champagne. 'He keeps telling me he'll leave her – thanks, Johnny,' she smiled at the waiter as he emptied the champagne bottle into their glasses.

'Want another one?' Johnny's voice was as posh as Douglas's. He must have been about eighteen and Kate could see that he wasn't comfortable serving.

'Why not?' said Louisa. 'Thanks.'

'Rory Talbot's younger brother,' she added to Kate when he was out of earshot. 'Sweet, don't you think? Kept me company before you arrived – telling me all about who was in here last night and what they were drinking.'

Kate smiled as she listened – she was beginning to feel very drunk, now. It was as if the room was floating on water. 'Go on about Richard,' she said.

'The thing is, I'm not sure I *want* him to leave his wife.'

'Have you told him this?'

'Yes – and he just tells me to stop pretending.'

'Pretending? You're saying he thinks you're faking indifference, and that you really want him to end it with her and marry you?'

'Yes.'

'The arrogance!' Kate laughed. 'And you don't?'

'No.'

'Oh dear.'

She was finding it hard to take Louisa's problem seriously – and so, in fact, was Louisa. Both of them were laughing as Johnny opened the second bottle and refilled their glasses.

Later, as she sat in the cab that took her home to

Tom, Kate's slurred brain wondered if that was part of the problem. Louisa was a professional partygoer. Was her designer lifestyle, with days centred around preparing for night, so removed from the ordinary business of living that it encouraged her to take the trivial things seriously, and the serious things with a pinch of salt? Kate wasn't sure. This was a side of her friend she was still discovering. Of course, she'd known Louisa since they were children. But at school they'd had identical workloads. And at university, she hadn't seen so much of Louisa. It was only now that they were living together as adults – maybe only now that Kate's job was so serious – that she felt the difference in Louisa. She knew that, at heart, Louisa was sound, that she did care. She did have principles. It was just the lack of work in her life that made it seem superficial.

Because Kate was only around at night – and, even then, she was late – Tom found that he saw more of Arabella.

This was partly because he couldn't resist her, and partly because there wasn't much else for him to do. Half-heartedly, he flat hunted and applied for jobs, but that couldn't keep him occupied all day. Even if it had kept him occupied, he would have been lonely.

In the past, Tom had always been happily conscious of having too many friends – not too few. He'd even quite enjoyed complaining that he never had any time to himself. Now that he had all the time in the world, Tom realised he was bored. He wasn't used to a girlfriend who worked. His idea of romance was unbroken togetherness – not hurried cups of coffee in the morning and dinners that were either cancelled, or slotted in between office and sleep.

To make matters worse, the people who didn't work – the people he would otherwise have played with in the day – played expensive games. Tom knew he wouldn't be bored if he was with Heinrich and Eva in Morocco, or if he'd been able to join Philip Westerland in Australia, scuba diving the Great Barrier Reef. But he couldn't afford it. Even when these people were in London, it was lunch at Kaspia Caviar, followed by shopping – and that was as expensive as the skiing holiday he'd had to refuse.

He knew Charlie Reed was around sometimes – between shoots in Guatemala and Egypt – but he was hardly going to want to see Tom after what had happened with Arabella. Douglas came up occasionally, but projects at Waveney meant that he was never able to manage more than a couple of days a month in London. And who else was there – apart from Arabella?

They'd meet for coffee at eleven, in the new coffee house next to the Italian restaurant at the end of Tom's mews. They'd read the papers and go back to his house. After the first time, they decided to use the spare room. It was only a single bed, but that way the chances of Kate discovering were reduced, and there was no need for complications over the sheets. Afterwards, they'd lunch together and then she'd leave.

It riled Arabella that Tom should have it all his own way. But she'd made it clear that she'd have him on his terms, and these were them: she had Tom's weekdays, Kate had his evenings and his weekends.

And Tom's libido soared. The more sex he had, the more it seemed his appetite for it increased. But he was no closer to finding a job or a flat. The money he had set aside for the flat, the money he'd inherited from his maternal grandparents, was disappearing. When his August bank statement arrived, Tom had to call his stockbroker. Philip Barclay had been a friend of his father's. He was red-faced from good living, and proud of it.

'Philip. It's Tom Faulkener.'

'Tom, dear boy,' the voice boomed back. 'How are you?' Philip was used to these calls. He began working out what price he could get for the BT shares.

'I'm well. And you?'

'Splendid! What can I do for you?'

'Money again, I'm afraid. Do you think it'd be possible for you to arrange for another five thousand to be put into my account?'

'Of course.'

Tom stretched out his legs and admired his shoes. 'How much does that leave me with?'

'If you'll just bear with me,' said Philip, leaning across his large desk. 'I'll get your details up on screen.'

Tom waited, still looking at his shoes. He bent forward and rubbed a speck of mud from the leather.

'It won't be entirely accurate, of course,' Philip went on, 'but there's about forty thousand there at the moment, so—'

'Forty thousand?'

'Thereabouts.'

'But I thought there was more like eighty . . . seventy.'

Philip began explaining that while the market had not been good, he'd managed to get quite a pleasing performance from Tom's portfolio. Tom had extracted twenty thousand in March, and a further ten at the end of April.

'Oh yes.'

'You needed ten in June and . . . again, ten about two weeks ago. So that's fifty gone.'

Tom sat forward. 'So there should be fifty left.'

'Well, Tom. Let's see. You started with ninety-two . . .'

The flat was very quiet when Tom put down the receiver. He sat staring at the dead television screen, remembering what it was like never to think of money, remembering his flat in Rome.

Kate was too busy to notice Tom's preoccupations. She had enough of her own. The Project Cannon II meeting with Henry and Margaret had gone well. They were going to need corporate restructuring documents and separate loan documents. Simon had already sent her first drafts of the loan documents. To her irritation, Kate could tell they were just basic adaptations of the Fraser Cummings' model forms. In other words, entirely favouring Simon's client – the bank.

'You were supposed to base them on the documents we agreed in the last project, Simon. Don't you ever look at the term sheet?'

'But they are based on the last ones.'

'Only insofar as the last project documents began with Fraser Cummings' model form documents. And we then spent months negotiating. Remember?'

'How could I forget?'

'Well, isn't it in all our interests to cut that out this time?'

Simon just laughed. 'Not in my interests,' he said. 'I wanted more time negotiating with you.'

'Don't think I'm that easily flattered.'

'Why don't you just mark up the documents as you think they should be and send them back?' he suggested.

'No, Simon. *You* send me documents based on the last project. *Then* I'll mark them up . . . and can you get them to me tomorrow?'

'Tomorrow?'

'You could meet me for a drink and hand them over then.'

'All right, all right. Jesus. Twist me round your little finger, why don't you . . .'

And not only was Kate in the middle of dealing with Simon, she was also trying to organise her thirtieth birthday party.

She'd agreed to let her mother give her a drinks party. Tom had said that she could hold it at Gibbs's, on the back of his membership, and that she could then pay him back. He'd taken her there for dinner, and while they'd both found the food revolting, she decided to go ahead and have it there anyway on account of the rooms, and the beautiful staircase. It was only a drinks party. And perhaps the club would let Sarah Knowles do the canapés.

Kate had invited everybody she knew, regardless of whether they'd get on. She wasn't quite sure what someone like Douglas would have in common with her colleagues at work, or what her rather intense friends from university would think of Arabella, but these people were her friends, and she wanted them there to celebrate with her. The only person she decided not to ask was Simon. He'd never know she was having it, and things were going so well at the moment it seemed a pity to spoil it by introducing him to Tom.

Kate's mother wasn't sure she should come. 'I'll only get in the way.'

'But you're paying for it, Mum. Of course you must come.'

'But—'

'I can't celebrate my birthday without you. Peter won't come all the way back from Hong Kong – not for just a drinks party – and I'll be miserable if neither of you are there. Please . . .'

Elizabeth said she'd come, but only for the start.

After quite a lot of begging, Gibbs's agreed to let Sarah Knowles do the canapés. 'Only because Miss Knowles is a member herself, you understand . . .'

Sarah's mother thought she shouldn't do it. 'Darling, you're a Cordon Bleu,' she said, flicking through her diary. 'You should be doing corporate lunches, or cooking for house parties on Scottish estates. You'll never meet someone eligible slaving in the kitchen at Gibbs's.'

Sarah said nothing.

'When did you say it was?'

'The seventeenth of June.'

'Well, you definitely can't do it then. It's Ascot. The Beaumonts have a horse running that day, darling. They've invited us all to join them for lunch. Roddy'll be there, I'm sure.'

'Mummy, I can't.'

'No such word as *can't*, darling. Why don't you do our lunch instead? The poached salmon you did last year was very good.'

But Sarah was adamant. Kate would be paying her enough money to join a gym, and it gave her exposure to a new market. Perhaps some of Kate's City friends would notice, and then she'd have as many corporate lunch commissions as her mother liked.

So while Davina Knowles explained to Imogen Beaumont that her daughter was doing a frightfully important party – it had to be, for her to miss the racing – Sarah spent a happy week checking the kitchen facilities at the club, peeling hard-boiled quails' eggs, and practising new ideas. Would crispy sage on warm chicken squares fried in butter and liquid seasoning actually work in bulk? Could she do sushi, or would that seem wrong with the miniature fish and chips she knew everybody loved? And should she do haddock for those, or could she get away with cod?

London was on the brink of a heatwave. Douglas would infinitely have preferred to go back to Norfolk after Ascot, but he'd accepted Kate's invitation, and he was much too polite to back out the day before. He was flattered to be asked, but he knew she wouldn't have time to speak to him. He didn't want to be, to her, just one of a mass of guests. He'd want to have a decent conversation – find out what she'd been doing, what she was working on, what she felt about being thirty – not a, 'Oh Douglas, hi – have you met so-and-so . . .'

He rang Tom to ask if he could stay for it.

'Of course you can,' said Tom, making a mental note to arrange Arabella.

Tom prepared carefully. The sheets in the spare

room were clean, and Arabella was to wait for Tom to call when Douglas left.

When, some weeks before, Kate had sent Arabella an invitation to her party, Arabella had shown it to Tom and laughed.

'Why on earth is she inviting me?'

'She said she would, didn't she?' said Tom who, relaxed and empowered after an afternoon of vigorous sex, was half-enjoying the recklessness of his position. He was tempted by the idea of being in a room with both of them, of all that surface-politeness and underlying passion. 'And anyway, she likes you.'

'Well,' Arabella had raised a glass of champagne to her lips and taken a gulp, 'that's a pity, because I don't like her. Not at all.'

Tom had smiled and pulled her on top of him, spilling champagne over them both. 'So you won't be coming?'

She'd put the glass on the floor, taken the stiff white card from him and examined it. 'To a drinks party at dull old Gibbs's? Full of lawyers? I don't think so.' Arabella had laughed again and then, kissing Tom, she'd lost the invitation in amongst the sheets.

But the truth was that Arabella was fascinated by Kate. What made her so special? What did Tom see in her? Arabella felt that if she knew the answer to this, she'd see a way to getting him back.

But on the day of the party – the day when she couldn't see Tom because he'd gone racing with Douglas, and Douglas' parents – Arabella began to reconsider. Ascot week had always made her feel an outsider. She loved the idea of herself dressed in a big hat and holding up a pair of delicate binoculars in a gloved hand. But Tom had told her that it really wasn't worth her while going unless she could get into the Royal Enclosure, and Arabella wasn't eligible for that. Tom couldn't sponsor her, Douglas wouldn't sponsor her – it was better if she stayed away.

But they would all be at Kate's party tonight and she was, at least, invited to that. She went over to the mantelpiece and sifted through her invitations. There it was, a little crumpled. Tom would be there. And Douglas. Maybe even Charlie.

Not seeing Tom that day, Arabella had been bored. Worse than bored. She'd had all day to herself to think that – well, that she had all day to herself. She switched on the television and turned to the racing, which bored her even more. Only the fashion commentary interested her, and even that was disappointing. She opened and finished an ironic bottle of champagne. And after that, when she'd searched and discovered there was none left, she'd moved on to vodka. The bottle was almost finished. It wasn't full when she'd started, but Arabella was having trouble remembering how empty it had been then.

She looked at the invitation, holding it in both hands so that she could read it. Why shouldn't she go? She was invited. And the moment he saw her, he wouldn't be able to resist her. She'd wear that dress again . . .

Twelve

Kate couldn't get away from work as early as she'd have liked. She'd invited everybody for seven, and it was exactly seven when she herself arrived.

The Ladies' Sitting Room had been rearranged. The round table had been pushed to one side and covered with white damask. Behind it, two club waiters were filling glasses with champagne. To one side, on a silver oval tray that had been covered with a thick bed of rucola leaves, miniature goat's cheeses melted on miniature toasted baguettes.

Tom and Louisa – who'd also spent the day racing, and who was feeling slightly drunk – were standing on the floorboards in the middle of the room, answering Elizabeth's questions about Ascot. They were comparing their day's losses, each lecturing the other on the evils of gambling, when Kate rushed in, still dressed for work and laden with her Harvey Nichols bags.

'Everything all right?'

'Where've you been?' said her mother, eyeing the clothes she had on.

'Sorry, Mum. I . . .'

Elizabeth then noticed that Kate's bags contained

the new clothes, and she brightened. 'It doesn't matter,' she said. 'You're here now. That's the main thing.'

Kate let Elizabeth kiss her, and smiled back at them all – particularly at Tom. She'd never seen him in a suit before, and it made her see him fresh. It had obviously been made for him – it lay over his shoulders like some second skin, emphasising the perfection of his proportions in the quietest possible tones. To think that this was her boyfriend, to think that everybody would know it, would see them together – it was going to be a great evening. Even the sight of Louisa's skin, lightly tanned and glowing against lilac silk, failed to depress her.

'Darling,' Tom kissed her. 'Happy Birthday!'

'Hi,' said Louisa, laughing, as Kate kissed her. 'Lou – you look stunning.'

'So do you – and anyway I'm afraid neither of us compares to this one,' said Louisa, prodding Tom. 'You're going to have to keep a firm hand on him, Kate. Every woman in the room's going to want to steal him from you.'

'Not when I tell them about the noises he makes in his sleep.'

'What noises?' said Tom. 'What noises? I don't make noises.'

Picking up one of the goat's cheeses, Kate grinned at him and put it into her mouth. 'Wow.'

'Aren't they incredible?' said Louisa, helping herself to one too. 'I've had three.'

As she said this, Sarah carried in two square dishes of little foie gras slices on very thin toasts and offered them to Elizabeth. Elizabeth, who was smoking, refused with a smile and turned to Kate. 'You must go and change, sweetheart. It's almost . . .'

'And what are *those*?'

Sarah held one of the plates towards Kate and told her. 'Try one.'

'I'm so glad I don't model any more,' said Louisa, helping herself, and then grabbing another one quickly before Sarah whisked it away. 'These are great. You don't want to cook for my parents in Italy this summer, do you?'

'Love to,' laughed Sarah, putting the dishes down and heading back to the kitchen.

'I mean it,' Louisa called after her. 'You're a genius. You must give me her number,' she added to Kate. 'Mum'll adore her.'

Kate was about to take her bags to the Ladies' Powder Room and change when she heard a familiar voice say, 'Darling!' Looking up, she saw Charlie, followed by a man she didn't recognise. They were both immaculate.

Elizabeth, Kate, Louisa and Tom all stared.

'Happy Birthday!' Charlie gave Kate a flamboyant kiss, and introduced his friend. 'Darling, this is Guido Mazzini. I hope you don't mind me bringing him, but he's only in London until the weekend, and I simply haven't had a second to call.' Kate was so surprised, she could only nod. 'It's naughty of me, darling. I know. We told the man at the door that he was your brother. You don't mind, do you? He'll be very good – won't you, darling?'

Prodded by Charlie, Guido dragged his black eyes from Tom and started telling Kate how grateful he was and what a wonderful place Gibbs's was and . . .

Kate stared at him. Was this a boyfriend?

Anxious to avoid appearing homophobic – which she wasn't, but she felt that Charlie would be particularly sensitive – Kate stopped staring, hid her surprise, and gave Guido a warm smile.

'It's lovely to have you here,' she said. 'And lovely to meet you. But now I must go and change – before anybody else catches me like this.'

Guido took in the Harvey Nichols bags, and quite understood.

'But of course you must,' he said, nodding. 'Go, go . . .'

Michael – who'd also been at Ascot, hosting a client day in one of the firm's corporate boxes – had rung Heather to say that he couldn't make the party because he'd been forced to join his guests for dinner. Gavin and Annette were still working. So Janet, Heather and Adam decided to share a taxi.

They arrived at the same time as Arabella and followed her up the steps. All three of them stared at her red rubber bottom.

'I knew I should've worn mine,' said Heather.

Adam felt in his inner pocket. He pulled out his invitation and looked again at Arabella, standing at the door.

'You've got a dress like that?'

'A white one.'

'Nice . . .'

Heather nodded. 'I think white's a bit less tarty.'

But she changed her mind when she saw that Arabella had been stopped. Rubber wasn't allowed at Gibbs's – at least, not rubber clothes.

'But I'm here for Kate Leonard's party,' Arabella's drawl reached the others as they passed. 'I have an invitation.'

'Yes, madam. Your name's on the list. But your clothing . . .'

'What's wrong with my clothing?'

'It's the rubber, madam. Ladies and gentlemen are expected to wear formal dress inside the club and I'm afraid that rubber clothing's not considered – suitable. I'm sure you understand . . .'

Arabella stared hard at him.

'I'm sorry, madam. The dress code is very clear. We really can't let you in like that.'

'What is this? You're saying I don't know how to dress? You think I don't know what looks right? Christ, take a look at yourself . . .' Arabella stood resting on one leg, her voice getting louder.

Janet nudged Heather. 'Isn't that . . . ?'

Heather had been about ten when Arabella had been in the papers. 'Who?' she said.

'What's-her-name. The bra model.'

Heather and Adam turned and stared at the sight of Arabella and the doorman. Arabella stared back at them fiercely.

'She's never a model,' Heather muttered.

'Come on . . .'

But Adam was going back down the stairs towards the door. 'You go on,' he said to the others. 'What's the problem?'

'This – man – won't let me in.'

'The club dress code is very strict, sir. There's a list of unsuitable materials, sir, and rubber . . .'

'Then what have you got on the soles of your shoes?'

The doorman frowned and checked. He looked back at Adam with a thoughtful expression. Adam thought he might have swung it, but then Arabella started laughing. 'She's not allowed in dressed like that, sir,' his voice was final. 'I'm sorry.'

'What is it, Adam?' Kate, who'd changed into the tight black satin trousers, the silvery silk jacket, and the pair of Gina shoes she hadn't been able to resist, clattered across the stone hall towards the noise, and recognised the dress.

'Arabella?'

Her brain exploding with a sudden rush of alcohol, Arabella squeezed her eyes tight for a second and refocused on Kate, who was coming closer.

Kate saw straight away that Arabella was drunk.

'He's not letting her in wearing rubber,' said Adam, indignant. 'I pointed out that the soles of his shoes were . . .'

'Thanks, Adam. I'll sort it out.'

Arabella stared at her, and the doorman coughed.

'I'm sorry, madam. There's nothing I can do . . .'

'I have some clothes with me,' said Kate, looking from the doorman to Arabella. 'Would you like to borrow them?'

Kate had left her work clothes in a plastic bag, hanging on the back of the door in the ladies'. She took Arabella there and put the bag into her hands with an apologetic smile. 'Not very exciting – but it will get you in.'

Arabella started rolling the rubber dress upwards and Kate looked away, only to see her naked body just as clearly in the reflection in the mirror on the wall opposite. In contrast to her face, it looked very healthy and very toned, and there was a small black tattoo on her right buttock.

Dropping the roll of red rubber to the floor, she pulled Kate's grey cotton skirt out of the bag. Unimpressed, she held it out for a second. Then she stumbled into it, pulled it up over her naked bottom and looked at her reflection. 'Ugh.'

'The zip's at the back.' Kate could see it was still too big for her and the waistline hung round the hips. 'Will that be okay?'

Fighting the swell in her head, Arabella grunted and bent for the jacket.

'I'll leave you to it, then.'

After Kate had gone, Arabella stood there for a second, swaying, looking at her reflection. Grey suit, grey skin. She looked every bit as queasy as she felt. And then she was sick – all over the basin and a bit on the floor.

Annette, who'd just arrived, and who wanted to change too, went down to the ladies' and was nearly sick herself at the smell. Arabella lifted her head when she heard the door open, and saw the revolted expression.

Annette turned and went into a cubicle, closing the door behind her.

Richard took a baby blini, ate it whole, and washed it down with champagne. He couldn't see anyone he recognised. Not even Louisa. But spotting Heather's white-blonde hair, flicked back as she helped herself to more champagne from a bottle on the round table, he went over.

'Let me.'

'Oh,' Heather let him take the bottle. She watched him fill her glass, tilting it expertly so that the fizzing was reduced. 'Oh, thank you. What a gentleman . . .'

Richard grinned at her. He was old, but his face was fat and round and cheerful. Heather smiled back. 'Hello,' he said. 'I'm Richard.'

Sipping her champagne, she looked at him from the rim of her glass and said nothing.

'And you're . . . ?'

'Heather. Heather Franks.' She put out her hand and Richard shook it. 'Pleased to meet you.'

'Well, Heather, I'm pleased to meet you too. You're the prettiest girl here. By far. Certainly the only one under thirty.'

Heather was the only one under twenty. She didn't know what to say. After a bit of nervous giggling, she pulled herself together and asked Richard what he did.

'He chats up pretty girls half his age and leads them to their ruin,' said Kate, coming up with a plate of canapés. 'Want one? They're delicious.'

'What are they?' Heather's perfect nails hovered over the plate.

'Foie gras.'

'Oh.' Heather knew about foie gras – what they did to those poor little geese – and removed her hand.

'Well, I'm having one,' said Richard. 'In fact, I'm having two.'

He grinned again at Heather and ate them both at once. Kate took Heather's arm.

'You don't mind if I take her away for a second, do you, Richard? You'll find Louisa over there by the flowers.' She turned to Heather. 'Now . . . do you know

262

who I mean by Charlie Reed?'

Heather looked blank as she followed Kate to the opposite corner of the room.

'You know, Heather – the photographer. Did that thing in *Catwalk*, I think it was, last month, those pictures of models underwater.'

'Oh yes – I saw that.'

'I thought you might like to meet him. And he's always looking for new faces. Charlie?'

'Darling.'

'Charlie, this is Heather Franks.'

Leaving Heather in total safety, Kate moved away. She looked across the room – catching the sense of her party, full now. Everybody here. The most unlikely people talking to each other. There was Douglas – angel – talking to her mother. And there was Guido chatting to *Adam* – Kate laughed to herself. Perfect ammunition for tomorrow morning.

And there, in the distance, was Tom – chatting to someone she couldn't see. Louisa was right. Tom was dangerously good-looking. But there was nothing that she, Kate, could do about it, except feel proud that he'd chosen her.

———— ◆ ————

Richard picked up the half-full bottle of champagne and went over to where Kate said he'd find Louisa. Under the flowers, and talking animatedly to a plain girl in an apron.

'It's a wonderful house,' she was saying. 'Overlooking the sea. Only an hour or so from Pisa. You'd have your own flat. And there are some unbelievable restaurants, so it's not as if you'd have to cook every evening –'

'Would you be there?'

'Don't know,' Louisa let Richard fill her glass. 'It depends if I get any *better offers* . . .'

Richard pinched her lilac bottom.

'And that depends how nice you are to me,' he said into her ear and then licked it.

Louisa drew away, bending her neck to wipe her ear with her shoulder. 'This is Sarah Knowles. Sarah – Richard Hastings.'

'Hello,' said Richard. 'Do you want a drink?'

Sarah sighed. 'I'd better not. In fact I'd better go. The sausages . . .'

'I'll get my mother to call you tomorrow,' said Louisa after her.

'What a dog,' said Richard, once Sarah was out of earshot.

'Richard.'

'I don't care if she cooks like a dream. She's still pig-ugly.'

Nearby, Arabella was talking to Douglas and looking over his shoulder for Tom. Her back was to Richard, and she overheard his remark. Watching Sarah head back to the kitchen – her shoulders bent, her flat face sweaty and tired – Arabella was inclined to agree. Pig-ugly.

Douglas had left his conversation with Kate's mother – a naughty conversation about Norfolk's do-gooders and worthies, and one that he was enjoying hugely – to speak to Arabella because he could see that she was looking so awful, so totally run down and lonely.

He was beginning to wish now that he hadn't. Having been introduced to Guido, he'd drawn the

264

natural conclusions about Charlie, and felt really sorry for her. But when he'd said how brave he thought she was being, and how difficult it must be for her having them both there, she'd just laughed at him and told him to pull himself into the twenty first century.

Douglas didn't know what to say to that. Fed up with Arabella continually looking over his shoulder – or round the side of his arm – Douglas looked over her head towards the door. There, he noticed Kate standing next to Tom – holding his hand as she kissed her mother goodbye – and wondered if it was worth hanging around to speak to her, or whether he should just leave too.

Arabella followed the direction of his attention.

'They look good together,' said Douglas, deliberately. 'Don't they?'

'Mm.'

'Doesn't look thirty, does she?' said Douglas. 'Looks ten years younger.'

'Thanks to me. I helped her choose that jacket.'

'Did you?'

'And those trousers, and – I think – yes, and those shoes.'

They watched as Kate and Tom turned to come back into the room. Kate looked up. She smiled at them both, and brought Tom over.

'Hi again!' she said. 'Hi, Douglas.'

Douglas kissed her. 'Hello, Kate. I was just admiring your,' he waved a self-conscious hand up and down, 'your get-up.'

'All thanks to Arabella . . .'

'She was just saying.'

'. . . who, poor thing, has been forced to wear my

hideous office suit because of those absurd club rules. Looks ten times better on her than it ever did on me, of course, but I'm sure that doesn't quite compensate for not being allowed to wear your own dress, Arabella. I'm so sorry . . .'

Arabella hauled a smile to her face – a smile that seemed to twist as she turned it on Tom. 'Hello darling – I'm just trying to think of the last time I saw you? It must have been . . .'

Tom felt suddenly sick. The stream of recklessness drained from his blood as he understood the desperate levels in Arabella's. This wasn't fun any more. 'It was at Waveney, I think,' he said.

'Really? I'm sure I've seen you more recently than that . . .'

'You must be thinking of when you ran into me,' said Kate. 'God, you were kind – but you couldn't make lunch, remember? You had someone to see.'

'Oh yes. That was it. Someone to see.'

Tom turned to Kate. 'Wasn't there someone you were taking me to meet?'

'Oh yes,' she smiled. 'My mind's like a sieve tonight. Rob wanted to meet you.' She turned to the others. 'Sorry. See you two later. Don't leave without saying goodbye, will you?'

Douglas and Arabella stood together for a second, both drinking from their glasses. They had nothing to say to each other. Deciding that he might as well leave, Douglas steeply tipped his glass, polished off the rest of its contents and swallowed a burp.

'Well,' he said. 'I think I'm off. Got an early start tomorrow.'

But as he bent to kiss Arabella goodbye, he looked

out and happened to catch Louisa's eye. Louisa smiled and Richard turned to see who she was smiling at. 'Look,' she said. 'It's Douglas, remember?'

'Hello,' she kissed Douglas. 'You were racing today, weren't you? Wasn't it boiling?'

'Ten times worse if you're in a top hat.'

Louisa laughed. 'That's exactly what Richard was saying.'

'Apparently tomorrow's going to be even worse,' said Arabella, but nobody heard.

'You remember Richard?' Louisa continued. 'From our dinner party?'

As Richard and Douglas shook hands, Arabella lingered to one side.

'Of course I do,' said Douglas. 'There was the two of you, Kate and Tom . . . and me.' He pulled a gooseberry expression and they all laughed.

Arabella smiled with empty eyes.

'We got your letter,' Louisa went on. 'So good of you to write . . .'

'Not at all,' he smiled. 'Should have written sooner. It was weeks ago. Must get you to come down to Waveney sometime soon. Come for the weekend.'

'That would be wonderful.'

'And Richard.'

Richard smiled and drank some champagne, thinking that his chances of a weekend away from Anne during the school holidays were virtually zero.

'Kate and Tom are coming down the second weekend in September. Why don't you . . .'

Kate and Tom. Kate and Tom. Kate and Tom.

Arabella couldn't stomach it. Everybody was talking about Kate and Tom – how good they looked together, how clever Kate was, how perfect Tom would be for her – and Kate was loving every minute, hanging onto Tom's arm, smiling her heart out like a radiant bride.

Drifting away from the others, aware of their lack of awareness that she was leaving, Arabella headed for the door. She should never have come. She didn't even want to see Tom any more. Not with him looking so devastating, and her in this dreary suit.

She'd left her red rubber dress in a plastic bag under the stairs, and went to fetch it. But as she searched through the other bags and cases left there, she suddenly heard his voice.

'Let's leave now. Just go home, or to Caratello which you *still* haven't been to. I'm sure they'd give us a table. Would you like that?'

'But I can't just leave everyone . . .'

'It's your birthday, darling. Your mother's left now. You can do what you like. There's champagne and a birthday present for you back at home.'

'A *present*?'

Arabella waited in the shadow under the stairs, and heard them coming down, directly above her head. Broken, she stood there, her eyes swimming with silent tears, while Tom persuaded Kate to leave with him.

When Douglas discovered from Louisa that it was Sarah Knowles who was responsible for the canapés, he went straight to the kitchen with a glass of champagne.

Sarah was alone, sticking cocktail sticks into sausages, with her back to the door. She was wearing a pair of navy trousers stretched tight over a bottom, that shook as she moved.

He stood watching her.

'Hello,' he said, when she'd finished the plate she was doing. 'Drink?'

Sarah turned, saw him, and smiled back. 'Hi . . .'

He offered her the glass.

'Thanks.' Sarah took it, but didn't drink. She looked exhausted.

'Isn't anyone helping you?'

'Not really. I don't think the club likes outside caterers. Not even *member* outside caterers.'

'Can I do anything?'

'Don't worry,' she smiled again at the thought of John Douglas, under-chef. 'I'll be fine.'

'I'm very good at sticking in cocktail sticks,' he said. 'Really I am.'

He wasn't, but she didn't care.

The party was over by nine-thirty. Douglas stayed until the end. He waited until Sarah was ready to leave, and then trailed behind her, carrying her dishes out through the tradesmen's entrance, along an alley, past a couple of industrial dustbins, to the end – where her Volvo was parked – and helped her load them in. Sarah slammed the boot, leant on it and looked at him.

'Thank you.'

'That's all right,' he said, but went on standing there with the hard light from the club kitchen windows full in his face. 'I was wondering. You're probably too tired . . . but would you like dinner? We could grab something here at the club.'

'I'm not properly dressed,' she pointed out.

'Yes you are,' he bent his chin to scratch the back of his head and, half smiling, caught her eye. 'At least you're not in rubber.'

269

Sarah had heard about Arabella. She laughed and pulled at her old shirt. In spite of the apron, it was covered in marks.

'Come on,' she said, 'look at me.' Douglas looked at the shirt. 'And it's almost ten. They'll never serve us.'

'What about somewhere else then?'

He took her to an Italian restaurant in Jermyn Street.

Later, she offered to drop him off outside his house in Knightsbridge. It was on her way home, anyway. Douglas pushed the passenger seat right back to make room for his legs, and gave her directions.

The car rolled slowly over the cobbles of the mews, past the coffee shop and down towards the black lacquered door.

'Here it is,' he said, and Sarah braked. 'Thanks.'

'Not at all. Thank *you*.'

Douglas knew he should be opening his door. Opening his door, or kissing her. Not just sitting here. He'd had all evening to decide and still he didn't know which. What was he doing? What did he want? If in doubt . . . he felt for the handle.

'Thanks,' he said again.

'Not at all. Thank *you*.'

She was laughing at him. Releasing the handle, he looked at her. You're thinking the same, they both thought. Sarah's smile faltered. And then, tentatively, Douglas leant over the gearbox and kissed her.

'You *didn't*.'

'I did.'

'Was it awful?'

'No, it was sweet.'

270

Tom was waiting for Douglas to find his wallet. He laughed, and then suppressed it as Douglas came back into the hall wearing an injured expression he'd learnt from George.

'I'm sorry, Doug. I just can't imagine it.'

'Why not?'

Tom chuckled, and opened the door for his friend.

It wasn't eleven o'clock, and already they felt the warmth of the sun on their backs as they walked to the end of the mews. They turned the corner together, and approached the coffee house. Douglas could smell the coffee from outside.

'Is this it?'

'Yes.'

'You come here every day?'

'Yes. I read the papers and gear myself up for job hunting.'

Douglas opened the glass door. 'Any luck?'

'No,' said Tom, following him in.

They joined a queue. A young man was serving from behind the pastries counter. He waved at Tom, greeted him in Italian and then said, in English, that he'd bring Tom his usual to his table.

'. . . and your friend?'

'What do you want, Doug?'

'Whatever you're having.'

'He wants the same, Enrico. Okay?'

Enrico nodded.

'Come on, Doug. There's a free table at the back.'

They settled at the table and waited for their coffee and croissants.

'What kind of jobs have you been looking for?'

'Auction houses,' said Tom. 'Unfortunately, it seems

everybody in London has read History of Art, and at better universities than me. The fact I spent three years in Rome doesn't seem to count for much. I've got someone to see at Phillips next week, so maybe . . .' He smiled at Douglas helplessly.

'It must be hard,' said Douglas. 'You know my parents are very keen to help. Sam Phipps works at Speke's, and they could easily put you in touch.'

'I'd like to be able to do it myself, if I can.'

'Of course.'

Douglas moved aside to let Enrico put their coffee and croissants on the table.

Enrico talked to Tom continuously as he wiped the table and put down the cups. '. . . so ee left. Like that!' Enrico snapped his fingers. 'An' now ees just me.'

'Disgraceful,' said Tom.

'An' where ees your beautiful girlfriend?'

'She has to go to work.'

'To work? What work does she do?'

'She's a lawyer.'

'A lawyer? That beautiful girl? Ees not possible!'

Tom smiled and picked up his coffee. 'Thanks, Enrico.'

'I'm surprised Kate has the time to come here for breakfast,' said Douglas, looking at a menu, and noticing that the place didn't open until ten.

'She comes at weekends.' Tom steered him onto another subject and out of the coffee house as soon as he could.

That night, however, Kate came back early. Tom was in the bath and Douglas, dressed in black tie for a livery dinner, let her in. She was wearing a knee-length slip of a dress, and carried a jacket over one

272

arm. In spite of the summer clothes, her skin was white from working inside.

'Douglas!'

He kissed her hot cheek. 'You look well.'

'You flatter me. I look like a drain.'

Douglas shook his head. 'You couldn't look like a drain if you tried.'

'You haven't seen me first thing in the morning.'

'Ah, but I know a man who has.'

She laughed. 'Tom's biased.'

'I don't mean him.'

Kate frowned. 'Who do you mean?'

'Enrico.'

'Who?'

'The boy in the coffee shop. He thinks you're beautiful.'

'The coffee shop at the end of the mews?'

'Yes.'

She laughed. 'But I don't even go there.'

'Don't you go there at weekends?'

'At weekends, if I'm not working – we . . .' she smiled at him, 'we don't really get up for breakfast.'

'Never?'

Kate was amused by his expression. Was it really so shocking? 'Never,' she said, dropping her briefcase by the umbrella stand. 'Now tell me all about Sarah . . .'

———◆◆◆———

'Are you still seeing Arabella?'

'Of course not.'

Douglas was standing by the mantelpiece, looking at Tom's pile of invitations, feeding the envy he felt at Tom's popularity. Tom was at his desk. Kate was in the bath.

'Why do you ask?'

'Kate was saying she doesn't go to that café.' Douglas kept his back to Tom – he began flicking through the pile of cards propped against the mirror and spoke very quietly. It took Tom a few seconds to understand what Douglas was saying. If Kate didn't go to the coffee house, then who was it Enrico was asking after? Not hard for Douglas to figure it out.

'I wish you'd stop interfering,' said Tom.

'I was concerned for Kate . . .' Douglas broke off as the pile of invitations slipped from his hand and fell like a large pack of cards into the fireplace. He bent to pick them up. Brushing ash off a cheap wedding invitation from Lord and Lady Lincoln to the marriage of their daughter Flora to some Italian, Douglas read the looping print. He was the one who'd introduced Flora to Tom, and he didn't even know that she was engaged. He tried to put it back, but it wouldn't stand up properly.

'Kate's not your friend. I am.'

'You're both my friends.' Douglas tried to straighten it.

'It's because you can't stand Arabella, isn't it?'

'No,' Douglas gave up. He let the wedding invitation rest against an ashtray and bent down for the others. 'I just . . .'

'Just because you're helping me out financially that doesn't give you the right to choose who I see, to lecture me, or creep around spying on me like a . . .'

'I wasn't spying, Tom. I . . .'

Tom put his head between his hands. 'Stop it! Stop trying to control me.'

'I'm not trying to control you,' Douglas stepped out

of the fireplace, 'and money's got nothing to do with it.'

'That's easy for you to say.'

'What do you mean?' said Douglas.

'You, who have so much money you can afford to throw it at desperate friends, buy their friendship, control their lives . . .'

Douglas felt his spine chill. 'I'm late for my uncle,' he said. 'We'll talk about this tomorrow.'

But by the time Tom got up the following morning, Douglas had left. There was just a note on his bed, written in biro on the back of his invitation to Kate's party.

Dear Tom,

The way you're treating Kate (and Arabella) is wrong. That is my opinion as your friend, and I won't apologise for voicing it.

On the subject of friendship, the financial arrangement we had was supposed to make your life a bit easier at a difficult time. It was not an attempt to buy you. I rather thought that a bit of financial support would give you more freedom, not less, but it is now clear that you must be independent from me if we are to remain friends.

I'm planning on spending more time in London and if it's all right with you I'd like the house back some time before the beginning of August. That should give you enough time to find somewhere else. The arrangement with the credit cards can be stopped at the same time.

Yours,
Douglas

Thirteen

The office reaction to Kate's party was mixed. Adam had loved it. He'd found an Arabella web-site on the internet, printed off the picture of her sprawled in a taxi, and stuck it up on the wall by his desk. There was one where they'd digitally removed the underwear, but he decided that there might be some objections to that.

There were quite a few objections to the original one, in any case – particularly from Janet and Heather.

'Honestly.'

'Men.'

'Just one thing on their mind.'

Heather leant close to the picture and frowned. 'Wouldn't recognise her. Would you? She's not a bit like that in real life.'

'But she's not bad,' said Adam, coming in with a fresh cup of coffee. 'You should see the one where they've digitally removed her bra.'

Janet sighed forcefully, and left.

'Wouldn't be her tits anyway, would they?' said Heather, still looking at the picture. 'She's probably got saggy ones.'

'No she hasn't.'

'How do you know?'

Adam laughed. 'I don't need to see her with nothing on to tell what kind of tits she has.'

Heather left the room feeling vaguely self-conscious.

Annette hadn't liked the party. She hadn't wanted to talk to Adam, or the secretaries, and she didn't know anybody else. She was cross with Gavin for not coming with her, and she was cross with Kate for not talking to her. All Kate had done was introduce her to Douglas, and disappear.

Recognising him from the same magazine article that Louisa had read, Annette had stared at Douglas and said, 'Didn't I see you in *Tatler* a few months ago?'

Douglas had quietly offered to get her another glass of champagne and not returned. She couldn't find him anywhere. After about half an hour of searching, she'd collected her things and gone home.

When they saw Adam's picture, Michael and Gavin both said they wished they'd been there.

'Didn't know you knew people like this, Kate.'

'You should give parties more often . . .'

Kate was glad it had gone well, and glad that it was over. It wasn't that her work was suffering – it was better than ever – but it was important to be completely free from distractions as Project Cannon II approached completion.

She was flicking through the latest drafts from Fraser Cummings. Her desk was covered with piles of paper. At the top of the highest pile, a half-eaten prawn sandwich hardened in the air conditioning.

She was holding a pencil in one hand and a glass of water in the other, and she was smiling.

Without being asked, Adam had arranged for the drafts to be copied. He'd then filed the originals, and gone through the copies, highlighting outstanding issues with a fluorescent yellow pen. It was these copies she was looking at.

She was experiencing a pleasurable sense of everything slotting into place, of lights shifting from amber to green, as far as the eye could see. Not only had she streamlined Adam so that they were an efficient team, she'd got Simon eating out of her hand. There were hardly any yellow bits, and the ones that were still yellow would be easy to negotiate.

Since that lunch with Simon, Kate had got into the habit of meeting him for the occasional drink after work. Each time, Simon would suggest they go on somewhere for dinner and, each time, Kate would look sad and say that she'd already made plans. Simon wasn't the sort of man to ask, directly, if she had a boyfriend. She'd said nothing, and her elusive manner intrigued him. It made him take a more co-operative line with her, and this had affected his negotiating style.

Kate had decided not to tell Tom. She was sure it wasn't the kind of thing that would upset him, but she felt that telling him might distort its significance. She saw no point in making an issue out of nothing. But still, for all her reasoning, Kate was uneasy. She wasn't sure whether this was because she'd been using more than just her brain to help Henry Hazel cut a good deal, or whether it was because she wasn't being entirely straight with Tom.

She put down the glass of water and flicked on through the document. Adam came in as she finished.

'God it's hot out there,' he said.

'Is it?'

'Boiling.' He sat at his desk and undid his tie. 'I can't imagine how they survived before air conditioning.'

He watched Kate pile up the Fraser Cummings documents and put them on the floor by the door, ready to take to the meeting in the evening.

'Thank you for doing these,' she said.

'You're welcome. Hardly anything to do.'

Kate grinned. 'Did you see that Simon accepted limited title guarantee in the fixed and floating charge?'

Adam laughed. 'And he took virtually all your deletions from the Borrower's Covenants. Is that normal?'

'It must be my feminine charm.'

'What feminine charm?'

'Piss off.'

'Exactly.'

Telling Adam that, as punishment for his insolence, she was taking him with her to the meeting that night – to show him feminine charm in action – Kate decided not to tell him that he was also acting as chaperon.

'Who's going to be there?'

'Just Simon.'

Carrying a box of documents, he followed her through the revolving doors and out into a wall of heat on the other side. It was six o'clock. Kate could only guess at how hot it must have been earlier.

Janet had ordered a cab, and it was waiting for

them in the street. Adam put his box on the pavement and opened the door for Kate.

'I don't understand why you need a meeting,' he said, shoving the box past her feet and stepping in behind. 'Everything's agreed.'

'Nearly everything.' As Adam closed the door, she leant forward to give the driver directions, and then slid shut the partition. 'I set up the meeting last week, expecting Battle Royal. It now looks as if this'll be more like a skirmish, or an outright surrender, but I don't want to alert them to anything by suggesting a change of plan.'

'But you didn't need to bring me.'

'I needed a box carrier.'

'You don't need this,' he laughed. 'You won't even open it.'

He was right. The box contained four correspondence files and some previous drafts of documents, none of which were necessary. Kate had a fear of being in a meeting without the right papers and invariably brought too much.

'Come on, Adam,' she countered. 'Where's your enthusiasm?'

Adam decided not to push it.

Simon was waiting in reception. His face lit up when he saw her, and then dimmed at the sight of Adam and the box. He shook hands with Kate, nodded at Adam and swept his arm in the direction of the conference rooms.

'This way.'

Kate was home in time for dinner with Louisa. She let herself into the flat and ran up the stairs.

Louisa was lying on her stomach on the floor with the portable telephone glued to her ear. She looked up at Kate without smiling.

'She's just this second come in. I'll pass you over.'

Kate took the receiver. 'Hello?'

'It's me.'

'What's up?'

'Douglas wants me out of the house.'

She accepted a cold glass of wine from Louisa. 'What?'

'He asked me to get out. In two weeks' time.'

'Have you fallen out?'

'It's ridiculous . . .'

'What was it about?'

There was a pause, and then Tom said, 'It's to do with Arabella . . .'

Kate took a sip of wine and said nothing.

'She's been pestering Douglas to get us back together. You know that's the last thing I want, but Douglas won't let it drop.'

'Are you saying that Douglas has been trying to split us up?'

'He believes very strongly in marriage.'

'What marriage? You got divorced years ago.'

'Really Kate, he . . .'

'How dare he interfere like this? Jesus. And there he was being charming last night, and all the time thinking about ways to split us up. He even tried to suggest some guy in the coffee shop at the end of your mews fancied me. No doubt to steer me away.'

'My darling, he's got nothing against you. He just . . .'

'Fuck him. Why don't you come and stay here with us? Come tomorrow. I'll take the day off work and help you move your stuff.'

Tom hesitated. 'Would Louisa mind?'

Kate looked up. Louisa was staring at her.

'Please?' she mouthed.

Louisa frowned.

'Hang on.' Kate put her hand over the mouthpiece. 'Come on, Lou. He's got nowhere else.'

'The flat's not big enough. I don't want to feel like a gooseberry.'

'*Please*. It won't be forever . . .'

Louisa capitulated.

Kate squeezed her hand. 'She says that you can come. But only if you're good and you don't steal her make-up.'

Tom, who'd heard everything, laughed. 'Will you thank her for me?'

'Of course.'

Louisa refilled Kate's glass, and smiled. 'I don't want any alien hairs in my bath.'

'I heard that,' said Tom, and they all laughed.

Kate felt buoyant. 'Why don't you come over for dinner?'

'No,' Tom replied, 'I'm taking you both out. Get dolled up, and meet me at the Pacific in half an hour.'

<hr />

He moved in at the weekend – filling the flat with a luxury presence that continued to fascinate Kate.

She cleared some cupboard space for his clothes – rows and rows of laundered shirts in fine-weave whites and pinks and blues with starched collars and sharp iron-lines down the arms, heavy suits in special

282

Savile Row suit-bags, shoes preserved with strange-looking wooden shoe-trees from Lobb's, endless pairs of bright white boxer shorts cut from some soft, fine cotton – and found that there still wasn't enough room. So she put her winter clothes in the cupboard under the stairs, to give him the extra space. She sat on the bed and watched him at the cupboard, slipping darker-coloured shirts onto hangers and slotting them in with the other fluid, disembodied shapes – a wardrobe full of potential Toms.

His ties had a special hanger all to themselves, and the silken splashes of colour flipped like tropical fish as he scooped them all off the bed in one movement, and put them neatly next to his suits.

A leather cufflink case sat on her dressing table. A bag of dirty laundry – discreet, closed – lay against the wall. His washbag had been left open on one of the shelves in the bathroom. It wasn't crammed full like hers, but contained only toothpaste, toothbrush, the squat and bushy shaving brush with its ebony handle, the circle of sandalwood shaving soap, a packet of Neurofen, and his glass bottle of cologne with its chiselled edges and its Fabergé-style label, worn thin with watery hands.

She took her heavy law-school books from the shelves in the sitting room, to make room for Tom's collection of novels and biographies of people she'd never heard of – some of them in Italian, all of them hardback. Much later, after an expensive dinner out, she sat on the sofa and let her eyes travel along the abstract pattern of their perfect spines – the varying rectangles of ivory, orange, black, maroon – wondering briefly how many of them he'd read, before taking the glass of whisky he offered, making room on the sofa for his body next to hers and coming forward for a kiss.

———•◦•———

Louisa had been at a party in Germany – given by a friend of her brother's – and came home on Sunday to a flat full of the smell of frying garlic. Kate was making spaghetti in the kitchen, and Tom was reading the papers.

He looked up. 'Hi.'

Louisa gave him a tired smile and sank into a chair.

Tom put the papers to one side. 'Good weekend?'

'No. A complete waste of time. The only person I spoke to was Alex, so it was hardly . . .'

'Alex?'

'My brother, who was full of news about his kids and his divorce. Which was fine – but hardly worth travelling all the way to Munich to hear. Could've gone to Dorset instead.'

'And why didn't anyone else talk to you?'

'They didn't speak English.'

'What did you expect?'

Louisa pulled a face.

Kate came in, holding a drying-up cloth.

'Hi,' she said. 'Good weekend?' Then she noticed Tom laughing. 'What is it?'

'She's had a miserable weekend, because she went to a party in Germany, where – shock of shocks – they all spoke German. How dare they?'

Over supper, while Louisa and Tom bickered, Kate's mind filled with thoughts of work. There was a meeting at Fraser Cummings at nine tomorrow morning. Should she go to her own office first thing, or could she go directly to Fraser Cummings? Had she got all her papers with her?

'. . . and look at the way you're eating that spaghetti. You practically need a bib.'

'This is the way you're supposed to eat it, Louisa.'

'And what makes you such an authority?'

Kate poured some more wine into their glasses. 'He's Italian.'

'Really?' Louisa swung to Tom. 'Are you really Italian?'

'*Si, signorina.*'

'Anyone can say that. Say something else.'

Tom rattled off a couple of sentences.

'What does that mean?'

'I'm telling you that you are cultured and well educated and beautiful.'

Louisa was about to take another mouthful of pasta. She stopped, mouth open, fork poised mid-air, and frowned at him.

Tom caught Kate's eye and laughed.

'Louisa goes to Italy every summer.'

'Then her Italian should be better.'

'There's nothing wrong with *my* Italian,' she grinned at him. 'It must be your provincial accent I didn't understand.'

'Her parents have a house – where is it, Lou? I can't remember.'

Louisa told her and, to her surprise, Tom knew it.

'I've been there,' he said. 'Do you know the Bertorellis?'

'You know Stefano?'

'I know Maya, his half-sister. She's my mother's god-daughter.'

'How extraordinary,' she laughed. 'Maya Bertorelli . . . Wow. Alex used to lust after her every summer. She's married now, isn't she? Or was that the younger one . . .?'

Kate thought again about the office. She was conscious that nothing had been done on Project Galaxy for weeks, and made a mental note to chivvy Adam tomorrow.

'Is she still going out with what's-his-name?'

'What's that?'

Kate was going to have to get up early and she didn't want to wake Tom, so she was trying to decide now what she was going to wear – which was difficult, when she didn't know how hot it was going to be. She stood at her wardrobe, wondering if she could get away with wearing no shirt beneath her pinstripe jacket and wishing her breasts were just a little bit smaller.

Tom repeated the question.

'You mean Richard?' she said, taking out the pinstripe suit on its hanger and checking it for marks. 'Yes. I think so.' She hung the suit on the hook on the back of the bedroom door and returned to the wardrobe for her summer sling-backs. About twenty pairs of shoes lay higgledy-piggledy at the bottom of the wardrobe. Kate saw one and knelt to find the other. It was musty down there. She should clear it out. Most of them could be thrown away, or taken to a charity shop. But when would she find the time?

'Of course, it's only an affair,' she added. 'He's married, remember.'

Tom pushed the duvet from his body and lay, half-covered, flat on his back, staring at the ceiling. 'I don't understand it.'

Stretching to the back of the wardrobe, Kate yanked the other sling-back free from a hanger that had fallen down. With a shoe in each hand, she turned and smiled at the sight of Tom sprawled on the bed.

'What don't you understand?'

'Why a stunner like Louisa ends up with an asshole like Richard.'

'I don't think they'll *end up* together,' said Kate, taking the shoes and placing them just outside the bedroom door. 'He'll go back to his wife, and she'll move on. She's just wasting her time.'

'But she's going to get hurt.'

'Yes.' Kate stood at the door with her hand on the light switch. 'Okay?'

Tom looked over. 'Fine.'

She pressed the switch and the room was dark. Kate made her way over to the bed, got in and lay there beside him.

He was very still.

'I know she's going to get hurt, Tom. But every time I say anything, she tells me to mind my own business . . . how would I know what it's like for her . . . that kind of thing. I end up feeling guilty for having you as a boyfriend.'

She felt him turn to her. Raising himself on an elbow, he put his free arm over her and pulled her gently towards him.

———◆◆◆———

Louisa was due to spend the next weekend with Richard. They were going to New York, and she'd

287

spent most of the week preparing. Tom came back from an afternoon at Arabella's to find the hall full of shopping bags and Louisa on the telephone.

'No. No, I don't need a bikini line, just a full leg wax. And underarm. You really can't do Thursday? It absolutely *has* to be before the weekend. What about today then? Great. I'll see you in half an hour.'

Tom grinned at her and went into the kitchen. He took a can of Coke from the fridge. 'You get your *underarms* waxed?'

'That's none of your business.'

'Isn't it terribly painful?' he said, coming back into the sitting room.

'Agony,' she said, smiling.

'Is Richard worth it?'

Louisa watched him sink into the chair by the window and open the Coke can. 'I don't do it for Richard.'

'Of course you do it for him. Why else does it *have* to be done before the weekend?' Tom sat in the chair by the window and pulled a brand-new suitcase towards him. He fiddled with the catch and looked across at Louisa, on the sofa. Louisa couldn't think of a reply.

'How did you meet him?'

She looked out over the rooftops, at the early evening sky.

'I've known him all my life. He's a friend of Dad's.'

'So when did . . .?'

'Oh,' she smiled, 'it was only a few months ago – at one of my parents' parties in Dorset. I was going out with a French guy. But he – Georges, that is – wasn't there and anyway, it wasn't really working. He was such a baby. Anyway, I was sitting next to Richard at dinner. I hadn't seen him for a while, and so we were catching up, and then we were clearing away the plates – both of us loading them into the dishwasher – and he started to say these incredible things to me . . .'

Tom sat listening as Louisa told him of Richard's seduction. It seemed that all Richard had had to do was lean over Louisa as she loaded the dishwasher, tell her exactly how beautiful she was, then follow it up by staring at her for the rest of the evening. By the time he crept along the passage to her room – a room he'd probably known when it was covered with animal alphabets and pictures of My Little Pony, a room he bloody well knew was out of bounds – she was more than ready to let him in.

'Kate doesn't approve,' she said.

'She's damn right.'

'But . . .'

'You're mad to let that man anywhere near you. Must be having the time of his life with a wife for the house and the kids, and you for the bedroom – feeding his sad little fantasies, spending a fortune, going through physical *agony* – your words – to keep your body hairless and faintly childish so that you'll turn him on . . . can't you see he's using you?'

'I'm using him too.'

'Right,' Tom laughed. 'You're using him. For what? What do *you* get out of all this?'

'I love him. I get his company, his time.'

'I see. And how much, exactly, of Richard's precious time do you get? One – maybe two – dinners a week, Saturday afternoons if you're lucky?'

'It isn't like that.'

'It's exactly like that, Louisa. You see more of me than you do of Richard, for God's sake.'

289

'Well – you see more of me than you do of Kate. It doesn't mean a thing.'

'The difference is that Kate and I are living together.'

'With me, too,' Louisa pointed out.

'But at the end of the day Kate is in bed – alone – with *me*. Kate doesn't have some other life. There isn't some other man I have to share her with.'

'There's her boss.'

'Don't be stupid.'

They sat together in silence for a second – Louisa looking at the links on her watch strap, Tom looking at the dark distorted room reflected in the blank television screen, and wondering if he'd gone too far. Then Louisa sighed.

'You don't understand,' she said.

'No. I don't – but I'm sorry. It's none of my business, and anyway,' he smiled, 'I'm sure there must be something good about the man.'

'Oh but there is! He's one of the most generous people you'll ever meet. Did you notice the bottle of wine he brought to that dinner party? And you should have seen what he sent me on Valentine's Day. And the dresses he's given me – we went to Bond Street last week and you wouldn't believe the things we bought. Not just clothes, Tom, but proper presents – these little matching diaries from Smythson's, look . . .'

She bent into her bag and pulled out what looked like a crocodile-skin diary and flipped along the familiar grey-blue paper.

Tom wished he could buy things like that for Kate.

'He gave me that pair of earrings you said you liked. And believe me, he really knows what he's doing in bed.'

Tom had the depressing feeling Louisa might be right. Richard must have had hundreds of affairs. He'd know exactly what he was doing – in bed, and everywhere else.

Louisa was lying on the floor, smoking her fourth cigarette and remembering her first date with Richard, when the beautician called to find out where she was.

'Oh shit. Estelle, I'm so sorry. I can be with you in ten minutes. Is that okay? Half-leg is fine. *Thank* you.'

Tom offered to drive her to the salon.

That night, Tom took Kate out to dinner. He knew Richard Hastings was a bastard, but he couldn't help admiring the man's style – the way he spoilt Louisa – and he desperately wanted to do the same for Kate.

Tom had once been a regular at the Caprice. He dined there twice a week in the early days with Arabella – and the Caprice made a point of remembering its patrons.

'I know it's last-minute, Angelo. And I'm sure you're fully booked – but if you did have a table for two? *You do?* No, of course we don't mind ten o'clock! Ten o'clock will be perfect. Perfect. Yes, and you. See you later!'

Sitting at the table, waiting for Kate to arrive, Tom knew that this was where he belonged. Here – this little paradise where he was made to feel every bit as special as the notorious actress in the corner, or the ex-politician-cum-journalist and his third wife, grabbing a quick post-theatre supper before driving down to Hampshire for a long weekend.

Suspended in amongst the bubbling voices, the

ribbon of ragtime notes floating and curling out over the restaurant from the white piano by the door, the tip-tip of silver on porcelain, and all the gentle noises of appreciation, Tom Faulkener was warm again. He was back.

'Hey!' Kate was suddenly next to him, in the black suit he liked – severe or sexy – day or night. Undoing the collar, she sat next to him while he filled her glass.

'Drink,' he told her, and she did.

In fact, she drank a lot. They got through two bottles of claret, two glasses of pudding wine, and then two glasses of whisky to send them on their way.

'I shouldn't be doing this,' she laughed. 'I really shouldn't. I've got Janet's annual appraisal to do tomorrow.'

'Janet's what?'

'It's when we look at what she's doing right – and what she's doing wrong. It's an utterly pointless exercise, since she knows exactly what I think already, but it's supposed to make her feel noticed. We both fill in forms – Janet has to assess herself – then we go through them together, and I write a final report.'

'And you're doing this tomorrow?'

Kate grinned at him. 'Well, I had planned to have a stab at her form tonight, but something tells me that's not going to happen.'

She finished her glass of pudding wine, and went back to finish what was left in the bottle of red. It was swept from her hand by a beaming waiter, who filled both her glass and Tom's – and removed the empty bottle.

'Have you got it with you?'

'Should be there,' she gestured towards the briefcase under her chair, 'somewhere in that mess.'

'Get it out. Let's do it now.'

'Now?'

'Go on.'

Laughing, Kate got the forms out.

'Please indicate in the boxes below,' she read, 'whether you think your secretary scores – Excellent, Fair, Adequate, Inadequate, or Poor – for the following. One: Written Work – Well, she's pretty good at that. I'll give her *fair*. Two: Telephone manner . . .?'

'Poor,' said Tom, taking the paper from her.

'Tom!'

'Angelo – have you got a pen?'

Tom started to complete the form. He wouldn't let her have it. And it wasn't the kind of restaurant for making a scene – so Kate gave up. Toying with the base of her glass, she laughed at Tom's running commentary as he completed Janet's form, pointing at the box he should tick, adding the odd remark, explaining some of the work methods, and generally helping him to produce the most insulting appraisal possible. It wasn't that clever, or that funny, but Kate was doubled up, wiping her eyes, by the end of it.

Tom loved it when she was silly. He loved making her laugh. And he loved the fact that she was drinking one of the best wines on the list as she did so. He should have brought her here months ago.

It was after one o'clock when they got home. As the cab drove away, Kate unlocked the door. Tom followed her in, and up the stairs.

'Thank you,' she said, twisting back to smile at him. 'That was fun. I'm going to have a stinking hangover in

293

the morning – that whisky's a killer – and I'll definitely have to postpone poor old Janet, but it was worth it.'

'You were being funny,' he said. 'Mad and funny. I love you like that.'

'Well, it's very easy. Go on taking me to restaurants like that, and I'll go on being mad and funny. In fact, I'll be whatever you want.'

She was fooling around, he knew – but he couldn't help thinking there was a grain of truth in there somewhere. Look where Richard had got with Louisa.

'I'd take you to the Caprice every night,' he said, 'if you were – if you weren't forever working.' Kate opened the upper door to the flat. The light switch at the bottom didn't work. She walked up a dark flight of stairs.

'I don't have the choice,' she said. 'You know I don't.'

'But I miss you. I miss you in the day. You see more of your boss than you do of me.'

They got to the top. Kate turned on the light and looked at him. 'Listen to me, Tom. My boss is one of the least attractive men I know. He's unfit. He's going bald. His idea of a good time is a round of golf on Saturday mornings. If I could spend every second of the day with you, I would. But I can't. Please don't ask me.'

Tom understood. He knew that she meant it, and a part of him resented what it implied. She was more committed to her job than she was to him.

On Friday morning, Louisa realised she couldn't find her passport.

'What did you do with it when you got back from Germany?'

'I can't remember.'

'You must have had it with you at Heathrow. Did you get a cab home from there, or the train?'

'My brother gave me a lift.'

'Could you have left it in his car?'

'I don't know.'

'Can you call him?'

Alex didn't have it, so Tom helped her search. He then rang to find out what to do to replace it. And while she had new photographs taken, and spent hours queuing at the Passport Office to get it replaced, he agreed to wait in the car and then drive her to the airport.

But he could tell something was wrong the second he saw her coming out of the Passport Office building. She wasn't running. She had her head bent, and was putting a mobile telephone into her handbag. Tom leant across the passenger seat and opened the car door for her.

'Can we just go back to the flat?' she said.

'What? After all that, they didn't give you another one?'

'No. No, I've got the passport,' the new maroon booklet in her hand confirmed this. 'It's Richard.'

Tom drew in his breath and started the car engine. 'What's the bastard gone and done now?'

Richard had cancelled. He'd forgotten it was the start of Christopher's school holidays. He really had to be there.

───────◆◆◆───────

At least, that's what he told Louisa.

But the truth was that Richard had been caught – and Anne Hastings was not the kind of woman to take it lying down.

295

She'd discovered a week ago. Richard couldn't have been playing tennis at the club on the day of the charity celebrity tournament, so what had he been doing? Anne didn't ask. She waited until he said he was playing tennis again, and followed him. She had to sit in the car in that quiet street, waiting for about an hour, and Anne was not a patient woman. Her resentment built until the car was like a pressure cooker. And then when he emerged, contented, into the sunshine – when she wanted to yell at him and scream at him, and tear out what was left of his hair, and much much worse – she'd had to duck as he came straight towards her with . . .

Jesus. Anne's face distorted with rage as she forced it under the steering wheel. It couldn't be her, could it? Not little Louisa Edwardes.

'. . . if only you could stay the night.'

'But not long now until New York, sweetheart, is it? Not long at all . . .' Richard's voice faced as they walked behind a van.

That night, Anne cooked him dinner, gave him wine, and then – later – she gave him the best blow job of his life. In the end, she didn't have the courage to threaten him with the penknife (the one he usually kept on top of his chest of drawers, along with a torch and a photograph of her). But she had it in her hand.

She was still holding it when he came back from the bathroom and got into bed. He cuddled up to her back.

'Thank you, darling. Thank you. I love you . . .'

For a second, she let him hold her – and then she sat up. She turned on the light and got out of bed.

'What are you doing?'

296

Dressed in the butterscotch silk nightdress he'd given her for Christmas, Anne put the knife back next to the torch and told her husband that unless his affair with Louisa Edwardes stopped – now – she was leaving him. She'd sue him for every penny, and make sure he was disgraced. She'd go on television chat shows about peculiarly satisfactory ways of getting revenge.

No more family.

No more home.

No more friends.

No more job, perhaps.

And certainly no more blow jobs (at least, none from her and none like that).

And if he lied to her, if he tried to trick her and go on seeing that bimbo – or anybody else – she might find she wasn't able to control herself with his little Swiss Army penknife.

No more . . . yes, she meant it. Richard said he'd sort it out.

But instead of meeting Louisa, to explain properly, he just rang to cancel New York, and then simply didn't call back.

To begin with, she thought it was because of it being the beginning of Christopher's summer holidays. Of course he wouldn't call then. And then, as the week ended and he still didn't call, she wondered if it was work. Or maybe he was waiting for her to call? Unusual, but . . .

She rang and left a message.

When he didn't reply, the fear began.

Kate told her not to be ridiculous – he was nuts about her, there was bound to be an explanation – but Tom didn't agree.

'Gone back to his wife,' he said. 'Men like Richard always do.'

Louisa waited a week and left another message. But by then she knew – and Richard could tell from the tone of her voice that she wasn't expecting a response. He deleted the message, and then deleted Louisa from the memory system of his telephone in the office.

In some ways he was grateful to Anne for finding out. It wasn't that he'd had enough of Louisa, but all that subterfuge had been a terrible strain. He was better off like this.

Fourteen

'Do you really want to be living with him, sweet-heart?'

It was Saturday and Kate was in the flat. She shut the kitchen door so that the others wouldn't hear. 'I'm not *living with him*, Mum. It's just convenient to have him here at the moment.'

'Convenient for him.'

'Convenient for all of us. He's cheering up Louisa, which means that . . .'

'Cheering up Louisa?'

'. . . which means that I can focus on work. I don't need to worry about neglecting her.'

'I see,' said Elizabeth, and then, 'Don't you think you're being a bit naïve?'

'What do you mean?'

'Louisa isn't exactly plain.'

'Nor am I.'

'I know, darling. But . . .'

'Listen. Apart from the fact that Tom's my boyfriend and Louisa's my best friend – and apart from the fact that she's just been dumped by someone she adores – if Tom and Louisa are going to have an affair, they'll have an affair, regardless of whether he's living with us.'

Elizabeth decided to let it drop. 'Tell me about Louisa,' she said. 'What happened?'

Kate sighed. 'He dumped her, and it's – I don't know – it's like someone died. She can't sleep, she won't eat – lost a frightening amount of weight . . .'

She stopped suddenly as Louisa came into the kitchen. 'Yes. Yes, okay, Mum. We'll talk tomorrow then. Bye.'

Kate put down the receiver and watched Louisa open the fridge. Taking out a carton of cranberry juice, she opened it and poured some into a tumbler.

'Want any?'

'Thanks.'

Louisa poured a second glass and handed it to Kate, who took it and put it to one side.

'Tom and I thought we might go to a movie tonight, Lou. Want to come?'

Louisa stood with her arms folded, tumbler in one hand, staring out of the windows at the gardens at the back. 'I don't know . . .'

Kate looked at her there. She longed to fight her – make her see that Richard simply wasn't worth it – but with these thoughts came an understanding that this wasn't about whether Louisa was right. The point was that Louisa wasn't happy. She was going through the hopeless misery of rejection, and she needed time. The best Kate could do was support, not intrude – which meant offering continual, unforced distractions, while allowing Louisa space.

'It's Woody Allen,' she said.

Louisa shook her head. 'I'm sorry I'd probably still burst into tears.'

'It would be dark.'

'I'd really rather be here.'

'Sure?'

Louisa said that she was sure. Later, as she watched Kate and Tom leaving and heard the door pulled shut behind them, she was glad she'd said 'no'. It was hard enough to see them getting ready together. To be with them all night – well, it would have been intolerable.

During the week, however, it was a bit better. When Kate wasn't around, their being a couple was less obvious – less forced down her throat. Tom was less intense. He never mentioned Richard – except, occasionally, to be very rude and very funny at Richard's expense. He just chatted to her, teased her, and made it easier for her to forget.

Louisa found herself wishing he was there more often. 'Where do you go?' she asked.

Tom put the spare set of keys that were now his into his coat pocket and picked up his wallet from the table in the hall. 'To a café. I find it easier to concentrate.' He began walking down the stairs.

'But what do you have to concentrate on?'

'Letters, bills, finding work . . .'

'Can I come?'

'No.'

'Why not?'

He stood by the door with his hand on the latch and smiled up at her, leaning over the banisters. 'It would rather defeat the object of going.'

'I'd be very quiet.'

'No you wouldn't. You'd chatter.'

'I do not chatter.'

301

'Yes you do,' he said, opening the door. 'See you later.'

Tom left the flat, thinking he'd much rather stay. Although this was in part because he enjoyed teasing Louisa, it was mainly because Arabella was getting so much worse again. All the problems with Douglas, and then moving house, had meant that the few times he'd seen her since Kate's party had been difficult.

Although they continued to meet beforehand in the same café – Knightsbridge was (sort of) halfway between Bayswater and Chelsea, and they both liked the coffee – they'd relocated the rest of their relationship to Arabella's house.

Tom apologised for the upheaval. But thinking that she'd be pleased that he'd fallen out with Douglas over her – that it was his continuing relationship with Arabella that had forced him from the house in Knightsbridge – he was surprised by her reaction.

'Douglas doesn't approve of me,' she said, her eyes filling with tears.

Tom didn't know what to say.

'Why won't your friends accept me? What have I done wrong?'

'Darling, you've done nothing wrong. He just doesn't approve of me seeing you and Kate at the same time. That's all.'

'Then tell me why you're still with Kate. Why? Why not me?'

Tom sighed. Arabella hadn't told him what she'd overheard under the stairs at Gibbs's. She hadn't revealed how hurt she'd been at his offering to take Kate to Caratello, and giving her presents. Caratello was their – Tom and Arabella's – restaurant. Presents were their thing. And it hadn't helped that Kate had looked so disturbingly pretty. Arabella had not, until that night, seen Kate as much of a threat. She'd written Kate off as a plain, uptight lawyer and she hadn't understood, hadn't been forced to acknowledge until then, the intimacy that existed between Kate and Tom – and shut out the rest of the world.

Knowing nothing of this, Tom couldn't understand why she'd become so much less easy about the situation, less accepting. At Waveney, he'd told her he wanted them both, and she'd said she didn't mind. But now, it seemed, she did.

He got out of bed and started to get dressed. Arabella lay watching him. The curtains were closed, but the afternoon shone through them and she could see him easily in the strange yellow light. As she watched, a gust of wind blew against the curtains and direct sunlight spilt over the bed.

In the far corner, Tom pulled on his trousers and did up the zip. He picked his shirt up off the floor, shrugged it on, and sat on the edge of the bed to do up the buttons. 'Would you rather we stopped?' he said at last.

Arabella sat up, staring at him. Feeling the movement, he stared back at her troubled face – then down to where the vulnerable swell of her breasts curved out over a small ribcage, and softened. 'I'm sorry,' he said quietly. 'I take it back.'

He held her, and another gust of wind blew sunlight over them.

'What you and I have,' he said, 'has nothing to do with Kate. This is for us.'

'For us.'

'We don't need to be married, or going out together, to share this. Do we?'

Arabella clung to him and made a small 'Mm' of agreement into his shirt. It was easier to agree than risk him leaving her. She lifted her face and smiled. 'I love you.'

Tom kissed the top of her head and detached himself. He went over to the window and opened the curtains. Below him, a row of plane trees rustled in the cemetery.

'When's that shoot coming out?'

'Which one?' said Arabella, knowing there was only one.

'The cemetery one.'

'September. It's the September issue, so it'll be out some time towards the end of August.'

'It's almost August now.'

He could see a couple of men in leather, walking with pert strides, side by side, under a canopy of cedar. Was it easier being gay, he wondered. Was sex without commitment more understood when it was between men? Were feelings less hurt? He thought of Charlie Reed.

'What are the pictures like?' When Arabella said nothing, he turned round. 'Bells?'

'Don't know – haven't seen them.'

'They were taken ages ago.'

'I know.' She got out of bed and into her dressing gown. 'But I can't get hold of Charlie. His mobile doesn't work. The girl at his studio keeps taking my messages and telling me he's abroad, but he never gets back to me,' she joined him at the window. 'He's probably too busy.'

Tom turned back. The men had gone.

'But it is coming out,' she went on. 'They sent some spotty nerd I'd never heard of to come and interview me last week.'

———— ◆◆◆ ————

Douglas was unhappy.

He and Tom had never fallen out. In fact, until now, he'd not fallen out with anyone in his life, and he didn't know how to handle it. The instinct to make amends fought hard with the memory of Tom's accusations, and Douglas hadn't really recovered from the shock he'd felt at the idea that he was, in some way, buying Tom's friendship.

The unravelling of their arrangements had been achieved by a series of messages passed through Douglas' agent, and by the occasional cold note left at the flat – the last one accompanied by Tom's set of keys. And that had been it. Silence.

Douglas knew that Tom had gone to live with Kate, but he had no idea what was happening with Arabella. Surely it was beyond even Tom to have an affair with one woman while deceiving and living off another.

On the other hand, Tom was in a crisis, a crisis that had not been helped by their row. With his self-respect worn down by the loss of all that money, by having to depend on other people, by not having a job, a house, a life of his own – it would take enormous guts for Tom to turn his back on Arabella. Douglas could see how tempting – how interesting – it would be for Tom to live a double life. He didn't think that Tom, right now, was strong enough to resist. Sadly, he realised that Tom didn't seem to care if he behaved badly any more.

And yet, in spite of everything, Douglas missed him.

He missed being teased by Tom. He missed hearing about the helter-skelter life Tom led. And he missed hearing news of Kate. He realised how much he'd depended on Tom as a link to his own generation. That birthday weekend in Waveney would not have been possible without him. Kate, Arabella and Charlie had all come because of Tom. Not because of Douglas.

It was bearable when he was in Norfolk, because he tended to be busy, and there were very few reminders. But when he came to London – which he did quite a lot these days, to visit Sarah Knowles in Fulham – it really hurt. Every room in the flat held memories of Tom. And it wasn't just the flat. Douglas couldn't walk past the coffee shop on the corner without thinking of him. There was the little news-agent that stayed open late, where Tom would get his cigarettes. There was the Italian restaurant at the other end of the mews – the one Tom loved so much.

Eventually he stopped using the flat. Instead, he'd base himself at Gibbs's or stay with Sarah, and even that didn't shield him completely. The club was full of reminders – and he'd never forget the time he actually saw Kate.

It had been on the underground. Douglas didn't usually take the tube but the traffic had been terrible and he was late for dinner with Sarah. He'd left his car in the Gibbs's car park, and walked up to Piccadilly, but as soon as he got to the westbound platform, he'd realised his mistake. Trains had been cancelled. There were long delays. Passengers were being advised to take alternative routes – or take the first train that came along, and then change where necessary.

Douglas had managed to get to Earls Court. He was waiting for a District Line train to take him to Fulham Broadway when he saw her standing at the edge of the opposite platform, holding her briefcase in both hands so that it hung flat over her knees as she looked at the mice on the rails. She was tired, he could tell. Either tired, or sad. And he thought again of Tom – of Tom and Arabella deceiving the poor girl and breaking her heart.

Douglas fought through the crowds on his platform until he was standing directly opposite her. 'Kate?'

He thought for a second that she hadn't heard, and then she looked up.

'Kate!' he smiled. 'How are you? How's Tom?'

She went on looking at him for a moment, and then she turned her back, closing her eyes in an expression of utter contempt before a train swept between them.

It wasn't Kate's fault, he knew – closing a door on his heart with a mind that looked to understand and excuse. It wasn't her fault. Tom must have decided not to tell her the real reasons Douglas had for throwing him out of the flat. It was mad of Douglas to think that he might. He realised now that she would never know. She'd never know that Douglas had been trying to make Tom give Arabella up – that it had been, in part, for her. All she'd think was that Douglas had abandoned his friend.

Project Cannon II was approaching completion.

As Louisa recovered from Richard, Kate was in the middle of a final fortnight of drafting meetings, and redrafting meetings, of waiting until two in the morning for calls from the States, and then staying until five to make changes to the documents which were then rejected by the bank. She and Simon were spending hours on the telephone, working for a document that would suit both their clients, working together.

Michael had noticed the long hours she was working and, over the course of that fortnight, he deliberately took a more hands-off approach. To begin with Kate worried that he was failing to give her enough support, but although he was never present at meetings or during telephone conversations, she became aware that he always took time to go through the latest drafts with her and that he was impressed by them.

Michael had been taking her to beauty parades for new clients ever since she'd qualified. She'd always suspected that this was because of her manner and her looks, rather than anything more academic, and joked about it with him one evening when they were walking back from the canteen together, clutching paper bags filled with sandwiches and Kit-Kats. Michael slowed his pace.

'You don't really think that, do you?'

'A bit,' she said, laughing. 'I don't mind.'

'But if that was true I'd be taking Heather to the beauty parades. Not you.'

'Heather?'

'She's certainly more to the taste of our potential clients.'

Heather was still in the office. They lowered their voices as they approached her station. She was leaning forward, squinting at her screen. She had stuck her chin right forward and was biting her upper lip. Kate waited until they went into his office and closed the door.

'That?' she demanded. 'Prettier than me?'

'Well, maybe not when she's . . .' Michael was at his desk, opening his bag of food. He looked up. 'I take you to beauty parades because you've got what they call in personnel, *good communication skills*.'

'I'm not that easily flattered.'

'Okay. How about I tell you that we're considering you for the Singapore office?'

Kate stared at him.

'Well, it's going to be either you or Annette,' he smiled. 'So you see, we do appreciate you.'

'But I . . .'

'You'd rather not go.'

Kate hesitated.

'Oh well,' he shrugged. 'Think about it.'

'Yes. Yes, I will.'

Michael opened his can of Coke, drank about half of it in one go, and wiped his mouth. 'Right. Where are those drafts?'

———— ❖ ————

Louisa was finding it easier than she'd expected to get over Richard. She missed their illicit dinners, and she still thought about him last thing at night, but that was more of a ritual than profound longing for him to be there with her.

As the weather improved, she took to sunbathing on the roof. She waited until Tom left the flat and then, in a black bikini, she climbed up through the hatch to the little roof terrace above. She'd take a couple of magazines, a bottle of mineral water and the portable telephone, but most of the time she'd just sleep.

Louisa had the kind of skin that tanned quickly, and Kate couldn't help feeling drab in comparison. Having Tom around only made it worse.

'You look fine.'

'I look awful. Look how pasty I am.' Kate pulled up her sleeve and held her arm against Tom's.

'I'm half Italian,' he reminded her.

'But Louisa's not. Her skin's beautifully tanned . . .'

It was two in the morning, and Kate was sitting on the bed, still dressed. She could never just go straight to sleep. It took over an hour for her to wind down once she got home, however late. If that hour was spent having sex, Tom was happy. But, increasingly, Kate didn't have the energy. Instead, her tired brain would attach itself to an insecurity and run with it. She'd pester him about it, not listening to his suggestions.

'You're every bit as pretty as Louisa. Tan or no tan. What's more, she spends all day lazing in the sun. You spend all day working.'

'I want to spend all day lazing in the sun.'

Tom was tired. He hated conversations like this. 'Why don't you? I keep saying you should take some time off.'

'There's too much for me to do. I can't . . .'

'Well,' he said. 'Either you give up your job and get a suntan, or you keep your job and stop hankering after what will only make you look twice your age in ten years' time. Now take off your clothes and get into bed.'

Louisa sunbathed only while Tom was out of the flat. She knew he got back between two and three and made sure she was down before then. She wasn't sure enough of him, or herself, to risk being alone together in the heat, wearing almost nothing.

But one day, after an unsatisfactory session with Arabella, Tom came back before lunch.

'Hi!' he yelled as he ran up the stairs. There was no response. 'Louisa?'

A bright pool of light surrounded the step ladder leading up to the roof. Climbing up, he found a languid body, draped across the wooden slats.

'Hi there.'

Louisa didn't reply. She was wearing sunglasses, and he couldn't see her expression.

'You're burning.'

She didn't move.

'Louisa?'

Louisa grunted.

'You're burning.'

'I never burn.'

'Yes, you do. You're burning now.'

'Where?'

'The tops of your legs.'

Louisa sat up and bent forward. 'Where?'

'You're dazzled. Go down to the bathroom and take a look in the mirror.'

Louisa pulled a sarong round her and went down.

Tom stood looking out at the cityscape, shimmering.

'I don't know what you're talking about,' Louisa's voice sailed up through the hatch. 'I'm not remotely burnt.'

When she came back, Tom was in her place and there was nowhere else for her to lie out flat. 'Tom . . .' His eyes were shut, but he was laughing. '. . . that's my place.'

She picked up the bottle of mineral water and poured it over him. He just went on laughing. 'You must learn not to get physical when you don't get your own way, Louisa. It's very childish . . .'

Louisa perched on a chair and scowled at the roofs. 'Why are back so early?'

Tom laughed. 'It was too hot.'

'So now you're here, getting in the way . . . I knew we shouldn't have let you move in.'

Tom opened one eye, noticed her expression and sat up, his wet shirt dirty from the slats. 'Louisa,' he said. 'I was joking.' He stood up.

Louisa scuttled back into her place, smiling broadly. 'So was I,' she said and, lying down, put on her sunglasses.

After that day, she stopped coming down at two. Instead, Tom would join her on the roof. She would lie in her patch, and he would sit in one of the deck chairs. Sometimes they'd talk, but often they didn't.

Louisa told herself it was fine – it was no worse than being on the beach – and it was better than being alone. She liked Tom's company. She liked him teasing her. And, if pressed, she'd probably have admitted to liking the sense that she was being watched.

When he was asked to contribute to the flat bills, Tom rang Philip Barclay.

'Tom, dear boy. Glad you called. We need to speak about tax.'

'Whatever. I was calling because I'm going to need more . . .' Tom paused. 'Tax? Surely there can't be inheritance tax. I inherited nothing.'

'It's capital gains tax on some of the sales you

requested this year.'

'Capital what?'

'Capital gains tax. It's a tax against any gain in capital you've made since the shares were bought. It's levied when you sell them . . .'

Tom said nothing.

'. . . so, for instance, if the shares were bought for a pound a share in 1990 and sold this year for five pounds a share then you must pay tax on the four pounds difference.'

Tom sat down and opened a new packet of cigarettes. 'Go on.'

'The tax people here have been looking at your portfolio and they estimate that you're going to have a bill for something like twenty thousand.'

'What do you suggest I do?'

'You could sell more shares.'

'If I do that, what will there be left?'

'About three thousand.' Philip took off his glasses and held them in his fat fingers. 'It's frightening how quickly money can disappear,' he said. 'The same thing happened to my cousin years ago . . .'

Tom was silent.

'. . . you won't have to pay the tax bill immediately, if that helps.'

'When will I have to pay it?'

'Not until something like this time next year. I just thought you should know where you stand.'

Tom swallowed. 'Can you postpone things until then?'

'Of course we can, dear boy. Now tell me. What were you calling about?'

Kate had agreed with Simon that, when Project Cannon II completed, she would let him take her out to dinner to celebrate. She told Tom and Louisa that it was a business dinner, and said she'd be back by midnight. Tom and Louisa decided to get *Raiders of the Lost Ark* out on video. They put it on, ordered pizzas, and opened a bottle of wine.

Simon had asked his secretary to book a table for two at a Japanese restaurant in Mayfair. He collected Kate from her office at eight and they went on by taxi.

'Here we are,' he announced, leaping from the taxi and holding the door for her. 'I hope you like Japanese food.'

'I love Japanese food,' she said, getting out, 'but my boyfriend hates it, so I hardly ever get to indulge . . .' She waited for Simon to pay the driver, glad that she couldn't see his face.

'Your boyfriend?' He took his change and turned to her.

'Yes,' she said firmly. 'Tom. Haven't I told you about him?'

'No . . .' They walked together into the restaurant. '. . . what does he do?'

'Nothing.'

The restaurant was white throughout, with a bar at the far end, rimmed in blue light. Kate handed her coat to the attendant and allowed herself to be led to a table. Simon followed, his long fingers pressed together.

'Nothing?'

'Yes.'

'Is that because he's phenomenally rich, or phenomenally lazy?'

She laughed. 'Both, I expect.'

Simon ordered sake, and gave her a menu. 'Do you live with him?'

'He's living with me and my flatmate, Louisa, at the moment. But that's just a temporary measure until he finds his own place.'

Kate watched his fingers stroke a pair of chopsticks in the blue light.

'Does he know you're here?'

'Of course.'

'And he doesn't mind?'

'Why should he? Does your girlfriend mind you going to a business dinner?'

'I don't have a girlfriend.'

Kate looked down. 'Perhaps I should introduce you to Louisa . . .'

'Your flatmate?'

'She's stunning. An ex-model,' she smiled, 'and, as from only a few weeks ago, single.'

Simon returned the smile, and changed the subject.

But later, while they were drinking jasmine tea and waiting for the bill, he returned to it.

'Tell me more about your flatmate. What does she do now that she's an *ex*-model?'

'Nothing.'

Simon held his left hand with his right and sat forward. 'And you're happy for your boyfriend, who does nothing, to be living with you, a busy lawyer, and your beautiful, recently single, flatmate, who also does nothing?'

Kate reached for her bag, and took out a packet of cigarettes. 'Yes. I am.'

'What are they doing tonight?'

'Watching a video.'

'Together? Alone?'

'Yes.'

Simon passed her the matches. 'You're very trusting.'

Kate lit the cigarette. 'We trust *each other*,' she said, tossing the match into a designer ashtray. 'It's mutual. How's he to know what I'm up to now? The situation is the same for us both.'

'But I'm not an ex-model!'

Kate had laughed, but her face was dark when, later, she climbed the stairs to the flat. Her reflection in the black window on the stairs was strained in the hard light. And her brain, not sober, distorted the image yet further. She let herself into the flat, feeling resentful and not knowing quite why.

The television was off. Tom was sitting on the sofa in front of it, and Louisa was lying on her back, on the floor. Kate noticed the finished bottle of wine, and the empty pizza boxes.

'Hi,' said Tom, smiling at her. 'How was it?'

'Dull.'

'We've had a lovely evening,' said Louisa from the floor, 'and I'm drunk.'

Tom laughed. 'You can't be drunk, Louisa. You've only had a couple of glasses.'

Louisa was wearing a pair of white jeans shorts and a pink linen shirt, sleeves rolled to the elbow. Her long legs, brown from spending the last month on the roof terrace, bent at the knees. Her long arms, even browner, draped along the floor. ''Smore than enough,' she said.

Kate made herself smile. 'I'm going to bed.'

'Already?'

'Stay and have a glass of whisky.'

She turned and walked out of the room. 'I've got to get up early tomorrow.'

'I'll be up later,' Tom called after her.

She heard Louisa's voice saying, 'Is she all right?'

'She's fine. Where's the good whisky?'

'None left.'

'Louee-sa . . .'

Giggles.

'No wonder you're so pissed.'

More giggles.

And Kate went upstairs, hating herself, and hating Simon.

Arabella liked making a point of arriving at the café after Tom. She liked the sensation of him watching her cross the floorboards; she'd pause at the pastries counter and stretch out her arm – her gold bracelet clinking slightly on the glass – and ask Enrico for a café latte, before turning. Only then would she appear to notice him sitting at his table at the back. Sometimes Tom would be watching her but, more often, he was reading the papers.

'Sorry I'm late.'

'Were you at the gym?' Tom folded his paper away and looked at her. Beneath a sleek black leather jacket, she was dressed in supposedly casual T-shirt and jeans that he knew were far from cheap. Arabella took off the jacket and flexed an arm. It wasn't as slim as Louisa's, and it wasn't as soft as Kate's, but it was much more toned.

'What do you think?'

Tom tried to squeeze it. 'Impressive,' he said, thinking he could still flatten her in seconds, and that he'd show her later.

Arabella dropped her elbow and smiled. 'The best thing's just happened.'

She paused to give Tom time to say, 'What?'

'Joe complimented my abs. At last. I mean, my biceps have never been much of a problem, but my *abs* . . .'

Still, Tom didn't respond. He'd never heard her talking about her muscles at all. Let alone like this – *abs* – as if she was suddenly an authority.

'You know Joe,' she continued.

'Er . . .'

'You've heard me talking about him, Tom. I know you have.'

'Oh yes,' he lied, thinking that, when Arabella was happy, he really found it more exhausting than when she was depressed. She demanded equal excitement from him, and he couldn't bring himself to get excited about Arabella's abs and her biceps, or yet another guy she thought fancied her.

Arabella gave Tom the wonky smile that told him he really must pay more attention, but she'd indulge him today. 'My new trainer. Remember? The one just over from LA? He brought some new guy over, all flabby, *obviously* not a member. I was there on the rowing machine, pumping away, and Joe said, "Excuse me, darling, let me show this gentleman what we can do with his belly." So I got up and stood there while Joe ran his hand up and down my stomach and to show old blubber-belly the ultimate . . .'

Tom couldn't help suspecting that Arabella timed

lifting her T-shirt to reveal her abdominal muscles exactly to coincide with Enrico bringing over her café latte. He watched Enrico's expression with interest, and wondered if Enrico still thought that Arabella was a lawyer.

'. . . then Joe says, "Now I know I shouldn't be asking a lady her age", so I tell him I'm about to be thirty-two and the other guy's eyes pop out of his head. He says he's only . . .'

'Thirty-two?' said Enrico, putting down the coffee and staring at her.

Arabella dropped her T-shirt, lifted her chin and smiled at him. 'Well, thirty-two *next week*. Awful, isn't it?'

'I don' believe you!'

'It's true,' she said, glancing at Tom. 'Next Wednesday.'

Tom gave her an absent-minded smile.

In his other hand, Enrico held a bowl of sugar in wrappers. He put them in front of Arabella who thanked him, and told him that he should know by now she never took sugar.

'Ah! That because you sweet enough weethout eet!'

'You've run that line before, Enrico. Now bugger off.'

'Okay, okay!' Enrico grinned at Tom and left.

Tom turned back to see Arabella smirking into her cup.

———◆◆◆———

Kate, meanwhile, was at her desk, holding a cup of coffee and staring into space.

Following the completion of Project Cannon II, Adam had taken a week's holiday and, in spite of humming from her computer and muffled noises from outside, the room felt silent in his absence.

She turned to her task list. First item: check Adam's report on Project Galaxy.

Adam's report on Space Vortex's financing documents was sitting in her in-tray. It was over 100 pages long. She picked it up. No summary – which meant that she'd have to wait for him to get back, ask him to do one, and then she'd go through the report with him.

Kate started a new list headed, Tasks for Adam. First item: summarise Project Galaxy Report.

'*You're very trusting . . .*'

Shaking her head, Kate turned to the second item on her list: prepare presentation on Fixed and Floating Charges. Ugh. When was that?

Searching for her office diary, Kate remembered the trouble Tom had taken to separate Louisa from Richard. Why had he done that? Why had he got so involved? She was opening the diary when her telephone rang.

It was the in-house lawyer at Space Vortex. There were more financing agreements he'd unearthed. Would it be convenient if he sent them over today? Of course. Would he prefer it if she sent someone to come and pick them up? Of course. She'd send a trainee round before lunch. How many boxes were there?

Kate put down the telephone and went in search of someone else's trainee. When she came back, the message light on the telephone was flashing. Simon.

He'll call again, she thought, returning to her list. Presentation on Fixed and Floating Charges. Flicking through her diary, she checked the date. It wasn't for a month. She smiled as she put a second item onto the Tasks for Adam list, and turned to the third item on her own list: Bank of Tyrol Refinancing – speak to Michael. Not one for Adam, this time. Where was the file?

Later, she called the flat.

Eyes shut, Louisa stretched for the portable.

'Is Tom there?'

'Hi. No. He's not usually back until after lunch.'

Why did Louisa know all his movements?

'*You're very trusting.*'

'Could you ask him to give me a ring?'

'Of course,' Louisa rolled onto her stomach. 'Anything wrong?'

'No,' said Kate.

Louisa was silent. She couldn't make out Kate's tone – it was as if Kate was angry about something, something to do with Louisa, and it was making her feel apologetic. But why? She'd done nothing.

'Does there need to be something wrong for me to call him?' Kate went on.

'No . . .' said Louisa. 'I just thought. Perhaps. Are you upset?'

'I can't hear you. The line's bad.'

'Are you upset?'

'What makes you think I'm upset?'

'I don't know . . .'

'I'm not upset. At all. There's nothing wrong. I just wanted to speak to Tom. And he's not there, which is fine. I don't know what you're going on about.'

'It doesn't matter. I'll get him to call you.'

'Where are you, Lou? I can hardly hear.'

321

'On the roof . . .'

Kate looked out of her door, across the pool of secretaries and through the window beyond. Outside, the geometric horizon of white city buildings cut into a cobalt sky.

Louisa shifted position and the line cleared. 'Is that better?'

'Yes.'

'I'll get him to call you then?'

'Thanks. And tell him I'll be back at about eight.'

Kate put down the receiver and dialled Janet. 'Where's the Bank of Tyrol file?'

'Which one?'

'General Banking.'

'Oh yes,' Janet's tone was chatty. 'I saw that recently. Where was it? Let's see . . . Oh yes, Annette was looking for it.'

'Annette?'

'She wanted to look at the side letters you drafted.'

'Why?'

Janet said nothing. How should she know why Annette wanted to look at some side letters when she didn't even know, or want to know, what made a letter a side letter?

'Would you get it off her? Now? I need it.'

Janet collected the file and took it into Kate's office. Kate was bent over her work. Approaching quietly, Janet placed the file on the side of the desk. Kate's back remained bent, but she lifted her head from the judgement she was reading and gave Janet a smile. 'Thank you.'

'Is there anything wrong?'

Kate sat back. 'Why is everybody asking me that?'

'You don't look well. You're pale. Too thin. You're
. . .'

'Really? Too thin?' Kate's tone was pleased.

'It's not healthy. You look exhausted. You should
be at home, asleep.'

'There's too much on.'

Janet opened the door. 'When isn't there?'

She didn't wait for a reply.

Simon Dalziel did call back.

'It's a beautiful day. Let's have lunch.'

'I've got a meeting.'

'A drink, then.'

'Tonight?'

'Why not?'

Why not? Tom hadn't returned her call.

She agreed to meet Simon at seven in a bar they'd
been to before.

They took their drinks onto some steps just outside
the bar and sat with their briefcases at their feet,
looking at the commuters striding home. Kate took a
gulp of Chardonnay and let it trickle down her
throat. She shut her eyes.

'Did you know that research studies have revealed
that the members of our society most likely to become
alcoholics are professional women in their thirties?'

Kate kept her eyes shut. 'I'm only just thirty. And I
read that article too.'

'Then you'll know that this is because they get into
a cycle of drinking at lunchtime meetings, and then
in wine bars after work, to be with the lads, and then
during dinner . . . it's really not that difficult to get
through three bottles a day.'

323

Kate opened her eyes. Simon's small face was turned in profile.

'I wouldn't say that drinking with you was exactly being with the lads.'

'But you admit you drink too much?'

'No.'

'Classic symptom.'

Kate laughed. 'This is today's first drink,' she said, draining the glass, 'but I'll confess I needed it.'

'Bad day?'

She nodded and let him refill her glass.

'Want to talk about it?'

'No.'

Simon said nothing.

'I'm sorry, Simon. I'm not much company at the moment. What I meant was that it's . . .'

'Private. I understand.'

Kate smiled. 'Thanks.'

Simon finished his glass of wine and refilled it. 'On the other hand,' he said, 'sometimes it helps to talk about it with someone dispassionate.' He put the bottle back on the step beside him. 'I mean, it's not as if I know him.'

'You might.'

'What's his surname?'

'Faulkener.'

'Never heard of him.'

Smiling, Kate shook her head. 'I'm sorry, Simon. Anyway, it's not just Tom. It's work, too . . . you know how it is. Some days race by with lots on, and you love them. Other days just drag and drag. I used to like having not much on.'

Simon looked at her. 'Time to think and dream.'

'That was why I liked them.'

'Why don't you like them now?'

Kate's eyes followed the zig-zag line of the steps. She sighed. 'Perhaps it's just boredom.'

'Well,' he said, 'we all know the best cure for boredom.'

She laughed, drained her second glass, and held it out. 'Alcohol!'

'Or an affair.'

Her second laugh was less easy. 'Come on. Fill my glass. I'm going for the former.'

'Where the fuck have you been?'

'Just let me in, Tom. I can't find my keys.'

'You're holding them.'

Laughter.

'Who's that with you?'

Tom heard the door below open. He heard footsteps on the stairs, and voices, and then the key in the door to the flat.

Louisa looked at him questioningly.

'She's got a man with her . . .'

Louisa hadn't removed the expression of surprise from her face when Kate entered the room, smiling carelessly.

'Hi.'

'Where's your friend?'

'Gone. Just dropping me off – so sweet – completely the wrong direction . . .'

Louisa stood up and looked at her watch. 'I'm off to bed.'

'Night,' said Kate after her.

Tom closed the door. 'So,' he said, sitting on the

sofa. 'Did you have a nice time?'

Kate dropped her briefcase by the door and ran her hands through her hair. 'I'm sorry. I got caught up.'

'You were working?'

'No,' she kicked off her shoes and sat next to him. 'I was drinking.'

'I can tell.'

'I didn't realise the time.'

'You *didn't realise the time*' he shook his head. 'It's after midnight, for God's sake. And who was that guy?'

Kate said nothing.

Tom took a cigarette from the pack on the sofa table and lit a match. 'Where did you go? His place?'

Kate watched him inhale the cigarette to life. 'Why don't you trust me?'

He shrugged.

'Can't I go out for a drink with a friend, without you assuming I'm having an affair?'

'You didn't call.'

'Don't you think that if I was having an affair I'd go out of my way to call, so as not to make you suspicious?'

'You could be double bluffing.'

'Yes,' she said, 'or I could be double double-back bluffing, with an extra bluff.'

This made him smile, and they looked at each other for a second.

'Just call next time.'

It was, for Kate, as if she'd been falling hard, and she was now suddenly weightless. She'd not consciously intended to provoke his jealousy but now that she had, she was no longer afraid – it told her that he minded.

'Of course I'll call,' she said, turning her wrist so that her palm was exposed.

Louisa, who'd heard all of their conversation from the bathroom, frowned at her reflection in the mirror and wondered again where it was Tom went in the mornings.

Fifteen

Before that evening, it hadn't occurred to Tom that Kate could be anything other than his.

The next morning, he woke early and lay with her in his arms, thinking about her. When her alarm went at six-thirty, he switched it off as quickly as he could. He tried to get her to go back to sleep. Why didn't she take the day off?

'I couldn't possibly . . .' Kate heaved herself up and sat on the edge of the bed. Tom pulled her arm.

'Come back, just another five minutes . . .'

'Tom!' she said, laughing and pulling away, 'the longer I stay with you this morning, the less time I'll have with you tonight.'

Tom let her go. But he thought about her all day. He left a message on Arabella's mobile, saying he couldn't make lunch, and then spent most of his time trying to decide what to do. When he called Kate at work, she was either in a meeting or on the other line. That night, she was late home. And then again the following night.

Kate wasn't having a particularly difficult week, but her nights were late. She made a point of calling Tom, to reassure him she wasn't out drinking and to let him know what time she'd be home, but still he felt neglected. Kate spent more time at work and with that Simon than she did with him. He wanted her to try harder for his attention – like Arabella did.

Tom's disposition managed to combine laziness with impatience. But he didn't see it like that – he thought he was relaxed and decisive, and once he realised he wanted more of Kate, it became very clear to him, very quickly, that he wanted much, much more of her. And he wanted it now. Why not? he thought, imagining her pleased expression. Why not?

The following Tuesday, he took Louisa out to lunch. At the end of their second bottle of wine, Tom told her he was thinking of asking Kate to marry him.

'Kate?' said Louisa, stupidly.

'Well, who else would it be?'

Louisa laughed through the nails in her throat.

This couldn't be happening. Not yet. Of course Louisa wanted Kate to be happy – and she was sure nothing would make her happier than a proposal from Tom – but it was too soon. Kate and Tom would want their own place. They'd move out. Who would she live with? Who'd sit with her on the terrace? Who'd talk with her about whether it was better to dine at the Caprice or the Ivy? Who'd give her a hard time about her latest boyfriend? Who'd laugh at her for not knowing that rhythm was a six-letter word with no vowels, let alone how to spell it? Who'd be there when she got in from a party? Who'd tell her how she looked before she left?

'Wow . . .' was all she could say, followed by, 'Wow,' and then, 'why are you telling me?'

'I want to get it right. Shall I ask her in a restaurant? Or on a beach? Or after sex?'

Louisa said she was sure Kate wouldn't mind where or how.

'And what about an engagement ring? Arabella never forgave me for not having one with me when I proposed to her. Do you think Kate would want a diamond?'

'I'm sure a diamond's fine.'

'Isn't it a bit unimaginative?'

Louisa didn't know.

'Would you mind coming shopping with me for one this afternoon,' Tom persisted. 'I need your help.'

'I'm sure Kate would want to choose her own.'

'If she doesn't like it, we can take it back. But it would be great to get her one she loved straight away. And she'll probably never have time to find one she likes if we leave it to her . . . Oh come on, Louisa. Please?'

When Kate got home – at midnight – Tom and Louisa were still up, playing backgammon in silence. Tom got to his feet when he saw her standing in the doorway, her eyes half shut.

'Poor darling,' he said, 'let me get you a drink.'

Kate sat in the chair by the window. Tom put a glass of whisky in her hand and kissed the top of her head.

'Busy day?'

'Hell,' said Kate, not wanting to talk about it. 'What did you do?'

Tom and Louisa's eyes met briefly.

'Nothing much . . .'

'We went shopping.'

'What did you buy?'

'Oh,' absent-mindedly, Louisa started packing up the backgammon pieces and stacking them back in their box, 'I needed to get something to wear for Charles and Janey's wedding.'

Charles and Janey's wedding was in November. It wasn't so unusual for Louisa to be buying clothes four months in advance, but there was still something unnatural about the way she was behaving. Kate drank her whisky in one gulp and stood up.

'I'm going to bed.'

'I'll come with you,' said Tom, quickly. 'Night, Lou.'

Louisa said goodnight and watched them leave. Then she put the rest of the pieces into their slots and shut the board with a snap. As she put it back in the games cupboard underneath the drinks' tray and began turning out the lights, she wondered wearily how long it would be before she'd have to find another flatmate.

Upstairs, while Tom was in the bathroom, Kate was taking off her jacket and thinking that he had called her 'Lou'. Hating her suspicious mind, Kate wiggled out of her skirt and decided that she, Kate, was the one with the problem. She was tired and paranoid. In fact, she thought, as she unsnapped her bra and dropped her knickers, the real person she should be blaming was Simon Dalziel – for infecting her head in the first place.

She was still standing there when Tom came back in, smelling of toothpaste.

'What are you thinking?' he said.

'Nothing,' she smiled. 'Just tired thoughts. I won't be long . . .' Wrapping herself in his dressing gown, Kate went along the passage to the bathroom.

331

Back in her bedroom, Tom sneaked another look at the ring he and Louisa had chosen. Although Douglas had stopped paying off his credit cards last month, the limit on his MasterCard was still huge, and easily accommodated the price of the ring. Seeing the diamond wink at him from its bed of velvet, he was reminded of the last time he'd bought an engagement ring and his smile faded.

Tom snapped shut the box and put it at the back of his boxer shorts drawer. He really wanted this one to work, and he felt it was very important that he resolve things with Arabella before he asked Kate to marry him. It wasn't going to be nice. Arabella would be angry and upset, but she'd get over it – she'd got over the other times – and then there'd be no more guilt.

The mere thought of having done it lifted him. He'd do it tomorrow.

———————

Birthdays, particularly her own, were important to Arabella.

Coming into the café, she could tell that Enrico had a card for her, and she took it from him, smiling. 'Enrico! How on earth did you know?' she said, opening it. 'Thank you . . .'

Enrico smiled back cheerfully.

Arabella couldn't resist a glance at the table at the back, to see if he'd noticed. But someone else was sitting there. Turning her whole head to get a proper look, Arabella saw an enormous woman with short hair and trainers, reading a guide book to London.

Enrico watched her eyes flicker over the other tables. Most of them were empty, and there was no sign of Tom.

'Ees not 'ere yet.'

Arabella said nothing.

'I bring café latte?'

'Thanks,' she said. 'I'll be over there.'

'And a leetle chocolate croissant as well? On your birthday . . .'

Arabella took the croissant over to the window and sat down, looking at Enrico's card.

Tom was in the park, walking fast with his head bent. A hot grey sky closed over him. No wind. No roller-bladers. Only listless tourists with sulky children, gazing through the railings of Kensington Palace while, on the round pond, the swans sank their heads and necks beneath the surface of the water.

He could say that Kate was pressuring him into it. 'I know it's inconvenient, Bells. But she's given me an ultimatum . . . and I suppose I think we may as well call it quits at the same time. You don't mind, do you?'

Of course she'd bloody mind.

Perhaps he could sort of – let it out. Like it really wasn't such a big deal. 'Oh by the way, darling, Kate and I are getting married.'

What he wanted to do, he thought, as he passed the Albert Memorial, was to present it to Arabella as if it was somehow the best possible thing for her, too. He could say she was limiting herself, staying with him – perhaps even suggest that she wasn't getting any younger – and offer to introduce her to someone. And he could point out at the same time all those admirers she kept banging on about – Joe at the gym, for instance. He could say he was ending it for her sake. That was okay, wasn't it?

Tom strode into the coffee shop, nodded at Enrico

333

as he passed, 'Bottle of mineral water, thanks . . .' and then stopped suddenly when he saw the woman at his table at the back.

Enrico, grinning, pointed him to the table by the window. Tom noticed the signs of Arabella – that handbag she was so proud of, slung over the back of a chair, and her Silk Cut pack of ten sitting on the wooden surface of the table. Realising she must be in the loo, he sat on the other chair, the one looking out into the street, and waited, one of his legs jiggling as he ran over what he was going to say.

But he couldn't concentrate. He picked up the cigarette packet and opened it, just to see how many there were in there. Four. Tom took one out and put it to his lips. He was looking for her lighter when he found the card.

'What kept you?'

'Hi,' putting down the card, he took the unlit cigarette from his lips, and stood up with a jerk. 'Happy Birthday!' He kissed her cheek.

'Tom darling – where've you *been*?' Arabella was looking at him eagerly.

Tom couldn't bear it. He just wanted to get the whole thing over and done with. Hanging his jacket on the back of the chair, he sat down again and told her they needed to talk.

Arabella sat opposite him, against the light. With her forefinger, she wiped at the crumbs left by her croissant, and then put it into her mouth. 'What about?'

'Well,' he said, tapping his unlit cigarette on the wooden surface of the table and staring at the point it struck. 'Us. I suppose.' Tom found he couldn't breathe in properly. 'I'm worried about you, Bells. You're thirty-two. Thirty-two today, as it happens. You're not getting any younger and I think, perhaps . . . I don't know. Don't you think you're wasting your time with me?'

He put the cigarette back into its box. 'I'm no good. You know that. And there are so many men out there who'd . . .'

Arabella's hands were very still.

'. . . you know. Enrico. Joe at the gym . . .'

'Tom . . .'

His eyes swung into her uncertain smile and then back to the surface of the table.

'What are you saying?' Arabella fixed her eyes on his until he looked at her again. 'Are you telling me it's over?'

He looked back at the surface of the table and said nothing.

'Tom?'

Still, he said nothing.

'What's brought this on? Has she found out about us?'

'No. She . . .'

'She what? What, Tom? *What*?'

'She wants to get married.'

'And *you*?' she said slowly. 'You want to marry her?'

'I'm sorry.'

Enrico put Tom's water on the table. He heard Tom say, 'I'm sorry,' and hated him.

'I'm sorry,' he repeated.

But she loved him.

'I'm sorry.'

She was his wife.

'Ex-wife.'

Didn't he think she deserved to be treated better than this?

'Yes, Arabella. Yes, you do.'

'Then . . . ?'

'I'm sorry.'

'But . . .' Arabella trailed off. But it's my birthday, was all she could think. There must have been hundreds of better reasons for him not to be doing this to her, but her mind wasn't working properly.

'I'm going to marry Kate,' he said again. 'It doesn't mean I don't feel for you. You're very attractive, Bells. But I . . .'

'Then why do you have to finish with me?'

Tom hesitated.

'You could marry Kate, and still see me,' she went on – pulling at him with her eyes. 'Come on. Come back with me now. Give me a chance, Tom. Let me show you . . .'

Tom finished his water and stood up. 'I don't think you understand,' he said. 'I love Kate. I love her. I can't help it.'

'You don't want me *at all*?'

He shook his head.

But it's my birthday.

He shouldn't have looked at her then, but he did. She was bent over her lap, putting the cigarettes back into her bag and wiping tears from its leather surface.

'Arabella?'

She didn't hear him.

Tom put some coins on the table for his water, and left.

But something about the coins cut into her. To Enrico's admiration, she picked them up and threw them at Tom. They shot across the tiled floor of the café, clinking and spinning as the door swung shut behind him.

'Wait!'

Tom heard her in the street and kept walking.

'Fucking wait!' She ran after him.

'Arabella – don't. Please. I'm sorry, but I . . .'

'Stop saying you're sorry. You're not sorry.'

Tom hailed a cab.

'Stop running away. Talk to me.'

'There's nothing more to say.'

Hating himself, Tom got into the cab and shut the door.

'Where are you going?' Arabella banged on the window. 'Why won't you talk?'

Tom didn't look at her, he just leant forward and gave Kate's address to the driver.

Hearing the name of the street, Arabella hailed her own cab and followed Tom back through the park.

Louisa was stretched over the wooden slats. She knew there was no sun, but she hadn't got the energy to collect her things and go back inside. She was smothered by the lethargy in the weather.

Hearing the engine of a taxi in the street below, she wondered if it was Tom. And then another taxi. A door slam.

'Fucking wait!'

'Arabella . . .'

'Will you stop for a second and speak to me?'

'I think your driver needs paying.'

The voices were distant but clear.

'Why are you doing this to me, Tom?'

'Darling, I'm sorry. Really I am. But I think it's best that we –'

'I don't understand what you see in her.'

'I –'

'Come back with me. Come on – just one more time. Just . . .'

The voices dropped and then rose again.

'No, Arabella. No, stop it. I won't. I can't . . .'

Louisa sat up, listening. When she'd heard enough, she collected her things, threw them back through the hatch, and leapt down. As she closed the hatch above her, she could still hear them. Tom's low voice, and Arabella's, full of edges.

When Tom came into the flat, Louisa was in the sitting room, reading yesterday's *Telegraph*. She didn't look up.

'Not sunbathing today?'

'No sun.'

Louisa turned a page of her newspaper. Fixing her eyes on the print before her, and her attention on Tom's presence, she heard him sit in the armchair by the window. There was a faint rustle followed by a click, as Tom found and lit a cigarette. And then an impossible silence.

Louisa put the paper on her lap and looked at him. She wasn't smiling and something in her expression made Tom shrink.

He stubbed out the cigarette and quickly lit another. 'Did you . . . ?'

'Yes.'

'It's not . . .'

. . . what it sounded like? His expression finished the sentence.

Louisa said nothing.

'It's not,' he insisted, and she shrugged.

'Will you tell her?'

'Will you?'

Would she? Should she? Would Kate want to know? Louisa felt the question wrench things open, diluting the strength of her disapproval.

With the cigarette still dangling from his fingers, Tom opened the window. 'Well?' he said. 'Will you?'

As he sat down, crossing his legs at the ankles, Louisa watched his feet stretch out towards her. She looked from the soles of his shoes, up the attitude of carelessness to the concentrated expression in his eyes.

'Yes,' she said at last, 'I will if you won't. I think she'd want to know the kind of man she'd be marrying. Don't you?' She looked back at his face, chalk-grey through the smoke.

'But she'll never take me . . .'

Louisa shifted her gaze five degrees and looked out of the open window, behind him. The light was hard and flat on the opposite ledges. All week, her heart had been sinking at the thought of Kate married to Tom. Now she felt it thudding.

Louisa knew that to nurture this feeling was wrong. But was it right to say nothing? She tried to think of Kate, of what she'd want, and it seemed to her that it was even more important that Kate should know about this side of Tom. So it was right to tell her. But she was finding it hard to separate her sense of duty as a friend from these other feelings. And the more she

339

tried to suffocate them, the more excitedly they forced themselves through.

'I can wait until tomorrow before telling her, if you like.'

Tom wasn't listening. 'But why,' he demanded, 'when it's all over with Arabella? Why tell her now? What good will that do anyone?'

Louisa's handbag was sitting at the foot of the sofa. She leant for it and stood up. 'Kate's my friend,' she said. 'I think she'd want to know.'

Tom agreed to confess on condition that Louisa find something else to do that night. 'I don't want you here.'

'Okay,' she said. 'I'll go to a film.'

'No. It's going to be hard enough as it is. I certainly don't want you coming back in the middle of . . .'

'You want me out of the flat all night?'

'I don't want you interrupting us.'

'But . . .'

'Can't you go to your parents' flat or something?'

Arabella asked the cab driver to drop her at the gates to the cemetery. She couldn't go home just yet – not with all those reminders.

The traffic was bad. As she sat there, slumped along the back, she noticed the driver looking at her in the rear-view mirror. Realising suddenly how raw her face must be – all the tears, and her make-up must be all over the place – Arabella felt in her bag for a pair of sunglasses.

But that wasn't why he was staring. He waited until the traffic stopped again, and turned round to get a better look. 'You're that model, aren't you?'

Arabella said nothing.

'The bra-ad model,' he chuckled. 'Well I never. Last time I saw you laid out on the back of a cab seat, love, you were wearing a bit less than you are today . . .'

'I'm surprised you remember me,' she said, without smiling. 'That was almost ten years ago.'

He laughed. 'Oh I know they're all saying you've changed, love, but don't you listen to 'em. Never forget a body, me. Never. All right, so your face's a bit more – mature, shall we say? But you've still got a great body on you. Let's face it, love, they're just jealous.'

'They?'

The driver patted his tabloid paper. 'And I'll tell you something, I bet it was a woman that wrote it. Bet you anything,' he turned in the Old Brompton Road and pulled up outside the cemetery. 'Here you are, love. That'll be six pounds forty.'

There was a newsagent's shop a couple of hundred yards back up the road. Arabella paid the cab fare and walked towards it. Inside, she picked up a copy of the tabloid her cab driver had been reading and opened it. Page five. *Graveyard for Arabella*. A large colour picture of her – although it might as well have been in black and white – lit hard from the left, drained, lined, old.

Inset, was the picture of her in the taxi, modelling the bra.

Millionaire model Arabella Dean is making a comeback. But judging from these pictures – published today in Dream Magazine *– it could be the death of her career.*

Former bra-girl Bella (35) trusted her lover, top photographer Charles Reed, to take the snaps in London's Brompton Cemetery. But time has caught up with the girl dubbed 'the body that caused a thousand traffic jams' in 1984. The pair's short-lived romance seems to be over, friends tell me.

Simon Dalziel stood on the platform at Bank underground station, waiting for the next Central Line train to take him to Holborn. He'd forgotten how irregular the trains could be when it wasn't rush-hour, and he was late for his lunch appointment.

When the next train arrived, he got on quickly and fought his way to a seat. Deliberately ignoring the large belly of a woman who got on behind him – it might just have been fat – he concentrated on the *Hello!* magazine being read by the person sitting next to him, and thought again of Tom Faulkener.

After that evening with Kate, Simon had given a lot of thought to him. Still convinced that he, Simon, was the one Kate fancied, he concluded that the only reason she was with Tom was because he was loaded. He had to be, to do nothing all day.

But if the guy was so rich, why was he living with Kate? Why didn't he have his own mansion (or whatever it was men like Tom Faulkener lived in)? And why wasn't he jetting off to exotic places? It struck Simon as odd that he just seemed to hang around Kate's flat all day. Okay, perhaps it was the model flatmate. But even so. Men like that could get all the models they wanted in places like Monaco, couldn't they?

Simon was on his way to meet Toby Williams for a

pint. Toby was one of Simon's clients, but he was also a friend. They'd been at law school together. But Toby, having qualified, decided there was more money to be had working for a bank. He'd spent a few years at one of the major city banks before moving to the Commercial Property department of Cheape & Co. Cheape's was one of London's oldest, most prestigious banks, but it was famous for exclusive, tailored, private banking – not for its commercial property department.

Simon got out at Holborn station and made his way back along High Holborn. He cut up the narrow lane which led to a pub, and pulled open the door. Raucous laughter spilled into the street as Simon went in, letting the door swing shut behind him. He looked over the heads of barristers' clerks, secretaries, court reporters, bankers – all shouting over one another – and spotted Toby at the bar. He'd put on weight and his hair looked as if it had just been cut. Scuffing the wood shavings as he pushed his way through the din, Simon reached Toby just as he was getting up to leave.

Toby gave him a long-suffering look. It wasn't the first time this had happened. 'Thought you weren't coming, mate – they stopped serving lunch ten minutes ago.'

'I'm sorry,' Simon loosened his tie. 'The tube took ages. Want another pint?'

'Just the one,' Toby eased his large behind back onto the bar stool. 'Thanks.'

Behind the bar, a girl was pulling a pint. She was skinny and strong, and her head was bent. Simon leant forward, trying to catch her eye.

'Got another job for you,' said Toby.

'Great. Who's the borrower?'

Toby named a developer Simon knew well and for some minutes they discussed the deal. He then removed an early copy of the *Evening Standard* from his briefcase and pointed to the man on the front. It was a recent picture of Lord Lincoln, dressed for Ascot. His debts had run into millions, according to the headline.

'There's another one,' he said.

Simon dragged his attention from the girl. 'One of yours?'

'His family banked with us for over two hundred years.'

Ashamed he'd never made it at his major city bank, when Simon was obviously doing so well at Fraser Cummings, Toby habitually stressed the exclusivity of Cheape's. He enjoyed telling Simon about the famous people who banked there – how he had complete access to their accounts, how most of them weren't nearly as rich as the public thought they were. Simon had never taken much interest in this, until now.

'What'll it be then?' The girl stood in front of Simon, pushing back a strand of hair.

'Pint of Best, and . . .'

'Oh, make that two,' said Toby, grinning at her, 'and a packet of cheese and onion.'

She managed a smile. With her left hand, she stretched above her for two pint glasses. With her right, she pulled a green packet of crisps from the green box wedged under the bar. She tossed it down in front of Toby and went to pull their pints.

'What happened to him?'

Toby handed him the paper and opened his crisp packet. 'Lloyds, mainly. In return for a fat cheque every quarter, men like Lincoln agreed to insure oil rigs and whatnot through Lloyds. But they had to accept unlimited liability . . .'

Simon knew all about Lloyds, but he let Toby prattle on.

'. . . which sounds crazy until you think that, while the going was good, Lincoln and his mates never had to do a stroke of work. They just raked in the cash. Then everything blew up, claims were made . . .' Toby looked at Lord Lincoln, beaming in his top hat and tails, and put another crisp into his mouth. 'Got what was coming to him, if you ask me. Arrogant sod.'

The girl brought their pints and Simon handed her a twenty pound note.

'Anything smaller?'

'Sorry.'

Waiting for his change, Simon turned to Toby. 'Has a family called Faulkener ever banked with you?'

'I can't tell you things like that.' Toby offered him a crisp.

'Of course not,' said Simon, taking one.

'. . . officially.'

Not looking at him, Simon ate the crisp and picked up his pint.

'Why d'you ask?' said Toby.

Still saying nothing, Simon drank from his pint and licked his lips.

'Faulkener, was it?'

'Mm.' Simon took his change – all in pound coins – from the barmaid, and put it in his pockets.

'How d'you spell that?'

––––––––––

Later, back at his desk, Simon swivelled his chair round and sat with his back to the desk and the room, gazing out at the building site. Then he reached for the telephone and dialled Kate's direct line. She answered immediately.

'Kate, it's Simon. I was wondering if you were free later – just a quick drink. There's something I need to talk to you about.'

'What is it?'

'It's a bit, er – sensitive – to talk about on the phone. Could you make six-thirty at the wine bar?'

'Not today, Simon. I've got mountains of work to do, and I promised Tom I . . .'

'Oh yes, Tom.' Simon clicked his stapler and took out the squashed staple. 'Well Tom's the reason I wanted to see you.'

Kate waited for Simon to go on. Simon waited to be asked.

'Well?' she said eventually. 'What about him?'

'You really can't make lunch?'

'What about him, Simon? You can tell me over the phone.'

'His surname's Faulkener, isn't it?'

'Yes.'

'F-A-U-L-K-E-N-E-R?'

'Yes. Yes, I think so.'

'Did you know about his debts?'

––––––––––

Kate got home to the smell of caramelised sugar, and to the sound of falling water from the power shower in the bathroom.

'Hello?'

Both hands occupied with briefcases, she pushed open the door to the sitting room with her shoulder. It was empty. Kate dropped her briefcases by Louisa's desk and headed for the kitchen.

'Tom?'

Tom pulled the grape brûlée from the oven and turned round. He was wearing Louisa's red apron and smiling. 'Hi.'

Kate put her arms around him and looked up into the smile. 'What's all this?'

'I'm cooking you dinner.'

Still holding him, Kate looked again at the kitchen surfaces. They were littered with Harvey Nichols wrapping, ceramic bowls of chopped vegetables, dirty knives and spoons, spilt wine and smears of oil.

'Just me?'

'Just you.'

'All this?'

'I'll be eating some too, I expect.'

'What's the occasion?'

'Just off,' said Louisa's voice, and Kate turned round.

'Look,' she said. 'All this – for me!'

'Yes,' said Louisa, briefly. 'I know.'

She was wearing an oriental dress of emerald silk, knee-length and short-sleeved, with cherry blossom embroidery and asymmetrical fastenings.

'That's new . . .' Kate broke from Tom to touch it. 'It's stunning.'

Tom picked up his grape brûlée and took it to the fridge.

'Look, Tom. Look at this colour . . .'

347

Tom opened the fridge. 'Stunning,' he said, not looking.

Later, still wearing the red apron, Tom poured out two glasses of white wine and took them to the bathroom.

Kate liked her baths very hot, and the room was full of steam. Tom, already warm from cooking, sat on the white wicker chair by the bath and began to sweat.

'Here's your wine.'

Kate – relaxed, wet, naked – sat up and took the glass. Her pink face smiled at him through the steam. 'Should I be . . .'

'No hurry.'

She lay back, her wet hair smooth over the crown of her head, and took a sip of wine. 'This is so spoiling,' she said. 'Thank you.'

'Kate . . .'

'Yes?' Kate picked up the soap and began rubbing it between her hands. Tom watched her work it into a lather. 'I've got a confession.'

Kate looked up with a sympathetic smile. 'Yes,' she said gently. 'I know.'

'You *know*?' he watched the soap run in streaks down her breasts as she rinsed it away. 'Who told you?'

'Simon – that solicitor I was drinking with the other night – he'd managed to find out all about it. Some contact of his works at Cheape's. *God* it makes me cross. I'm wondering whether I should report him to the Disciplinary Tribunal for breach of confidentiality,' Kate looked up at him and he watched her indignant expression melt. 'Darling . . .

it really couldn't matter less. To me. In some ways I prefer you poor.'

Smiling, she got to her knees in the bath. She bent forward to where he was sitting and kissed him, drenching the apron with soapy water. 'I don't care if you're millions and millions of pounds in debt, like poor Lord Lincoln. I still love you.'

Tom smiled helplessly. 'He – he told you about my *financial* situation?'

Kate pulled the plug and heaved herself out of the bath. 'Appalling isn't it?'

'Yes,' he said, passing her a towel. 'Yes it is. I can't think how I let myself . . .'

'Oh Tom.' Kate began to rub herself dry with a towel. 'I was talking about Simon – not you. I always thought there was something untrustworthy about that man.' She wrapped herself in the towel and went into the bedroom with Tom following her – wondering how he was going to bring himself to confess about Arabella now.

'Of course, there is a problem with your spending, darling,' she continued. 'You're going to have to do something about that. But I –'

'My spending?'

'I mean, you're not exactly economical at the moment, are you?'

'Most of it goes on you.'

'Well from now on, that will have to stop,' she smiled. 'I don't mind.'

'I'll spend what I like.'

'No, Tom,' she said, missing his tone as she dropped the towel and put on a dressing gown. 'No you can't – unless you get a job.'

349

'I am getting a job.'

Kate did up the cord, tied it into a bow, and said nothing.

'I *am* getting a job. I've been trying bloody hard for months to get a job. You have no idea how difficult it is – breezing along with your high-flying career . . .'

'Breezing along? It's hard work – not something you seem to know much about.'

Downstairs, his mobile was ringing.

'Is that your . . .?'

'They can leave a message,' he said, sitting heavily on the bed.

She waited until the ringing stopped, and then continued, 'Tom, listen. I'm not getting at you about finding a job. I'm not. I'm just saying that, until you do, you'll have to watch what you spend.'

'You think I don't know that?'

'Well, you . . . I . . . well, yes. I mean – you've been spending money you don't have, you've obviously been doing it for months, and I'm sorry but I don't think you have thought it through. Don't look at me like that, I'm trying to help you. I don't mind about you not being rich. Really I don't. And I can look after you until you're on your feet, so you mustn't worry. But in the meantime you've got to stop shopping at places like Harvey Nichols. You've got to stop eating out the whole time. You've got to . . .'

'Oh for God's *sake*. Stop nagging. You sound like –'

'I'm not nagging,' she said. 'I'm telling you – it's very hard to pay off debts. Believe me. It took something like five years for me to pay off the bank loan I needed to get through university and law

350

school. And I was really careful. You're not. You're exactly like Louisa – both addicted to spending.'

On the table in the hall, his mobile rang again.

'Your –'

'Whoever it is can bloody well wait.'

Kate sighed. 'Can't you understand what I'm saying?'

Tom looked away. 'Please,' his voice was cold. 'Please – don't – patronise me. Of course I understand. Don't you think I know – better than you – what I've got to do?'

'So why don't you do it? You must see that if you go on spending the way you do, you'll run up debts that you'll never be able to pay off.'

His laugh was empty. 'You think I'm never going to get a job. Is that it?'

'I didn't say that, Tom.'

'Yes you did. You said I'd never be able to pay off my debts.'

'What I meant was that, unless you get a job, you'll run up debts, and that's why you need . . .'

'What I need – what I *need* – is a girlfriend who trusts me – not some Miss Perfect. If you're going to start nagging and criticising and getting at me, then . . .'

Kate sat at the dressing table and rubbed moisturiser into her cheeks. Tom watched her. The skin was completely clear. The cheeks were still pink from the bath and her hair hung back over her shoulders, squeaky clean. '. . . then what?'

He wanted to kick at her complacency. Infuriated by the absolute confidence Kate had in herself, infuriated by the patronising concern she expressed for him, Tom wanted to pour his drink all over her hair. He stood up so that he could at least speak down to her.

'Then perhaps I should find someone else – someone a little less demanding than you – someone who *can* take me as I am.' He made for the door.

Kate stopped rubbing the moisturiser. 'Someone like Louisa?' she said to his back.

He turned. 'Why not? At least Louisa wouldn't nag at me.'

Kate simply stared. But before she could speak, there was a knock at the door to the flat.

'Leave it,' he snapped.

The knocking went on.

'I'd better go,' said Kate.

It was Mrs Banks from the flat below. 'Hello, love. Sorry to bother you, but I thought I should let you know I'm going away for a month. To see my daughter. You know. The one in Yorkshire. She's about to have her first baby . . .'

Mrs Banks beamed, and Kate said, 'That's nice.'

'Isn't it? Of course it'd be better if the father did the decent thing and married her. But we can't expect miracles these days, can we, love . . .'

'So you wanted us to keep an eye on the flat?'

'Would you?'

'Of course we will,' Kate smiled. 'Good night.'

Mrs Banks stopped the door. 'Sorry, love. There was just one other thing. My post. I was wondering if you'd do us a favour and forward it? Not that it'll be much, I expect. Nasty bills and so on,' she laughed. 'But as I'll be gone for a month, I suppose I'd better deal with that, too. Would you mind?'

'Not at all.'

Mrs Banks didn't have any pen and paper, so Kate invited her up.

'Oh,' said Mrs Banks when she got to the top, breathing heavily, leaning on the banisters and looking through the double doors into the drawing room where Tom, unsmiling, sat at the table. 'It is nice up here, isn't it?'

Kate introduced them, and Mrs Banks shook Tom's hand.

'I'm so sorry, interrupting your supper . . .'

'That's okay.'

Tom sat down again. As Kate found her a pen and pulled an old envelope from the bin by the desk, Mrs Banks hovered by the table, unsure whether to sit down too. She could see the table was laid for two, and she could smell lamb and rosemary cooking in the kitchen. She smiled at Tom.

'It is good to see a man cooking,' she said, indicating the red apron. 'My late husband couldn't boil an egg.'

Kate handed her the pen and paper.

'Thank you, love.'

'Do sit down.'

'Now. My daughter's name's Sandy. Sandy Banks,' she started writing. 'And her address is . . .'

As Mrs Banks dictated to herself, Tom picked up his mobile. He took it into the hall and shut the door. Checking to see who'd rung, he stared for a second at 'ARABELLA' on the display panel – and then he slowly pressed redial.

Mrs Banks was giving Kate Sandy's boyfriend's telephone number when he came back in, still holding the mobile and trying to undo the apron knot at the back at the same time. Something about the way he was moving, the urgent way he was tugging at the apron, made them both look up.

'What is it?'

'I'm off.'

'Now?'

'Yes, I . . . blast.'

He let Kate tackle the knot, and stood facing Mrs Banks. She was looking at him with interest. 'Oh dear. I hope it's nothing serious.'

Kate undid it. She followed him into the hall and stood there, watching him search for his keys and his wallet, and tuck in his shirt.

'*Tom*,' she said in quiet fury. 'Don't just *leave*. We have to . . .'

He looked at her for a second, and then turned and ran down the stairs.

Returning to Mrs Banks, Kate heard the door slam hard, and then distant fading steps as he ran down to the street.

* * *

The alarm was going. Kate sat up in bed and switched it off. Uneasy, but for a second not knowing why, she felt for the light. Slowly, she got out of bed and walked out of her room towards Louisa's. The light was on in there. She knocked and went in. No Louisa.

She tried Tom's mobile, but it was switched off.

So was Louisa's.

Her mind stumbling in the attempt to find some ordinary explanation, crashing into memories of glimpsed moments that seemed to point in only one direction, Kate walked to the kitchen and stood in the doorway, staring at the scene. Tom had left the window open and stupid over-priced wrappings whispered and rustled in the morning air. There were smears of cold-pressed extra-virgin olive oil from some aristocratic Tuscan estate, and an extravagant sprinkling of sea-salt where Tom's careless hand had missed a pan and scattered the crystals all over the hob. And there was all the washing up still waiting in the sink. It looked wrong in the morning light, but Kate turned her back. The others could do it, whenever it was they decided to return.

It was the day she'd allocated for Janet's appraisal. The appraisal had been postponed twice now, and Janet was losing patience. Heather had had her appraisal with Michael over a month ago. Michael, as usual, had told her she was wonderful, had taken her out to lunch and even – Janet suspected – upped Heather's pay. Janet knew she was a much better secretary than Heather. She had seven years more experience, and it always irritated her that Heather was Michael's secretary while she, Janet, was only Kate's.

Janet wanted to be told she was the most efficient secretary Kate had ever had, and she wanted to see it in writing. She didn't care much about the lunch – five minutes out of the office and they'd probably have nothing to say to each other – but she wanted her pay increased by whatever percentage Heather's had been, and she wanted it now.

Kate was hurriedly completing a clean form and trying not to think about Tom as Janet knocked on the door. She was looking very smart, and she'd put her form in a special plastic folder.

'I'll be five minutes.'

'Don't forget you've got that meeting at eleven.'

Kate looked at her watch. It was nine-thirty. How long did Janet think her appraisal was going to last? 'Yes,' she said. 'I know. Five minutes – all right?'

Janet shut the door.

Kate finished the form. She wrote 'Excellent' in the summing-up section – where half a page had been left for extra comments – and hoped Janet would buy it. She was about to ask Janet to come back in, when she saw the form that Tom had filled out that night at the Caprice – lying face up on her desk.

Wondering if personal distractions were making her into too much of a liability – if it wouldn't be the responsible thing for her just to go home – Kate rushed the offending form to the shredder. She watched the ribbons of paper fall into the bin – scattered fragments of Tom's handwriting falling in strips across themselves – and felt that she was shredding him, too. Not passionate tearing. Just thirty seconds of calm, monotone buzzing to achieve comprehensive destruction. But her mind was crackling. She wasn't calm. Beneath that hard expression, she was burning.

Maybe there was an explanation. They wouldn't be that – that *obvious*, would they? Unless – oh God – unless he was angry with her for getting at his spending, for telling him what to do . . . and what was it he'd said about Louisa? Something about not trying to change him, taking him as he is?

'Kate?' Adam was there beside her. 'Janet's waiting.'

Forcing out images of Tom and Louisa, Kate returned to her desk. She asked Adam to leave her and Janet, and to shut the door behind him. Then she smiled at Janet. 'So . . .'

'Well, here's my bit,' Janet put her plastic folder on the desk.

'And here's mine.'

Kate took Janet's self-assessment form out of its folder and laid both forms side-by-side. At a glance, they could see from the ticks in the boxes that Kate's view of Janet and Janet's view of herself differed by one, if not two levels. Wherever Kate had given Janet "Fair", Janet had given herself "Excellent". Janet grabbed the form Kate had completed and looked hard at the rest of it.

'Janet —'

'Hang on.'

'It's not as bad as —'

'Just hang on, will you? . . . I don't get it,' she said at last, looking at Kate with a face that was genuinely confused. 'I don't see why you've gone and done *Fair, Fair, Adequate* in all these boxes. And then you write that,' pointing at the 'Excellent' at the end, Janet thrust the form back into Kate's hands.

Kate put the form down. 'Because I think you *are* excellent,' she said. 'You combine all these qualities – technical skills, telephone manner, organisation and so on. You're better than average at almost all of them. That's rare – and it's what makes you so good. I don't want someone who's charming on the telephone but who hasn't got a clue about filing – or vice versa . . . I'm sorry—' she broke off to answer her telephone.

'Yes?'

'Sweetheart. It's me.'

She said nothing.

'Kate?'

'I'll call you back,' she put down the receiver.

357

'Where was I?' she looked down at the forms. They swam in front of her for a second.

'You were saying that I was excellent – generally.'

'That's right.'

'But not for any of these areas?'

'No, Janet. No. Don't you see . . .?'

'All I know is that Heather gets straight "Excellents", and I get this.'

'Heather?'

'I work ten times as hard as Heather does. I'm more efficient, more experienced, more – everything. It's not fair.'

Kate sighed. She looked from the form she'd completed to Janet's self-assessment form, and then across at Janet's round indignant face. Compared to Heather, Kate could see that Janet was "Excellent". It wasn't fair. But she couldn't tell Michael to redo his appraisal of Heather. She was going to have to stand down.

'It's not fair,' Janet said again.

'All right. All right. I see what you're saying. Give me another day and I'll do your form again.'

Later, with the office to herself, Kate sat staring at the revised form she'd half-started, and thought about Tom. He'd be waiting for her to call but Kate wasn't sure she could bear to hear it. The defeated tone in his voice had made her more, not less, worried. What was he going to tell her? What possible explanation was there – other than that he and Louisa . . .

When the telephone rang, she thought it would be him again, but it wasn't. It was Simon.

'Kate? I'm sorry you didn't like what I said yesterday, but you must see I was trying to do you a favour.'

'A favour?'

'The guy's a fraud. He's thousands and thousands of pounds in debt. Surely, you . . .'

'What do you take me for? I don't care how poor Tom is. That's not the problem.'

Simon was quick. 'What *is* the problem?'

'There isn't a problem.'

'Yes, there is.'

'No, Simon. There's not.'

'Is it the model? Larissa? Lucinda? . . . If he lies to you about money, what's to stop him lying about women? I don't know how you begin to trust a man like that.'

'More than I'd trust a man like you,' she yelled and put down the receiver.

She looked at it for a second, and then went to the loo. Her reflection was marble in the mirror over the sink: the skin on her lips almost the same colour as the rest, and cold. Her hands shook as she pushed back her hair. They were clean, but she held them in warm water, and felt comforted.

He's wrong, she thought, tugging at a paper towel from the chrome holder by the Tampax machine, and wiping her hands with it. He's wrong.

But the idea of Tom and Louisa alone in the flat tormented her. She couldn't work. After lunch, she decided to go home – to go and see for herself.

<hr>

It was almost three o'clock. Full of quiet warmth absorbed from the height of the day, the street now dozed in a gentler light. With doorkeys at her fingers, Kate hurried past Louisa's car, parked badly on the corner, and up the steps to the door of their building.

359

From an upper window, the waves of Capital Radio were being converted into sound and dispersed back into the afternoon.

Kate unlocked the door. Then she walked upstairs, past the large window overlooking the gardens at the back, past the first-floor flat, then the second floor, up, up to her own: the music getting louder with each step.

'Tom?'

'No,' said Kate, pushing open the door. 'It's me.'

Louisa was in the sitting room, wearing a black bikini and eating pasta while she waited for the varnish on her toenails to dry. She looked up in surprise.

'Kate . . . ?'

Kate switched off the radio. 'Where is he?'

'Haven't seen him all morning . . . what's wrong?'

Kate was staring at her, noticing how lovely she was.

'Oh dear,' said Louisa, putting down the pasta bowl with a sigh. 'He told you. Jesus, I'm sorry. I really am.'

'You're sorry?' Kate laughed and turned her back. She stood at the window, looking out at the irregular shapes of the gardens.

So it was true. All that happiness was gone. Worse than gone – it had depended on things that didn't exist. There had never been a best friend. There was no perfect boyfriend. Just a conspiracy.

She wondered at the gardens – they looked exactly the same as they'd been looking all summer, as if nothing had happened. That door still banged. The cat still crept along the wall and slept in the sun on the flat shed roof. Easy breezes from the open window still brushed across her skin – still warm, still kind.

But all of it was false. From behind the shapes and

light came a kind of darkness Kate had not known existed.

'You think – you think that saying sorry will make it okay?'

'What else can I say?'

'You say it like you'd say sorry for forgetting to empty the bins.'

I . . .'

Kate turned back. Louisa was testing the varnish, delicately tapping her toes with her fingers.

'You don't have the faintest fucking idea you've done anything wrong, do you?'

'But I haven't done anything wrong. Tom's the one you should be . . . ?'

Kate was starting to feel sick – but there was too much for her to say. 'Oh God!' she spat. 'How could you? What kind of woman are you? I thought your behaviour with Richard was bad. But this – *this* – this is a different league.'

Biting her lower lip, Louisa took the pasta bowl into the kitchen. 'I don't quite see what Richard's got to do with it,' she said, filling the kettle with water. 'I was trying to help. I thought you'd rather Tom told you himself, than that you heard about it from me. Of course, it's awful for you,' she took the kettle back to its base and switched it on. '. . . but it's completely unfair to take it out on me.'

Kate followed her into the kitchen. 'You . . . How dare you tell me what's fair and not fair – when you're the one fucking her best friend's boyfriend?'

'What?'

'Or was it *making love*? Somehow, I doubt it, if it was anything like the racket you made with Richard

361

– why can't you keep away from other women's men? – and don't think that crying'll make me feel sorry for you,' she yelled, as Louisa pushed past, back into the sitting room – where Tom was standing, dressed in the clothes he'd been wearing the night before. They hadn't heard him come in.

Louisa went up to him. 'Tell her. Tell her it wasn't me.'

Tom stared beyond her, at Kate, and then shut his eyes.

'Go on,' Louisa urged. 'Tell her about that woman – whoever she was – shrieking at you in the street.'

'You don't understand,' he spoke indistinctly. 'There's . . .'

'What I understand is that you had all last night to tell her about your sordid affair, and it's clear you haven't said a word.'

Tom opened his eyes with an effort. 'It wasn't sordid . . .'

The fragment of hope that lay in Kate's mind – that there had been some misunderstanding and that, in spite of everything, her world was as before – disintegrated with his words. It may not have been with Louisa, but one thing Kate now knew for sure was that Tom had not been faithful.

But instead of an emotional response – instead of the natural feelings of betrayal, anger and loss – this limited but certain knowledge caused in Kate a kind of overload-impact, a system crash that pushed her into shutdown. Everything went very quiet in her head. She felt nothing beyond a cold, fixed, all-consuming desire for the truth.

'Where've you been?'

'I've been at the hospital.'

'The hospital?'

'Arabella took an overdose last night.'

Kate and Louisa looked at one another.

'Is . . .'

'Is she okay?' said Louisa.

'No,' said Tom, staring at the carpet. 'She's dead.'

Sixteen

In August, the beaches on the Waveney stretch of coastline were dotted with holidaymakers. They'd park their cars along the sides of the road and trample over the dunes with picnic baskets and plastic bags, dragging their wind shields, deck chairs and spades.

Douglas was standing at a window in the dining room, looking out. 'I just wish they'd take their rubbish away with them,' he said.

'What about those industrial bins,' said Jane from the table, 'the ones you installed last year.'

'They're never used.'

'I used one the other day,' Sarah Knowles poured some milk into her cup of coffee and took it from the sideboard to the place next to Jane. Stretching forward, she helped herself to butter and marmalade and began spreading it onto her toast. 'I put my can of Diet Coke into the one at the far end of the bay.'

Douglas turned from the view and came to the table. 'Where are the papers?'

'Here,' Sarah, her mouth full, pointed to the pile on the chair to her left. 'Can I keep the *Mail*?'

Douglas extracted the *Mail* and handed it to her.

'Of course you can,' he said. 'No-one else reads it.'

'No-one else admits to reading it,' said Jane, winking at Sarah. Sarah grinned back. She finished her toast, wiped her buttery fingers on a napkin and opened the paper.

Douglas extracted the main section of *The Times* from the pile on the chair with uncharacteristic impatience. He didn't like her getting on so well with his mother. There was something irritating about them ganging up against him like this. He was about to leave the room when an exclamation from Sarah made him stop.

'My God . . .'

'What is it?' Jane asked. 'Someone you know?'

'Did you know about Arabella? Arabella Faulkener?'

Douglas came over. 'What's she done now?'

Sarah gave the paper to Jane, who read the article with Douglas leaning over her shoulder.

Two pages had been given to the story of Arabella's death. There were lots of photographs of Arabella, including the recent ones from the Brompton Cemetery shoot. The article concentrated mainly on Arabella's life and how she'd been betrayed by ex-boyfriend, Charles Reed. Tom was mentioned only as a former husband. An inquest on Friday had confirmed that it was suicide. The funeral would be held on Monday.

'Will you go?' said his mother.

Douglas considered it for a second. There was so much he'd disliked about Arabella. On the other hand, perhaps it was right to bury that dislike along with her body – pay his respects, and remember what

365

was good. He thought of the funeral – Tom would be there, for sure, and so would Kate. But then he remembered the way Kate had looked at him that day on the underground, and shook his head.

'No, I won't,' he said and, picking up *The Times*, quickly left the room.

Sarah drank some more coffee – she swallowed it with difficulty. It was lukewarm, and the brown bitterness washed over her tongue. Holding the cup in both hands, she looked out through the imperfect glass of the dining-room windows. Far off, too far to hear its engine, another car – a red estate – was moving very slowly down the narrow beach road. It found a place to park, and backed in. The doors opened and a couple of children burst out. Another child, smaller than the others, was let out of the boot. She watched them running over the skyline.

'Obviously all of us would rather lose a few pounds – a few stone in my case – and we'd all like a perfect complexion. But if I looked like Arabella, I'd be wanting to show myself off, not kill myself.'

Douglas reached the gates at the end of the drive. He slowed the car down and shifted gear. 'I think her situation was a bit different,' he said, turning out. 'You know. It's – relative, isn't it?'

Sarah sighed inwardly at what Douglas had, unconsciously, implied and looked out over the fields. The sun hadn't yet risen and pockets of mist lay faint in the hollows round the river. But the landscape was rosily expectant.

She didn't want to be going to Italy. She could sense unspoken problems, and wanted to air them.

366

She wanted to understand why it was that however hard she tried – however good she was with his parents and so on – Douglas seemed to get more irritated rather than less so. She'd lain awake last night – in the room she'd shared with Kate the first time she'd come to Waveney – wondering why he wasn't visiting her. It was her last night in England for three weeks. He said it was because his parents were there, but Sarah couldn't help thinking that Jane and Henry wouldn't have minded. Anyway, they were at the other end of the house.

She began to wonder if it had something to do with her.

They drove in silence until they reached the motorway, when Douglas put on the radio. The deep pink light of the sun crept into the car and lay across the windscreen, showing up the smudges of George's nose-marks, and still they didn't speak. They listened to the shipping forecast, and then to the news.

When Douglas stopped at a petrol station, Sarah decided to say something. She switched off the radio and waited for him to come back from the kiosk, trying to think of how to put it without sounding desperate. He walked across the tarmac, blond hair lit pink. Sarah noticed the shadow of his body crinkle for a second as it moved over the petrol pumps and then flatten again as he approached. He carried two paper cups of coffee and gave them both to her through the window before coming round to his side of the car and getting in.

She gave him back his cup.

'Thanks.' Douglas took a tentative sip but it was too hot. He looked at his watch. 'What time's the flight?'

'Eleven,' she said, watching him. 'We should be fine.'

'I was wondering . . .' he began.

'Yes?'

He attempted a second sip. 'Would you mind if I dropped you? Rather than coming in. It's just a nightmare parking, and I do have a lot to do in London . . .'

Sarah said nothing.

'Of course, I don't have to if you need a hand with your things, but I—' he broke off as she turned away from him and looked out of the window, 'Sarah?'

In the wing mirror, she could see a man in a boiler suit, winding up a hose in great rubber loops.

'Is there anything wrong?'

'It's not working,' she said, watching the end of the hose jerk away across the tarmac. 'You're not in love with me. I mean, you like me, but you're not . . .'

She turned back and, for a second, they looked at one another. Douglas tried to feel some sort of loss. Instead, all he felt was relief that she was the one who'd brought it up, and Sarah read it in his face.

'It doesn't matter,' she said quickly. 'I mean, I do understand. And it's quite all right. Really. I'll be fine. And so much better that it happens now than . . . I don't know. Whenever. It's fine. Really.'

'Are you sure?' With his free hand, Douglas took hers and pressed it.

'Yes. Yes, of course I am. And it's not as if we were going to get . . .'

'No,' he agreed.

Swallowing away the lump in her throat, Sarah watched him throw the remains of his coffee onto the

368

tarmac, and stuff the paper mug between the dash-board and the windscreen.

'You'll really be all right?'

'Oh Douglas,' she managed a laugh, 'don't flatter yourself. I'll be *fine.*'

He smiled automatically and felt for his keys beneath the steering wheel.

'Really, I'll be fine. I'm going to Italy, for God's sake. And they say it's lovely at this time of year – not quite so hot. It'll hardly feel like work. The only thing I'm worried about is shopping in the market – I must remember to buy a proper phrase book at the air-port. Remind me, will you?'

When they arrived at the airport, Douglas left the car on a yellow line and helped her find a trolley. He loaded on all her bags, and wheeled it in. He found the right check-in desk, queued with her, and bought her a phrase book. He knew it wouldn't make either of them feel any better, and it didn't.

Discovering he'd escaped a parking ticket actively made it worse. He shouldn't have got off so easily, and lack of reprimand – any reprimand, however disconnected – only increased his discomfort.

Although it was now September, the day of Arabella's funeral was if anything even hotter than the day of her death. The light was brighter, more intense, but it had yet to penetrate the sepulchral spaces of the church. It made weak patterns across the stonework on the upper walls, but left the main body of the interior very dim – lit by occasional low-watt lamps, or left in darkness.

Kate and Tom were sitting at the back. Although

he was still living in her flat, they'd hardly spoken since that afternoon. And now they sat side by side like strangers on a bus, watching the others arrive. Preoccupied with her own state of ignorance, Kate found it hard to concentrate on Arabella.

All she knew was that Arabella had taken an overdose. Taken her life. Committed suicide. Topped herself . . . There was no nice way of saying it. And that Tom was involved. But how involved?

Kate thought back to when, after telling them that Arabella was dead, Tom had left the flat – and she'd followed without thinking.

'Tom!' she'd called as she ran.

'Leave me alone.'

'Tom – just tell me – what affair? What did Louisa mean?'

'I don't know what Louisa meant,' he'd stopped his striding and looked at her. He'd been close to tears and, looking back at him, Kate had felt the anger seep away.

'All I know,' his voice had stumbled and recovered, '. . . is that someone I once loved very much, loved enough to marry, has just died. I – I have to be by myself. Please . . .'

She couldn't force it from him. She didn't have the heart. And thinking that, anyway, she'd be able to ask Louisa when she got back to the flat, Kate had done as Tom asked – only to discover that Louisa had gone. Gone – with a scrawled note to Kate that said how betrayed Louisa had felt at what Kate had said, at Kate's total lack of trust. She wasn't sure that she and Kate would be able to live together after this. She'd be in touch.

Kate had waited for Tom to come back. She'd waited the whole weekend and then she'd had a call from the police. They'd got Tom at the station. No, he wasn't in any trouble, but he was obviously quite distressed – had someone close to him died recently?

'Yes,' Kate had said. 'His ex-wife.'

'Oh. Well, love, we could arrange for him to spend the night at hospital – but perhaps it would be better, now we've reached you, if you just took him home . . . ?'

'Yes, of course,' she'd said. 'I'll come now.'

So she'd picked him up and driven him home. He'd sat in the passenger seat of her car – ghost-grey, smelling of urine, unable to look her in the eye.

'It's okay,' she'd found herself telling him. 'You don't have to say anything. You can have a bath, and go to bed in Louisa's room. I'll bring you a cup of tea if you like, and something to eat. The funeral's at midday tomorrow – but you don't have to go if you . . .'

'I'll go,' he'd said.

'We'll both go – and then, if you're up to it, we'll talk.'

And so she sat there, out of touch with the mood of the church, outside Tom's despair, consumed by an inappropriate desire for information. Kate looked at his hands, clasped to a copy of the Order of Service. She'd guessed that, if it wasn't Louisa, then he must have been having some sort of affair with Arabella, but she couldn't be sure. Perhaps Louisa had been mistaken. Perhaps it hadn't even been an affair. And even if she was right about Arabella, Kate still didn't know how much Tom was really to blame. Nothing was certain any more.

Only Tom could tell her – and it wasn't something she knew how to ask. Not now, after everything that had happened. She felt that to put it to him directly would have been violently insensitive. It would be thrusting her suddenly petty fears about infidelity right into the heart of his bereavement.

Then from behind, coming through the doors, she heard someone saying, 'It's the pew at the front, I think. On the right . . .'

Turning her head, she saw the figure of a tall, thin man dressed in an ill-fitting plain black suit. He was helping a woman in grey up the aisle. The woman wasn't old – she was younger than the man. She was in no physical difficulty. But the expression in her face was so completely lacking in direction, it was as if she was blind.

Kate turned quickly back, conscious again of a kind of intrusion. As they passed her, making their way up the aisle, she concentrated instead on a pregnant woman in the row in front of them.

'Are they the parents?'

The husband leant closer to her. 'I can't hear you.'

The woman did not raise her voice. She spoke instead at half-speed. 'That couple – the woman just sitting down – are they Arabella's parents?'

'Yes – yes I think so, darling. Can't see properly from here.'

Tom was staring forward at the altar, completely still, except for the movement of his fingers over the white card in his hands. Kate looked from his fingers to what had to be Arabella's father. He was coming back up the aisle. As he got closer, it was clear from his expression that he was coming to speak to them.

His steps slowed, and he stopped next to Tom, at the end of their pew.

'Hello, Tom,' he said, bending forward and speaking very quietly. 'I was wondering, would you come outside for a second?'

'Of course . . .'

The three of them moved out of a door at the right, back into the hard light of the street. Arabella's father scratched the back of his neck and blinked in the glare. He looked older in the sunlight. They could see the red-sore rims of his eyes and rough patches on his skin.

'I'm so sorry,' he said at last. 'It's Hilary. She . . .' Tom and Kate waited for him to collect himself. 'I think she'd prefer it if you – you and –'

'She'd rather we weren't here?'

William Dean liked Tom – what little he knew of him. He'd been genuinely sad when the marriage hadn't worked, and this was proving more difficult than he'd realised. He put a hand on Tom's shoulder.

'We're not holding you responsible. Really, we're not. It was that article – and Charles Reed's appalling photographs. But it's just – you know – the will and everything.'

'Her will?'

'And of course there's all that stuff she wrote in her note about you and . . .' He glanced at Kate. 'And . . .'

Kate looked from him to Tom, and then back again. The darkness that, ever since the afternoon at her flat, she'd been trying so hard to ignore fell over her once more.

'She loved you,' he was saying to Tom. 'Maybe it's

not your fault. I mean, she does,' shaking his head, he corrected himself, 'she did – have an overactive imagination. I mean, an affair's an affair, right? But with an ex-wife? Of course, I don't know what really happened – and perhaps you thought it meant as little to her as it did to you. But Bella's what I call a romantic. She might seem tough, but she's not – she wasn't. I think she really thought that it – you know – it – it meant you were getting back together. I don't think she understood that you were only . . . frankly, Tom, none of us understand it. Least of all Hilary. Which is why she – why we'd prefer it if you – if you . . .'

Kate was running. Running the full length of the street in her black heels and her black court suit. She was sweating by the corner. Cars and buses sped past her in both directions. Running up the pavement, in search of a cab, conscious of shouts and steps behind her.

'Taxi!'

The door handle was stiff, and she had to battle with it.

'Give it a good pull, love.'

Kate pulled, and jumped in, followed by Tom.

'Fuck off.'

Tom was inside. He shut the door. 'I didn't know about the money.'

'What money?'

'Arabella's will. I didn't . . .'

'Jesus, Tom. I don't give a flying fuck about money. Bayswater,' she said to the driver, who nodded, executed a U-turn and headed north.

Tom closed off the glass between them and the

driver. 'Will you listen to me?'

With her right hand, Kate held tightly to the knuckle at the end of the middle finger on her left and watched it go white as Tom tried to explain.

'She wouldn't leave me alone.'

'Oh, poor you.'

'I'm not saying I wasn't wrong. But I did end it with her, sweetheart. I ended it because I realised I . . . I was never in love with her. It was just . . . I chose *you*.'

He looked at her profile: still, against the blur of shop fronts beyond.

'Listen to me, Kate. I wanted to marry you. I still do. And that's why she . . .'

'Your affair with her meant nothing?'

'Nothing,' he took her hands. 'You're the one I . . .'

But Kate leant forward and opened the glass partition. 'Can you stop?'

The cab pulled in at the side of the road.

'Get out.'

'But . . .'

She leant across him and opened the door on his side. 'Go on. Get out. I wouldn't marry you if you were the last person alive. Your last wife preferred to die, rather than live without you – and it meant nothing?'

Tom stumbled into the gutter.

'How could you think you'd be welcome at her funeral?'

'I was talking about the affair, Kate. Not her . . .'

But she'd pulled shut the door.

'. . . not her death,' he murmured, watching the taxi pull out.

Back at the flat, it was quiet – there was no sign of Louisa. And Kate, her face covered in tears, was glad of the space. She sat at the table they'd used for dinner parties and scooped Tom's pack of cigarettes towards her, half expecting it to be empty, and it was. Screwing it up in the palm of her hand, she tossed it in the direction of the bin and missed. The packet landed on Tom's overcoat, hanging over the back of the sofa.

Kate got up from the chair. She put the packet in the bin, and picked up the coat. It smelt of Tom, and Kate's reaction was a confused mixture of attraction and repulsion.

It's over.

And then again, out loud, 'It's over.'

Dropping the coat in the middle of the floor, she set about amassing a pile of his things. His CDs, his books, his shoes, his toothbrush – all in the same pile. She threw open his side of her cupboard, hauled out the pressed shirts, suits, coats . . . and dumped them, still attached to their hangers, on top of the rest.

The pile was high when he rang. He was in a bar.

'Kate . . .'

'I'm packing your stuff. Can you collect it tomorrow?'

Tom paused and then said, 'Yes, of course.'

'About eight in the evening would be best. I'll have some boxes by then.'

'Okay. I was hop—'

She hung up.

———◆◆◆———

Kate was in early the day following Arabella's funeral.

She'd not been in since the day Arabella had died

and, with the exception of calling to check that the Forms 395 had been dispatched, and Adam was getting on with the Project Galaxy summary, she'd done nothing for days.

With a paper-cup espresso in one hand, and her briefcase in the other, she struggled to find her security pass. The man at the desk waved her on.

'Don't worry, love . . .'

Walking past the cool greys and blues, the glass walls and the thin metal of the filing cabinets that made up the offices and secretarial stations in her department, all empty at this time of day, Kate felt calm again. Somehow, the very lack of character she'd once disliked was what now made it attractive.

At nine o'clock exactly, her mother rang. She'd been away, visiting Kate's brother and his family in Hong Kong, and had only discovered about Arabella's suicide from references to it in the newspapers on the aeroplane home. She wanted to talk about it to Kate. How well had she known her? Was Tom all right?

Kate was silent.

Was Tom all right? No. Probably not. But then, she didn't care any more, did she? Because it was finished, and the last four months had been a sham. She thought of Tom – not all right, somewhere, alone – and began to feel the weight of what had happened.

In the end she just said, 'That's over,' and hoped her mother would understand.

'You've split up?'

'Yes.'

'Oh darling.'

'Adam, would you . . .?'

Adam picked up his drafting papers and left the room, closing the door with a quiet click.

'Was he . . .?'

'He was having an affair with her.'

'Oh God,' Elizabeth shut her eyes. 'I wish I'd been wrong, darling. Really I do.'

It took Kate a second to realise what her mother meant. 'No,' she said. 'It wasn't Louisa. It was . . .'

Elizabeth waited, and said nothing.

'. . . I feel such an idiot. Why didn't I see? And why do I always find myself being treated like a—'

'You trust people.'

'I trust the wrong fucking people. I trust men. I let them mess me around like this was some sort of game, and—'

'Not all men are like that.'

'Yes they bloody well are,' Kate shouted, tears pouring down her face. Looking up as someone came in, she found she couldn't see who it was and bent her head. The door closed again.

'Was it someone you knew?'

Kate pulled a tissue from the box beyond her computer, 'It was his ex-wife, Mum. It was Arabella.'

There was a pause as Elizabeth digested this.

'I don't think you should be at work.'

'It's better than being at home.'

'Would it help if I was with you?'

Kate had some trouble convincing her mother that she was fine. She had to lie about Louisa leaving, but she really didn't want Elizabeth watching her through all this. Worrying about her mother worrying would only add to the stress. It was better she stayed in Norfolk – Kate would come and see her, instead. Some weekend soon.

The second she put down the receiver, the telephone rang again. It was Janet.

'Henry Hazel rang,' she said, cautiously. 'He said it was important – something about today's meeting. I said you'd call him back this morning. Will that be okay?'

'I'll call him now.'

'Are you okay? Can I get you anything?'

'I'm fine.'

Henry was calling to say that his trip to Dubai had been extended. Could they have the meeting on Friday instead?

'That's fine with me.'

'I've spoken to Ross, and he's happy to come then. It's just Dalziel.'

'I'll sort it out.'

Louisa had gone home to her parents. That day at the flat – the day Kate had accused her of having an affair with Tom – she'd packed two suitcases, thrown them into the boot of her car, and headed home.

Louisa's parents had two houses in England but were forced for tax reasons to spend most of the year abroad. Although they had the house in London, they preferred to spend what time they could in Dorset, and it was to Dorset Louisa went. After three hours on the motorway, she was driving her car under the stone arch of the gatehouse entrance and up the long straight drive.

In the mid-eighties, Louisa's father had sold his electrical company and made thirty million pounds. With it, he'd been able to buy and retire to Falcombe

Abbey. It had been a school before he'd bought it and, although a lot of time and money had been spent making it into a private house again, Louisa didn't like it. In an attempt to rid it of its institutional air, her mother Mary had gone overboard on the upholstery. Wall to wall carpets covered the floors. Eighties-style pelmets and festoon blinds blocked the already-small Elizabethan windows, making the rooms even darker. To compensate, she'd had the whole place rewired with bright, obvious lighting and the result was that Falcombe Abbey now looked and felt like a hotel.

With the exception of its park, Falcombe had no land. Nigel Edwardes wasn't interested in farming. He realised too late that the only thing he was really interested in was his electrical company. And while everybody envied him his smart move, selling before the crash, Nigel was bored. He couldn't go to the City. He couldn't even stay in the country for more than three months of the year. He'd fork out vast sums of money taking Mary to exotic parts of the world only to spend his time searching – often with poor results – for the English broadsheets.

Louisa arrived just before seven to find the hall full of luggage. Evening sunlight lay in a pattern of bright blue squares on a child's pair of flippers by the door. Those flippers, and her mother's straw sunhat sitting on one of the chairs to the left, reminded Louisa that her parents were going to Italy and that her brother Alex and his children, Tim and Polly, were going too. Judging from the luggage, they were leaving tomorrow.

Voices were coming from the mock-Victorian

conservatory her parents had added some years earlier. She could hear Alex laughing, and her mother talking in a ridiculous voice that told her his children were still up.

'Time for beddy-byes.'

This was followed by a series of violent screams.

'Give it back, Timothy.'

'Won't.'

'Timothy . . .'

'Do as she says, Timbo.'

Alex and Nigel sat at the table with a bottle of rosé between them, looking out. The glass doors had been opened to their widest and, there on the lawn, Tim was handing his grandmother a doll.

'Thank you, Timothy.'

Tim watched her take the doll, twist the head back round and give it to Polly – who ran with it clutched to her chest back into the conservatory, fell at the feet of her father, and burst into tears. Alex bent to pick her up.

'There, darling. Come on. Daddy'll take you upstairs . . .' He stood up with Polly weeping over his shoulder and spotted Louisa. 'Hey! Hey, Pol. Look who's here . . .'

Louisa smiled at her brother. He was tanned from sailing, and what was left of his hair had gone very blond. But he'd lost a lot of it since the divorce. He turned slightly so that Polly could see.

'Do you recognise this person?'

Polly stopped making a noise. She stared at Louisa with tearful eyes.

'Who's this?'

'Aunt Loui.'

'She's just jealous of you, darling.'

'She's got no reason to be.'

Louisa stood by the Aga, testing the béarnaise sauce while her mother checked the lamb.

'Darling, I know you don't realise it, but she has *every* reason to be. You're beautiful, and she's not.'

'She is, Mum. And she's clever. And she . . . but that's not the point.' Louisa moved the sauce-boat closer to the Aga and began ladling in the béarnaise. 'How could she think I'd steal him?'

'Because she's jealous,' her mother said, again.

'Who's jealous?' said Nigel, coming in with the empty bottle of rosé.

'Kate seems to think Louisa tried to steal her boyfriend.'

'Oh God,' said Nigel, putting the bottle next to all the other empty bottles. 'Did you?'

'Of course I didn't.'

'Darling, could you tell Alex dinner's ready?'

Louisa and Nigel looked at one another.

'Which darling?'

'I don't care. One of you . . .'

Later, over dinner, it occurred to Mary that Louisa could come to Italy with them. They hadn't been on holiday as a family in years, and if Louisa didn't want to be in London, what was stopping her?

'Will there be room?' said Louisa, considering the idea as she picked at a French bean and dipped it into the lamb juices on her plate.

'You can move into Polly's room, and Polly can move in with Tim . . .' Mary turned to Alex, who was at the sideboard, helping himself to more potatoes. 'That's okay, isn't it?'

'Fine,' Alex drizzled the remains of the béarnaise over his plate and brought it back to the table. He picked up his napkin and sat down. 'Come on, Lou. Keep me company. I'll be the only one under fifty.'

'Apart from the cook,' said Nigel, filling his glass and grinning at him.

'Is she pretty?'

'No.'

'Dad,' Louisa gave her father a reproachful look. 'Alison's not bad. The cooking's crap, but . . .'

'It's not Alison.'

'It's the girl you found for us, darling,' said Mary. 'How awful, I can't remember her name.'

Louisa put down her glass. 'Kate's friend? Sarah? Is Sarah Knowles cooking for you?'

'That's the one. We got her to do a dinner for us in London. She was simply brilliant.'

'Come on.' Alex put a potato into his mouth and leant forward. 'It'll be fun. I know the Westons are going to be out there. Susie was saying they've bought a new boat. And I expect Hugh Bowman will be there with that crazy Italian crowd . . .'

'I don't like Hugh Bowman.'

'Nor do I, but his friends are great.'

'You just like looking at the girls,' said Nigel.

'And you don't?'

Nigel laughed and turned to Louisa. 'You'll be bored silly down here by yourself . . .'

As Alex ate his last potato, Nigel and Louisa both reached for their cigarettes.

'When are you going?'

'Tuesday morning.'

'And you really think Tim won't mind?'

Italy had always been a family holiday. It hadn't occurred to Louisa that anybody else would be invited, and it wasn't until they arrived at Heathrow that she realised Richard Hastings was coming too, with his wife.

'They said they'd meet us at the check-in desk,' said Nigel. 'Where the hell are they?'

'Perhaps they're going Economy.'

'Who? Who are you meeting?'

'Richard and Anne,' said Mary, heading for the Economy desks, where she thought she recognised Richard's battered panama.

'*Who?*'

Louisa watched her mother approach what could only be Anne Hastings, dressed in a fawn Armani trouser suit and wearing her sunglasses inside the terminal.

'Don't worry,' said her father, 'Richard managed to convince Anne's parents to take the children – so it's just them. He thought she needed a proper break.'

Every summer, Louisa's family went to the same part of Italy – to a fishing village on the western side, south of Pisa.

But to call it a fishing village was an understatement. If you took the coast road north along an avenue of aromatic pines – with rocks rising high to the right and, far below to the left, a flat sea, strangely solid, stretched taut to the horizon – and braved three or four miles of hairpin bends until the village was no longer in sight, you'd come round the edge of a rocky headland and see beneath you a group of about twenty villas – overhung by a mountain the fishermen still used as a landmark when coming in from a haul.

From above, you'd see that each villa had its satellite turquoise rectangle pool, and that each one nestled in the privacy of gardens kept rigorously green by the constant use of sprinklers. But the buildings themselves were so different from one another and spread so generously apart that, were it not for the same security-enclosed area they lay within, you'd think they'd grouped themselves there by chance and not design.

These villas – and their class of occupant – had turned the fishing village into one of the smartest resorts on the Italian Riviera. The harbour sparkled with yachts. The stone houses on the waterfront, originally for the boatmen, now accommodated some of the most expensive restaurants and bars in the country.

Anne Hastings hid rising excitement behind her dark glasses as they drove through the security gates.

'Which one is us?'

'You can't see it yet,' said Nigel, waving at one of the gardeners. 'It's beyond the row of cypresses up to the right.'

'Will anyone be there?'

'Only Sarah. I hope she arrived okay,' said Mary, checking her list.

'Is Sarah the cook?'

'It sounds terribly extravagant,' Mary turned round, an apologetic expression on her face. 'But it's really very difficult to do these things oneself out here. I find the markets impossible.'

'Oh, quite,' said Anne, in what she hoped sounded like knowing agreement.

Sarah had arrived late the day before. She'd been instructed to hire a car at Pisa airport and get herself to the resort. After a nerve-wracking drive, she'd been met by Caterina at the security gates and taken up to the house. Caterina was the maid. She was fat and friendly, but spoke no English. As Sarah spoke no Italian, they communicated in signs and smiled a lot. Caterina showed Sarah where she was sleeping – in a room next to Caterina, separate from the main house – and left her to unpack.

To Sarah's dismay, her room was also next to the swimming-pool pump house. But when she woke the next morning it wasn't to the churning of the pump, but to light coming in from the windows of a door that led directly onto the garden with views beyond that to the sea. She lay in bed for a second, gazing into the blue distance, thinking of Douglas, and wondering if there was anything she could have done.

She should have stopped herself from telling him she loved him. Or waited at least until he said it to her. That was what the magazines said, wasn't it? Her friend Camilla Davis had a book in her loo called *The Rules* that told you exactly how to avoid situations like this. Camilla swore by it, but Camilla's success rate had been pretty poor and Sarah had been scornful. She'd said that any man who fell for that kind of treatment wasn't worth having. Was Douglas that kind of man? Or was it just that he'd never really fancied her?

386

Sarah heaved herself out of bed.

She'd been told to have a late lunch ready when they arrived. After an exhausting morning in the village, using her phrase book to shop for food – but ending up by pointing – and searching for a shop that sold fresh basil only to discover a patch half the size of a tennis court in the villa's own garden, she was now frying prawns in chillies and garlic. She'd managed to get Caterina to help her lay the table, but that was it. For all her warmth, Caterina preferred entertaining the security guards to helping the English girl in the kitchen.

There were slices of fresh bread left in a basket in the middle of the table. There were two salads: one, plain rucola with oil and balsamic vinegar; the other, cold penne pasta with the basil she'd picked, shreds of Parma ham and sundried tomatoes. Then there was a fresh tomato salad – the tomatoes were warm from the sun when she'd picked them – with red onions and pepper. And two little pizzas for the children.

She was at the critical stage with her prawns when she heard the cars arrive. Squeezing in lemon juice, and tossing them around the pan a few seconds more, she tipped them onto a plate. She was resting a sprig of oregano on top when the door opened and a man's voice said, 'Well, something smells amazing.'

Sarah turned. He looked exactly like Louisa, but without the hair. Same baby nose. Same long limbs. He was with two small children.

'Hello,' he said, holding out his hand. 'You must be Sarah.'

Sarah wiped hers on her apron and shook it.

'. . . I'm Alex. This is Tim, and this is Polly. I was wondering if you had anything for them to drink.'

Sarah smiled at them and raised her eyebrows. 'Coke?'

'Coke! Coke! Coca Cola!'

'Come with me . . .'

Polly hadn't wanted her pizza, and Anne Hastings didn't like fish. But as she waited in the kitchen, reading Louisa's *Hello!* magazine, Sarah thought that lunch hadn't been bad.

Louisa had been a bit distracted, but friendly. She wasn't sure about Anne Hastings, who'd looked through her. Or her husband, who – well, who hadn't. But the others were nice.

Now they were all drinking coffee and planning their afternoon. Sarah had already decided what she was going to do with her afternoon. She was going to sleep, and then she would think about dinner. She'd wanted to give them fish originally but thought that, after Anne Hastings' complaining about the prawns, they could have veal tonight, and the fish tomorrow. She could prepare sage and butter ravioli for Mrs Hastings separately.

Sarah listened to them talking. Alex wanted to go sailing. Tim wanted to do whatever his father was doing, and Mary wanted to sleep. Nigel didn't really mind, but what did Richard want to do? Richard, who was standing behind Anne's chair and leaning on it restlessly, said he wanted to go down to the beach.

Anne picked at Polly's pizza and turned to Mary.

'He just wants to gaze at all the girls.'

'Right now the only girl I want to gaze at, my darling,' said Richard, massaging Anne's bony shoulders and looking over her head at Louisa, 'is you. In fact, why don't we have a siesta, too . . .?'

Sarah heard a chair scrape and Louisa appeared in the kitchen, visibly upset. She was holding her coffee cup.

'Thanks. That was great.'

She dumped the cup on the side and went to her room.

Seventeen

Douglas had not been back to his London house since his decision not to use it, to stay instead at Gibbs's, and he had difficulty opening the door. It was blocked by a pile of unopened mail. He leant hard with his shoulder, but it wouldn't budge. In the end, he had to put down his suitcase, stretch round the door, and yank out the mail from the inside.

Once through the door, he swept up the mass of envelopes into a big pile and took it into the study. He separated the free property magazines and circulars from the rest, and threw them into the bin. Of the remaining envelopes, four were addressed to himself. The rest were for Tom. Douglas picked up one of Tom's and looked at the name – T.A. Faulkener – printed in familiar square-shaped type-set. It was his Barclaycard bill.

Putting the envelope down, he turned to his own letters. He'd arranged with the Post Office for his mail to be forwarded, but these ones must have arrived before that had happened. There was a council tax statement, a water bill, a Littlewoods competition and a residential notice about lamp-posts. He threw away the Littlewoods offer, and put the others in a folder to take back to Waveney.

Tom's pile sat there on the desk, with the Barclaycard bill at the top. Douglas picked it up again. Pressing hard, he could almost see the figure. Resisting the temptation to open it (so easy to say that he'd made a mistake, that he'd thought it was for him) he put it back with the others and took them into the hall. As he lifted his suitcase, he made a mental note to forward them to Kate's address – quickly, before he gave in – and then wondered if it might not be better to take them round himself. Perhaps now was a good time for him and for Tom to put their row behind them. Perhaps Tom needed him. And it wasn't as if there was . . . well, the poor girl was dead now. Best not to think about it too much.

For some months Douglas had been wondering whether he should put his mews-house on the market. He wasn't sure the limited time he spent in London justified the expense of maintaining it – unless he let it. And, if he let it, Douglas couldn't quite see what point there was in having it at all. There were so many other things he'd rather invest in, like that farm the other side of Burnham Market that had come up for sale. Or that estate near Inverness – the Saville's particulars had arrived over a month ago. They were losing their gloss a bit, but they still occupied pride of place on his desk at Waveney. Douglas hadn't quite been able to shift them into the bin.

Working out that he came to London no more than eight times a year, and for no longer than two or three nights at a time, Douglas and Sarah (who was good with numbers) had calculated that it was cheaper and more convenient for him to stay at Gibbs's on these occasions. This had decided him in principle to sell the flat, but his agent had suggested he take advice from someone who specialised in London property, and he was expecting a visit from Rod Maris of Maris Property that afternoon. Putting thoughts of Tom and his mail to the back of his mind, Douglas set about preparing a list of suitable questions for Rod.

Douglas had not expected to spend more than half an hour with Rod Maris. In the end, he'd spent all afternoon with him and his assistant, Fiona – who was supposed to be taking notes, but who kept interrupting to correct.

They advised him to turn the property back into the family house it had once been. The study needed to look like a dining room again. He should put back that wall upstairs, so that there was an extra bedroom. Fiona thought he might like to decorate it as a nursery. They suggested that he convert one of the walk-in cupboards in the master bedroom into an en-suite shower room. Much easier to sell, Fiona said.

And the garden was a mess. Ideally, he should make the kitchen door into a French window, leading onto a raised terrace, with steps down to the grassy area at the back – and that definitely needed replanting. It looked like a bog. Douglas had said he rather liked it like that, but Fiona had been firm.

They thought the conversions and redecoration would cost ten thousand – the garden, another five – and that he'd be able to get at least another hundred thousand when he sold it.

All of this meant that Douglas was forced to spend the week in London arranging for funds to be made available and getting quotes from contractors –

letting them in, seeing them out, and making them cups of coffee from the old machine that Tom had used. He could tell they would have preferred Nescafé, but there was none to offer and, after a couple of days, they started bringing their own.

Douglas kept coming across reminders of Tom. It wasn't just the coffee. It was the fliers pushed through the door from expensive-looking shops Douglas hadn't even heard of. It was the yellowing invitation to Flora Lincoln's wedding, still there on the mantelpiece; the half-empty bottle of cologne by the bath; and all those half-read copies of the *Spectator*, in a pile by the television. He'd come across an old message from Kate on the answerphone saying that she was running late. Had Tom remembered to tell Gloria – the cleaning lady – that Douglas was coming to stay for her party? Could he get Gloria to make up the bed? She'd see him at Gibbs's at seven . . .

And then, of course, there was Tom's mail.

On Thursday, Douglas decided to call Kate's flat. He left a message for Tom, referring to the mail, and asked Tom to give him a ring. When he got no response, Douglas decided to go round himself. He was still unnerved by the memory of Kate at Earls Court, but there was also a part of him that simply wanted to see her again – even if she cut him. He'd made plans to visit Maris Property's offices on Friday night to give Fiona a spare set of keys so that she could oversee the works while he returned to Norfolk, and Maris Property was based in Kate's part of town, sort of. Whatever. It was close enough to give Douglas the excuse he needed – to convince himself that it made sense to deliver the letters at the same time.

Kate spent Friday morning examining a new set of instructions from Henry Hazel, pleased that the letter was addressed to her. Later, that evening, she took the letter, and a photocopy for Michael, into Michael's office, and asked if he had a moment to go through the main points.

'Oh Kate,' he looked up. 'Yes, of course. And I'm afraid there's something I must talk to you about. It's something a bit – er – well, perhaps it would be better if you shut the door.'

Closing it quietly, she came back in and sat opposite him, with the desk between them. 'What is it?'

'Just a second . . .' Michael pressed the forward button on his telephone and looked at her for a moment.

She tried to think what she might have done wrong. 'You did know about the funeral, didn't you? I'm sorry if that put me behind with matters, and . . . well, it won't have given Adam a very good impression, I know. But I . . .'

'Of course I knew. Janet told me.' He smiled. 'If anything, I'm wondering if you should be back so soon.'

'It was only a friend.'

Kate waited for him to speak. Michael looked at her, and then at the pair of glasses he held in his hands.

'So,' he said. 'Everything all right?'

'I'll catch up on the days I missed over the weekend, and you'll never know I've been away.'

'That's not what I meant,' he said gently.

'Then what . . .?'

'I mean, you're happy with your workload and stuff?'

'Yes, Michael. It's all fine.'

'And the funeral? You're sure you . . .?'

'I'll be fine.'

Michael put his glasses in the middle of his blotter, looked at her and sighed. 'The thing is, Kate, we've got to start thinking about Singapore.'

Kate looked blank.

'The new Singapore placement, remember? I mentioned it to you a couple of months ago. We can't send a partner, so that means one of you lot has to go.'

'Of course. Sorry.'

Michael ran through the choices. 'As you might imagine, Annette's so keen she can hardly concentrate on anything else right now. So's Gavin, but he doesn't have quite enough experience. And Steve's not – well, we really need someone a bit more outgoing.'

Kate smiled.

'I expect the last thing you feel like doing right now is uprooting to the other side of the world, but you should think about applying. It's an opportunity.'

Kate pushed back her hair and looked at the floor. 'How long would I be out there?'

'Two years.'

'And then?'

'Of course, after that you'd have the option to come back. If that's what you'd like.'

'Who else is out there?'

'Well, I'd be around to begin with to get you settled. And Tim Cheung – know him?'

'I know who you mean.'

'He's already there. He's been flooded with

business – not only from Singapore, but India, Sri Lanka, and God knows what other exotic places – mainly project work, and there's a bit of securitisation. He needs someone with him by the end of the year at the very latest. I know that sounds ages away, but arrangements have to be made.'

'What else?'

Michael picked an internal memorandum headed 'Singapore Placement' from one of the trays and read from it. 'It says here you get a twenty per cent pay rise, your own apartment, free gym membership, satellite TV, maid service . . .'

As Michael listed the perks, Kate thought what it would be like to uproot, to leave behind her home (a lonely flat with nothing but memories of Tom and Louisa hardly counted as a home), her friends (what friends?), and her life. She realised that the only person she'd miss – the only person who'd miss her – would be her mother, and that wasn't a good enough reason to stay. She was thirty. She had a life to lead, and it was time for her to take control of it again.

'Okay.'

'Okay?'

'I want it.'

Michael smiled. 'Good. I'll put your name down.' He took the top off his ink pen, and Kate watched him write her name beneath 'Annette Latham' on the memorandum.

'It's just between me and Annette?'

'Looks like it.'

'When will we know?'

He handed her the memorandum. 'It's all here. Why don't you take a copy and give me back the original. Tim'll be coming over some time at the beginning of October. He'll want to meet you both then. I guess he'll make a decision after that.'

Kate took the Singapore memorandum to the nearest photocopier, made a copy for herself, and returned the original to Michael. Then she put her copy in the side-pocket of her briefcase, took her handbag from underneath the desk and left.

It was getting dark, and the wine bar on the corner was overflowing with Friday night business. Men and women of varying ages and at varying stages of winding down clustered round the outside, smoking and drinking. They were still dressed for the office, but ties had been loosened, top buttons undone, jackets removed, make-up retouched. Some were sitting at the tables outside, others were standing in whatever groups they could make between the tables, onto the pavement, into the street.

Kate scanned them as she passed, looking for Adam and her colleagues. They were there somewhere, but Kate couldn't see them, and she didn't feel like fighting her way to them, perching on a wall with a glass of mediocre wine and talking shop. She wanted to go home.

She went down the steps that led to the station, round a corner, and along a row of shops – newsagents, clothes shops, sandwich bars – places that, at lunch hour, bustled with suited shoppers standing aside for each other as they went in and out, all with different things on their minds, different packages to get, yet all with that pressing sense of the hour being up.

Now these shops were empty and locked, with night drawn out in lines of grey over the strong glass doors. The absence of colour and noise – save the sound of her heels on the wide flat stones, marking her steps like the ticks of a clock that someone forgot to wind up – meant that there was nothing to distract her. And the thoughts she'd successfully blocked out all day – with a barricade of handwritten tasklists and Post-it notes, with sketched plans and flowcharts, emails, faxes and quickfire calls – those unwanted thoughts now came at her, free and unimpeded. Kate slowed her steps to a halt, leant against the wall and, holding the old briefcase tight to her chest, she bent her head and cried.

Forgetting Arabella's death for a moment, Kate looked at last at herself. She'd been glad to leave the office before eight. Leaving work on time was one of the things that brightened her day. It was only now that she was here in the limbo between work and home that she understood the gladness had been hollow. Just habit – formed in the days when there was something to get home early for: the remains of a bottle of wine bought for 'only £80' at a Christies auction, some article in the *Spectator* Tom wanted her to read, '. . . and what's another word for DELEGATION? Ten letters . . .' Or Louisa's bright voice, demanding Kate's opinion on some moisturiser everybody was talking about. Stupid, trivial things . . .

How people would laugh at her. She was supposed to be professional. Responsible. Maybe even supposed to be lonely. People paid huge sums of money for her informed independent judgement. She was supposed to make wise decisions, see through deceit, understand limits.

And what had she been doing? She'd been out

drinking and laughing and dining and dancing with the madness of a teenager. Why? And why – the fuck – with *him*? Him of all people. He, whose very first words to her were those careless, shoulder-shrugging, make-hay-while-the-sun-shines-out-of-my-ass words that told her he did nothing. Was nothing. Why hadn't she seen the signs? Wasn't it obvious that a man who did nothing – and who was proud of it – would never take the serious things seriously?

And Louisa? Just the same. Flitting over the surface with a glorious weightlessness that only unearned money could give. Kate had delighted in the charm, the novelty, the full-hearted fun – but why hadn't she seen the risk, the absurdity? Wiping her eyes with her sleeve, she accepted that it was partly because Louisa and Tom had offered an antidote to work – a seductive alternative – and she'd fallen for it with the credulous longing of a little girl who dresses up in fancy dress and plays with imaginary fairies.

There was nothing to be glad about. The empty routine of the office lay behind her. And a cheerless flat lay ahead, at the other end of the Hammersmith and City Line tunnel. She could join the others in the yellow light of the wine bar, but that was just delaying the inevitable encounter with loneliness – loneliness that put its hands behind its head, stretched its legs into the darkness outside and patiently sat out the hours.

Male laughter and the debating tone of legal voices burst round the corner and into the street. Kate looked back and saw a number of indistinct silhouettes approach – people from the office perhaps, people she might know. Switching the briefcase from its place in her arms, back into her left hand, she made for the crowded anonymity of the station.

It was five o'clock, but the heat was still intense in the shelter of the mountain. Nothing disturbed the surface of the pool. Next to it, curled on her side, lay Louisa – alone. She was wearing her black bikini. In one hand, she held a paperback book. An upright rectangle of fading lilac in an otherwise passive scene, it blocked her face from the house. The other hand rested on the edge of her sunbed, fingers dangling over baking tiles. She'd been in the shade of an umbrella, but the sun had now moved round and only her left foot remained in shadow.

In the distance a door opened.

'God, that looks inviting.'

'I hope you're talking about the pool, my darling.'

Richard's laughter. 'I certainly am. I saw you at the Swiss Army counter in duty free, my love. I'm not going to do anything stupid.'

Their voices carried over the garden with extraordinary clarity, and the world of her book – a dark, wet London street, cobbled, lit by gas lamps – faded from Louisa's mind. Swiss Army? Not moving her body an inch, her focus left the print, swept across dazzling turquoise and rested on the green. She listened.

Anne was laughing now. 'I was looking for a present for Christopher,' she protested.

'Come here . . .'

Soft – but still just as clear.

Richard and Anne had addressed barely three words to Louisa since they'd arrived. They'd made a big show of togetherness that had pleased Nigel and Mary, but had left Louisa with a bleak sense of deserved loneliness. She hoped they'd change their minds about coming for a swim, but they didn't.

Anne arrived first, shuffling her flip-flops, and dressed in a crimson swimming costume with a very low back. She'd tanned quickly – suspiciously quickly, Louisa thought – in the last few days. The crimson made her brown skin look almost black. She was followed by Richard, carrying towels.

Louisa rolled onto her back.

'Hello,' Anne's shadow danced over her. 'You okay all by yourself?'

'I'm fine.'

Richard put down the towels and leapt straight into the pool. Anne picked one up and laid it out so that half of it was in the sun, and half in the shade of the umbrella. Then she sat in the shady part, searching her rope bag for sun-cream.

Louisa held up her book, but from behind her sunglasses, she swivelled her eyes. She watched Anne remove a tube, open it up and rub its contents onto her legs. Anne was small – not much over five foot – and for someone with three children, two of whom (from a former marriage) had left school, she was slim. Louisa wondered how old she was – she seemed so much younger than her mother. Her skin was brown and smooth and, with the exception of the area round her neck and the tops of her arms, she didn't look as if she was in her fifties.

But the really strange thing about Anne was that she looked nice. Her eyes were bright and appealing, and her smile was warm. It was hard to believe that this was the kind of person who'd tell you 'it's just us' for dinner, and then you'd arrive to a full-blown party for twelve hopelessly underdressed, or who'd say, 'well, if you can do it, I certainly can' in a tone that would make you think for a second that she might be paying you a compliment. She'd needle and pester. She'd tease in a manner she thought was lighthearted – but it was too much, too often, too close.

'You must be careful not to burn, Louisa.'

'I don't think I will.'

'You can never be too careful. What factor are you using?'

'Four.'

'*Four?* You'll be burnt to shreds.'

'I'll be fine, Anne. Thanks . . .'

She returned to the dark wet cobbles, carriages, horses . . .

'What are you reading?'

Louisa held up the book – a regency romance.

'Oh,' Anne put on her sunglasses and took the book from Louisa. She looked at the back. 'Oh yes. I used to read books like this before I got married.'

Louisa said nothing.

'Don't you have some dashing boyfriend coming out?'

'No.'

'Why ever not?'

Louisa didn't answer. She took the book back from Anne and found her page.

'Perhaps you'll meet someone here. Richard and I were just saying a pretty girl like you really should be married by now . . .' Ann squirted more Factor Two into the palm of her hand and began rubbing it onto her legs. 'Isn't there anybody?' she went on. 'I bet there is. You're just not telling. Perhaps you fancy someone you can't have?'

Louisa gave her a sharp look. But she just went on rubbing.

'Forbidden love is always so much more exciting. Your mother was telling me about the problem with your flatmate's boyfriend—'

'*What*?'

'Oh, don't worry, dear. I won't tell a soul.'

Richard reached the end of his second length. 'What are you two talking about?' he called.

'Louisa's love life.'

He heaved himself out of the pool. 'Sounds interesting.'

'Oh, it is. But she still won't tell me who she's in love with.'

'Really, Anne. I . . .'

'You must indulge us, dear. Now that we're boring and married.'

'You can read this after me, if you like.'

Anne took off her sunglasses and got up. 'No thank you,' she said in tones that added, 'I'm not that desperate,' and walked towards the pool.

Richard grabbed his towel and began drying himself. He and Louisa watched as Anne climbed down the steps into the water. Keeping her hair well out, she swam slow, deliberate breast stroke to the opposite side – and suddenly looked her age.

Louisa picked up her book again, but she was still searching for her place when Richard flopped down beside her with a sigh and murmured, 'When can I see you?'

Louisa tried to read on. But he rolled onto his side and stared at her until she looked back at him.

'What? What is it?' she snapped.

'When can I see you?'

'You're looking at me.'

'Alone.'

She shook her head and bent it to her book.

'Don't do this to me, Louisa. Please. There are things,' he lowered his voice as Anne approached, turned and set off to the other side again. 'There are things I have to explain . . .'

'I don't want to hear your explanations.' Louisa looked up and out at Anne in the pool: a poisonous tropical frog, her old brown skin, her crimson costume, her black eyes blinking.

'I'm sorry, angel. I am,' said Richard. 'But there's more to it . . . I had no option.'

'I don't want to talk about it.'

'All right,' Richard sighed and was quiet. He lay flat on his back and stared up at the sky. Louisa returned to her book, but she couldn't concentrate. His 'all right' had been too light, too easily won.

Richard knew that Anne would swim twenty lengths. She always did. When she started the seventeenth, he resumed his attack.

'You haven't heard my side of the story.'

'You've had months to give me your side of the story. The only reason you want to get me alone is so that you can try to seduce me again. I'm not falling for it, Richard. I'm not that stupid.'

She was still looking at the page of her book. He was still looking at the sky.

'You don't trust yourself alone with me?'

'I don't trust you.'

'You think I'd rape you?'

'Of course not. I just . . .'

'You just what? Listen,' he lowered his voice again as Anne approached, and waited until she turned. 'I could come to your room tonight. We'd talk freely, and you'd get to hear the whole story. And if I make a pass at you – you're extremely tempting, sweetheart, but I'll try not to, I promise – if I make a pass, you can say no, reject me, and I'll be gone. Easy – unless of course you're worried you might enjoy it.'

Under her tan, Louisa flushed. She hadn't had sex for months. 'I'd hate it.'

'Then what's the problem?'

As she struggled for an answer, other voices interrupted. Turning, she saw her parents coming through the garden: her father's pale body was in a pair of navy nylon swimming trunks she'd known all her life, her mother's straw hat bobbing behind him. They were talking about schools.

'. . . same problem of distance. Frances'll never agree to drive six hours every time she wants to see him. Hello, darling!'

'Hi!' Louisa called back. 'Sleep well?'

'Not bad. Goodness, it gets hot, doesn't it?'

Anne was on length nineteen.

'I'll see you later then,' said Richard, under his breath.

Before Louisa could respond, he got up and jumped into the pool – splashing Anne's hair, laughing, blocking her twentieth length.

It wasn't until that evening that Louisa was able to catch her mother alone.

'How *could* you?' she said.

Mary took out the last curler, brushed the roll of hair lightly into place and reached for her hairspray. 'She said you were looking so sad, and I . . .'

'It's got nothing to do with her.'

'Yes. Yes, I see. I'm sorry.'

Louisa stood back as the spray flew into the air around and behind her mother's head and then settled. 'I came here to get away from all that. Not to have it forced down my throat.'

'I'm sure she meant well, darling. You must try not to be so oversensitive . . .'

Louisa watched her correct a couple of stray hairs. Was she really being oversensitive? If that was true, then why was it only with Anne?

Mary put scent on her wrists and neck, and stood up. 'Let's go down.'

Louisa followed her out of the room.

Sarah had done canapés for them to pick at before dinner every evening since they'd arrived. She'd done mozzarella and basil, and melon balls wrapped in Parma ham. But today she thought she'd try something different. They were selling mushrooms in the market – huge, fleshy ones called *funghi porcini*. Sarah bought masses. She'd tried them in a restaurant and loved them. But she hadn't cooked with them before, and she thought it best to experiment with canapés before moving on to more ambitious things.

She was putting them next to the drinks tray on the stone table by the pool, when Louisa drifted out. She was still wearing the black bikini, with a short black mesh sarong tied around her hips. 'Seen Alex?'

Sarah shook her head.

'He's been ages. Poor Tim will be exhausted. What are *those*?'

'Mushrooms – *funghi porcini* – cut into pieces, on toast, with truffle oil.'

'God, you're brilliant,' said Louisa, taking one and pouring herself a glass of wine. 'Want one?'

She and Sarah stood at the table, looking out to sea, with the pool behind them – drenched in pink evening light.

'Isn't that them?' said Sarah, shading her eyes.

Louisa looked below to where she was pointing. Coming up the path, she could see what looked like Tim – his snorkling goggles on the back of his head, carrying his flippers and a pile of towels. Behind him was Alex, talking to a wiry woman in a pink sundress and a man in dark glasses.

'Who's . . .?'

'That's odd,' said Sarah, narrowing her eyes, trying to see better. 'He looks exactly like Tom Faulkener.'

As if reading their thoughts, the man took off his sunglasses and looked directly at them. It was.

'How lovely,' said Sarah. 'Did you know he was here?'

Louisa didn't reply.

'Will they stay for supper, do you think? I've only got seven veal portions . . .'

But as she spoke, the beach party halted. She and Louisa watched as Alex tried to persuade the others to come up, but Tom was shaking his head and looking at his watch. They then shook hands, and Tom set off alone in the direction of the Bertorelli villa.

'Oh no,' said Sarah, waving vigorously. But Tom's back was to them and he didn't see. To her embarrassment, Alex waved back instead, and got Tim to wave too.

The woman in pink remained. She looked over to where the others were waving and smiled warmly. Remembering in a flash what Tom had said about coming here, and that he knew the Bertorellis, Louisa realised that the woman was Maya – and guessed that she must have brought Tom with her from Rome.

'What a pity,' said Sarah, as Tom disappeared around a bend in the road. 'It would have been great to see him.'

'I'm sure we will at some point. It's a small place.'

'I wonder why he's here . . . I expect it's to get away from all that awfulness over Arabella, don't you?'

Louisa shrugged and said nothing.

'In fact I'm sure it's that. Poor man. Probably can't face anybody at the moment,' Sarah remembered how she'd felt when her father died. 'No wonder he didn't want . . .'

'I'd better get changed for dinner,' said Louisa, closing the conversation, and heading back to the house.

Maya Bertorelli was exactly Tom's age and she was single. She and Tom had known one another for too long to consider themselves as anything more than friends, but that did not stop them from taking a keen interest in each other's relationships.

Maya had not liked Arabella. Arabella had not liked Maya much either, and while she was married to Tom he'd seen very little of his mother's god-daughter. Maya was sad for Tom when she heard about the divorce, but she wasn't surprised. It was Maya who'd encouraged him to come back to Rome – she'd helped him find his apartment. Three years later, she'd helped him make the hard decision to sell it.

When she heard that Arabella had committed suicide, Maya's gut reaction was, 'how typical, how selfish,' but she could see that Tom was devastated. It didn't occur to her that Tom had left England because he was ashamed. Tom had not been able to bring himself to tell her about the affair, and she assumed instead that he had come home to Italy to recover from the shock. When she heard that, on top of all of this, Tom had been dumped by his girlfriend, Maya cursed English women and saw it as her responsibility to comfort him and help him through. Perhaps even find someone new for him – although it was way too soon for that, of course.

With a bit of persuasion, Tom had agreed to come to the beach for a long weekend. She wasn't inviting anyone else. They could just go sailing, and get away.

Leaving Rome on Thursday night, they were able to spend all Friday on the water and it was after six when they brought their boat back into the harbour. Tom was steering with his back to the evening sun, and Maya was at the far end of the boat, putting out fenders. She looked up as they approached the pontoon, and spotted someone she knew.

'Alessandro!'

Alex looked up, shaded his eyes and waved.

'Help us in, will you?' she shouted.

Alex took the rope Maya threw him and told Tim

to tie it to the ring, '. . . like I showed you the other day, remember?'

Tim squatted over the ring, while Alex fended the boat off with his hands.

Maya clambered off, rocking the boat, and threw her arms around him. 'How long have you been here?'

'Couple of days,' said Alex, smiling at Tom. 'Hi.'

Maya introduced them, but Tom wasn't paying attention.

He'd heard Alex's surname, but it wasn't until he saw Louisa on the terrace that he understood who Alex was. As he saw her expression harden in recognition, Tom realised he couldn't take a whole evening of it. He invented some story about having to ring his mother, told Maya he'd rather have dinner on his own – he was fine – and left.

Kate put down the telephone. She kicked off her shoes and went into the kitchen. There was half a bottle of wine in the fridge, and she poured herself a glass with a shaky hand.

She'd managed to put off visiting her mother until the end of the month. She'd told Elizabeth it was because there was too much for her to do at work and Elizabeth had sighed heavily. Explaining that it was crucial for the next Hazel Industries deal to run smoothly if she was to stand any chance of going to Singapore, Kate had realised too late what it was she'd said.

'Singapore?'

'It's not certain yet. But I . . .'

'*Singapore*? How long for?'

'I don't know, Mum. Couple of years, maybe.'

'Darling,' Elizabeth's eyes swept frantically over her kitchen to a fading photograph she had of Kate and Peter when they were small: Peter, concentrating on the tower of wooden bricks they were building and Kate, smiling at the camera. Losing Peter and his family to Hong Kong was bad enough, but *Kate?* 'Darling, you can't go to Singapore. What about . . . what about the flat?'

'I can sell the flat.'

'*Sell it?*'

'Or let it. Whatever. But it does mean that I . . .'

'And *when?* When would you go?'

'Not for ages.'

'But when?' Elizabeth persisted. 'When?'

'Calm down, Mum. I'd go some time after Christmas – if I go at all. Nothing's definite. They're considering quite a few people for the job.'

'They're bound to choose you.'

'No they're not. There's—'

'I'm sorry. I'm sorry, darling – but I can't bear it. I can't bear to see you do this to yourself. You won't be gone for two years. You'll be gone indefinitely. They'll offer you huge incentives to stay out there, year after year,' she stubbed out her cigarette and reached for another, 'Just think about it.'

'I have thought about it.'

'No you haven't. You've got no *idea* what this is going to do to you.'

'I'm sorry, Mum, but I have thought about it. I've thought about it a lot.'

'It's Tom, isn't it?'

'It's got nothing to do with Tom,' Kate replied in a firm voice.

'It's about Tom. I know it is. And all that rubbish you were saying about men and trust.'

'It's about my career,' said Kate, anger straining at every word. 'If I was a man – if it was Pete and not me – you'd understand. You'd probably be pleased for me. It would mean success. But because I'm a girl, you think that it means I'm a failure – don't you?'

'I . . .' Elizabeth said nothing. She was crying, and didn't trust herself to speak.

'Mum?'

'Oh darling,' she took a breath. 'I don't think that at all. I think you've had awful luck – really awful – but I don't think you're a failure. I'm just asking for you to think – think more – about whether Singapore is right for you. Will you do that?'

Kate had agreed to think about it, but not now. She was too tired. She was going to ring for a pizza, and watch television.

She ordered a large pizza with pepperoni, mushrooms, and extra cheese – and felt a bit better. With a glass of wine in one hand, and the remote control in the other, she lay along the sofa, waiting for the pizza to arrive. She aimed at the television and it sprang to life. Kate liked Friday night TV.

She was about to pour herself a second glass, when the doorbell rang. Kate put the glass down and picked up the intercom receiver. 'Hi,' she said. 'I'll come down.'

Hoping the man had change, she grabbed a ten pound note and the set of keys from her bag and ran down the stairs. She opened the door to the street and there, on the step, was Douglas.

'Oh.' Kate flapped the ten pound note. 'I thought

you were the pizza man.'

Douglas smiled. 'No,' he indicated the pile of envelopes in his hand. 'No, I'm just the postman. There was some mail at the house for Tom and I wanted to give it to him.'

'That might be a bit difficult. You see he . . . Ahh!'

A man in a helmet and biker boots came up the steps behind Douglas. He was holding a large square red bag, flat, in both hands.

'Hello,' said Kate. 'That's for me.'

Douglas stood aside as the man opened his red bag and gave her the pizza box. Then he felt in his pocket and produced a slip of paper. 'Eight pounds fifty.'

'For one pizza?'

'It's a large one,' she explained, giving over the ten pound note. 'Keep the rest . . .'

The pizza man nodded and left.

Kate looked at Douglas. 'Tom's not here,' she said.

'Oh.' Douglas looked at her. She was standing there at the top of the steps, holding her pizza and looking back at him. Douglas hadn't eaten. He could smell the extra melted cheese and mushrooms. He held out the envelopes. 'Then would you give them to him – and let him know I . . .'

'I don't know where Tom is. We split up.'

'Oh Kate,' he said with feeling. 'I'm so sorry.'

'Are you?'

He frowned. 'Yes. Yes, of course I am. Very sorry. I thought . . .'

'You thought Tom would be happier with Arabella.'

'What?'

'I'm right aren't I? He told me that was why you

kicked him out of your house. He said you wanted him to end it with me. You wanted him to "give his marriage another try". You . . .'

Douglas was shaking his head. 'No, Kate. That's not right. I asked Tom to leave the house because he . . .'

'Yes?'

'Because he was . . .'

Kate looked at his expression, felt his difficulty, and began to understand that Tom had lied about this too. 'Do you want to come up?' she said.

Shutting the door behind him, Douglas followed Kate up the stairs, overwhelmed by the smell of pizza.

'Drink?'

'Whatever you're having.'

Kate gave him the bottle. 'Glasses are in the cupboard next to the fridge. Help yourself.'

Douglas went into the kitchen. It took him a bit of time to find the fridge because it was concealed behind a cupboard door. As he searched, he could hear Kate opening her pizza box.

'I read about Arabella in the papers,' he said, returning with a glass, filling it with wine, and then topping Kate's up.

Kate chewed at her pizza and looked at him.

'Awful,' he said, not sure how much Kate knew.

'Awful,' she agreed.

'I was worried about Tom . . .'

Kate finished her mouthful and took another.

'. . . he was so close to her.'

'I think it was more than just close, Douglas. Don't you?'

Douglas looked at her, and then at the floor. 'Is

that why you spli . . .?'

'I do wish you'd sit down Douglas. You're making me uncomfortable, standing there watching me eating.' Kate swallowed hard and cleared her mouth. 'Just sit over there, drink your wine, and give me your side of the story.'

Douglas sat where she'd indicated, in the armchair by the window. He sat on the edge with both feet on the floor, and leant forward, swilling his wine. 'In some ways, it was my fault,' he said, looking at the whirlpool he'd made in his glass. 'I lent Tom some money . . .'

By the time Douglas finished, Kate had lost her appetite. Still holding the remains of the second slice of pizza in her left hand and a full glass of wine in her right, she decided that what she really needed was a cigarette.

The only ones left were Louisa's Mexican brand.

'Want one?'

'No thanks. I . . .'

'Of course. You don't smoke. Another drink?'

'Thanks. I . . .'

'Here. Let me.' She took his glass and emptied the remains of the bottle into it. Her hand still shook. 'I'm so sorry,' she began. 'So sorry that I was rude to you that day – on the underground. I didn't know. And of course I thought . . .'

'I know. You thought I was trying to steer Tom away from you, and back to Arabella.'

'Tom told me you were. He said . . .'

'I know.'

'He lied,' she said, her voice upset. 'I trusted that man – I loved him – and all he did was . . .'

'Whatever he did,' said Douglas. 'You must believe me when I say that he adored you too.'

'Right.'

'He was just weak.'

Saying nothing, Kate wiped her face with the back of her hand and picked up a yellow box of matches from the sofa table.

'It wasn't anything to do with you,' he went on. 'He just couldn't say no to her.'

Kate took out a match, scraped it on the side of the box and brought the cigarette close to its flame. It was bitter.

'Or to the money,' she said as she exhaled. 'Did you hear about that?'

'About what?'

'Arabella's will. It seems she left him hundreds of thousands of pounds.'

'No . . .'

Kate nodded.

'But why?'

'She never got round to changing it.'

The ringing of the telephone cut into this thought, and Kate got up to answer it.

'She's not in. No. I'm not entirely sure when she's coming back. Could you try her parents? Yes I have, somewhere . . .'

Douglas couldn't hold out any longer. As Kate gave the caller Louisa's parents' number, he broke off a slice of pizza and brought it to his mouth. It was still warm. He was halfway through it when the call ended. Kate turned round and smiled at him as she rang off. 'Shall I heat that up for you?'

Eighteen

'You're sure you won't have any more?'

'I couldn't,' said Maya.

'What about you, Anne? Louisa?' Mary went round the table, 'Come on Richard. I know you do.'

Richard grinned.

'Darling . . .' said Anne. 'You'll burst.'

'That's what you say to Christopher, angel, and he never does.' Richard got up and went over to the sideboard where Sarah's frozen chocolate pudding melted in the hot night air. He cut himself a third slice. 'Anyone else? Alex?'

'I couldn't.'

Richard brought his plate back to the table. 'It's just too good,' he said, stretching over Louisa for the jug of cream and pouring its contents over his pudding.

For a second, no-one spoke. With the exception of Louisa, who was looking out into the darkness of the garden, the entire table watched Richard's plate.

'Darling . . .'

Richard went on pouring.

'Darling, that's too much.' Anne leant forward and snatched the jug from Richard's hand. 'He's got a thing about cream,' she said to Maya.

'So have I,' said Maya to Richard. 'I love it.'

'You do?' said Richard, his mouth full.

Anne put the jug beyond Richard's reach. 'Well, you obviously know how to control yourself better than my husband.'

'I'm not sure about that. You should see me in my bikini.'

'I'd love to see you in your bikini,' said Richard.

Maya turned from him to Alex. 'What have you got planned for tomorrow? Tom and I thought we might take a picnic and sail right round to the cove. You could come too.'

Alex thought this was an excellent plan. Why didn't everybody go?

As he and Maya discussed it, Louisa tried to think of a way out. The idea of spending a whole day squashed on a boat with Tom, and Richard, observed by Anne – it was enough to give her a headache, even without pretending.

'There are nine of us,' Alex was saying, 'including Sarah, and two of you – we'll easily fit on two boats if we take the Sunseeker.'

'What's a Sunseeker?' said Anne.

'It's a speedboat,' said Louisa, opening a packet of cigarettes and offering one to her father.

'A speedboat with an engine the size of a rocket,' Maya added. 'We'd never keep up with you, Alessandro.'

'What's your horsepower?' he asked her.

'Donkey.'

Louisa decided to wait until plans were firm before excusing herself – that way she could find some reason for not going that they couldn't accommodate. As it happened, she was given a perfect way out by her mother.

They were sitting outside on the wicker chairs, drinking coffee and limoncello, and talking softly. Sarah had found night candles that acted also as insect repellents. They flickered in the hot wind and gave off a strange smell – half-aromatic, half-petrol. Louisa rather liked it. She sat back in her chair and put her feet up on the edge of her father's. Neither of them said anything. Half-listening to the others, they smoked their cigarettes and looked out into the dark and up at the stars. Half of Nigel's raised face jumped and flickered with the candles, and half of it was black.

Beyond him, and beyond the silhouettes of the cypresses, tall and rustling, lay the sea. Louisa looked out at it, and extended her ear to all the noises of the night – an insistent cricket, a car in the distance, the wind in the garden.

They were sitting slightly apart from the others – away from the lights of the house, so that they could see the stars more clearly – but close enough for Louisa to hear that Maya was leaving. She'd been leaving for over half an hour, and the tones of their voices were now building up to a finale.

She turned and saw that Maya was standing, a straw bag slung over her wiry shoulder, pulling at one of her pink straps to reveal a darker pink bikini underneath. She was laughing and thanking Mary. She kissed Alex goodbye, waved to the others, 'See you tomorrow!' – and let Nigel show her out.

In the brief vacuum left by Maya's absence, Mary sat down next to Alex and picked up her coffee cup. She was about to take a sip when she was struck by a thought. 'Oh God,' she said, lowering the cup. 'What about the children?'

'They'll love it. Tim's been pestering me all week.'

'But Polly's had sunstroke, darling. And all day on the water? They'd both . . .'

'Tim would never forgive me. Can't he just wear a hat?'

'But there's still Polly. She's only three.'

'Can't what's-her-name take care of Polly?' said Anne, giving Richard her other foot to massage.

'Are you talking about Sarah?'

Something in Alex's tone put Anne on the defensive. 'Well, isn't that what she's paid to . . .?'

'Sarah's not a nanny, Anne. She's a cook.'

'I suppose I could stay behind,' said Mary.

'If you're worried about space,' said Richard, scrunching Anne's toes, 'and Sarah doesn't come, there'll be room for at least three more.'

'Don't be bitchy, darling,' Anne's eyes sparkled. 'The poor girl can't help her size.'

Nobody said anything while Sarah came out to clear away the last of the wine glasses so that she could put them into the dishwasher before she went to bed. There was only the scratching sound of Nigel lighting himself another cigarette. Holding the remaining glasses in one hand, Sarah closed the outside door behind her, and returned to the kitchen.

'Oh God,' said Anne. 'Did she hear?'

'Of course she heard.' Alex rose from his chair and followed Sarah inside.

'I'll look after Polly,' said Louisa after him.

'Really?' he paused at the door. 'But why should you?'

'I'd like to. I'm not feeling a hundred per cent myself, and I've got a good book.'

'Are you sure you're able to do it, darling?' said Mary. 'Three-year-olds need constant attention.'

'I'll manage.'

Mary smiled. 'All right,' she said, 'but don't expect a peaceful day.'

Inside, Sarah was loading the machine. She looked at Alex and smiled. 'More coffee?'

'No . . .' he couldn't think of what he wanted to say and ended up offering to help. Sarah rinsed a cloth under the tap and wiped around the sink. 'Everything's done. I was just going to do this and go to bed.'

Alex watched her. 'Did you hear what we were saying out there?'

'No,' she squeezed the cloth, opened it out and hung it over the tap. 'Should I?'

Alex found himself relieved of one problem and facing another. He hesitated. 'It was just – well – we were thinking of going out on the boat tomorrow – the speedboat. We're going to the cove – it's not far – and we thought we might have a picnic—'

'You want me to do you a picnic?'

Alex grinned. 'Well, that would be fabulous. And – well – we thought that perhaps you'd like to come too . . .'

Louisa went to bed pleased that she'd managed to escape the boat party, and forgetting what Richard had said by the pool about coming to visit her later. Her room was on the ground floor, on the far side of the house. It wasn't large, but it had its own shower room and glass doors that slid open onto a private terrace.

It was so hot, she decided to have a shower before getting into bed. Because her windows were open and she didn't want to attract mosquitoes, she undressed in the dark. She was pinning up her hair so that it wouldn't get wet when the door opened and Richard entered with the bottle of limoncello. Louisa snatched up her towel. 'What are you . . .?'

He shut the door and came further in.

'What are you doing in here, Richard?'

'We agreed . . .'

'We did *not* agree. You know we didn't . . .'

Richard sat on the bed. He put down the bottle and picked up the shirt she'd been wearing at dinner. 'This is new,' he looked at the label, but it was too dark to see.

'Richard.'

He tossed the shirt aside and looked at her. 'I wanted to see you alone.'

Bending her neck, Louisa pulled the towel around her more firmly and tucked in the end. 'Well now you've got me,' she said, 'why don't you say whatever it is you want to say – and then go?'

'I will. I will in a minute . . .' He picked up the bottle, drank from it and offered some to Louisa, who shook her head.

'Richard – I'm tired. Just tell me why you're here . . .'

Richard sighed and looked at her, waiting, standing with her back to where the glass doors opened to the terrace – wrapped only in the towel. There was no moonlight, but nor was it completely dark and a strange blue light touched her hair.

'Oh Louisa . . .' he breathed.

'What?'

The weary tone did nothing to put him off. 'I can't stop thinking about you. You have no idea . . . and it's driving me mad having you so close and not being able to touch you.'

'No,' she drew away from his outstretched hand – back into the curtain. 'No. No, I'm sorry. You don't understand. I'm not . . .' She broke off as, in one surprising movement, he stood up from the bed and grabbed at her.

'Stop!' she cried. '*Stop it.*'

Holding her tight by the arms, he stopped her from struggling and faced her. They were the same height, but he was twice as large in terms of body weight. She felt his belly pressing in on her, hot and lumpy – all that pudding – pressing her against the curtain, and the wall beyond. Then she remembered sex with him, and felt sick.

'I can't stop it,' he whispered, easing the pressure on her arms and stroking them. 'I love y-uh.' He lurched as she brought up her knee. 'What th-uh.' Straining like a constipated dog, Richard doubled up. 'Nn. Uh . . . *Ow.*' From his curled position he looked at her. 'What the hell did you do that for?'

'Get out,' said Louisa, faintly exhilarated.

The next morning, with Polly's considerable weight in her arms, she waved the departing cars out of the gates and turned to go in. At last. No Richard. No Anne. Nobody but Polly, whose probing fingers were in her hair.

'Now Pol,' Louisa heaved her down and squatted to her level. 'What shall we do today?'

'Sand.'

'Sand?'

'Sand.'

'You want to go to the beach?'

Polly's brown curls fell about as she nodded.

'Is that what you do with Granny?'

More nods.

Louisa looked at her watch. It wasn't ten yet. If she took Polly now, they'd have at least an hour before it got too hot.

Five minutes later, with her beach bag full of high-factor water-resistant sun-cream, her novel, her sunglasses, a blue plastic bucket and two spades, and towels for them both rolled under one arm, Louisa was walking Polly very slowly down the narrow path that led to the beach. Most of the path was sloping, but steps had been made where the gradient demanded. Polly was wearing a white cotton sunhat and a serious expression, and taking each step by putting her right leg first.

'Four . . . Five . . . Well done, darling. Only three more to go.'

She was on the last step when Louisa heard someone coming up the path. Raising her head to check the path was wide enough, she saw that it was Tom – dripping, and wiping his face with a towel. He brought the towel down and saw them.

'. . . Eight!' said Polly, all by herself.

Louisa took the little hand. 'Come on, Pol. We're nearly there.'

'Louisa.' Tom blocked their way.

'What is it?'

'Can we talk?'

'I don't want to talk to you.' Louisa continued

along the path at Polly's pace, with Tom taking small steps behind and rubbing himself dry. *'I don't want to talk to you,'* she repeated.

'I know. But I—'

'That's why I'm here and not at the picnic.'

'And that's why *I'm* here, Louisa. How was I to know you'd . . .'

Louisa stopped and looked at him. 'I expect you thought you'd escape it all by coming to Italy. You thought: nobody here will know what I've done, nobody here will despise me. Well bad luck. I'm here, and I despise you.'

Tom followed her onto the beach. It wasn't large and it was getting crowded. Children chased each other over and around a row of bodies, stretched out on multicoloured mats and towels in various shades of flesh. In the water, heads bobbed, and lilos tilted with the waves. Louisa looked for a spot by the rocks and made for it, guiding Polly with her hand. Tom stood still.

'You can talk,' he flung back.

Louisa stopped and turned. 'What was that?'

'When it comes to extra-marital affairs, you're hardly perfect – a nice holiday in Italy with your lover, and all right under his wife's nose?' He looked down at Polly and was unable to stop himself, 'Is Richard the happy father?'

'How dare you?' Louisa dropped her bag and stood facing him with her hands on her hips. 'Polly's my niece,' she said.

'But Richard's here. From Maya's description, it couldn't have been anyone else.'

'There's nothing – absolutely *nothing* – going on.

Just because you behave disgracefully, don't assume the rest of us do.'

'Then why are you here with him?'

'I'm not *with him*, as you put it. My parents invited him.'

'And you thought you'd come along for the ride?'

'For God's sake. I didn't realise Richard was coming until I saw him at the airport.'

'You think I'll believe that?'

'I don't care what you believe,' she said, spinning round, back to Polly.

But Polly wasn't there.

'Where is she?' Louisa's voice was very controlled. 'Where's Polly?'

Tom dropped his towel. He ran in the direction Louisa had been walking. 'Polly?'

'Oh God, Tom. Didn't you *see* . . .?'

'Polly?' He raised his voice, '*Polly?*'

They searched around the rocks, but there was no sign of her.

'Polly?'

Willing her eyes to see further, see clearer, Louisa stared down the length of the beach. 'She can't have gone that far, can she? We were only talking for a second.'

'Polly!' shouted Tom.

'Oh God.'

'Come back to the beach, Lou. She must have wandered towards those . . .'

Louisa ran after him, stubbing her toe on a rock, and gritting her teeth as she ran on.

'*Mi scusi, signora . . . ha visto una bambina? . . . una* piccola *bambina . . . si . . .*'

Louisa stood, half-listening as Tom asked a middle-aged lady if she'd seen Polly, her eyes darting from group to group.

'What was she wearing? Lou?'

'White hat,' Louisa sobbed. 'White hat, and flowery swimsuit. Pink and green . . .'

'. . . *con un cappello bianco . . . bianco, si. Si . . .*'

The woman hadn't seen her, and nor had her husband.

Tom ran on to the next group. Louisa followed and stood there with him for a second – unable to follow the flow of information, but reading from the blank, concerned expressions that they hadn't seen her either. Where could she have gone? The water?

Shadowy people were swimming and shouting in the bright round sparkles. She couldn't have gone that far, could she? But perhaps she had, and perhaps she'd fallen over. What if she drowned? What if someone had taken her?

Feeling every second, Louisa ran down to the edge and splashed in. She stood with her feet in the water, searching hopelessly. Why had she let Tom distract her? Why? What could she have been thinking of? And what was Alex going to say if . . . ?

'Polly –' she cried in all directions. Pol-ly!'

Nothing.

Up on the beach, Tom was working his way systematically through the crowds. Louisa waded back out of the water – back towards him. He was talking to a couple of girls – both topless – and one of them was pointing. Louisa ran up.

'. . . *si . . . si, grazie, signorina. Mille grazie. Grazie,*' he turned to Louisa. 'She says she saw the coastguard with a little girl.'

'Does she know where the coastguard is?'

'*Dilà*,' said the girl, pointing again. '*Sotto – sotto l'eucalipto. Riesce a vederla?*'

'*Ah. Ah, si*,' said Tom. 'Over there, Lou – see? By that eucalyptus?'

Louisa looked again. Under the canopy, in patchy light, stood a very brown man in a crisp shirt and navy shorts – he was bending forward, and talking to a little white hat.

After that, it was rather difficult to be cross with Tom. With Polly in her arms, Louisa returned to the villa. Tom came with her – carrying the beach bag, the bucket and the spades. He put them by the front door and turned to go.

'Wait.' Clinging to Polly, Louisa stood in the doorway and looked down at her bloody toe. 'Don't you want any lunch?'

Louisa sank her head well below the surface, held her nose, and resurfaced with her chin up, using the natural weight of the water to smooth back her wet hair.

'I can't bear to think about Alex's reaction – just imagine it, Tom – to come back and be told that I'd lost her.'

'Don't think about it, then.' Smiling, Tom refilled her glass of wine, refilled his own and drank. 'Anyway,' he added, 'she was fine.'

'But how long would it have taken me to realise that?'

It was three o'clock. He and Louisa stood in the

shallow end of the pool, drinking and talking while their skin darkened and their fingers turned to prunes. Tom knew he should be leaving, but he couldn't. Not yet. He couldn't drag himself away from the intoxicating gratitude.

Louisa pushed aside the wine, and heaved herself out of the water.

'Where are you going?'

'I'd better check on her.'

'Again? You only went up ten minutes ago.'

'Won't be long.'

Noticing her wet footprints – already beginning to dry – Tom's eye followed them to where she was, walking back into the house. As if she knew she was being watched, Louisa brought her left hand round and, with her middle finger, adjusted the bottom half of her orange bikini so that it sat straight. Tom watched – appreciating – until she turned a corner.

Polly was asleep. Louisa returned via the kitchen, thinking about Tom. She could think more clearly out of the sunshine, and away from his eyes. He'd told her about what had happened at the funeral, and about Kate's reaction. 'You were right,' he'd said, 'about escaping.' And because he was so upset, and so ashamed, Louisa realised that she didn't despise him at all. She felt sorry for him.

Opening the giant fridge, she took out a bottle of water and poured herself a glass – still thinking about him – and about her reaction to him. It's only because of Polly, she insisted.

But it was the knowledge that Tom was free – that Kate didn't want him now – that had changed the experience of being with him. There were – possibilities – that had not been there before, in London, when she'd sat with him on the roof. Standing in the dim of the kitchen, lit by the open fridge and feeling its frosty air, Louisa accepted the truth of this, and felt a sense of dread – that the terrible things Kate had suspected of her might actually happen. And what kind of person did that make her?

She came back into the sun with another bottle of wine, and was struck by the sight of Tom swimming – crawl – reaching through the water with his elbows and shoulders positioned for maximum power. She watched him get to the shallow end and stop, standing tall, pushing his wet hair from his face, wiping the water from his eyes.

Louisa covered an involuntary smile with her hand – but failed to suppress the feeling of anticipation that radiated excitement from every other part of her as she approached.

She sat on the edge of the pool with her feet in the water while she opened the bottle. Tom came towards her, swimming lazy breast stroke and laughing. 'Not more wine?'

'I thought you'd need it.'

'Me?'

There was a loud squeak as the cork left the bottle. Louisa put the corkscrew to one side, brought a glass to the bottle and began pouring.

'I want you to tell me more about Arabella.'

For a second, Tom said nothing. He simply turned and rested his back on the edge of the pool. Louisa bit her lip – was it too soon for this? She was about to apologise when he replied.

'Not much to say – except of course that you're

right. And I can't forgive myself . . .' He took the glass from her and continued. 'I couldn't resist her. And I couldn't give Kate up either. It seemed easiest just to go with it – you know – let it happen. I did try ending it with Arabella once before, but that didn't work. And then,' he drank quickly and put down the glass hard on the concrete, chipping the base. 'I'm so completely to blame for this. I didn't realise until the funeral, and then of course Kate's disgust . . .'

'What did she say?'

Tom couldn't reply. He put his head in his hands, and shook it.

'It doesn't matter,' Louisa touched his shoulder and slipped down into the water beside him. 'You don't have to say anything. Just listen. Listen when I tell you you're not to blame. Not for Arabella's suicide.'

Tom released his face but continued to look down. He looked at the distortions being made to the floor of the pool by the bright blue ripples on its surface. 'I humiliated her,' he said.

'All right. You humiliated a lot of people. In fact, you've been a complete shit. You've betrayed people, and you've lied and God knows what else. But you weren't to blame for her death.'

'I was. I was.'

'You weren't. Look at me, Tom . . . Tom?'

Tom looked. She was much closer than he expected. In the turquoise light thrown up from the pool, her eyes were startling. Gas-blue and serious and looking back at him.

Both of them thought of Kate, and both were relieved to hear the cars – wheels crunching over the

431

gravel, doors opening – and Alex's voice, over the others.

'Pick those up, Timbo. No. Do it now – we don't want to see them in the sitting room. Put them in the pumphouse. Then you can have your ice-cream.'

———————

Kate had not set her alarm, but she still woke at 6.45 on Saturday morning. It was dark outside, and intermittent footsteps on the pavement below, followed by the sound of a car engine spluttering to life, prompted her to check her clock.

Lying there, watching the dim blue rim round the edges of her bedroom curtains turn white, she ran her mind over the catching up she needed to do in the office. There wasn't that much. Just the points from yesterday's meeting, and pushing on with Project Galaxy.

The window rattled and Kate, shivering in response to the sound, pulled her duvet up closer under her chin. Deciding not to go in that day, she nestled in the warmth of her bed and waited for the foliage pattern on the curtains to appear.

It was never completely quiet in the flat. Even when there was no activity in the street, even when there was no wind to rattle the windows, an ever-present city hummed beyond: the flow of cars over the West Way, of water along the pipes, of trains underground, aircraft overhead – trailing their brief lines of white, crisscross across the sky. Everywhere, a kind of traffic pressing up the density.

Despite all that, to Kate the place was silent. The absence of Tom and Louisa disturbed her far more than the alarm of a neglected car, parked in the square at the end of her street – and she did not get back to sleep.

Later, she ran a bath. After her bath, she made herself a cup of coffee and some toast. She ate and drank them without pleasure, sitting on the sofa, full of weary restlessness. There were things she should be doing. The floor needed hoovering, the bins needed emptying. There were bills that needed to be paid, bills that needed to be opened.

When the telephone rang, it was for Louisa. Searching again for Louisa's parents' number, Kate noticed that Douglas had left his wallet behind. He'd be wondering where it was, she thought, as she relayed the number and hung up. He said he'd be going back to Norfolk today. She should call him now, before he left.

'I've got your wallet,' she said, without first saying who she was, but Douglas recognised her instantly.

'My wallet?'

'Well, I think it's yours. It's stuffed with cash.'

Douglas laughed. 'How embarrassing. I hadn't even missed it.'

'Do you want to pick it up? Or I could drop it round? Or what?'

Douglas decided he had nothing to lose. 'Are you free for lunch?' he said, in a voice that didn't sound like his at all.

He was waiting at a table for two.

Kate walked towards him, shaking out an umbrella and smiling. After he kissed her, she felt in her bag for his wallet and gave it to him. 'I've been very

433

honest. You'll find all your cash and credit cards exactly where you left them.'

Douglas raised his eyes from the wallet, open in his hands, and gave her an uncertain smile. 'I wasn't checking.'

'Yes, you were. You thought I'd pinched a tenner.'

'No, Kate. I promise. I was . . .' Douglas looked up and saw that she was laughing at him. Smiling in defeat, he shut his eyes, and shut the wallet. 'Drink?'

As he went to the bar, Kate noticed that he'd lost weight and that it made him seem very tall. His shabby country shirt was loose on him. He'd rolled up the sleeves. She watched his back, bent slightly, as he stood waiting. He leant on the bar with arms rod-straight from his shoulders to where his hands held onto the edge – the undersides of his wrists facing forward – like he was going to lift it and shove it somewhere. The barmaid came to him and smiled as she took his order.

Kate sat back and looked round the pub. It was empty, for a Saturday, and she was glad. When Douglas had suggested it, she'd imagined a smoke-filled, beer-bellied place with Sky Sports hanging from every corner of the ceiling. But it was fine and warm and comfortable – not noisy at all. And something smelt very good.

Douglas came back with a bottle of wine, two glasses and a basket of bread balanced on his left forearm. As he got closer, she looked at him and smiled – and all the feelings he'd experienced when he'd first seen her in the Savoy flooded back. Kate, noticing, looked away.

She took the bread from him and watched him pour out the wine. They both took their glasses and drank.

'How's Sarah?'

'Fine. I think. Cooking in Italy.'

Kate put down her glass. 'You must be missing her.'

'We've split up.' Douglas kept his gaze on his fingers, at the base of his wine glass. He parted them around the stem and pulled the glass towards him. 'My decision. I think it's better.'

It was still raining hard when they left the pub. They walked under Kate's umbrella to where Douglas had parked his car, past people sheltering in doorways, waiting for the rain to stop – or at least for the weight of it to ease. It fell in sweeps of grey, pummelling the pavement, the trees, the roofs of the cars. Above them both, the umbrella crackled and rattled like something on fire. Douglas was holding it – feeling Kate's hand light in the crook of his arm.

Kate was glad she'd had lunch – a normal weekend lunch, with good wine and hot bread. She was glad she hadn't gone in to work. Shifting her hold on Douglas' arm, she thought how kind he was – and how wrong she'd been. She'd thought of him as a manipulative, interfering snob. Remembering this, she bent her head in shame and smiled at her lack of judgement.

'It's just here on the corner.'

Looking up, she saw a green Land-Rover with Countryside Alliance rally stickers all over the rear window, and a dent in the bumper.

'Not usually this clean,' Douglas confessed, finding

his keys with his left hand and opening the passenger door. 'It's the rain.'

He held the umbrella for her to get in and, once inside, she could see what he meant. Dry mud-dust lingered everywhere and a pile of dirty papers occupied the passenger seat – land agents' particulars covered with George's paw marks, and what looked like a valuation of some furniture.

'Throw that rubbish in the back,' he slammed shut her door and went round to his side. Kate did as he told her and clipped in. At her feet was a large, scuffed road atlas. She put that in the back as well.

Douglas got in and handed her the umbrella. 'Sorry about the mess,' he said. 'I don't usually have visitors.'

The battering of rain was so loud, she had to shout directions. When they got back to her flat, he leapt out, went round to her side of the car and opened the door.

'Thank you.' She slid down, opened the umbrella and – before he knew it had happened – she'd kissed him on the cheek, and was making a dash for her door.

'Goodbye,' she called, running backwards for a second and waving. 'Have a good trip back!' Her voice carried down the empty street, through the rain, towards him.

Douglas watched her open the door, umbrella collapsing as she went inside.

* * *

The dining-room table at the Edwardes' villa was long and thin. It was also extremely heavy, as Nigel and Tom discovered when they tried to heave it across the garden to the flat terraced area by the pool. In the end, they'd had to admit defeat. The round stone table would do – everybody would just have to squash up. Four people would fit on the curved stone seat, and they could put out chairs for the others. Sarah and Louisa had taken five of them from the house and arranged them around the remaining half of the table.

The day was fading now, drifting and cooling. But a mass of burning candles threw the table into a pool of apricot light – light that flashed from a fork, or the arc of a wine glass, and spilt out onto the terrace, across the shiny surface of the swimming pool, leaking into the garden, over the wall and onto the empty road, where the air was quiet and dim.

Anne was thrilled to be sitting next to Tom – she knew all about him from the papers. Did he know the Redesdales? No? But he must have been at school with Johnny. Or was it Guy who'd gone to Eton? She could never remember . . . No? How odd. Well anyway, they lived in Audley Crescent too – only a flat, of course, but *stunning* proportions. Number twenty-six. She remembered that because she'd been twenty-six when Johnny's father, Reedy – Seedy Reedy they'd called him because his clothes never looked clean, and he had terrible wandering hands . . .

Tom smiled, but he wasn't listening. He was looking through the candles – barely flickering, now that the wind had dropped – looking at Louisa, who was sitting opposite, leaning back on the stone seat with her face in shadow, listening to Alex's account of the picnic and playing with her napkin.

Seedy Reedy wasn't the only one with a wandering

hands problem. While Louisa listened to her brother, Richard had leant forward so that nobody could see and was touching her thigh – running a finger slowly up from her knee, dragging with it her flimsy skirt. Louisa pushed the finger away and crossed her thigh over the other one. But that simply meant that the finger could wander down the outside of her leg and practically under her bottom. Leaning for a better angle, Louisa rammed her fist down hard – hard as she could without anyone seeing – and crunched the finger under her knuckles against the stone.

Richard's wandering hand wriggled free, and vanished back into his lap, accompanied by a sharp intake of breath. Looking up to see if anyone had seen, Louisa saw that Tom was looking at her – and that he'd been looking at her for some time.

'. . . and what about the Beaumonts? Surely you know them.'

'What?'

'Freddy and Imogen?'

Tom dragged his attention from a smiling Louisa. 'My father might have known them. Are they horsey?'

'My dear!' Anne laughed. 'Are they horsey? They're obsessed.'

'Then I expect he did know them.'

'Completely obsessed. Freddy lost God knows how many millions . . .'

With a large bowl of butterfly pasta in her arms and a small jug of olive oil hooked around her little finger, Sarah walked up the path towards the pool. She walked through the garden – darkening, and silvery with dew. She could hear Alex's laughter, and the amber warmth of the table seemed to come towards her, out of the evening. She put the bowl beside Anne, the oil in the middle of the table, and went back for the ravioli.

Tom held the bowl for Anne. With both hands, she gripped the wooden handles of the spoons and began to help herself.

'When I was thirty, I was pregnant with my second child,' she was saying. 'Of course, it's fine for you men. But the girls . . . I mean, look at poor Louisa. I do wish we could find someone for her. Sad, don't you think, to come all the way out here, with no dashing chap to whisk her off her feet. It breaks my heart. Why don't I hold it for you? There . . .'

As Tom lifted a pile of pasta onto his plate, Anne observed him for a second. She looked at Louisa, and then back at Tom again.

'Why, of *course*,' she exclaimed. 'What about *you*?'

'Me?'

Tom put the spoons back into the bowl, took it from Anne and held it for Maya, on his other side. 'You and Louisa,' said Anne, delightedly, to his back. '*Perfect!*'

Tom said nothing, until Maya had taken the bowl from him to hold it for Alex. Then he turned back to Anne and said that he didn't think Louisa would consider him.

'But why ever not? You're frightfully glamorous. Louisa?'

Louisa looked up from her napkin.

'Louisa, what's wrong with Tom?'

'Nothing.'

'He says you wouldn't consider him.'

439

Louisa hesitated. But before she could reply, Richard had leant forward and told his wife to shut up. 'You silly woman. It's none of your business.'

'But darling, I was only . . .'

'It's just meddle meddle meddle with you, isn't it?'

'I get into trouble for meddling too,' said Mary quickly. She looked round the silent table and rested her eyes on Richard. 'It can be hard to stop oneself, you know, once one has an idea. One means well, but sometimes it comes out all wrong.'

'I'm sure *you* mean well, Mary.'

'We all do. It's just sometimes – well, anyway. What shall we do tomorrow? Another trip?'

Dinner was short. At the first available opportunity, Anne said that she was tired and went to bed. Maya said that she was quite tired as well. Did Tom want to come back with her now, or . . .? Tom said he'd stay a bit longer, if that was all right.

After she left, Richard and Alex went to the kitchen in search of brandy, and came back noisily with an unlabelled flagon-shaped bottle, a tray of fresh coffee, and Sarah.

Thinking that it might make Louisa jealous, Richard encouraged Sarah to stay. He got everyone to shift round so that Sarah was sitting between himself and Alex, turned his back to Louisa, and began asking Sarah about herself. Where had she learnt to cook so exquisitely? What did she do with herself for the rest of the year? Was it terribly hard work?

He was so engrossed in this, he didn't notice Louisa get up.

She took her glass of wine to the far side of the pool and sat there, dangling her feet in the warmth of the water, half-transfixed by the reflection of the table – upside-down, golden now, and streaked with black. She waited patiently for Tom to finish his conversation with Mary and come to her.

Tom was wearing a pair of trousers he'd borrowed from Alex – to save returning to Maya's villa for his own. Rolling them to his knees, he sat down next to her. He put his feet into the water and marvelled at the temperature. 'How warm it is,' he said.

Louisa nodded, and looked out to where the ripples from his feet sent the gold reflection into chaos.

Mary did not turn to look. She poured milk into her coffee, watched it whirl as she stirred, and listened to Sarah's conversation with Richard.

'. . . and a couple of drinks parties. But I'm really just starting out.'

'And what about over here? Isn't it a nightmare in the market? All those Italian men . . .'

'Not at all. In fact they're incredibly helpful. Especially the fishmonger.'

'I bet he is,' said Alex, offering her a chocolate.

Nigel, who'd been by himself, examining the sky, came round and sat down next to Mary in the chair that Tom had left vacant.

'Hello, my darling,' he said. 'It seems you've been abandoned.'

'I don't mind. I think he's charming.'

'Oh *good*,' said Nigel. 'So do I.'

Nineteen

To begin with, Kate thought that it was just her. The suicide, the split with Tom, the absence of Louisa – they all must have affected her concentration.

She must have received Simon Dalziel's fax – the one outlining MetBank's objections to her amendments to the latest loan documents. She must have just put it to one side for some reason, and then forgotten about it. After all, everybody else had it. And her name and fax number were there, clearly, on Henry's copy, as one of the addressees. It was embarrassing of course to skim through it while the meeting waited, but not critical. She'd just have to make sure that Janet brought her attention to all Hazel Industries correspondence – perhaps make a separate pile – so that it didn't happen again.

But when Janet did that, and still she failed to receive certain faxes and messages – and when she realised that it only happened with Fraser Cummings documents on the Hazel Industries file – she began to suspect that Simon was deliberately cutting her out of the loop.

Following her reaction to his efforts to expose Tom, Simon had been cool towards Kate. He couldn't believe how ungrateful she'd been – especially since she and Tom had now split up. He'd saved her from being shackled to a phoney loser, and all the thanks he'd got was to be told that he was lucky she wasn't going to report him for conspiring in a breach of confidentiality.

Simon took to ignoring her. But there were few opportunities for him to do this effectively and, when he did, Kate didn't seem to mind. If anything, she was amused. He began to see that she'd led him along with the last deal. His client hadn't realised what an unsatisfactory position he'd negotiated, but that didn't stop Simon from feeling a fool. This time, it was going to be different. She'd have to fight him for every point.

Sometimes, when he circulated revised drafts or comments, he didn't copy her in at all. But most of the time he'd just get one of the girls to send all items to Kate at eleven or twelve at night – when everybody else got theirs twelve hours earlier. Make her wait for it. Tire her out. Kate would then be forced to read his comments and consider her response that night, in case her client rang in the morning to discuss it – which, invariably these days, he did, to make sure she was on the ball.

Henry was beginning to have doubts about Kate. It wasn't that he didn't like the girl. She was bright, and personable, and so on. But she was, as he'd always suspected, *unreliable*. He was disappointed with her performance. No stamina, he thought, watching the pale face concentrating – struggling to take all Simon's points on board as she read his latest fax. And there were a lot of points. It had taken Henry the best part of yesterday afternoon to go through that

443

fax. The girl was quick, yes, but it was asking the impossible to expect her to do it in five minutes.

And she wouldn't be in this unfortunate position if she was properly organised. Maybe she had a lot on her plate. Maybe she wasn't experienced enough to handle this level of responsibility. But whatever it was, he wasn't paying them millions in fees to be given this kind of service. It was unacceptable.

'But it's not – my – fault,' said Kate for the third time, her eyes fixed on Michael's.

'Yes, Kate, I understand what you're saying.'

'I don't think you do understand. He's cutting me out deliberately – and you're punishing me for it.'

'I'm not punishing you.' Michael looked at her and sighed. 'It's the client we have to consider. You know that.'

Kate was silent.

'And Henry's not satisfied. From his perspective, you must see your performance has been sub-standard.'

'But only because of Simon. Can't we take it up with Fraser Cummings? Or report him?'

'If you like, but that won't make a jot of difference so far as Henry's concerned. I've got no choice, Kate. I have to take you off the file.'

'It's because I'm a woman.'

'Now come on, Kate. That's unfair.'

'You're too right, it's not fair. Simon's behaving like this because he fancies me, Michael. And because I'm not interested.'

'That's as may be – and I feel for you, Kate. I really do. But the client has to come first.'

It was late. She'd been shut up with Michael in his room for over an hour, battling for the file – and now they both wanted to go home. Kate was exhausted, and that made her tearful. She was determined not to cry in front of him, but Michael could see she was upset.

'What else can I do?' he said at last.

Kate put herself into his position. What else *could* he do? She stood up. 'All right. But I want it documented exactly why this is happening. I don't want this going on my records as something to be ashamed about.'

'Of course.'

'And I want to make an official complaint. He's not getting away with this.'

'Absolutely. So you should. But we can talk about that tomorrow – yes?'

Kate nodded and opened his door. 'Who'll get the file?'

'Me,' said Michael, putting on his coat. 'And Annette.'

Kate returned to her office to find Annette in there, going through her in-tray. She stopped at the door and stared in disbelief.

'Just looking for Dalziel's fax of the fourteenth,' said Annette, not looking up.

Michael must have told her. He must have told her hours ago – before Kate had any idea.

'We didn't get it,' she said dully. 'If you read my attendance note on the meeting of the fifteenth, you'll see why – and there's a photocopy of the one he sent to Henry Hazel stapled to it.'

'Where's that?'

'I think you'll find it in the file, Annette, between the fourteenth and the sixteenth.'

'Are you sure?'

Kate approached the desk. 'Don't push it,' she said.

Annette bridled. 'I just wanted to be clear – completely clear. Henry's been quite – er – specific about efficiency and I do have a nine o'clock meeting with Simon Dalziel tomorrow morning.'

'Lucky you.'

Kate stood aside for Annette to leave. She went to the door and held it for her, but Annette wouldn't drop it. She knew this was difficult for Kate – she even felt sorry for her – but Annette's gladiator instinct compelled her to remain, to consolidate her victory.

'Do you think you can let me have the code numbers for all the Hazel Industries files – all of them – on my desk when I get back? Should be around eleven. I'll need an up-to-date list of telephone numbers. And I do need to go through where you are on billing. Perhaps Adam could help with that, now that you're less busy – and he should come to meetings with me . . .'

'Annette – please. I have to make a call.'

'Mike did say he could, you know. For the sake of continuity.'

Too flat to be angry, Kate closed the door behind her and returned to her desk. Sitting at it, she looked around the room – at the rows of books and legal journals shelved along the wall to her left, with the odd page marked with a yellow Post-it note. She looked at the grey and white Willis & Storm cardboard boxes, piled up on the chair between her desk and Adam's – at the details of their contents, scrawled along the outsides in a black marker-pen that was obviously drying out. She looked at the scuffed picture of Arabella – the one Adam had put up – still taped to the wall.

And then she looked at the calendar, hanging from a drawing pin nearby – and she thought of all the lost evenings, the lost weekends.

What *was* the point? What had she gained from committing to this life, to a career that seemed so indifferent to her?

Kate stared at the mess Annette had made of her in-tray. Picking up the *While You Were Out* slip of paper that had fallen out, Kate read in Heather's writing that Douglas had called at ten-thirty that morning. Was she free for dinner tomorrow night?

You bet I am, she thought, reaching for her telephone.

———————◆◆◆———————

When Annette and Adam returned from their meeting the following morning, Adam moved into Annette's room – temporarily – to help with the Hazel Industries file transfer. And while this meant that Kate was deprived of Adam's services, it also meant that Annette had no reason for coming into her office. Kate had silence, and privacy.

When her mother rang, she was able to talk.

'Any news about Singapore?'

'No – but Tim Cheung's in London. I'm being interviewed tomorrow.'

With the speaker-phone on, Kate was able to use the computer and talk at the same time. She came out of the document she was working on – a lecture to the department on Private Finance for Hospital and Prison Projects: the Borrower's Perspective – and waited for the 'Automatic Save' function on her

447

computer to finish before checking her e-mail.

'You're still applying?'

'Mum . . .'

'I'm sorry, darling. It's just I can't believe that you really want this. Why Singapore? You've never been there. You don't know anybody living there. You're running in blind . . .' Elizabeth sighed and softened her tone. 'Don't you think that this is less about Singapore, and more about giving up on life here in London?'

'I am not.'

'Darling, you are. You never go out.'

'I do go out.'

'Then tell me when you last let anyone take you out to dinner. It's been months . . .'

'I've got a date tonight, as it happens.'

'Really?' said Elizabeth.

'Really.'

'Who? Who with?'

Kate checked her e-mail. There were eleven new messages – all from people in her department. The first one was from Adam and headed, 'I thought lawyers weren't your type . . .'

'You don't know him.'

'What's his name?'

'All right, it's Douglas. But I . . .'

'John Douglas?'

'That's right. And it's not . . .'

'But I do know him. I met him at your party, darling. He was charming.'

'Mum – there's nothing between us. Nothing at all. It's only dinner . . .'

Kate could sense her mother smiling.

'. . . it *is* only dinner,' she insisted, highlighting and double-clicking the first of her eleven messages.

'*So,*' Adam wrote, '*is it true? Have you finally succumbed?*'

'Whatever you say, darling. I'm just glad that you're . . .'

'Hang on, Mum – something very odd's just . . .'

Kate clicked on the next one – from Michael. '*Who's the lucky fellow?*'

These messages were being circulated to everybody in Kate's group. Looking up, she saw Heather, Gavin and Steve making faces at her through the glass door – with Janet just behind. It opened, and Gavin came in first – aiming a rubber band at Kate's face.

Kate ducked and grabbed the receiver. 'Mum – I'll call you back.'

'What's so special about Simon Dalziel?' said Gavin. 'Apart from his ridiculous name.'

'What?'

'Haven't you read your e-mails?' said Heather.

'What – what is all this? What about Simon?' Kate looked from them to her screen and back again. 'I don't understand.'

'Oh, she's very good, isn't she?'

'Very good *what*, Gavin? What are you talking about?'

'Very good – very convincing – but we know better, don't we? We know all about what you get up to when nobody's looking.'

Kate shook her head. 'I really don't know what it is you're all on about. Either tell me, or leave. Some of us have work to do.'

'Maybe she didn't actually sleep with him,' said Heather.

'Sleep with . . .? You think I got it together with Simon Dalziel?'

'We know you did.'

'What do you mean, you know I did? Take it from me, I didn't. And I think I'd remember if I did – don't you? And there's no way,' sensing that the more fuss she made, the harder it would be, she forced a smile – but inside she was raging. 'If you saw him, you'd understand.'

'Is that right, Adam?'

'What's he look like?'

'He's not my type.'

'But he might be Kate's type.' Gavin aimed the rubber band at Kate's face again.

'Gavin,' she laughed. 'Stop it.' If she hadn't raised her hand, he'd have got her on the nose.

'You still haven't answered my first question, Miss Leonard. Why Simon Dalziel? Is it the irresistible mystique of Fraser Cummings? The nice little edge it adds to your late-night meetings? What?'

'I don't know who's feeding you all this crap, Gavin – but you need to check your sources.'

'My sources are impeccable.'

'Your sources are defamatory.'

'Kate,' his voice was mock-shocked, 'are you telling me that Annette and Adam are guilty of defamation?'

'Annette? Adam? Yes, they bloody well are . . .'

Gavin perched on the edge of Adam's desk, facing Kate, and took another rubber band from his pocket. 'I think we need Annette in here, don't we? Somebody get Annette.'

Heather went.

Annette came in, unable to look at Kate. 'I only told Adam what Simon told me,' she said.

'And what was that?'

'He told me he took you out to dinner.'

'Yes,' said Kate. 'Yes, he did. A business dinner, Annette – not a date.'

Annette shook her head and looked at Gavin. 'But Simon told *me* that she – she . . .'

'Yes?'

'She . . . well – you know.' Annette couldn't say it, so Gavin did.

'She shagged him. Right?'

'He was very complimentary.'

'Rea-lly?' said Gavin, looking at Kate and stretching the rubber band as far as it would go. 'How interesting? Are you free tonight?'

'No.'

'Hot date with Simon?'

'No!'

'All right,' said Michael, coming in. 'The rest of you – out. I want to talk to Kate.' He held the door for them, and then closed it. 'I spoke to Adam,' he said. 'Are you okay?'

Kate looked at him for a second. 'I know,' she sighed. 'I know you'll say it's not such a big deal. I know other people have affairs, one-night stands – whatever – in and around the office all the time. But this kind of gossip, Michael – particularly when it's connecting me with someone on the other side of a transaction. And on top of everything that's happened . . . no. No, I'm not okay. It's bloody unprofessional, and it's . . .'

'It's undermining your reputation?'

'Yes.'

'You want to make an official complaint?'

Kate nodded.

'Put everything in a memo to me – get your facts straight with Annette – and we'll take it from there.'

Kate spent all day on her memo. Then, at six-thirty, as she was printing it off, she was told by Heather that Tim Cheung wanted both her and Annette to write a short piece on why they were applying for the Singapore position, and why they thought they should get it. On his desk. First thing in the morning.

Kate rang Douglas on his mobile. 'I'm running late.'

'Would you prefer another night?'

'Certainly not. Just don't worry about picking me up.'

'Are you sure? I'm more than happy to . . .'

'Sure. I'll get a cab and meet you at the restaurant. Is nine okay?'

'Nine's fine.'

Douglas gave her the name of the restaurant, the address, and told her he'd be there from nine on. 'Don't worry if you're late. I'll bring a newspaper.'

———◆———

Kate walked down a flight of stone steps towards a heavy wooden door. The steps were slippery, and she trod carefully, holding onto the cold, wet rail. It must have been raining all day, she thought. Yet again, she'd been too office-insulated to notice.

Inside the restaurant it was so dark that, for a second, it was hard to work out the arrangement of the room at all. But as her eyes became accustomed,

Kate saw that the tables were set deep into the rough stone walls, so that each one could be private. The walls of each flickering hollow were covered with gilded mirrors, side-lit with candles. And at the far end, she noticed a short flight of stone steps leading down to another table, slightly larger than the rest, and set about with orchids.

It had to be the wrong restaurant.

Kate turned. She pushed open the heavy door and walked out, back up the steps again into Douglas, coming down.

'Hey. Where are you going?'

'Douglas . . .'

From his upper step, he had to bend double to kiss her cheek.

'I thought it was the wrong place,' she said.

'They didn't take my booking?'

'I don't know,' she muttered, following him back in. 'I just . . .'

Douglas took her coat and umbrella. 'Where's Philippe?' he demanded of the teenage waiter, passing them with his hands full of dirty plates and glasses.

The boy nodded. Then with a professional thrust of his elbow, he flicked open a tapestry curtain to their left to reveal, for a second, the sharp-lit engine of the restaurant, caught in a blue flash of chrome and ultra-violet.

They waited, looking at the curtain. But Philippe appeared from the other direction. He greeted Douglas, took the umbrella and their coats, and led them to the table at the far end. Without reference to Kate, Douglas ordered two glasses of champagne. Then he turned his attention to her.

'Have you been here before?'

'Never.'

'What do you think?'

Kate hesitated.

'You don't like it.'

'No,' she smiled. 'No, I do. I like it very much. I'm just surprised.'

The teenage waiter brought their glasses of champagne – long, slim flutes, precarious on their tray. Conscious of the fragile stem of hers, Kate held it in a hand knotted tight from hammering a computer keyboard all day – and wondered if it would break. She noticed how Douglas brought his easily to his lips. He gave it a swift unthinking tilt and asked her about her day.

Sipping in jerks, Kate told him. She explained about Simon Dalziel, about losing the file to Annette, and about the gossip. Douglas listened – vicarious indignation swelled with every word.

'And weren't you furious?' he said.

'Of course I was furious. But I couldn't let the others see that. If I made an issue of it, if I showed them that I minded, I'd be mincemeat.'

'Because it's your reputation at stake? You think the less people talk about it, the less damage you'll suffer?'

'Exactly.'

'You can control yourself that much?'

'Just about.'

'If I were you, I'd have exploded without thinking.'

Kate laughed. 'No you wouldn't,' she said. 'You'd have reported him to the Disciplinary Tribunal – which is what I'm going to do.'

'So he'll get his knuckles rapped?'

'With the stuff about delaying faxes – withholding information – I hope he'll get struck off. But it'll take forever, and in the meantime I've lost a client and my reputation's in shreds.'

She didn't smile. Looking at the dejected slope of her shoulders, Douglas longed to lift her free. He wanted to say to her, 'Don't worry about it any more. Leave it with me.' But he couldn't, because that wasn't the way things were done any more, and because he wouldn't have the first idea how to bring an official complaint to the Disciplinary Tribunal.

'I'm so impressed,' was all he could say. 'So impressed by the way you cope with things.'

'Not coping so well at the moment.'

'Rubbish. When I think of what you've been through – what with Tom and Arabella, and losing your best friend, and now this . . .'

Kate was biting her lip.

'. . . it's incredible. Where do you find the stamina? How do you keep going?'

Kate said nothing. She'd felt his sympathy, and all her efforts were concentrated in an internal struggle to dam up the surges of self-pity.

Douglas interpreted the silence. 'Or is it sometimes too much,' he said, 'even for you?'

'I . . .'

'Would you prefer to go home?'

'I'm fine.'

But Douglas could see that she wasn't. Here at last was something constructive he could do for her. 'We'll cancel the order, and my car's just outside. You'll be much better off with a decent night's rest. Not sitting here listening to me.'

'But I . . .'

'You're exhausted.' Signalling to the surprised waiter for his bill, Douglas got up and went round to her side of the table. 'Come on,' he said, easing Kate's chair back as, still unsure, she stood.

'It seems an awful waste.'

'Not at all. I'll get your coat.'

Climbing into the Land-Rover, she had to squeeze her legs in next to George, whose body filled the footwell of the passenger seat. After a display of sniffing and wagging, George settled his warm weight back down over her feet. She felt his wet nose through her stockings and reached to stroke him while Douglas got in.

Inside, it was tidier. There was still a smell of petrol and straw, but Douglas had removed his papers and it seemed that some attempt had been made to get rid of the mud – although that could have been just because it was dark.

He had to reverse to get out of his parking slot. Putting a consciously platonic arm along the back of Kate's seat to steady himself, he turned and the car rolled back.

'Now you're not going to starve, are you? You've got food in the fridge? Or do you want me to order you one of your pizzas on this thing?' Braking decisively, facing forward again and switching gear, Douglas pointed at the mobile phone on a pod between them.

Kate smiled. 'I'll be fine.'

Their Land-Rover worked its way through the grid of streets just south of the Cromwell Road, into Gloucester Road, heading north. They stopped at the

456

traffic lights – a light rain tapping on the windscreen – and Douglas switched on the wipers.

'I'm so sorry about this,' said Kate, as they moved north over the Cromwell Road, then west – more rain with every wipe.

'Not at all. You need your sleep.'

She nodded, and stared at the black stretch of railings, at the row of doorways – each with a pair of pillars and worn stone steps – repeated to the end of the street. It did something odd to her eyes.

'Busy day tomorrow?'

'Not busy,' she blinked, 'but important. I've got an interview.'

Douglas turned left into Queensgate and then quickly right – heading for where Exhibition Road led into the park – before registering what it was she'd said.

'An interview? You're leaving Willis & Storm?'

'No,' Kate smiled. 'Not yet. It's for a job in our Singapore office.'

'*Singapore?*'

'You sound like my mother.'

Douglas stopped at the lights to the park, and looked at her.

'What?' she demanded. 'What? And don't *you* tell me I'm giving up, or running away or whatever. I'm not.'

'Have you thought of what you'll be leaving behind?'

'Oh, I know: the empty flat, the broken relationships, the miserable weather. I must be mad.'

The lights went green. Douglas released the brake and drove slowly into the park. He said nothing and, in the space he'd left her, Kate had to acknowledge that, all right, so it did sound a bit like . . .

'I'm moving on.' She looked at his profile, wondering if he'd heard her. 'I'm moving on, Douglas. What's so wrong with that?'

They drove through the park in clattering rain, both of them looking ahead – both focused on the red tail-lights of the car in front, blurring and then clearing with each wipe.

There was a parking space directly outside her flat. Douglas reversed into it, and turned off the engine. He turned it off halfway so that the noise from the motor died, but the steady click and rub of the windscreen wipers remained, along with the apple-green spots of light on the dials and digits in front of them.

Kate undid her seat belt.

Douglas looked at his hands, still on the steering wheel.

Holding the end of her seat belt, Kate heard him sigh and turned. 'What is it?'

His arms were straight, parallel and straight from shoulder to wrist, like they'd been at the bar the day they'd had lunch. Her eye followed the line of his shoulder up over the collar of his shirt, up his neck to where the clean hairline met his ear. He was very still.

Kate sensed his difficulty. She knew he minded about Singapore, and she knew why. What surprised her was that she wasn't shrinking from it. 'What is it, Douglas? What's wrong?'

'I don't know what to do,' he said at last.

'What about?'

'About – about the way I feel about you.'

'How do you feel?'

Relaxing his arms, he dropped his hands to the

bottom of the steering wheel and looked at her. 'Can't you tell?'

'Yes,' she said. 'Yes, I can.'

Douglas sighed again and bent his head. 'It's no good, is it? I mean, why on earth would someone – would you – consider . . .'

Kate opened her heart to his total lack of arrogance. 'What makes you think that I wouldn't?'

He was looking back at her – stupidly, miserably. 'Wouldn't what?'

'I feel the same,' she said – hoping, as with absolute sincerity he kissed her, hoping fervently that she did.

Douglas couldn't believe it. He was actually kissing her. This wasn't in his head – this was happening – and she was kissing him back, and smiling at him, and touching him with her hands. Pulling back to look at her, trying to take it in, he felt weightless. No more need for concealing, or pretending, or holding back from kissing her, touching her. He could put his hands, his lips, here – or here – or anywhere. He could do anything – say anything.

'I love you,' he confessed freely, between kisses. 'I love you.'

He watched her smiling face come up close again to kiss his mouth. She hadn't said it back to him, but that didn't matter. It was enough to have her here with him.

After an indefinite stretch of time, Kate stopped kissing him. With her face still very close to his – their noses almost touching – she suggested they go inside.

'Aren't you tired?'

'Yes – but that's not . . .'

'I think you're tired,' he said. 'Don't get me wrong

459

– I could go on like this forever. But you, my poor overworked darling . . . you need your sleep, and I'm going to make sure you get it.'

'But I want . . .'

'No buts.' He got out of the Land-Rover on his side and came round to let her out. 'Come on – get out.'

Kate slipped out, lifting her feet round a very quiet George, who snuffled at her as she left and then watched them from the footwell, past the open door.

Douglas brought her to him, and held her there. 'Get some rest,' he said in her ear, and then kissed it. 'Get some rest, and I'll call you first thing tomorrow. We'll make a plan for tomorrow night – are you free?'

'Yes.'

They kissed again.

'Good night.'

He stood watching as she let herself in – a waving silhouette before the door closed. Shutting the passenger-seat door, he went round the front of the car to his own side, got in, and drove back to his room at Gibbs's.

———— ◆◆◆ ————

Douglas did exactly what he said he would do. He rang her first thing, checked that she really was free, and told her he was picking her up at seven – which he did – and then took her to a small restaurant at the bottom of Kensington Church Street. It wasn't one he knew, but he'd noticed it from the outside and thought it looked nice. And it was close to her flat – but not so close as to seem presumptuous.

After all, she might have had second thoughts. She might have woken up in her flat this morning – wishing *wishing* that last night hadn't happened.

460

Douglas was very glad he'd resisted the temptation to go inside with her. Imagine if he'd spent the night – imagine if he'd woken up next to her, with her thinking, Oh my God. What have I done? – a bit like the way he'd felt the first morning he'd woken up next to Sarah, still liking her but knowing it was wrong. It would have been awful. Better to do it like this – take it slow.

When she saw Douglas waiting for her in the Willis & Storm lobby – tall and attractive, and smiling – Kate was relieved. The truth was that she *had* woken up with second thoughts. It wasn't that she hadn't enjoyed kissing him. And as for being kissed by him – she'd loved that. Thinking about it that day, she was reminded of a pianist – an American – she'd heard play at Oxford. The man's hands were built for hard labour. He was tall and slightly clumsy, with an uncomplicated expression on his face. But he'd played with dazzling sensitivity – with all the wonder of someone discovering those notes for the very first time – and Kate had been transfixed.

She didn't wish it hadn't happened, but she was bothered by the lack of balance – concerned that, in spite of the physical connection, she wasn't keen *enough* – and that, perhaps, she was leading him on. What worried her was Douglas confessing that he loved her – his sincerity, his restrained intensity. She hoped she hadn't made a terrible mistake.

Seeing him there at the bottom of the escalator, talking happily to the security guard, she realised instantly that she hadn't. He kissed her on the cheek, the way he'd always done – but with a private flicker of amusement in eyes that acknowledged the difference between that kind of kiss, and the kissing from last night. She knew exactly. She saw straight in to where he was busily imagining shocked reactions to the latter – here, in the very serious lobby of Willis & Storm. He walked with her to the revolving doors, standing aside for her to go first. Following him to his car, she had the sense that he was in control – of himself, and of the evening – and she found his confidence infectious.

Later, after dinner, he didn't leave her at the door. He didn't try to, and – even if he had – she wouldn't have let him.

––––––◆◆◆––––––

From the moment he started going out with Kate, Douglas went back to Norfolk only once – to collect more clothes, and George's basket. He justified his absence to his father and his agent on the grounds that it was important for him to be on-site while his house was being converted. He pointed out that he hadn't used London builders before, and said he didn't think that Rod and Fiona were sufficiently capable of getting tough with them.

Kate thought that it was ridiculous for him to stay at Gibbs's when he could stay with her for nothing, so Douglas and George had moved in – temporarily.

Douglas kept all his things in Louisa's room, out of Kate's way, but he worried about George. He knew that, in spite of looking quite clean on the surface, George was filthy underneath (Mrs Brady was always complaining about the dirt he spread). But Kate didn't seem to notice or, if she did, to mind. In fact, she loved having them there. She loved coming back in the evenings to a home full of life, to welcoming yelps and presents of socks, and a cool glass of wine.

Often, they'd order pizzas and sit with them on their laps, watching television. And George would watch them. He'd watch their hands, the bits of pizza in their fingers, the food going into their mouths, the wrappings going into the kitchen bin. Sometimes Kate gave him something, but Douglas was very strict.

Some weeks after he arrived, he caught her feeding George scraps in the kitchen – George's nose snuffling busily over the pizza boxes as Kate held them out. But Douglas couldn't bear to get angry with two sets of anxious eyes. He just looked at them with a defeated expression and then laughed. 'It's not fair. I can't fight you both.'

Later, while Kate had her bath, Douglas took George out. He waited for George to sniff at a couple of lamp-posts, cock his leg on one of them and wander back. George took his time, and Douglas had to haul him off the dustbins, pull a triangular plastic sandwich container from his mouth and scold him before they both returned.

Douglas then poured himself another glass of wine and settled at the desk to do his correspondence. There seemed to be so much of it – so many letters, projects, lists, reports, statements from stockbrokers, accountants. He switched on the light and bent over his papers.

When Kate came back from her bath, into the sitting room, she saw him at the desk – his shirt always seemed to get untucked at the back, but she liked the way it did that. She liked the genuinely unself-conscious way he wore his clothes.

George lay directly under his chair, apparently

asleep. He looked up when Kate came in, but Douglas hadn't heard her. The wine glass was empty. He was sitting back in the chair, examining a letter with some figures at the bottom. She watched him pick up the pen – pushing off the lid with his thumb – then he leant forward and made some adjustments to the figures. He put the letter on a pile to his left and took another one from the pile on his right. It was a big pile.

Kate smiled. She could understand that kind of concentration – the kind that meant you didn't hear when someone came into a room, the kind that meant you weren't even aware of getting uncomfortable – and she liked seeing him like that. She liked the fact that his life did not revolve entirely around her. And yet, in another sense, it did. He knew far more about her daily life than anyone else – even her mother. He made it his business to find out if she'd eaten, if she was tired, if her glass was empty. But he knew when to leave her alone.

Seeing Douglas sitting there like that made all of this clear to her – and Kate felt something shift inside. She loved him. Just having him here in the flat made her problems at work – the disciplinary issues with Simon Dalziel, the Singapore application – all of them less crucial, less traumatic. Of course they were still there, still important – particularly Singapore. If she was accepted for Singapore, then the other problems would disappear, she'd have the confidence of the firm, and she'd be a million miles away from Simon Dalziel. But, in the meantime, there was nothing like sex with Douglas to put the rest of the world into perspective.

'Come to bed,' said Kate.

He turned round and smiled at her. She could see in his eyes that she was pretty.

'Come on,' she said again.

'No, you come here.'

She came over, and put a hand on his shoulder.

'What do you think?' he handed her the letter. 'Rod Maris is charging me twenty grand for extra work in the garden.'

Kate read it quickly. 'It's because he knows how much you're making with the conversion, isn't it? You can tell from the letter.'

Douglas pulled her onto his lap. 'You smell lovely,' he kissed her, 'and you taste lovely . . .'

'You taste of wine.'

'. . . and you're absolutely right about Rod,' he took the letter from her and dropped it to the floor so that he could get both arms round her properly, 'although I expect it's Fiona. She's going to get an earful from me tomorrow. I'll tell her. My girlfriend's a hot-shot lawyer, I'll say, so don't even think of . . .'

He broke off to let her kiss him.

'Come to bed.'

'Insatiable,' he said as, laughing, she wriggled from his grasp and forced him from the chair.

Douglas slept lightly when he was with her. Sometimes, not at all. He'd lie on his side and hold her – with her back to him, her hair wound over her shoulder – and time his breathing with hers.

Twenty

'That's all right. I've got pots.'

'You really don't mind?'

'I love you, Tom Faulkener. And I love you all the more for refusing Arabella's money.'

'Well, it wasn't mine. Not really. I couldn't . . .'

'Of course you couldn't. And you couldn't help the fact that your father lost everything with Lloyds. So please, let's not talk about it.'

Tom stood back for Louisa to go first as a doorman held open the door. Louisa sped in and headed straight for the shoes. Smiling, he followed. He loved Gucci. He loved Prada. He loved this street in Rome, and it was fabulous to be here – to be here for real, with real money to spend.

Affectionately, he watched her work the shop. She was as good at it as he was. She knew exactly which shoes to linger over, and which ones to ignore. She knew the importance of soles that were made from one seamless cut of leather, knew to check the pressure points, and how to spot shoddy craftsmanship.

As her slim brown fingers with their pale rounded nails crept, caressed and pressed their way over the shoe – turning it, and marvelling at it – Tom couldn't help but think of the way she'd been doing that to him recently. It had felt so right. He wanted to take her back to their hotel right now – take off the pink linen shirt that had been fluttering against her all morning, brushing against the brief line of a breast, or shifting slightly to give him a glimpse of the fine hair on the back of her neck – the wisps that hadn't made it up into the tortoiseshell clip. He wanted to bury his nose in her skin again, and inhale that addictive combination of Chanel, Louisa and warm Rome dust. He was looking at that part of her neck as now – with her back to him – Louisa held the shoe under a light and bent her head to inspect the price tag on the bottom.

'Will you ask her how much that is in pounds?'

Tom looked at the price himself and told her.

'Really? Only that? You're sure they haven't missed off a couple of noughts?'

'I'm sure,' he laughed.

She bought three pairs in as many minutes and waited for the cashier to deal with her credit card. The sight of that card brought Tom back to thoughts of money – and what Louisa's parents would say when they found out that he had none.

'It may not matter to you,' he said, 'but what about your father? He's hardly going to approve of you choosing a man without a penny.'

'Stop it, Tom. Dad's been desperate for me to get married, desperate to give a massive wedding ever since I can remember. And now – *at last* – the missing element is here. Believe me. He'll be on his knees to you with gratitude . . . where do I sign?'

Tom watched the flowing lines and the happy dot fall from her pen.

They left the shop with their crisp new bags and headed for the restaurant, accompanied by their reflections – dark and expensive – shifting in flashes with the varied angles and tints of the windows as they walked to the end of the street.

Nigel and Mary had exchanged glances when Louisa announced that she wouldn't be staying the whole three weeks – that she was going to join Tom in Rome instead. She'd been to Rome before, but – well, she wanted to see it properly this time, and improve her Italian.

They weren't a bit surprised to get a call from her – a month later – to say that she and Tom were coming to England, together, and could they come to Dorset that weekend?

'Just us, Mum. Don't get anybody over.'

It was perfect, thought Louisa – her body chilling with the blast of air conditioning as they entered the restaurant for lunch – perfect, apart from Kate.

Douglas was in the Ladies' Sitting Room at Gibbs's, waiting. He was due to have dinner with Kate and her mother, but Kate had rung to say that she was going to be late. She had a last-minute meeting – something about Singapore – and Douglas could tell from her voice that she was expecting to hear tonight if they'd be sending her.

Douglas had not mentioned Singapore to Kate again. Not since that time in the car, except to ask, occasionally, how the application was going. He kept hoping she'd tell him that she was dropping it – that she didn't want to go – but she never did. If anything, she was getting more determined. Part of that determination, he knew, was down to the trouble with Simon Dalziel. Kate had something to prove. Her reputation was on the line, and she was looking to Singapore to restore it.

But it made him sad to see that he was, basically, irrelevant. Kate wasn't stupid. She could see that her going to Singapore would spell the end of what they had. He could just about arrange his life in line with hers when she was in London, but anywhere abroad would be impossible. It was him or Singapore – and she'd chosen Singapore.

Douglas thought back over the last few weeks. It was going so well. He and Kate had hardly missed a night together. Okay, so most of those nights had been in her flat, her bed – but she'd come to Waveney at the weekends. She'd loved it there. And yet, none of this was enough. It didn't mean as much to her as it meant to him, and he was going to have to live with that. He loved her – and if he loved her he should want her to get whatever made her happy. But how Douglas wished that it was having him that did that for her – and not some foreign placement.

More immediately, however, Kate being late tonight meant that he and Mrs Leonard would have to cope with each other, alone, until she arrived. And the longer Douglas waited, the more anxious he became.

He'd met Mrs Leonard before and liked her, but he was still uncomfortable. Now that he was Kate's boyfriend, he felt less relaxed about her mother. Would he hate her? Would she be another Mrs Knowles?

When it wasn't being used for drinks parties, the Ladies' Sitting Room fell naturally into four corners, and tonight each corner was occupied by people waiting for other people to arrive. At the other end of the room, a woman of about fifty was being led over to a group of three. Douglas smiled as he watched. She was pretty, and clearly from the country. It was the quality of her skin, the un-coiffed heavy grey hair, the sensible shoes and bag – and the crazy bright green power-suit that was much too big for her.

The other three stood up to greet her. They went straight in to dinner, followed by a group of people younger than Douglas that had been congregating in another corner.

That left Douglas, and one other person – a woman. She was sitting diagonally opposite with her legs crossed, and she was reading a magazine. Douglas looked again. He looked around the flowers in the centre of the round table, and almost dropped his glass. It was Davina Knowles.

At exactly the same moment, Elizabeth entered the room with a club waiter. 'Mr Douglas is over there in the corner, madam. By the desk.'

Davina Knowles stretched her neck round the flowers as Elizabeth came towards him, smiling. Douglas looked from one mother to the other.

'Hello, Douglas. How are you?'

He kissed Elizabeth's cheek. 'Very well. Very well indeed. Drink?'

He busied himself with the waiter, ordering Mrs Leonard's glass of champagne, explaining that they wouldn't be eating until nine. He was about to sit down when he heard the magazine shut. He heard

470

Mrs Knowles leave her chair and walk to the table – she was putting the magazine back on the pile, she was coming over.

'Hello.'

'Hello, Mrs Knowles. Do – do you know . . .?' It was obvious they didn't know each other, and Douglas introduced them. From all the smiling and nodding, it crossed his mind that perhaps Mrs Knowles thought that he and Sarah were still together, and then the smiling stopped.

'So . . .'

'So,' he echoed, smiling hard at Mrs Knowles in an attempt to bring back her former expression, 'are you in London long?'

'I suppose you thought that Sarah wasn't good enough for you.'

'It's got so much colder, hasn't it?'

'If you *knew* the pain this man has inflicted on my daughter,' she said to Elizabeth and then turned back to Douglas. 'Well, don't think she's missing you. She's not.'

'I'm really very pleased to hear that, Mrs Knowles. I was worried . . .'

'Then no doubt you'll also be pleased to hear that she's just had a lovely time in Italy – with the heir to Falcombe Abbey. *His* requirements are obviously less exacting than yours . . .'

'I'm glad – really glad. And it's lovely that she's doing so well with her cooking, isn't it? I'm sure they all adore . . .'

'You have a problem with that? You think cooking's insufficiently smart?'

'No. Not at all. Quite the rever . . .'

'I think that you must be one of the most arrogant men I have ever had the misfortune to meet,' she said, and then turned to Elizabeth. 'Good night.'

They watched her leave – and found they had the room to themselves.

Slowly, Douglas looked at her. Elizabeth had her head bent. She was feeling around in her handbag, beside her on the sofa. 'Well, after all that excitement, I definitely need a cigarette,' she pulled out a fresh packet. 'Want one?'

He shook his head.

She undid the wrapper and gave him a sidelong glance. 'Am I allowed? Or will she bite my head off as well?'

'You're allowed,' he smiled, and then shut his eyes. 'What must you be thinking?'

Elizabeth settled herself back into the sofa and lit up. 'I'm thinking, poor you,' she said, exhaling. 'I'm thinking, what an appalling woman.'

'She was angry. It's true, I was seeing her daughter, but I . . .'

'Stop,' Elizabeth waved him quiet with the palm of her hand – the cigarette filter poking out from between her index and middle fingers, 'please stop. You don't need to explain any of this to me. Really. It's none of my business – and from the little Kate's told me about you, I'm sure you behaved perfectly.'

'What has she said?'

'Oh, nothing. Nothing specific,' she smiled. 'But you do seem to spend your time picking her up from work, dropping her off – spoiling her, in fact. And you mustn't. It's very bad for her.'

'She works so hard.'

'Too hard . . . did I hear you tell the waiter she won't be here till nine?'

Douglas nodded. 'Something about Singapore. There's a meeting – I think she might hear tonight.'

Kate stood on the escalator, staring into space.

When she reached the bottom she began walking in the direction of the underground – propelled forwards by the automatic weariness of someone tied to a daily route. Kate knew that route better than any clause of any loan agreement. From the exact weight necessary to activate the revolving doors, to the number of strides she could fit into the break in the steps that led to that loose pavement at the bottom – the one that rocked – Kate knew that route so deeply that she'd long stopped noticing it, unless something got in her way.

Today, she trod it with the lifeless confidence of a sleepwalker, and it wasn't until she reached the underground – she'd gone through the barriers – that she remembered she wasn't supposed to be going home at all. She was supposed to be at Gibbs's, and that meant taking a taxi.

It was harder to walk against the flow of commuters – she had to dodge and react as she made her way out, up and into the street again.

Safe at last in the darkness of her cab, Kate let the disappointment surface. Only now could she see how much she'd depended on being chosen for Singapore. She needed to show everyone that, in spite of the problems, she was still a success. Instead, it was because of the problems – the gossip, the things Simon had said about her, the way she'd looked so unprofessional – it was because of these things that she had failed to get the placement. It was just too risky for them to send her to Singapore now. She tried to cheer herself up with thoughts that at least Annette would be gone – away for years. But that did nothing to lift the particular loneliness of her failure. Douglas and her mother would show sympathy, but at heart she knew they would be pleased.

Elizabeth could tell what had happened from the way Kate crossed the club dining room.

'Oh darling . . .'

Kate was glad not to have to find the words.

Douglas was still mesmerised by her face when he saw it in a room full of people. It didn't seem to matter if she was smiling or not – if she was dressed up, made up and sparkling, or if, like today, she wasn't.

He stood, waiting patiently for her mother to finish, before kissing her himself on both cheeks. He had to look away from her mouth – lovely, newly familiar, half-open – to stop himself from kissing that as well. Then he moved so that she could sit between them.

'Did they say why?'

'They just preferred the other girl.'

'How could they prefer her? How *could* they?'

'I don't know. They just did.'

Douglas' eyes darted from daughter to mother and back again as he read between the lines.

'Red or white?' he said.

'Red. Thanks.'

He filled her glass and gave her a menu.

Kate drank her wine and looked at it, while they both looked at her. There was a very long pause.

'Have anything,' said Douglas. He leant round to remind himself of the menu. 'The terrine's supposed to be quite good.'

'And the waitress was saying that the lamb looks nice today, wasn't she?'

Douglas nodded.

'All right,' Kate gave the menu back to Douglas, 'I'll have the terrine and then I'll have the lamb.' She could feel their relief – in the light way Douglas handed the menu to the waitress and relayed her order, in the springy tone of her mother's voice.

'Douglas was telling me about his garden.'

'Was he?'

'I do think you're clever,' Elizabeth smiled at him, and turned back to Kate, who was frowning slightly. 'You know, darling. The extensions to – the *kitchen* garden, is it?'

Douglas nodded. 'It'll be something like four times the size, by the time we're through.'

'And when do you think that'll be?' said Elizabeth, taking out another cigarette.

'Well, the whole area's a mess at the moment. We've got diggers and building contractors in there – putting up walls, constructing special hothouses and God only knows what else. It'll take at least three months just to get that done, and then we've got all the planting . . .'

'But when did you decide all this?' Kate stared at him. 'Why didn't I know?'

Douglas smiled. 'Well, it's mainly Chris, the gardener. I just okay his plans. And it was Mrs

Brady's idea in the beginning – so I can't claim much of the credit. It was only because your mother was asking about the lavender.'

'You obviously didn't ask him, sweetheart. You're too wrapped up . . .'

'She's had more important things on her mind,' said Douglas.

Elizabeth decided not to push it, more for Douglas than for Kate. He seemed every bit as nice as she'd remembered from Kate's party – good manners, kind, attractive, and his obvious love for her daughter only increased her liking for him. But Kate looked miserable. Of course that was due to the news about Singapore, but it was hard not to compare the way Kate was this evening with how she'd been with Tom, and Elizabeth knew that something was wrong.

It seemed to her that Kate wasn't giving enough of herself – and Douglas looked like the kind of man who'd let her get away with it. Elizabeth worried that, un-encouraged, he'd just give up. Kate wouldn't know what she was missing until it was too late, and then what would she do? Hong Kong, New York, Dubai? It seemed to Elizabeth that there was no limit to the number of Willis & Storm international offices that would take her, if Singapore wouldn't.

Douglas decided to say nothing about Singapore. He let Kate talk about her disappointment, but told her nothing of his. He supposed he was glad that she wasn't going, but he wished that it had been because she'd chosen not to – because of him – and not because she no longer had the option.

Kate's air of disappointment had not, however,

476

lasted as long as he'd expected – and in two weeks she was back to thinking how best to deal with the Simon Dalziel problem. She'd put all the facts in a memo to Michael, and Michael had suggested to her that perhaps it would be best for him to have a quiet word with Dalziel's superiors at Fraser Cummings, and see what kind of response it got. There was no point doing something that would attract publicity at this stage, in case the whole thing backfired. But Kate wasn't sure if she should let him go ahead, or just go straight to the disciplinary body. What did Douglas think?

Douglas thought it might be best to follow Michael's advice. What would she have to lose? But he didn't really know. He was just happy to see that she seemed to have moved on from the idea of Singapore – and pleased that she seemed to value his judgement. Perhaps there was nothing to worry about.

———— ◆◆◆ ————

Tom and Louisa had decided to spend an extra night in Dorset. This was partly because the atmosphere of celebration at Falcombe had given them all a sudden sense of holiday, and partly because Louisa was not looking forward to telling Kate.

She knew she had to do it before the engagement was announced, and she wanted to say it to Kate's face, but it was with a sickening back-to-school feeling that she drove Tom up to London on Tuesday morning. It was now October, and Tom sat beside her in the passenger seat, gazing at the display of autumn colour in the trees and bushes on the side of the motorway as they shot past.

'As I remember, it was Kate who chucked me.'

'I know.'

'So why would she have a problem with me getting engaged to you?'

'Because I'm her best friend.'

'Not any more,' he chuckled.

'It's not funny, Tom. She's going to feel so hurt – so betrayed – and I'm sorry, but I happen to mind.'

He put his hand up to her neck and stroked it. 'I know you do, sweetheart. So do I. But you have to understand – and so does Kate – that these things happen.'

Louisa said nothing. She was happy, of course. The idea of spending the rest of her life with Tom was sometimes too wonderful to believe. And perhaps it was because of this, because of things being so nearly perfect, that Louisa longed for a reconciliation with her friend. In spite of her happiness, Louisa still missed Kate – and she feared that Kate would never forgive her if she married Tom.

'What would you rather do?' said Tom. 'Call off the engagement?'

'No. No, of *course* not.'

'Then we have to tell her. The sooner the better.'

They'd decided that it would be best for Louisa to go to the flat alone, to get an idea of Kate's state of mind. Louisa wanted to be completely sure that Kate was not still in love with Tom. And it was important to them both to tell her at a good time – to check that she didn't have a big deal on, that she wasn't 'depressed or anything' was the way Louisa put it. Neither of them mentioned Arabella, but thoughts of her were there – troubling, and unexpressed.

Tom would wait in the car.

Kate got back on Monday night to an empty flat and a written message from Douglas – full of apologies – saying he hadn't been able to get through to her, that he was needed at Waveney, and that he'd be back for dinner tomorrow night. He'd take her somewhere nice.

There were three messages on the answerphone. The first explained why Douglas was needed:

'John, it's your father. Will you call me the second you get this? There's been trouble with the new manager you put in at Felton – can't remember the chap's name, but he seems to have fallen out with Bert and Brady's worried it'll get out of hand. Says the only person Bert'll take orders from is you. Doesn't want some namby pamby Essex man telling him how to operate a tractor . . .'

The other two messages were from Louisa.

'Kate? Kate, it's Louisa. Listen. I – would you – shit . . . Kate, I'm in London tomorrow and I really want to see you. Are you around tomorrow night? I thought I might pop in for a drink – but perhaps you're not there, or working late, or giving a party? But I do want to see you – and your secretary's being as evasive as ever. Can you call me? I'm in Dorset.'

'Me again. Sorry. Just to say, we're out to dinner tonight, so do try to call before seven – otherwise . . . shit. I don't know. I'll keep trying you at work, but it's not going to be very easy for *you* to reach *me* tomorrow – you can try the mobile, but I'm not sure it's working properly – or . . . I know. Why don't we say that I'll be at the flat at seven, whatever. Unless you call. Is that okay? Lots of love . . .'

Douglas was back in London at six-thirty the following night. He'd sorted the matter out, but he was tired and desperate for a bath. Kate told him that was fine. Louisa was coming over for a drink at seven. Why didn't he join them whenever he was ready?

'Louisa's back?'

'Yes.'

'And she's coming here in –' he checked his watch, 'in half an hour? But what about her room, and all my things?'

'It's okay,' Kate laughed. 'She's only coming for a drink. She can stay at her parents' flat until we sort something out.'

Douglas filled George's bowl with biscuits and water, and bent to put it on the floor. George barged a hungry snout between them in the direction of the bowl.

'So you've made up?'

'Maybe . . .' she said, over the crunching and slurping.

'But that's great.'

'I know,' Kate smiled as she popped the ice cubes out from their mould and into the ice bucket. 'We couldn't speak for long, but she sounded happy, and keen to talk. No doubt there's a lot of grovelling to do on my part, but I think she sounded ready to forgive me.'

He put an arm around her shoulders, waiting for her to finish, and then took the empty ice mould from her over to the tap. 'About time.'

'Come on, Douglas. I did accuse her – completely unjustly – of stealing him. She's got every right to feel wronged.'

'But it's a bit extreme for her just to disappear like that,' he said, putting the ice mould back into the fridge freezer, 'when she must have known what an awful time you'd be having.'

He was in the bath when the doorbell rang.

Louisa crept up the stairs, up and up to where Kate was waiting. They kissed at the top of the stairs, and went through to the sitting room.

'I'm so glad you came.'

'I'm glad you let me.'

Inside the sitting room, Louisa looked around – remembering. She took the glass of greenish white wine that Kate offered, and sat in the armchair by the window.

Kate smiled. 'Where've you been? Italy?'

Louisa nodded.

'Was it wonderful?'

'Wonderful.'

Kate sensed that Louisa had something to say. Louisa had carried her preoccupations with her into the room and, instead of feeling curious, Kate felt uneasy. Whatever it was, it was giving Louisa huge difficulties – controlling what she did with her eyes and her body, affecting her breathing and her concentration. Kate's anxiety grew until, without knowing it, she began to behave in a similar way. She began her apology. It had been there on her tongue all afternoon. She spoke quickly, and with emphasis – all the time checking Louisa's face for signs of forgiveness. The more she spoke, however, the more it seemed that Louisa wasn't interested in forgiving, that she was here for something more important, and Kate trailed off.

'. . . what is it?'

But before Louisa could answer, they were both distracted by the sudden arrival of George – wandering in from the kitchen, his bowl in his mouth.

'Who's this?'

Kate smiled and took the bowl. '*This* – is George. George, this is Louisa.'

'You've got a dog?'

'No,' she laughed, taking the bowl back into the kitchen. 'No, George belongs to Douglas.'

'Douglas?'

Louisa sprang up and rushed after her into the kitchen. 'Douglas?' she repeated.

Kate put the bowl in its place by the bins and turned, smiling. 'Yes. Douglas,' she smiled. 'He's just having a bath, but he'll be down in a minute.'

'You – and Douglas?'

Kate nodded.

'But what about Tom?'

'Tom? Tom who?' Kate gave Louisa a naughty smile and laughed as they returned to the sitting room.

'I forgot you left before it happened,' she went on. 'Well, what can I say? A bastard. A snake in the grass. You were absolutely right. He was unfaithful to me, he lied about his finances, he was responsible for his ex-wife's suicide, and – as if that wasn't enough – it now appears he's living off money wrongly inherited from her . . .'

Douglas came in as she was speaking.

'Just talking about Tom,' she smiled at him. 'You remember Louisa, don't you?'

'Of course.' Douglas kissed Louisa and helped himself to a glass of wine. He sat on the sofa and played with George's ears.

Louisa was too caught up in her own agenda to consider Douglas. 'You – you don't love Tom any more?'

Kate laughed. 'I know I'm a glutton for punishment, Lou, but even I have my limits.'

Louisa was smiling now – smiling and laughing – 'So you won't *mind*,' she was saying. 'Oh, I can't *begin* to tell you how relieved I am!'

'Mind about what?'

'About me and Tom. We . . .'

'You and – you and Tom?' Kate's smile emptied, but the shape of it lingered on her face while she took in the sense of Louisa's words. 'Well no – I mean . . .'

Tom and Louisa – she sounded the names in the front of her head. Louisa and . . . Oh God.

The new life that Kate had, with painstaking effort, constructed around herself was unravelling like crocheted silk. Just one catch, one small yank, at the bottom, and the intricate patterns were spiralling and wriggling – deconstructing themselves into a pile of thread, and leaving her standing there, totally exposed. What could she say?

'Do you mind if I run down and tell him? Bring him up? He's just in the car downstairs. We were so terribly worried about you, Kate. I couldn't sleep a wink last night, imagining how hurt you'd be, but it's all fine. It's wonderful. Here you are with Douglas – lovely Douglas!' she kissed him. 'I won't be a minute . . .'

As she ran out, thumping down the stairs, all the way to the bottom, Kate and Douglas looked at each other.

'Are you all right?'

'Of course I'm all right,' Kate grabbed at lies – at anything to hide the truth. 'I'm fine. You don't think she minded me being so rude about him, do you? I said some pretty insulting things.'

Douglas shook his head. 'No,' he said, 'she wouldn't have noticed. She's just worried about hurting you – worried, if anything, that you like him too much, that you'd mind . . .'

'*Like him too much?* Why? Why would I like him?' she was talking much too fast. 'Why would I mind? I think she's mad, but if that's what she wants, good luck to her. It's quite funny, if you think about it. Her and Tom. You and me . . .'

'You don't have to see him, if you'd rather not.'

'I don't mind if you don't mind. Do you mind?'

'No. But aren't you . . .?'

'Douglas, I'm with you now.'

But as she heard Tom's voice, coming up the stairs, up into the flat, Kate's heart skidded into a wall.

There was quite a lot of laughing and drinking after that – and clinking glasses, and smoking. Aware that Douglas was watching her, Kate anaesthetised her heart, and threw herself into congratulating them. How quick! How romantic! When was the wedding? December – at Falcombe? How lovely! Wasn't it funny? Weren't they all terrible? And what a relief it all turned out this way!

Nobody mentioned Arabella.

'Guy and Lucy,' said Mary, writing their names carefully onto her list.

Louisa looked up from *Brides* magazine. 'Do we have to have them?' she said. 'We hardly . . .'

'They're your cousins.'

'Second cousins.'

'Still family, dear. I'm afraid they've got to be there.'

Tom leant across and looked over Mary's shoulder. 'Who are Fred and Delia?'

'Delia's Dad's first cousin, and my god-mother. Never sent me any presents . . . come on, Mum. Let's scrap them.'

'She sent you that lovely necklace for your confirmation, didn't she?'

'You mean the coral one with matching earrings?'

'Scrapped,' said Tom, taking Mary's pen and running a line through Fred and Delia.

'Tom,' insisted Mary, taking the pen back and writing them in again. She was losing patience with his attitude. 'No. I'm sorry. They have to be invited. They probably won't come – Fred's still in Germany – but they've had such a hard time lately, and Delia would be so hurt . . .'

They were sitting in the conservatory. It was almost November. Outside, it was grey. A wind was drying and shifting the brown remains of autumn leaves across the lawn. Tom watched them – bored – and wondered what time lunch was.

Choosing wedding presents had been fun. So had deciding what flowers to have, what champagne, marquee, caterers . . .

After some discussion, they'd given Sarah Knowles

485

the option – did she want to do it? Or would she prefer to come as a guest? Sarah had told them, laughing, that she wasn't up to dinner for four hundred – not at the moment – but she'd love to do the reception canapés.

. . . especially on what seemed to be an unlimited budget. But he was irritated by the way they went and organised things without telling him. It was his wedding as well as Louisa's, for God's sake. Sometimes he felt he was being bought for her, and it took all his self-control to go on smiling when they told him that Nigel's favourite champagne was Pol Roger, so that was what they were having. No, not Dom Perignon. No, Tom – sorry. Darling, it is Dad who's paying . . .

He'd drawn the line at the photographer. Mary had gone ahead and booked one without discussing it with them – and Tom had exploded when he found out she'd got Charlie Reed.

'I'm not having that man at my wedding.'

'But he's an old friend of Louisa's – isn't he, darling? And he's doing so brilliantly at the moment – I thought it was incredibly lucky to get someone so prestigious . . .'

'I don't care. He's not coming.'

After busily raised eyebrows and short, quick, head-shaking between mother and daughter, they'd agreed to cancel Charlie.

Tom had thought that the guest list would, at least, be relatively simple. Nigel and Mary had said that they didn't mind how big the wedding was. The bigger the better. So Tom had happily invited all his friends – they included a lot of Italians who probably

486

wouldn't come, but it was nice to be able to ask them. He wasn't prepared for the Edwardes' guest list. With all the lists combined, Tom realised that over seventy per cent were names he'd never heard of – all of them seemed to be Nigel and Mary's greatest friends, and their numbers seemed to be growing.

They were silent as Mary rewrote, 'Fred and Delia'.

Then Nigel said, 'And have you remembered Richard and Anne?'

'Of course. Anne will definitely come and I expect Richard will too, if he's out of hospital in time . . .'

'Hospital?'

It sounded like a horrid operation. Anne hadn't been very specific, but Mary gathered it had something to do with an embarrassing injury and that Richard was being terribly brave.

———◆◆◆———

Annette wanted a big leaving party. She wanted balloons and free champagne. And she wanted to have it upstairs at the regular wine bar, so that everybody would see and ask.

Michael thought that this was a good idea. Her departure was certainly worth celebrating. The department might soften, lose its competitive edge, without her – but it was now December. The annual figures were in and they were way above target. In fact, they'd almost doubled last year's billing – and if he could get Henry to pay the Hazel Industries bill from Project Cannon II, they'd be there. He was sure he could find another Rottweiler for next year. Gavin was looking promising, and somehow it was less offensive, coming with a sense of humour, and coming from a man.

Douglas activated the burglar alarm and locked the door. It was ready now – a family house, ready to go on the market. Fiona was showing people round tomorrow. There were two appointments, and she thought both sets would pay the asking price.

The trouble was that Douglas didn't want to sell.

He'd thought it all through and he knew that what he really wanted was to move in himself, with Kate. Knowing she'd never give up her job, and that he'd never give up Waveney, Douglas had realised that the reality of their future – if they had a future – was weeks in London, and weekends in Norfolk. And that meant a proper house in London.

It was crazy to sell it – and crazy to keep it, on the off-chance that Kate and he would marry. An off-chance that was looking increasingly off, he thought, walking towards his Land-Rover and remembering Kate's reaction to the sight of Tom and Louisa's 'Forthcoming Marriage' in *The Times*.

He'd rung her at work. 'Have you seen the papers?'

'Yes?'

'Tom and Louisa?'

'I know,' she'd laughed. 'Extraordinary middle name – Aylwin. I looked it up,' she laughed again. 'It means *noble friend*.'

It was the determined carelessness, and all the deflections. What he wanted to hear was, 'They're getting married, and I feel hurt. It upsets me, not because I'm in love with him, but because they were shabby and they let me down.' Instead, he got dismissive remarks and jokes. Douglas worried that, for all his faults, Kate was still in love with Tom, and that was why she couldn't talk about it.

It wasn't that Kate was cold to him. Quite the reverse. She told Douglas that she loved him, she was physically affectionate, and she was happy to make plans with him – they were both going to visit her mother this weekend, and she was coming to Waveney for New Year's Eve – but he knew that Tom was always there in the back of her mind. Douglas wasn't sure he could spend the rest of his life being second-best.

The sensible thing to do was to wait – at least until Tom and Louisa were married. Perhaps she'd change then. But what was he going to do with the mews-house in the meantime?

Douglas opened the car door, frowning, and set off for the City.

He was on his way to collect Kate. He thought she was mad to be going to the party – to stand there drinking champagne, congratulating Annette, when everybody there would know that it should have been her name on the balloons. He told her he'd pick her up at nine, so that she'd have a decent reason for leaving early.

When he arrived, at ten to, there was no sign of her outside. He waited until nine and then found some-where to park. Squeezing through the groups on the pavement – wrapped up, cold, but determinedly drinking – and past the red-hot blasts from a pair of street gas-heaters, Douglas ducked to avoid the looping shiny-gold Christmas decorations over the door and went in.

Unaware of how out of place he looked in his worn burgundy cardigan and open-necked shooting shirt,

Douglas searched over the heads of the regulars for Kate's honey-coloured one and then realised that the party was upstairs. He excused himself through the roar of suits and made for the wooden staircase to the left of the bar.

'G - O - O - D - B - Y - E - A - N - N - E - T - T - E -!' had been hung up the wall in individual letters.

Douglas ran up, but he couldn't see her there either. 'I'm looking for Kate Leonard,' he said to a lanky man with glasses who wasn't talking to anyone.

'Oh,' said Steve, mentally emerging from his finance lease. 'Er – Heather?'

A stunning blonde, who seemed to be drinking from two champagne glasses, turned. 'What is it?'

'Seen Kate?'

Heather looked from Steve to Douglas – tall and tired, but smiling.

'I'm sorry,' it was a voice she recognised, calm and unforced, 'I'm supposed to be collecting her . . .'

'You're Douglas, aren't you?'

'Y-es,' he said, amazed.

Heather wasn't sober. 'Know that voice anywhere,' she said. 'Don't worry. For a posh voice, it's quite nice . . .'

Heather began jigging to the music in front of him and offered him one of her glasses.

Douglas smiled and shook his head. 'I'm driving. But is Kate . . .?'

'Oh yes – Kate,' Heather laughed and took his hand. 'Nearly forgot.'

She dragged him over to a group of about five people, all listening to a young balding man in a navy suit.

'Gavin?'

The man stopped his story, and they all looked at Douglas.

'Gav – seen Kate anywhere? Here's her gorgeous boyfriend looking for her and she's gone and disappeared . . .'

Annette walked away to greet Michael.

'Hello,' said Gavin, smiling slightly and shaking Douglas' hand. 'She's probably still working. Shall I give her a call?'

'No, she's not working,' said Adam, who was the last to leave. 'She must have gone home.'

'But it's only just gone nine.'

Heather thought that Douglas had a very nice watch. She turned to Janet. 'Did Kate say anything about not coming? About going home?'

Janet wasn't listening. She couldn't think why Kate didn't return Douglas' calls the second she knew he'd rung.

'*Janet?*'

'Oh,' she smiled. 'Oh yes. Come to think of it, I saw her leave. Saw her on the steps – you know, the ones down to the tube. And that was, well, that must've been when I was on my way here – about half an hour ago, I should think.'

Douglas could hear Kate's voice – bright and smiling – as he opened the door to her flat. 'Any time. I'm in all night – or you can try me at work tomorrow. All right? Bye.'

She was putting the receiver down as he came in. 'Hi.'

'Who was that?'

'Just leaving a message for Tom.'

'Tom?'

'Oh Douglas,' she smiled. 'Don't look so serious. He called and I was returning his call.'

'What did he want?'

'No idea.' Holding his shoulders with both hands, she stretched up and kissed him. 'And Mum rang. She's expecting us for a late dinner tomorrow night. Is that okay?'

'Fine.'

He threw his keys on the desk and looked at her as she bent to stroke George.

'Where've *you* been, Georgie darling. I missed you . . .'

'He came with me to pick you up from Annette's leaving party.'

Kate looked up. 'Oh God,' she said heavily. 'I . . .'

'You forgot.'

She nodded. 'What will they *say*? They're going to think I'm so rude – not showing – they're going to think I'm not there because I've got a problem,' she looked at her watch, 'and it's too late now, isn't it? Oh damn. Damn, damn.'

Douglas sat at the desk and said nothing.

'I can't believe . . . what can I have been thinking of? I know you think I shouldn't have been there anyway, but it was important to show them – show Michael – that I'm not beaten by it. And now he'll think that I'm sulking . . .'

Expecting sympathy, she released George and looked across the room. Douglas was playing with his keys.

'Douglas?'

He was concentrating on his fingers.

'What is it?'

'You knew I was picking you up.'

'Oh Douglas. Douglas, I forgot. I'm sorry – but you know it wasn't deliberate. I was just . . .'

'You were worried about the impression that this will make on your boss?'

'It's important to me.'

'Yes,' he sighed. 'Yes, I suppose so.'

'So? So . . . I don't understand. What's your problem?'

George got into his basket. He lay there watching his master, with his snout low and his ears flat down and back.

Douglas stood up, a set of keys in his hand. 'It doesn't matter,' he said, putting the keys in his pocket and looking around for George.

'Of course it matters . . . Douglas *please* tell me what's going on. I can't read your mind.'

He looked at her for a second and then went back to the desk. He stood at it, leant on it, and then pulled a Willis & Storm branded pencil from the tray. He brought it to his face and examined the silver print – the way it had been embossed into the wood.

'I've just driven halfway across London, to pick you up from a party of people I've never met before, to be told that you've already left. Which is, of course, frustrating and humiliating for me – but I don't really mind, because I love you and I know that you're overworked and distracted. What I do mind about is your complete indifference to what I do, or what I might be feeling . . .'

Kate had never been spoken to in this tone before.

It wasn't particularly loud or violent, but it was final. Tired, and final.

'And most of all,' he went on, 'I mind about Tom.'

'Tom?'

Douglas put the pencil back and looked at her. 'My darling, I'm not completely stupid. I can see through the bravado and the jokes. You're being wonderful about it, but the truth is that you still love him.'

He paused, but Kate said nothing.

'Well there. You do love him . . . and I mind. Maybe I'm not right for you – in fact, the more I think about it, the plainer it is to me that I'm not – but nor is Tom. He's weak and he's stubborn. He'd live off you, and hate you for it. You'd make him feel a failure for the rest of his life. And then one day you'd fall out of love with him and see him for what he is – and you'd despise him.'

Still she said nothing.

'I know you don't agree with me, but Louisa's right for him. She can look up to him. She goes for all those trivial values of his that pass for style in this city – and that dazzle us so much. Can't you *see* that you and Tom would make each other miserable?'

'It's all a bit hypothetical, isn't it? Given he'll be marrying Louisa the weekend after next.'

'I'm not talking about practicalities, Kate. Whether or not he actually marries her is irrelevant. I'm talking about what *you* want. I'm talking about what's going on inside your head. And I'm trying to show you that, when it comes to Tom, you're better off where you are.'

'With you, you mean.'

'No,' he looked terribly sad. 'No, I've had enough

of trying to make you love me.'

'I do . . .'

'No you don't. Not like that. Oh my darling – if you loved me, really loved me, you'd never have forgotten that I was coming tonight to collect you. You'd never have wanted that job in Singapore. And you certainly wouldn't be hankering after Tom,' he took a breath. 'If you love me, then it's just the way I loved Sarah, and it's not enough.'

'But you can't just leave. We need to talk. I need . . .'

'You need rest and space. You need to go home to your mother this weekend, alone. I'm sure she'll understand. You will, too, when you've had time to think it through.'

'So this is it?'

He nodded. 'Come on, George.'

Twenty-one

Kate woke the next morning to an empty bed, and remembered.

It was dark as she trod to work – trod in and out of the patches of light thrown down by the lamps in her street. Dark, dry and bitterly cold. The night had been clear and she noticed that the windscreens of the cars she passed were etched with the curls and fronds of a hoar-frost. Kate walked on, mouth almost white with tension, briefcase bumping at her legs.

There were no free seats, so she stood – suspended from the ceiling on the end of a dangling grip – while her train rattled east through the tunnels, wheezing and shrieking, the lights going and coming with a fault on the line.

At Liverpool Street, the doors hissed wide. And the weight of workers – workers at all levels – fell to the platform, brushing and touching with that cold proximity peculiar to strangers. The mass of stepping feet, the various shoes, thickened at the whirr of the ticket barriers – Kate's with them – and then spread out in various directions, through the station concourse.

She queued for her coffee, ordered it with a nod

and the briefest of smiles – they knew how she liked it. With her free hand – the one not holding her briefcase – she left the exact amount on the counter, and collected the paper cup with its trail of steam.

Then up to street level, along past the shops, and up the steps – stride stride stride – up again, and along to the revolving doors – wait, le-an . . . and round with a glide to the security man.

Adam was in – the light was on, his coat was there, and his squash bag. But he wasn't at his desk when Kate arrived. Kate shut the door, went over to her own desk and rang her mother before she took off her coat.

'Douglas isn't coming this weekend. It's just me.'

Elizabeth was still getting up. She sat in her dressing gown on the edge of her bed, with electric-yellow light warm in her lap, on her hands – but with her face turned to the cool winter day, breaking through the semi-opaque windows that gave onto her garden. Each glass pane was warming at the edges – melting and clearing – and as the bluish daylight spread across her room so the yellow light retreated to its bulb.

'I'll get the six o'clock if I can leave on time,' Kate was saying. 'Or it may be the one after. I'm not sure . . .'

'Douglas isn't coming?'

'No.'

'But I've just gone and done a massive shop.'

'I'm sorry, Mum. He . . . we . . .'

Elizabeth's attention left the window.

'It's over,' Kate's voice was very faint. 'He . . .'

'Darling, I can't hear you.'

'He ended it,' she said, close again to the receiver.

Elizabeth could hear the awful noises of her daughter crying.

'He ended it, Mum . . . thinks I don't love him . . . wouldn't listen. And I was . . . I deserve everything I . . .'

'Darling, he adores you. Ring him. Ring him right now and sort it out.'

'I can't,' she sobbed. 'It's too late.'

'What's too late?'

'Everything. He's gone.'

'It's not too late, sweetheart. Call him. Tell him.'

'Wouldn't listen. Wouldn't speak to me.'

'How do you know?'

'Not after what I said to him – or not said. Nobody would. I've been awful to him, Mum. So awful. And now I don't know what I . . .'

'Darling? Darling, listen. Get on whichever train you can – let me know – I'll meet you and we can talk about it at the weekend – sort it all out. But please don't –'

'You don't need to meet me.'

'But I'd like to.'

'The trains are never on time, Mum. And your car . . . I'll get a taxi. I'd prefer it.'

Elizabeth could hear the intransigence in her daughter's tone and decided not to press her. Kate said she'd try to catch the six o'clock, that she'd ring if she missed it, and promised that whatever happened she'd be home that night. '. . . all right?'

'Of course it's all right, darling. I'll see you later.'

'Saw your man last night,' said Janet, coming in

498

with a cup of coffee and smiling at Kate as she put down the receiver. 'We all thought he was lovely. No wonder Simon never got a look-in.' Then she saw Kate's face. 'Are you okay?'

'It's nothing.' Kate dropped her coat on her chair, turning her back to Janet. 'I'm just not feeling very well. Must be that bug going around.'

Janet laughed. 'There'll be a lot of people with *that bug* today. Daniella's already rung in sick, and you should've seen Heather at the end. She let Gavin dress her up like the angel Gabriel, with tinsel in her hair and a tablecloth over her shoulders and . . . oh my God, here she is. Heather! How are you feeling this morning? Bright and breezy?'

Kate heard a grunt that must have been Heather – but sounded more like Adam.

'Oh Heather, *look* at you! How did you get home?'

Laughing, Janet walked away from Kate towards the secretarial pool.

'Don't remember,' Heather's voice was quiet and croaky, but smiling. 'Don't remember much about last night, to be honest, except that nice bloke of Kate's . . .'

'Can you remember being an angel?'

'A *what*?'

'You were an angel, remember – and Annette was the Virgin Mary.'

Heather giggled. 'Who was Baby Jesus?'

'Steve.'

A telephone was ringing over their laughter.

'. . . and . . . o-oh, can someone else answer that? It's hurting my head . . .'

Kate picked up her receiver, murmuring her name.

'Kate?'

It was Tom.

'I need to see you,' he said. 'Can you make lunch?'

He knew a fashionable restaurant that had opened in the City. They agreed to meet at twelve-thirty.

Kate closed the door to her office and looked at her task list. She didn't have much on – nothing that had to be done before the weekend, except a ten o'clock appointment with Michael to discuss the Simon Dalziel matter.

She sat back in her chair and thought again of what her mother had said. Should she call? She thought of Douglas in his flat. Now was quite a good time – nine-thirty. He'd be up, and he'd probably still be in. But what on earth would she say?

The words'll come to me, she thought, reaching for the telephone.

She dialled the London number first – her heartbeat accelerating violently, then calming, then seemingly shutting down altogether as she realised he wasn't going to answer. She let it ring another five times and put the receiver down. There was no response at Waveney either – just an answerphone, and she couldn't leave a message. What if Mrs Brady got it?

She decided to try again, just before her appointment with Michael, but there was still no response.

Willing Douglas from her thoughts, Kate went to Michael's office, knocked and entered. Michael beckoned her forward. She sat in the chair opposite and listened to the voice coming out of the speakerphone. It was a man's voice – Irish – and one she didn't recognise.

'Of course the guy's happy to apologise – in writing if she likes. I'm sure we can agree the wording, can't we now? And leave it at that . . .'

Michael and Kate said nothing.

The voice sighed. 'D'you really want this thing to go to the Tribunal?'

'I've put you on the speaker-phone, Tony, because she's just come in.'

'Oh,' said the voice. 'Hi, Kate.'

'Hello . . .'

'It's Tony Cummings,' Michael mouthed. 'Simon's boss.'

'Now, Kate,' said Tony. 'The thing is, we've received notification of your complaint. I've spoken to Simon, and he's . . .'

'What I want,' said Kate, wearily, 'is a formal acknowledgement that Simon Dalziel deliberately withheld information from me at crucial stages in a transaction. I want an unreserved apology, in writing – for that. I want a separate statement from him to the effect that his claims that we slept together – that there was *anything* going on – were completely unfounded. And I want him taken off all the MetBank files before Christmas. I think you should also know that he was guilty of conspiring in a breach of confidentiality concerning a customer at Cheape & Co. He deserves to be given the sack. He deserves to be struck off. But if I get an apology and a statement, and if he's removed from the MetBank files then . . .'

'Oh, we're not keeping him on,' said Tony. 'No way. We just didn't want any unnecessary adverse publicity for Fraser Cummings.'

Kate looked at Michael.

'I think that should be fine, Tony,' he said, 'but we'll need to think about it over the weekend, if that's okay, and call you on Monday . . .'

He said goodbye to Tony Cummings and smiled at Kate. 'Well . . .?'

'Will you speak to Henry Hazel about this?' she said. 'I want that file back.'

'Already have. He's happy to have you. After what he was saying about Annette, I think he'll welcome you with open arms.'

'Having me back is fine. He can close his arms.'

Michael chuckled. 'And I'm sorry about Singapore,' he added. 'But there is a possibility of Hong Kong next year if you're interested.'

Kate sighed. 'I don't—'

'No need to decide now. Just think about it.'

She got up to leave – she was almost out of his room, with her back to him, when he said, 'Pity you weren't at the party.'

'I know,' holding the door handle, she turned to him. 'I was too tired.'

'Did you hear about Heather?'

She nodded, smiling.

'And I seem to remember someone telling me something about a boyfriend of yours . . .?'

'He . . .'

'Douglas, is it? The secretaries couldn't get enough of him – I'm telling you, I spent most of the evening being bored out of my mind, hearing all about him from Janet.'

Kate smiled a different smile, and left.

———◆◆◆———

She had to get a taxi to the restaurant. Tom had said

that it was in the City, but his idea of the City was anywhere beyond Covent Garden – and that included the Aldwych. Kate didn't mind. It meant that she was less likely to bump into anyone she knew.

Tom was sitting at the bar – a huge oval, surrounded by a range of City suits, and by the black polo necks and designer street-wear of film producers and fashion people.

He was dressed in a charcoal suit, a beautiful pink shirt open at the collar and no tie – and leaning over the bar giving very precise instructions to a Japanese girl. Kate knew exactly what he'd be saying. He liked his Bloody Mary very spicy, with horseradish sauce, double vodka, and did they have celery salt?

'Hello, darling,' he said, kissing her. 'Bloody Mary?'

'Love one – less spicy than his,' she added to the girl, who smiled.

He'd managed to get two bar stools for them to perch on. 'Sorry about the wait,' he said. 'I forgot to book, and they don't have a table until one . . .'

'That's fine.' She took off her coat, sat with it on her lap and looked at him.

He'd turned his stool so that it faced her completely. She had to shift to prevent one of his knees from touching hers. But she couldn't do anything about the way he was looking back at her.

'Are you well?' he said.

'Yes. Quite.'

'Only quite?'

'Douglas and I split up last night. So . . . so yes. Only quite.'

Tom put the brimful Bloody Mary into her hands – she had to use both of them to steady it.

'What happened? Who ended it?'

'He did.'

'*He* did? Why?'

Kate put the glass down. She rested her left elbow near it, propping up the left side of her head with her left hand, and spreading her fingers through her hair. She stared into space, somewhere around the edge of the bar.

'He doesn't think I love him – thinks I love you—' she shut her eyes. 'I've made a terrible mistake, Tom. I . . .'

Tom looked at her – the shiny drop of hair, the curve of her body against the bar.

'I had no idea I'd feel like this. So – empty. And, oh Tom, it's all my fault. I've got exactly what I deserve. I threw it all away – all that happiness – gone. Gone like that.' Tears sprung at her lashes. 'Gone. Gone forever. And now it's too late.'

'Oh darling,' he was touching her leg, her hand – Kate opened her eyes, wet and red – 'Oh darling,' he repeated excitedly, right into them, 'it's not!'

'It's not?'

'It's not too late.'

'But how do you know?'

'Kate,' he said, visibly moved, stroking her neck with his thumb, 'I know, because I feel exactly the same as you. I've been in agony – wondering whether to call it off, wondering what on earth to do – missing you, thinking about you continually . . .'

'Call what off?'

'The wedding. Oh, the doubts I've been having, the worry – and all the time, wondering if you'd ever . . . Kate,' his hand was right up round her neck – he

504

was going to guide her towards him. He was going to kiss her. Really going to do it – here and now.

'No,' she was on her feet, the bar stool toppling behind her into the legs of the man behind. 'No – you don't understand. Oh, I'm sorry . . . sorry – thanks . . .' she righted the stool and looked at Tom. 'No.'

'But you just said.'

'It's Douglas. I was talking about Douglas. Not you.'

'So you don't . . .' Tom felt for his cigarettes. 'You mean, you don't . . .'

She shook her head. 'No, I don't love you.'

It was only as she said it, that she realised it. Realised that Douglas was right about him. She saw in his expression – and in that beautiful pink shirt – the confusion of his values. The desire to be liked and admired, twinned with a child-like consumer-driven selfishness she couldn't hate, could even enjoy indulging, but could never live with.

She saw, too, that his weakness was not limited to shirts and coffee. It included women – and Tom would never be satisfied. She saw that it still had not occurred to him to think of Louisa, and what this might do to her. He was still thinking of himself. When it did occur to him, Kate was sure that Tom would hate himself – feel guilty, sorry and full of remorse, but by then it would be too late. He could only apologise.

And then she thought of Douglas.

'. . . driving me mad. She just sits around all day, reading magazines and watching television. I need someone I can talk to, Kate. I need you.'

'No you don't.'

'I do.'

She looked at his cigarette – lit, but unsmoked, burning itself into a grey line of ash. 'You need someone you can play with – someone beautiful, with beautiful things – and someone who can afford you,' they both smiled. 'You need Louisa. She's from your world, Tom. She understand you, she looks up to you – God knows why – and loves you.'

'And you don't?'

'I love Douglas.'

A waitress was standing near them, holding a pair of menus. 'Your table's ready, sir.'

They chose quickly – Tom, because he wasn't hungry. Kate, because she didn't care. All she could think about was Douglas. Douglas greeting her after work – picking her up – his Land-Rover, his shabby clothes, his warm, large presence and his open smile, so terrifyingly absent last night.

She picked at her food, and found she couldn't talk to Tom at all – she wasn't making any sense – and in the end she told him why.

'I'm sorry, Tom,' she pushed away her plate. 'I can't stop thinking about last night.'

'About Douglas?'

She nodded.

'You really want him back?'

'Weren't you listening to anything I said? Of *course* I do. I . . .'

'Then why are you sitting here with me?'

Kate frowned.

'Why are you sitting here?' he repeated. 'You should be telling *him* this. Not me.'

'He's not speaking to me. He won't pick up the phone.'

'Then you should go and find him. I'll take you now if you like.'

'But you haven't finished eating.'

'Sod that.'

He dropped his fork and opened his wallet, took out £100 in notes and put them on the table. 'Should cover it,' he grabbed his car keys. 'Come on.'

Tom had parked Louisa's silver Mazda on a yellow line. He yanked the cellophane-covered ticket out from behind the windscreen wipers, unlocked the doors and fell in behind the steering wheel. Swerving in and out of the traffic in distinct Italian style, he got Kate to Knightsbridge Mews in under twenty minutes – but Douglas wasn't there.

Kate rang and rang. She opened the post-flap and looked in – but all she could see was the legs of a new table in the hall, and smell the freshly painted walls. There was no sign of him or George – and no Land-Rover parked outside.

She came back to the Mazda and got in. 'Not there.'

'He must be at Waveney,' said Tom, looking at his watch. 'If we leave now, we'll get there at about six.'

Kate laughed. 'I can't go off to Waveney.'

'Why not?'

'I can't just drop everything. Unlike you, I have responsibilities at work, people depending on me to be there, to get things done . . .'

'Which is more important, Kate? Are you really going to tell me that some Psycho-Syncopated-Super-

Revolutionary-Fuck-me-this-is-so-NOT-A-LIFE document of yours is more important?'

'But I . . .'

'Shut up,' he said, reversing sharply, turning the car around.

Kate kept her eyes down, watching Tom's tanned hand struggle with the unfamiliar gears as he went back into first and drove up the cobbles, under the mews-arch and indicated left.

'What if he's not there?'

'Where else would he be?'

'What if he won't talk? What if he won't forgive me?'

'Of course he'll forgive you.'

'He didn't forgive you.'

'Well, he might just forgive me if he finds out I brought you to him . . . and if the worst comes to the worst, I'll drop you at your mother's, as planned. You've got nothing to lose.'

Nothing and everything, thought Kate as they set off.

'I should at least try calling him there . . .' she said as, twenty minutes later, Tom hurtled round Shepherd's Bush roundabout and then headed north. Feeling in her bag for her mobile, Kate realised she'd left it recharging in her flat. 'Can I borrow yours?'

Tom felt in his inside pocket and handed her an impossibly thin mobile telephone. It looked more like a calculator.

Mrs Brady answered. No, Douglas was out. Could she take a message?

'Do you know when you're expecting him back?'

'I'm afraid I can't be sure. Who's speaking?'

'It's Kate, Mrs Brady. Kate Leonard.'

'Ah. Could he call you?'

'Oh yes,' said Kate. 'Yes, he could try. It's a mobile. The number's oh-three-eight-five . . .'

'Oh-three-eight . . .?'

'Five . . . then what? Tom?'

'Not *my* number, you idiot,' said Tom, overtaking a Mercedes on the inside and jumping the lights, 'that would give completely the wrong message . . .'

'Oh-three-eight-five,' repeated Mrs Brady.

'I'm sorry,' said Kate. 'I'm sorry, Mrs Brady – that number won't work. I'll have to just keep trying him, or . . . or I suppose he could ring my mother. Leave a message with her if he likes.'

Kate gave her mother's number, and then rang work.

'Kate Leonard's office,' sang Heather, her voice slightly flat. 'How may I help you?'

'Heather, it's me.'

'Kate?'

'Yes. Now listen. I'm not coming in to work this afternoon . . .'

'Skiving off like everyone else? There'll be nobody left.'

'It's something very important. Something personal . . .'

'It's that boyfriend of yours, isn't it? Taking you somewhere nice?'

'Heather . . .'

'It is, isn't it?'

'Heather – I can't chatter. If you must know, it is to do with him. I'm going to lose him if I don't see him today – and that means going to Norfolk, because that's where he lives. But if you tell anybody – *anybody* – I promise you, I'll . . .'

'I won't tell a soul,' said Heather, excitedly. 'Promise. You leave it with me and don't worry – I'll say you were ill. You looked awful this morning . . .'

Kate pulled down the sun-flap, looked at herself in the little mirror – her eyes were bright now, her skin recovered – and told Heather not to be so rude.

Heather laughed. 'See you Monday. Good luck . . .'

The traffic was heavy with weekenders. Kate and Tom sat in it, in the low sun, winter-weak, touching the bare bark of the trees and the flat rows of plough-tips to a warmer brown, while the shadows froze in a lingering frost. After a few false starts, Tom found the car's central heating. He switched it on and they began to talk.

They spoke mainly of Louisa and the wedding – of the importance of not telling her about what Tom had said at lunch, about what he'd tried to do. Kate did most of the talking, and Tom listened – nodding, agreeing. He just accepted that he'd been useless, that Louisa was right for him, and that Douglas was – well, whatever Kate said he was.

Kate was getting hot. She took off her coat and threw it in the back, along with her handbag, talking at the same time. She criticised Tom's driving, she criticised his behaviour, his morals, his infidelity, his weakness, his lifestyle, his inability to get a job. He was irresponsible, charming, hopeless, impractical . . . he was a hedonist. A playboy.

By the time they got to Waveney, Tom was just glad to know that, when this journey was over, he'd be back with Louisa – comfortable, re-masculated, loved.

It was dark as they approached the gatehouse at the bottom of the South Drive. Dark and quiet. Kate fell silent, looking at the windows of the gatehouse – curtains drawn – and thought again of Douglas. Was she mad to come here? What if he refused to see her? What if he wasn't there?

'Stop a second, Tom.'

'What?'

'Just stop. Pull in here.'

'You're not going to chicken out now, are you?'

'No – no I just want to call – make sure he . . .' she broke off, bent her head to Tom's mobile and dialled the number.

'Mrs Brady? Hello again. It's Kate Leonard . . . is he there?'

'No.'

'No?'

'He went out again, I'm afraid. About an hour ago.'

'You gave him my message, and he's gone out?'

'That's right.'

'Will he be back tonight?'

'I'm sorry, Kate. I don't know. Why don't you try again tomorrow?'

'You definitely gave him my message?'

'I left it for him on the table in the hall,' the voice was beginning to lose patience. 'I'm sorry. There's nothing more I can do.'

'All right,' said Kate. 'Thank you.'

She switched off the mobile and turned to Tom. 'Not there. Or if he is, he's avoiding me.'

'I bet he is there,' said Tom. 'Let's go up and see.'

'Mrs Brady's just told me he's not. Tom – we can't. What if they find us?'

'I think we should check.'

'What's the point? Either he's not there, or he is. And if he is, then he doesn't want to see me – so what am I doing crawling around looking for him?'

'It's important to know which, isn't it? Otherwise you'll always wonder.'

Kate said nothing.

'Oh come on,' Tom started the car. 'We've come all this way.'

They crept forward, moving slowly past the gate-house and up the drive – headlights off, but it was a clear, cold night and the drive wound ahead of them, easily visible in the moonlight. They bumped quietly over the cattle grid, round a corner and up to the house.

But there was no sign of him. The lights were off, the windows dead, all over the vast black building – except in the kitchen, where Mrs Brady sat at the table, her head bent over something. There was no Land-Rover in the courtyard, and no sound of George barking.

'Where *has* he gone?' Tom steered the car slowly past the stables and onto the West Drive. 'Where else can he be?'

'Well, he's not here,' said Kate, exhausted.

'Perhaps he's gone to Gloucestershire – to his parents . . .'

'Just take me home, Tom. Please.'

They took the road to Diss and it began, quite suddenly, to rain. Kate watched detachedly as Tom grabbed at various levers, looking for the wipers. The headlights went off for a second and then on at full beam, illuminating a green road sign that ran with the unwiped rain down the screen in front of her. Then he found the right lever and everything stood out clear.

She wasn't going to think about Douglas. The important thing, right now, was her career – and that was going well. With Simon out of the way, and with the Hazel Industries file back on her desk, she was back on track. Watching the mechanical action of the wiper in front of her, Kate reminded herself to get Michael to call Tony Cummings on Monday.

And maybe she'd go to Hong Kong next year or the year after. Or maybe not. If she wanted to be made a partner – and she did – then perhaps it was better that she stay in London. Get promoted while Annette was away. That would serve her right.

In the darkness she smiled.

It wasn't so bad, she thought. It felt bad now, of course. It felt awful. It felt as if things would never be good again – but they would, she supposed. There'd be other men. She was only thirty, and there was plenty more time for marriage and children and so on.

And it was good to have resolved things with Tom. Douglas had helped her to see him clearly. He'd saved her from a potential nightmare and she should be grateful for that. At least she now knew the kind of man she wanted – but how many men like Douglas were there?

'Big sigh,' said Tom, and Kate said nothing.

'You mustn't give up,' he insisted. 'There might be a perfectly good reason. I don't know, maybe he had something to sort out, some estate problem.'

'Maybe.'

'You must call him. Call him tomorrow.'

'Whatever. I'll see.'

She wouldn't call him. He knew she wanted to see him, and it was obvious he didn't want to see her. It was over.

Staring through the wipers at the cats' eyes on the road, Kate let her mind shift forward. There'd be Christmas with Mum. Just the two of them this year as Peter was spending it with his in-laws. Then there was all that holiday time she'd taken from work, to be with Douglas over New Year – well, either she could cancel (give her a chance to catch up on the Hazel Industries file and all those other matters she'd put on hold to sort out the Simon Dalziel business) or she could take it and go somewhere hot – spoil herself. Kate wasn't sure who she'd go with – most people had already made plans for New Year – but that wouldn't matter. She could go alone, if necessary. Quite exciting to travel alone. She could go anywhere she liked. Anywhere in the world.

She swallowed – stared even harder at the little diamond studs – and tried to cheer herself with thoughts of Simon Dalziel. She imagined him being told that Tony Cummings wanted a quick word. He'd saunter in, expecting a new matter, or even an offer of partnership, and – yes – he'd be told to pack his bags and push off. He'd battle for it, she thought. He'd have to go through all of it – crime by crime – and there'd be nothing he could do! She couldn't wait to tell . . .

Well, she'd explain the whole thing to Mum. But Elizabeth didn't know that there had been a problem in the first place. And nor did Peter, or Tom, or Louisa. Kate acknowledged that, okay, so it would have been nice to talk about it with Douglas. He'd have picked her up in the Land-Rover this afternoon and they'd have driven out to Diss – as planned – and she'd have told him then. And he'd have smiled, and felt for her hand. He'd have understood completely.

She blinked to clear her vision and looked quickly at Tom – who hadn't seen. He was busy overtaking a lorry. The road was blank ahead, but Kate imagined a car coming towards them. She imagined a terrible crash, blue circling police lights, fluorescent jackets, medical equipment – but none of it necessary because she and Tom were dead. Killed instantly. Leaving everybody – Douglas – thinking that she and Tom were 'together' after all.

'Tom, please – please drive more carefully.'

'The road was empty.'

'Yes, I know that – but you swerved out without looking. You . . . is this the right road?'

'What do you take me for?'

'That sign said Thetford.'

'We have to go to Thetford to get to Diss.'

'How do you know?'

'I've looked at the map and I'm following the signs. We go along this road until we get to Thetford and then we take the A1066 to Diss. Just trust me, will you?'

Kate pulled out the map, opened it and said nothing.

'You wouldn't be questioning Douglas like this if he was driving,' he said.

'Of course I wouldn't. He lives here. He'd know the road . . .' Kate trailed off, realising that it wouldn't matter where she was in the world with Douglas – the point was that she could trust him. And not just with things like driving and directions. She didn't know anyone she felt like that with – not even her mother. She sat with the map open on her lap and looked at it without seeing.

'That's the north coast of Scotland you've got there,' said Tom. 'Try page thirty-eight.'

Kate didn't bother. She closed the map and looked again at Tom's profile. He turned to her for a second and then – noticing her expression – looked quickly back at the road.

'How far is it now?' she said.

'Ten minutes, I should think. Something like that.'

They were entering Thetford. Kate watched the grey-orange scenery, jaundiced in the sodium street lighting. Tom was indicating left at the sign to Diss.

She reached for the mobile.

'I must call Mum – let her know we're almost there. Do you mind?'

'Not at all. The batteries'll be quite low now, and I do want to speak to Lou, but . . .'

'I'll keep it short.'

Kate dialled her mother.

'It's me.'

'Darling! Darling where . . . ou *been?* Di . . . miss your train?'

'No, Mum. I've been to Waveney, looking for Douglas, but he's not there – so now I'm coming home. Should be with you in about fifteen minutes. Is that okay?'

'. . . can't hear . . . word y . . . saying, darling – you . . . break . . . g up . . .'

The line went dead.

'You were right about the batteries,' said Kate, closing the mobile and putting it in the compartment between them. 'I'm sorry.'

'Doesn't matter.'

'You can call Louisa when we get there. I'm sure Mum won't mind.'

Tom drove in through the outskirts of Diss, towards the Mere at the centre, past houses with Christmas trees in their front windows. And – in between the houses – where a gate had been left open or where a wall was low, Kate began to see the dark water of the Mere rippling in the wind, reflections of the town lights lost and then caught in the fine lines of its movement.

Tom let Kate direct him round the one-way system and they waited for the traffic lights by the church to turn green. To their left, Kate was conscious of the shadowy graveyard with its rustling trees and the moon hung high in a brief gap in the clouds. She thought for a second of Arabella, understood in that moment something of the sense of loss that had driven the poor girl to—

'Which way now?' Tom was saying. 'Kate?'

'Mm?'

'Which way?'

'Sorry,' she muttered. 'It's just down here – here on the right.'

He indicated, and turned.

'Third house.'

Tom braked slowly, and came to a halt outside a pair of white gates. They were blocked by a large vehicle.

'Oh dear,' she sighed. 'You'll have to park in the road.'

She then noticed that the car in front of them was a Land-Rover – and looked at it in disbelief, taking in the stickers and the dent.

She turned to Tom – and when he smiled, she knew.

'I won't park,' he said. 'I won't come in.'

'Is . . . real – really his . . .?' she found she couldn't speak properly.

She was choking, struggling to find the shoes she'd kicked off in the darkness, getting the left one onto her right foot for a second, pushing the road atlas from her lap, feeling for the seat-belt catch, and then struggling with the door, looking for the handle – unable to see in the dark, with everything blurring. Tom had to lean over her to open it.

She got out into the rain – closing the car door behind her – and the air filled with barks. A light went on in the porch, and she made for it, wiping her eyes with the back of her hand so that she could see her way through the gap between the gates and the Land-Rover. George was thumping and banging around in there, steaming the windows in his excitement, his tail wagging furiously – beating the floor.

Tom was calling her name.

'Kate?'

She turned.

'Your coat,' yelled Tom through the car window.

Kate threw out a hand, refusing. She didn't need her coat.

'And your bag . . .' He waved them at her.

Kate was really crying now. She ran back, grabbed